I0634163

O Negative

Cassandra Lynn King

CSJ King Publishing
Oregon, Wisconsin

This book is a work of fiction. Names, characters, businesses, organizations, places, events, and incidents either are the product of the author's imagination or are used fictitiously. Any resemblance to actual persons, living or dead, events, or locales is entirely coincidental.

Copyright © 2013 CSJ King Publishing
All rights reserved.

Cover by Ashley L. Steinberg

All rights reserved. No part of this book may be reproduced, stored in a retrieval system, or transmitted in any form or by any means, electronic, mechanical, photocopying, recording, or otherwise, without the express written permission of the publisher, except by a reviewer who may quote brief passages in a review to be printed in a newspaper, magazine, or journal.

ISBN: 0985622024
ISBN-13: 978-0-9856220-2-2

DEDICATION

To Karen King, the loved one I have lost.

CONTENTS

ACKNOWLEDGMENTS

There weren't many who contributed to the completion of this book, but those who did helped it come a long way. My parents, Jeff and Didi King, as always, supported me through the drafting and editing processes while I was away at school. I would like to thank them over everyone else for their love, help, and support of my writing.

I must also thank Deanna Blanchard for her contribution to the editing process. This book would have never been finished without you, Deanna!

Last, I must thank a wonderful friend of mine, Ashley Steinberg, for taking the time to design the cover. Ashley is busy with school but took time out of her schedule to design a magnificent cover for O Negative. I hope she will continue to stick with me.

For those who helped finish O Negative, thank you for your support. For those who have been nagging me to finish it, thank you for being my motivation.

1

Eight Days In

Walter Reifert

There used to be a genetic research facility about twelve miles outside of Philadelphia in a little town called Hatfield, or Hellfield, as it's called nowadays because of the massacres. The facility no longer exists. It was demolished long ago by angry protestors, but it was still standing when I was eighteen years old, and that's all that matters anymore. Hellfield was the birthplace of the virus, the Colician Strain. Nobody living in Hatfield really knew what went on inside that building, and honestly, none of them wanted to. I know I didn't. My Uncle Don worked inside as one of the genetic researchers or engineers. (I'm not really sure what his title was, even to this day.) I never dared ask him what he was doing in there. Ever since the night of the screaming, everyone in town avoided that building like it was infected with the Black Plague. When horrible screams came from that building all night long, the citizens of Hatfield knew something terrible was going on inside. My father, John, refused to let Uncle Don anywhere near me or my three brothers, and I wasn't allowed any contact at school with

1

my cousin Maia, Don's oldest daughter. It was almost as if my father knew what was happening inside the facility.

After the night of the screaming, when even the cops refused to go inside to investigate, my dad kept an annoyingly close watch over me, as if he knew something really bad was about to happen to me that he was trying to prevent. He also kept in close contact with my three older brothers, who were in college or had already graduated and moved on with their lives. Sometimes I wish my dad had decided to flee sooner. If he had, he and my brothers would still be alive. But had he done so, I never would have found Shauna, and our people may have never had a chance.

On April 4, 2018, at 2:16 a.m. I awoke to a loud bang reverberating across the town. I went to my window and could see the red-orange glow from behind the trees in my backyard. My dad scared me when he came up behind me and told me to go back to sleep. "There was an explosion," he said quietly. "There's nothing we can do right now." I went to bed as he instructed, the sirens of the fire engines already approaching.

Later that day, I heard rumors that there was a chemical leak and that was what caused the explosion at the research facility. I went to school in Philadelphia because my dad taught history at the University so I didn't learn much more about it. For the first time in weeks, I dared speak to my cousin Maia, who told me that Don was okay but there was something serious going on. "My dad thinks people in Hatfield are going to start getting sick," she told me, concern burning in her eyes. "He thinks some may even start dying. Don't be surprised if you're not allowed out of Hatfield tomorrow."

She was right. The next day, my dad and I left for Philadelphia like we did every morning. We were stopped at the edge of town by a barricade set up by the National Guard. The men who approached us had guns. Big guns. They said that Hatfield was being quarantined until further

2

notice. No one in or out. I started panicking on our drive back home, but my dad told me I would be fine. He didn't say that we would be fine; he just said that *I* would be fine.

That same night I woke up shaking with a terrible cold sweat. Something was wrong with me; I knew that much; and for the first time in twelve years I called out for my mother. But it was not my mother who came rushing into my room. My mom had died more than a decade earlier, and in my delirium I completely forgot she was gone. My dad came to my bedside to ask what was wrong.

"Something's wrong with me," was all I could muster. I couldn't give him specifics because even I didn't understand what it was. I wasn't in pain, but I was definitely uncomfortable. My head felt like it was vibrating, and my whole body had this pulse of buzzing energy coursing through it. I felt like I needed to get up and run a marathon, but at the same time I didn't want to move. I was hot, and my stomach was flipping over constantly, giving me a feeling of panic and dread. When I finally found my voice and could slow my mind down enough to form words, I broke down and told him what Maia had told me. "I'm sick," I whimpered after my story. "There was a chemical leak at the facility and now I'm sick."

"It's just the flu," Dad assured me, rubbing my shoulder and smiling. "The flu is starting to go around Hatfield and you've caught it is all."

A strange time of year for an influenza outbreak, I thought to myself, but I wanted to believe my dad. I didn't want to think I was sick and dying as the result of a chemical leak.

"Just try to go back to sleep," Dad said softly.

I didn't sleep. I couldn't, but my dad stayed by my side all night anyway. I didn't sleep for days after that. I didn't eat either, no matter how hard my dad tried to make me. My body was too restless to sleep, and my stomach was too uneasy to eat. Dad was getting really worried about me, especially on day four when I suddenly puked up blood with absolutely no warning. But I didn't feel all that bad by then. I just had this God-awful headache. It started the morning after I woke up crying for Mom and had been getting progressively worse with each passing day. By the seventh day after the explosion, I had no choice but to resort to bed rest, or couch rest. I stayed on the couch for fear of being alone. After five days of this strange internal feeling and splitting headache, I knew it wasn't the flu. I had suffered through my fair share of flu viruses, and this wasn't one of them. I had fallen ill to whatever Maia had been describing, and if I was going to die then I didn't want to die alone in my room, the way my mom had died alone in that car wreck. The thought of death didn't really scare me, at least not while I was with my dad.

Anyway, I had been lying on the couch in the living room, having taken as much Tylenol as Dad dared give me, when I heard my first words. For some time that afternoon I had been drifting in and out of a light doze (it felt nice after having gone four nights without sleep) when a loud rap sounded at the front door. By the time my dad reached the door I was wide awake. There was an unfriendly presence, and I could sense it. My dad sensed it too. The moment he entered the room he immediately ran to me and pushed me back down as I attempted to climb to my feet.

"Just relax," he said, his face creased with worry. "Let me deal with this."

I laid back down and watched from an angle as my dad answered the door. Dad was in the front entryway and I couldn't see him or our visitor, but I could hear their conversation perfectly. It was Uncle Don, and my dad was not happy to see him. Ever since Aunt Nicole—Dad's older sister and Don's wife—died six years ago due to complications during the birth of my younger cousin Marlena, Dad hadn't enjoyed Don's visits. I never asked him about it, but something happened between Dad and Don after Nicole's death and the two of them had never gotten past it. They never got along after that. Well, Dad never tried to get along.

"What are you doing here?" Dad demanded curtly.

"I just came to check up on you and Walter," Don replied casually. "Your neighbors say they haven't seen the two of you for several days."

"Would you let Maia and Marlena out on the streets with military tanks rolling around town?"

"Can I come in?"

"No, you cannot!"

"I just want to check and see for myself that Walter's alright."

Damn it, Don! Can't you just stay out of my life?

That was when I heard it. Had I not heard Dad say something else at the exact same time, I might not have noticed anything odd.

"Walter's fine, Don! Can't you just go away and leave us alone?"

When I heard my dad speak two phrases at once, I sat straight up and stared in shock in the direction of my uncle and father. How was that possible? At the moment, I was confused and didn't understand what exactly I had just heard, but I did know that I wasn't crazy. Whatever just happened, it was odd, but I wasn't going to sit around wondering about it. I cringed in pain as I forced myself to rise. I lost my balance at first from a wave a dizziness, but I managed to drag myself over to the front entryway to get a view of the conversation.

Uncle Don was a small man next to Dad. Dad was at least six-foot-two with wide shoulders, making him look even bigger. (I wish I had gotten my dad's strong build. I'm tall but skinny like my mom. I did get my dad's brown hair and green eyes but that doesn't help me with much.) Uncle Don is only about five-ten and quite thin. It's funny how much Don and Maia look alike; black hair, brown eyes, thin faces, always a small smile present. Looking at Don made me realize how much I missed Maia. Maia wasn't just a cousin but also a very good friend, and once this disaster was over we would have some serious catching up to do.

I watched my father as the conversation continued so I could see how my father did it. Don was sighing and saying, "How long is this thing between you and I going to last, John? Hasn't six years been long enough to get over it?"

My dad pursed his lips, but at the same time I heard the words, *"I'm going to kill you for killing my sister!"*

Gaping at my father in astonishment, I couldn't believe what I was hearing. It wasn't what he said, but the fact that he was saying it without actually speaking. I looked at Don to see how he was reacting, but then I realized that he wasn't hearing it. Only I was hearing it. I was hearing my father's thoughts. My headache must have been really bad.

I looked back to my dad as he answered Don, using actual words, "This will continue for as long as my sister is dead." *And until I kill you.*

Now I knew I definitely wasn't hearing things. I really was hearing my father's thoughts. Since I was now so focused on that and keen to understand how I was doing it, I stared hard at the back of my dad's head to try and hear more. I could, but it was all jumbled nonsense, and I understood why. Dad wasn't thinking a direct sentence; just random thoughts and images were racing through his mind. I picked out words that were being thrown around, none of them very nice. There were words like *murderer* and *psychotic* and *medical experiments*, and then I heard him think, *You killed my sister so you could screw around with your damn kids!*

Had these words actually been spoken aloud I would have been horrified, knowing now why Aunt Nicole didn't live through childbirth and also why my dad hated Uncle Don so much. Unfortunately, I had a much bigger crisis on my hands.

I was so panicked and focused on my father that I didn't realize that Don saw me until he spoke my name. "Walter?"

Startled, I jumped back a step and stared at Don's concerned expression. Don was dressed in a white lab coat that gave him the mad scientist look.

Okay, he is definitely not fine, Don said, speaking without speaking. It wasn't just Dad I could hear.

My dad whipped around. "Walter!" he said sharply.

I immediately knew my mistake. Don came to make sure we were alright because he was looking for sick people, and I knew how terrible I looked. I had made the mistake of looking into a mirror today. My face was exhausted from lack of sleep, my body was thin from lack of sustenance, my skin was a nasty gray color, and my eyes were curiously bright despite how sick I knew I must be. When Don took a step towards me, I knew it was wise to take a step back.

"Walter, what did I tell you?" Dad snapped, grabbing me by the shoulders and steering me back to the couch. "I don't want anyone seeing you like this!"

"Dad, something's wrong with me," I told him, and found myself crying. With the agonizing pain in my head and realizing that I was now some kind of freak, I couldn't contain my emotions any longer. "I need help!"

"Walter, you're just fine," Dad promised me, pushing me back down onto the couch. "You just need some sleep."

"Dad, I can hear your—"

I know what you can hear, Walter, Dad said in his mind, staring back intensely into my eyes. *And it's okay. But if Don realizes how sick you are, he's going to take you away from me.*

My eyes widened but I closed my mouth, frightened and angry that my dad knew what was happening to me but didn't tell me.

"John, Walter's sick," Don informed my father, as if Dad didn't already know. He had followed us into the living room. "You know that I need to take him in."

"You're not laying a hand on my child!" Dad snarled, rounding on him and shoving him back to the door. "You can mess with your kids all you want, but you're not touching mine!"

"John, please." He retreated, knowing he couldn't beat my dad in a fair fight. "Let's put our past behind us for one minute. This is about *Walter*."

"I know what's best for my son!"

"I can help him."

"You're not touching him! Get out of my house!" Dad shoved Uncle Don out the front door and slammed it shut before quickly clicking the three locks into place. Then he ran around the whole lower level of the house, locking every door, window, and closing every curtain.

"Dad," I called as he bustled about. The random thoughts from my father's mind were growing louder inside of mine. It was becoming painful. "Dad!"

"I'm coming, I'm coming!" Dad rushed back into the room and sat beside me on the sofa. "You're alright, bud. Just breathe. It won't be so bad for long."

"What the hell is happening to me?" I sobbed, knowing I looked absolutely pathetic.

"You're changing, Walter," Dad told me gently, placing his hand on the back of my head in an effort to soothe me.

"Yeah, no shit!" I squeaked. "How did you know?"

"You wouldn't believe me if I told you, so I'm not going to. All that matters is that I do, and that I'm here. I can't tell you exactly what to expect, but in a few days you should be feeling much better. I'm sure what you're going through is scary, but you just need to relax. Everything will be fine."

"I just need to relax?" I repeated in disbelief. "Why don't *you* start hearing what people are thinking and then try to relax!"

"Shh, shh, shh," Dad shushed, smiling back at my terrified face. "Freaking out isn't going to help you at all, now is it?"

"What is happening to me?" I shrieked, wincing from the pain in my head. "How am I changing?"

"That explosion at the facility last week? Well, Maia was right. There was a chemical leak and it's making people sick. I don't think anyone will die from this, but I don't know for sure. This chemical that leaked is a type of virus as I do recall, a virus that destroys sections of DNA in the body and then rebuilds it to be stronger and allow access to sections of the brain that we don't yet know how to control. Being able to hear my thoughts is a side effect of this virus. In a few days you may even be able to control my thoughts." He spoke as if I should be proud of it.

"How do you know all this? Did Uncle Don tell you?"

"Don doesn't even fully understand this virus yet," Dad said. "He and his buddies down at the facility were experimenting with it to see what it could do and now it's making people sick."

"But how do you know this?"

"It doesn't matter."

"Yes, it does!"

"Somebody told me this was going to happen!" Dad shook his head. "You wouldn't remember, but ten years ago we met someone who saved our lives. A girl, about the same age you are now. She told me about all of this, so that's how I know."

Ten years ago... somebody saved our lives? I'd had a crazy dream ten years ago about something like that happening. Was Dad trying to tell me that was all real?

I didn't have time to think about that. "So if this is just a side effect of being sick then it's only temporary, right?"

Dad hesitated. "I'm afraid that this is permanent. This gift you now have will be with you forever."

I dropped my head in my hands and allowed myself to cry. "I don't want this!"

"I know," Dad said, rubbing my back gently. "But it won't be this bad forever. Soon it will just feel like another part of you."

"There's got to be a cure for this though!" I cried, looking back to him desperately. "If it's a disease then there has to be a cure!"

"It's a virus," Dad corrected. "Not a disease. You can't cure a virus. You can only get a vaccine, and you're already sick. Don't think of your gift as something bad. It's a gift, after all."

"If you think this is so great, then you can have it!" I snapped, massaging my temples. My mind was still buzzing with everything going on in my father's. "This is terrible, and my head feels like it's going to explode!"

Dad didn't say anything for a while. When he did, his voice was grave. "Tomorrow, Don and the other doctors are going to process everyone in Hatfield, which means that the military is going to round everyone up to see who's sick and who's not. Don already knows you're sick and will send someone for you." Dad studied me for a moment. "You look terrible, Walter."

"Thanks, Dad," I muttered.

Dad patted my back and rose to his feet. "You get some sleep, and I mean that. Tomorrow, when you're stronger, we're going to make a run for it before Don sends someone."

"Where are we going to go?" I asked as my dad made me lay back down. "How are we going to get out of here in the first place?"

"Let me worry about that," Dad said and smiled. "You just worry about getting some of your spunk back."

"But where would we go?"

"Canada," Dad said. "Some place in the Rockies. I don't know exactly where yet, but the United States is about to become a very dangerous place and I don't want my kid being in the middle of it."

"Am I contagious?" I asked him, realizing for the first time that it was entirely possible.

"Yes, which is why we're going somewhere in the Rockies. Very few people live up there."

"If I'm contagious then shouldn't you stay away from me?" I asked cautiously.

"I'm already infected," Dad said mildly, as if it wasn't a big deal.

"How do you know?" I asked as my heart began to pound. He didn't look sick.

"It's a genetic virus," Dad explained. "It only affects people with a specific blood type, and we have the same blood type so I should start showing the same symptoms as you in a few days or maybe even sooner." He smiled at my horrified expression. "It's okay, bud," he reassured me. "We'll be alright. Just think of it this way; we can be freaks together."

I tried to smile as he left the room but I just couldn't. This was all too much to take in. Closing my eyes, I tried to push the never-ending buzz of noise from my mind. I could hear my neighbors, and even the people across the street. My head was pounding with these thoughts, and all I wanted was to find a way to block them from my mind. I wanted to be able to hear my thoughts and my thoughts only. With all the unwanted noise in my head, I haven't a clue how I fell asleep. I dreamt of whispers—whispers in the dark, inaudible and their origins unknown. I realized that I was dreaming about the inside of my own mind.

From the shadows on the wall, I knew it must have been late afternoon of the following day when I awoke. I rolled over on the couch and looked at the clock on the mantle over the fireplace. 4:17. How had I slept so long when I hadn't been able to sleep for days?

Shouts were coming from the kitchen. My dad was angry by the tone of his voice, and he was yelling at someone else in the room. I tried to figure out who it was by listening to their thoughts, but I found that I couldn't hear any more thoughts. The inside of my head was ringing with the silence. I couldn't help but smile, and I prayed that I wouldn't hear thoughts ever again. Or at least for a while.

Somebody stepped in front of me suddenly and crouched down beside me, making me jump almost a foot off the couch. "Hey, Walter!" my second brother Ethan said cheerfully, grinning at me.

"Ethan?" I said skeptically, squinting back at him. "What the hell are you doing here?" Ethan was supposed to be finishing out his senior year of college at the University of Wisconsin -Milwaukee. How he got here and what he was doing here, I had no idea.

"What, did you think I was going to let you and Dad be experimented on by Uncle Don while I studied myself to death in Wisconsin? I don't think so. We're going to get you out of here."

"How did you get through the barricades?"

"We didn't. We went through the woods and crossed the lake."

"We?"

Just then, the arguing in the next room became louder, and Dad and my two other brothers entered the room.

"This is the stupidest thing any of you have ever done!" Dad shouted. "And that's saying something! What were you thinking? Now you're all going to get sick, too! Don't touch Walter!" He slapped Ethan's hand away when he tried to help me sit up. "He's sick! Get out of this town before you all get sick too!"

"Relax, Dad," my oldest brother Tyler said and knelt beside me as well. "We knew the risks when we decided to come back. We discussed whether or not it would be worth it and we all agreed that it was. We're family, after all, and we have to stick together."

Tyler had graduated from college three years earlier and was happily married with a young daughter named Mari, so coming to Hatfield was taking a huge risk.

"And besides," Anton, who was a sophomore at Stanford, piped in. "Like you said, it's not like it's going to kill us. So we'll get a little sick? I just got over a cold anyway."

"Do you think this is a joke?" Dad bellowed. "This isn't the common cold! Walter's suffered through enough already and he's only just caught it!"

"So are we going to get out of here or what?" Ethan asked Dad, standing up and folding his arms over his chest. "Because we're not leaving unless it's with you."

Angrily, Dad said, "If Walter feels up to it…"

"I think I'm alright," I told him as I sat up. My head still felt like it had been run over by a semi, but I felt strong enough to at least make an effort.

"Then get in the car," Dad growled through his teeth at my brothers.

As the three of them headed to the garage, I heard Anton say, "I told you there was a reason why Dad bought that gas-guzzling beast!"

He was referring to the Hummer that Dad kept in the garage under a blue tarp. It was rarely driven, and I finally understood the point of having it. Dad had gotten it for now. Today. He was going to go through the woods.

Sighing in frustration, Dad grumbled, "They're never going to listen to me, are they?"

"Have they ever?" I chuckled as he helped me stand unsteadily.

"How's the head?" Dad asked me as I swayed dizzily.

"It still hurts, but at least I can't hear any thoughts right now."

"You can't hear anything?"

"No, I guess it turns on and off. I'd rather it stayed off."

"Huh," Dad muttered, and started to ease me forward. "I guess you'll just have to learn how to control it."

"I don't want to be able to control it," I said insistently. "I want to get rid of it."

Dad snorted. "Yeah, good luck with that one, bud."

I glared at him. "You talk like having this illness is a good thing."

"Isn't it?"

"When your head starts throbbing and you can hear people's thoughts, then you can tell me it's a good thing!"

"When you think of it as an illness, it seems worse than it really is." Dad opened the door leading into the garage. "This gift of yours may come in handy someday. You just have to learn how to use it first."

"You know what? I don't really want to talk to you anymore."

"Fine." The garage door was still closed, and Dad hit the button on the wall to open it. "But you're not going to have me forever, so you'd better listen to what I'm telling you."

"Whatever," I grumbled, hobbling over to the passenger door and watching my brothers as they stood at the front of the Hummer.

"Boys!" Dad snapped, giving them each a shove as he made his way around to the driver's side. "Get in or I'll run you over on my way out!"

"Hi, John."

Each of us jumped as Uncle Don appeared on the other side of the garage door. Behind him were at least eight armed men in military uniforms with a large truck waiting at the foot of the driveway, blocking our escape.

"What the hell do you want, Don?" Dad demanded, immediately stepping between the two of us.

Leaning to the side to get a good look at me, Uncle Don smiled. "Well, for one thing, I want Walter. Look at him. Can you not see how sick he is?"

"I know how sick he is," Dad snapped. "I've been looking after him through the worst of it."

"Don't you think that a proper doctor should be caring for him?" Don asked him, taking a step forward.

"If I can find a doctor that I trust, then yes." Dad glared at him. "You do not fall into that category."

"I had a feeling that you were going to try to make a run for it," Don said, staring evenly back at Dad. "I didn't realize that the rest of the family was coming to the rescue as well."

"You'd better watch yourself, you psychopath son of a bitch," Tyler growled, starting to get between Dad and Uncle Don.

"Tyler, get in the car," Dad instructed sharply, shoving Tyler back and waving his arm at the rest of us. "All four of you, get in the car."

"John, we don't want to hurt you," Don promised him, raising his hands to prove his good intentions. "Or your boys. We only want to help. But if you continue to resist us then we're going to have no choice but to detain you by force."

"You'd better tell *your* boys to get out of my way," Dad warned as he followed my brother to the car doors. "Because if they're not gone in ten seconds then I *will* hurt them."

"John, this is a huge mistake," Don said, gesturing for the soldiers to wait as they started to advance. "I'm only trying to help you. We're family, remember?"

"You killed my sister," Dad said and shook his head. "You're not my family anymore."

As Dad turned his back on Don, Don motioned for the soldiers to go, and then eight armed men were all running into the garage.

"Dad!" Tyler yelled, running to my father's aid. In an instant, all of my brothers and my dad were fighting the advancing soldiers. One huge fistfight, and I knew who was going to win.

I was the only one who had actually gotten in the Hummer, so when the fight broke out I simply clicked the locks shut. There was nothing I could do for my family now. Two soldiers got past the brawl and positioned themselves on either side of the vehicle, aiming their rifles at me. I kept completely still and watched my family as they lost their desperate battle. Ethan and Anton had already been carried away to the truck screaming, and Tyler was dragged away a minute later. That left my dad squabbling with the two remaining soldiers. Considering his age, he was putting up a hell of a fight. And I knew it was for me.

Uncle Don was the one to finally intervene. Walking up to the fight as one soldier got his arms wrapped around Dad's chest, Don pulled something out of a pocket of his lab coat, a syringe.

"Dad!" I cried in terror, reaching for the door handle.

"Don't move!" the soldier on my side of the car warned, cocking his weapon.

I watched helplessly as Uncle Don injected my dad in the upper arm as he continued to struggle. A few moments later, Dad's struggles stopped. I found myself crying again as Dad was carried away and Uncle Don walked over to my door. Watching Don carefully, I gripped my seat so hard that my knuckles began to tingle.

Uncle Don tried the door but found that it was locked. He gazed in at me as he knocked on my window. "Walter, open the door, kiddo."

Had my head not ached so bad, I would have shook it. Instead, I just stared back in fear.

Don turned and caught Dad's keys as they were tossed to him. Giving the remote a click, Don opened the door before I could lock it again. "Hey, Walter," he said, smiling in at me as I cowered in my seat. "How are you feeling?" He knew I wasn't going to answer him, so he didn't bother waiting for a response. "Why don't you come with me and I can see if I can make you a little more comfortable?"

I shook my head this time and winced from the pain.

Don saw the pain in my eyes. "That pain in your head, Walter? I can make it go away, but you need to come with me now." He took my arm gently and tried to coax me out.

"Please!" I managed to spit out, gripping the seat even tighter. I stared pleadingly into Uncle Don's eyes but didn't say anything else.

"I'm not going to hurt you, Walter," Don promised me, still smiling. "I want to help you feel better, but I need you to get out of the car and come with me, okay?"

I gave up against him as his grip tightened and his pull strengthened. There wasn't much of a point in fighting him anyway. I was weak and sick and there were several armed men ready to restrain me. With a soft whimper, I allowed Uncle Don to help me out of the car. Once I was out, I gripped the car door just as hard as I had gripped my seat. My heart was still thumping in my chest and I stared in terror back at Uncle Don's calm face.

"Are you going to escort him to the ambulance or do you want us to?" the soldier that had instructed me not to move asked.

"He's not looking quite as bad as I thought he was going to," Uncle Don commented, studying my face curiously. "He can ride with me. I'll drive him to the lab myself."

I wasn't sure what sounded more unpleasant; riding in an ambulance with a gun to my head or being trapped in a vehicle with my mad scientist uncle.

"Sir, that's not such a wise idea," another soldier said, eyeing me warily.

I almost laughed. The soldiers were all afraid of me. They kept their eyes and their rifles locked on me at all times. Even though their expressions were hard, I could see the fear in their eyes. Did they know what I was becoming, what I had already become? They must have known, but why was that something to be afraid of? It wasn't like I could hurt anyone with this ability...could I?

"He's my nephew," Don told him flatly, putting his arm around me protectively. "He's not going to hurt me. And besides, he's not in a condition where he can just take off running. Are you, Walter?"

I didn't reply.

"Whatever you say," the same soldier muttered, starting to back out of the garage but keeping his eyes and weapon trained on me.

Don turned back to me as the remaining soldiers retreated as well. "We're going to go for a drive, okay?"

"Where are we going?" I asked, my voice shaking. I realized that my whole body was shaking.

"Haven't you always wondered what's inside the lab?" Don asked, the smile still on his face. "Now you get to see."

He was talking about the research facility, and now that I was being invited inside, I really didn't have a desire to know. "What are you going to do to me?"

"I already told you," Don said. "I'm going to try to make you as comfortable as possible until we can figure out exactly how to help you."

I held my ground as Don tried to get me to move again. "So...this headache...it's bad, right?" I had already heard the story from Dad, but I wanted to hear it from the man who had helped to create the virus.

The smile left Uncle Don's face. He nodded solemnly. "Yes. It's bad."

That was when I gave up completely. I let go of the door and let Don start to lead me out to his black SUV. I was done for. I was infected with a man-made virus that had turned me into a freak. It didn't matter what Uncle Don told me; I was going to be poked and prodded for probably the rest of my life.

"Everything's going to be alright, Walter," Uncle Don promised me.

Just after he said that, my head exploded in pain. It hurt so bad that I couldn't even scream. I gasped and caught myself on the hood of the Hummer, clutching my head in agony.

"Walter, what's wrong?" Don asked, immediately concerned. His words echoed around in my brain and my mind barely registered his touch.

The whispers had started again. Thousands of indistinguishable whispers hissed through my head, making it pound and throb and scream. It went on for what felt like hours, but it couldn't have been more than a couple of seconds before they all cleared out again and the pain retreated to a steady pulse.

"Walter?" Don asked, peering into my face as I focused back on his. "Do I need to get you a wheelchair?" *These symptoms are even more erratic than I anticipated.*

"N-no," I stammered, realizing that I was going to be hearing both his voices for a while now. Maybe I could somehow use that to my advantage. "I'm fine. It's just this headache…"

Don nodded but continued to watch me. "Well, when I get you in my car I can give you something for the pain. Can you walk that far?"

"I…I think so." I managed to walk to Uncle Don's car. It was difficult to ignore the people that I knew were staring at me. The soldiers standing in my yard, my neighbors standing on their porches, people walking across the street. They all knew that I was sick, but they also knew that what was happening to me was also going to happen to many of them as well. I was only the beginning.

Uncle Don helped me into the passenger seat and left the door standing open while going around to get in on the driver's side. As he did so, a soldier came up and buckled my seat belt for me.

Once he was properly situated, Uncle Don took another syringe out of his jacket pocket and turned towards me. "I'm going to give you a shot of morphine. It should decrease the intensity of the migraine."

"I don't want that!" I shouted, making Uncle Don jump. I leaned as far away from him as my seat belt would allow me to, gazing back at him fearfully as my chest heaved up and down with each breath.

Startled by my seemingly unprovoked outburst, Uncle Don stared at me in bewilderment. "It's only a painkiller. It's not going to hurt you."

"I don't care," I told him stubbornly, not wanting any type of injection from my uncle. After just finding out that he had killed my father's sister while experimenting on my cousin, I was having some trust issues. "I don't want it!"

Someone from outside the SUV—presumably a soldier—took hold of me. One arm hooked under my left arm and held my shoulder down, and the other pressed against my head, forcing it away from the left side of my body. I was only slightly immobilized, but it was enough for Don to do his work.

I screamed bloody murder while Uncle Don injected me with the morphine. He tried calming me the whole time, but that only made me scream louder. "It's alright. It's alright! It's not going to hurt."

It did hurt, but that might have been because I was struggling. I stopped fighting after Uncle Don pulled the needle out and the soldier released me and closed my door. A few moments later, the pounding in my head began to lessen until all that remained of my headache was a dull throb. At the same time, I began to feel noticeably sleepy. Sighing wearily, I rested my head against the car door.

"Yeah, it was a high dose so it's going to make you feel a bit drowsy," Uncle Don explained as he placed the syringe back into his pocket. "Jeez, Walter. You're exhausted. You've completely worn yourself out." He turned the keys in the ignition. *He looks absolutely terrible.*

"Thanks, Uncle Don," I muttered sarcastically. I didn't understand my mistake until I had already made it.

Uncle Don's hand froze in midair as he was about to put the SUV into gear. He looked at me, his brow furrowed. "Thank you for what?"

My mouth opened, but I had no clue of what to say. Should I defend myself? Should I just say that I was grateful for him helping me? He would totally buy that one. I ended up answering his question with another question. "What exactly is this virus? I mean…what does it do to you?"

It was unnerving to see my uncle's usually calm and smiling face become so serious. He stared back at me with a very suspicious look in his eyes before he asked, "You can hear everything I'm thinking, can't you?"

"No," I replied, a little too quickly and a little too defensively.

Still eyeing me, he pressed further. *Are you sure?*

"Yes, I'm sure…" I shut my mouth mid-sentence, but it was already too late. I turned my head away as both of Uncle Don's eyebrows raised. How stupid could I be? Sighing, I rested my head in my hands and massaged my temples.

Uncle Don didn't say anything else. He put the SUV into drive and we headed for the facility. I tried my best to ignore what was going on inside his head. The fact that he wasn't speaking to me was making me uncomfortable enough. I didn't want to know what his plans for me were.

The facility was located at the very southern edge of town, surrounded on three sides by thick trees. My house was nearby, so we didn't have to drive far. There was a large parking lot in front of the lab with lots of military vehicles unloading other civilians. Some of them I recognized, some of them I didn't. Some of them were screaming; some of them were calm. I saw my family being unloaded from one and being dragged inside. I wanted to help them, but for now I could only pray for their safety. Uncle Don saw me watching them and assured me that they would be alright. His assurance didn't comfort me.

The feature of the facility that frightened people the most was the fact that it looked just like a school. It appeared so non-threatening, yet at the same time everybody knew that something terrible was going on inside. Its façade was red brick and it had eight doors at the front entrance. There were single doors all around each side but people rarely used them. Around the entire perimeter was an eight foot high barbed wire fence with big WARNING signs every couple of yards. Just inside the fence, close to the front entrance, were large tents with military personnel setting up equipment inside. They must have been preparing for the whole town to be brought in to get tested for the virus. I wondered if they had some kind of test that would tell the doctors who was sick and who wasn't. Some people—like me—would have obvious symptoms, but my dad claimed he was sick too and he wasn't showing it at all. Dad said it had to do with the person's blood type, so maybe they would just do a finger prick and check each civilian's blood type and detain people based on that. Was the virus spreading to surrounding areas? Hatfield wasn't far from Philadelphia, a city with millions of people. And I had been in Philadelphia after I was exposed. My father and I could have both spread the virus to other people. I could have given it to Maia…

I had lost myself so deeply in thought that I didn't realize we had stopped until Uncle Don came around and opened my door. Still feeling a bit disoriented, I just looked at him uncertainly.

He smiled up at me. "Time to go inside," he said, taking a step back as two paramedics wheeled a stretcher in front of the door. Patting the gurney, Uncle Don gazed at me expectantly.

My uneasiness was only made worse when I looked down at the stretcher. I even felt a little nauseous. It looked just like any old stretcher, but attached to it were wrist and ankle restraints. Making eye contact with Don, I refused to move.

Raising his eyebrows, Uncle Don patted the gurney again. "Come on," he coaxed, like I was some kind of dog.

Eyeing it warily, I asked, "Are the restraints really necessary?"

Don continued to smile. I wanted to punch him in the face. "They're just there to keep you comfortable." I heard murmurs in his mind about how they were also there to keep me from running.

Soldiers started to creep closer as they saw that I wasn't getting out. I didn't see a way out, so I regrettably eased my way out of the SUV and onto the gurney. I sat there for a moment, feeling completely helpless against Uncle Don and the other doctors I was sure I was about to meet. I considered running, but with the soldiers already wary of me I wouldn't get more than a few steps before I was shot in the back.

Uncle Don pressed on my shoulder. "Lie down for me," he said.

I did, but I didn't want to. I did my best to lay completely still while I was strapped in. The sky was a very pale blue, and I tried to think about that. It didn't really work.

Patting my shoulder, Uncle Don asked me, "You doing okay?"

"If I say no, will it make a difference?" I glared at him.

Looking away from my hate-filled eyes, Uncle Don extended his hand and took something from a paramedic. He then pressed it down on my forehead. It was a cloth soaked in cold water. I didn't realize how hot my skin was until then. It felt really good.

"Don't panic," Don said suddenly. "This is just a precaution." He pulled part of the cloth down over my eyes, completely obscuring the world around me.

My heart began to pound, but I held still. I hoped that I was only being blindfolded so I wouldn't know how to get out and not because they were about to do something unspeakable to me. If I could actually control this "gift" of mine, I could simply look into Don's mind to find the answer. Sadly, though, my new ability was erratic.

Without anything else said, Uncle Don and the two paramedics wheeled me inside. I did my best to keep calm despite the blindfold. The air inside the building was cold. I don't know why, but I had expected it to be warm, even hot. I shook my head a couple of times to try to knock the cloth aside, but it made my head start to throb again and Don put a hand on my forehead to keep me still. I kept still only to keep him from shooting me up with more drugs.

Voices of different tones and pitches were all around me. It was surprisingly noisy, but then I realized that half of the voices were actually thoughts. Many of the people were urgent, even frantic, about getting to their destination and completing their duties. This viral outbreak was stressing out the people who caused it, too.

I was wheeled down a long hallway and I felt a few direction changes every now and then, and then we entered an elevator. We descended a few floors, and that was when I realized that the facility was much bigger than anyone thought. There were a few floors above ground, but that was apparently the tip of the iceberg. What was going on here?

When the elevator let out a high-pitched *ding*, I was wheeled out and was pushed through a door I heard open to my right. The gurney came to a halt a few paces later and then Don took the cloth off of my eyes. Blinking at the harsh light above me, I gazed around at the small white room. I saw a tray full of syringes to my left.

Don gave me that smile of his once again. He had another loaded syringe in his hand. "I'm going to give you a sedative," he told me, snapping the syringe a couple times. "We don't want you to be awake for these procedures." He took hold of my left arm.

"Uncle Don!" I pleaded, bucking against my restraints. "Please don't do this!"

"I'm not going to hurt you," he promised me for about the sixth time. Honestly, he already had. He injected me in the upper arm.

"I don't want to sleep!" I cried, giving up again.

"When's the last time you slept?" he asked me, rhetorically, of course. "You and I both know how much you need it."

His last few words were foggy. I was already drifting out of consciousness. Don was right. I did need the sleep. I was so exhausted that the slightest push of the sedative sent me under as I wondered what would happen to me.

Shauna Skyler

The whole town heard the explosion eight nights earlier, but no one received an explanation for what happened. Some said there was a chemical leak and we were all being slowly poisoned, but after more than a week we were all still alive so that was unlikely. Other people said there were microscopic parasites that had escaped the facility and were taking over our bodies, but that was even more ridiculous than the first theory. Nobody knew what was really happening, but I knew that it was something serious. Why would the military quarantine Hatfield? Why would the entire town be forcibly taken to the grounds of the genetic research facility for "precautions"? What were we all doing here anyway?

"People from the front of the line have been passing back information about what's happening up there," my father, Eric, told my mother, Angelina. "All this madness that's been going on all week is because of a man-made virus that was created here. The explosion from last week let it out and it's supposedly infected some of the people in the town. Thankfully, it's not supposed to be fatal."

"Why some and not everyone?" Mom whispered in confusion.

"They don't know," Dad explained. "They think it has something to do with genetics. At the front they're splitting up children from adults. For some reason, it's much easier to detect in kids than it is in adults. The soldiers are scanning everyone's head, so this virus must manifest itself in the brain. They're also looking for other symptoms. Extreme fatigue but inability to sleep, dilated pupils, agonizing headaches..."

My heat skipped a beat and I panicked for a split second. For the past two days or so my throbbing headache was having an effect on my day-to-day activities. I wasn't sleeping well, but I *was* sleeping. I have had bad headaches in the past that caused my sleep cycles to be off. I calmed down as soon as I reminded myself of that.

I knew I wasn't supposed to be eavesdropping on my parents. Hearing that stuff was already making me uneasy. Glancing up at my older brother Russell, I saw that he was listening too. His eyes were wide and his body was tense. He looked down at me.

"Didn't you say you had a headache?" he asked nervously.

I shrugged. I didn't tell my parents because they were already worried enough with the quarantine. Russell had caught me downing a couple Advil the day before so he was the only one who knew. "It's not so bad," I lied.

My mom heard me and rounded on me, clutching my littlest brother, Sawyer, to her. "What did you say, Shauna?"

"Nothing," I said quickly, but she was already freaking out.

"You have a headache, don't you?" she demanded, pressing her palm to my forehead. "Oh God, and you're burning up!"

"Mom, I'm fine," I insisted, rolling my eyes at Russell.

"I should have known that one of them was going to be affected by this!" Mom cried. "We should have just left after the explosion!"

"There was no way we could have known," Dad said, rubbing her back. "Plus, we wouldn't have wanted to spread it around, whatever it is. Shauna gets headaches a lot. It's probably nothing unusual."

"Well, she has one now. Of all times to have one!"

"It's just a coincidence," I told Mom, wanting her to stop freaking out. Some of the soldiers were starting to get curious about the commotion. I really didn't want any false alarms.

"*There are no coincidences!*" Mom snapped, turning away from everyone.

Dad went to comfort her while I turned to Russell. "Does she have to freak out over every little pain I feel?" I demanded through gritted teeth.

Russell shrugged but also rolled his eyes. "She's a mom," he replied, and grinned. "Maybe you'll end up like that someday."

I gave a false laugh that caused my head to throb. "I'm not going to have any kids. That way I'll die of natural causes and not stress."

Shaking his head and snickering, Russell told me, "Make sure you always wear protection."

Making a face, I asked him, "Who are you, Dad?"

Russell's eyes got really big. "Wait...*Dad* gave you the talk?"

"Shut up," I snapped as Russell started laughing, but I, too, found myself laughing.

"*Dad* gave you the talk?" Russell repeated in bewilderment.

"It was God-awful," I told him, punching him in the arm.

"It couldn't have been as bad as Mindy Hernandez's dad's speech," Russell said with a grin.

"What?" I cried, remembering his first girlfriend at fourteen. "Russell, oh my God!"

We were both laughing, which felt strange given the circumstances. We received the occasional stink eye, but neither of us took any notice. Russell put his arm around my shoulder. "That was disgusting," he told me.

"I'll bet," I laughed.

"*Unbelievably* awkward."

"Is that why you broke up with her?"

"She broke up with *me*, remember?"

"Oh, right. Because you weren't *good enough* for her."

The laughing began again, but we stopped immediately as an uproar of shouting began in front of us. A few soldiers were marching down the line, separating children from adults. The mass of people had moved quickly. We were now near the front.

"If the children are healthy and not at risk of spreading the virus, they will be returned to their parents immediately following the testing," a soldier was yelling into a microphone.

"And what if they are a risk?" a man I recognized from my street demanded, clutching his little boy to him. "Huh? Then what?"

I didn't hear the reply. Mom and Dad had both turned to us. "Keep them safe," Mom was telling Russell, passing Sawyer to him. "Stay together."

"Don't let go of him," Dad instructed me, putting my eight-year-old brother Michael's hand in mine.

"We'll see you on the other side," Mom told us, but she didn't look so sure about that. A moment later, a soldier pushed her and Dad to the right and then shoved the four of us kids to the left. I lost sight of my parents almost immediately. I didn't realize at the time that I would never see them again.

My three brothers and I were shoved into the large tent and then the flap was closed behind us, sealing us in. I blinked in the harsh light and took a look around. Dozens of soldiers with weapons in their hands were standing around, some looking at us and some not. Three groups of siblings were in front of us, moving towards two five-foot tall pillars that looked strangely like metal detectors. The first group, a group of five, moved through the pillars and nothing happened. "Cleared!" a soldier yelled, and then the five rushed out the other side of the tent.

Russell bent his head down to whisper in my ear. "What do you think that thing is for?"

"I don't know," I muttered. "But I'm not getting a good feeling about it."

The second group, a group of two, went through the pillars. Once again, nothing happened. The soldier yelled, "Cleared!" again and the pair rushed out. There was one more set of siblings before us, another group of two. They were two boys about seven and ten, and they walked forward hesitantly. Unlike the two times before, when they stepped through, dozens of circular red lights began to flash on the pillars.

"Stop!" the soldier ordered, stepping forward. He had a wand shaped object in one hand, and he waved it slowly in front of the smaller boy's face. It beeped once, which must have meant that he was okay because the soldier gestured to the opening of the tent. The soldier waved the wand in front of the taller boy's face. There was an alarm that sounded from the wand, and when it did the soldier called out, "Sign!"

The boy tried to run, a terrified expression on his face, but the soldier caught him by the hood of his sweatshirt. Other soldiers moved in to restrain the thrashing, screaming boy.

I gasped as I watched the scene.

"Stay back!" another soldier warned me and Russell, aiming his weapon in our direction.

The soldiers carried the boy to the side of the tent, where another flap opened and they disappeared from sight. The boy's screams died away soon afterwards.

"Come forward," the soldier with the wand instructed, beckoning to us.

"Russell," I breathed, slipping my free hand into his.

"Just do what they say," he whispered back, but I could hear that he was scared too.

"Now!" the soldier snapped at us, growing impatient.

We slowly walked forward, each step I took feeling ever so fateful. As we stepped through the pillars, I held my breath and prayed for a miracle. I didn't get one. The red lights flashed again.

"Shit," Russell muttered.

"Stop!" the soldier ordered, stepping up to Russell.

I knew it was me. My headache wasn't just a coincidence. I just prayed that none of my brothers were sick as well.

The wand beeped once at Russell, and I heard my brother breathe a sigh of relief. To my dismay, I wasn't the only one who had caught the virus. The wand shrieked at Sawyer.

"Sign!" the soldier called at the same time that Russell shouted, "No!" and stumbled backwards.

Soldiers were immediately upon us, grabbing at Sawyer. Sawyer screamed and tried to hold on to Russell, but they easily pulled Sawyer away and started to take him away.

"Sawyer!" I cried, and rushed to his aid. Two soldiers caught me and pulled backwards. Russell and I were both fighting them with all of our strength. In the struggle I was knocked backwards. I fell directly between the pillars. The lights flashed again.

"She's got it too!" a soldier yelled, and they were upon me again.

I knew I was sick, but I still tried to run. Two soldiers caught my left arm, and with my right I tried to grab for Russell, who had come to my aid as soon as he saw the second set of flashing lights. My fingers grazed his, and then the soldiers picked me up off the ground and carried me after Sawyer.

"Russell!" I cried in terror, struggling against the strong arms that held me captive.

"Shauna!" Russell shouted, fighting the soldiers who were restraining him. Beside him, I saw Michael being led towards the far end of the tent. At least the two of them would be safe. As for Sawyer and I...God only knew what was going to happen to us.

The last thing I saw before I was carried out the side was Russell's face, desperate as he tried to get to his little sister. And that image was one of the last I would ever see of my older brother.

2

Inside the Lab

Walter Reifert

The third floor below ground was almost completely empty. That floor, and the eight floors that existed beneath the earth, each consisted of three dozen rooms that had been built in case an outbreak such as the one occurring should happen. Later that night, the rooms would quickly begin to fill up with the poor souls who had fallen prey to the Colician Virus. But as of that moment, late in the evening, the only sign of life on the third floor was a young man named Walter Reifert. The Colician Virus had already taken over his mind, and being the nephew of a creator of the strain had earned him a safe place to rest throughout the night. Unfortunately, several of those who had fallen ill in Hatfield would not survive the trials of that night, and those who did would be held prisoner underground. Don Rudolph knew the horrors that would come that night and over the next several weeks, which is why he placed his nephew securely underground; he could take care of him himself once that night was through. Dr. Rudolph had sedated his nephew and left him to sleep while he attended to others who were sick, but Walter was no longer sleeping. He looked like he was sleeping, but his mind was buzzing with activity.

Walter Reifert had fallen ill the night after the virus escaped the facility. Now that he had been sick for exactly one week, the virus had taken over his mind completely. And he was seeing things much clearer than ever before.

The young man now possessed the ability to reach into the minds of others. Although he could not quite control the ability, he did find a way to use it.

He woke from his slumber precisely three hours after his injection, but he chose to keep his eyes closed. While he kept his entire body still and cleared his head, he heard everything. He heard the thoughts of every single person in that building. There were a lot of voices. Most of them originated from above him on the ground floor, where the cataloging was taking place. Walter heard dozens of people from the town, their thoughts all terrified as they were held against their will, repeatedly poked by needles and having bright lights shined in their eyes. Among the ruckus, Walter heard his family. Ethan and Anton were being held together, so they were slightly calmer than Tyler and their dad. They were sitting side by side, and from what Walter could hear they were strapped to chairs. Walter's father was in a room away from them, his thoughts panicked because a couple of soldiers had just loaded Tyler onto a stretcher and then wheeled him away. Tyler was now in a different section of the facility than the rest of Walter's family. He was in one of the testing rooms, where there was little light and four doctors to each patient. His thoughts were the most terrified of the whole family. Doctors were drawing his blood and they weren't answering any of his frantic questions. He didn't know what they were going to do to him, and he was very scared.

In addition to hearing the thoughts of everyone in the building, Walter could also reach into the minds of individuals and see their memories. One mind in particular drew his attention. It was the mind of the man who was walking towards his room.

Frank Atkinson was not a doctor or a soldier. He was a medic, but he was going back to school to become a doctor. He was twenty-seven years old, unmarried with no kids, and although he was well liked by his co-workers he was not at all a good person. Nobody knew of the dark secrets of his past, nobody except for Walter and the people he had hurt. When he was nineteen years old, he was driving home from a friend's party while intoxicated and blew a stop sign, striking a mother and her two young children in the crosswalk. All three, the mother, the baby, and the four-year-old, were killed instantly. Frank fled that scene and left the three innocents to be discovered by someone else. He was never punished for his crime.

When he was twenty-one, he lost a game of poker to a man in a rival fraternity, losing five thousand dollars. The next evening, Frank followed him to a hunting range, and when his back was turned he put a bullet through his spine. The man didn't die right away, but after he took back his money and more, Frank left him there to die slowly. Once again, he was never caught.

When he was twenty-five, Frank made friends with a pretty girl named Kristin who was studying to become a doctor. After four months of just being friends, Frank told her that he wanted to be more than that. Kristin turned him down, because she was married with a baby boy. That night he followed her home to an empty house and raped her before strangling her and burying her in the woods. For a third time, Frank had gotten away with murder. Nobody alive had ever known about the horrible crimes Frank committed, until now. Until Walter reached into his mind and saw it all. Which was why Walter didn't feel a shred of remorse for what he was about to do.

Walter heard him enter his room a few moments later. It was three hours and thirty-eight minutes after he had been forced to sleep, which meant that Frank was late in delivering Walter his next sedative. He thought that being a few minutes late wouldn't make a difference. He was so, so wrong. Walter lay very still as Frank approached his side, but listened to his thoughts very, very closely. The RN reached into his jacket pocket, pulled out the syringe, snapped it twice, took hold of Walter's arm, moved the needle towards his arm, and that was when Walter made his move.

Walter's eyes snapped open and he looked Frank directly in the face. Frank hadn't been looking at him, but a second later his eyes landed on Walter's. He did a double take and then his eyes widened in shock. As their eyes locked, Walter grabbed hold of him with his mind and held on.

"Untie me," Walter told him quietly, and Frank's lips moved to form the same words simultaneously with Walter.

Walter didn't know how he was doing it, but he was. He could feel Frank's mind as part of his own. He was controlling Frank. Frank set the syringe down and did what Walter said. He looked different. His eyes were almost black, and it took Walter a second to realize that his pupils had dilated and were huge.

As his body was freed, Walter sat up and mentally instructed Frank to take a step back. He did, expressionlessly. Walter hopped off the bed and then instructed Frank to get on.

"Give yourself that shot," Walter told him sharply.

"But it'll kill me," Frank murmured, not really looking like the thought bothered him all that much.

Walter looked into his mind again and saw the truth in his words. The injection was double the concentration of a normal sedative. Walter now had a higher tolerance to drugs, so they had to give him twice the dose. Knowing everything that man had done, Walter truly considered pushing him to give himself the full dose. Walter now could see that Frank wanted to hurt more people. He wanted to hurt the younger girls that would be held prisoner in the facility. Walter wanted to kill him. He *wanted* Frank to die.

"Give yourself half of it," Walter said finally. Death didn't seem like a fair punishment for his crimes. "And when you wake up, you will tell everyone about the people you hurt. You will tell it all."

"I'll tell," Frank muttered, his eyes staring off. "I'll tell it all."

"And you won't tell anyone what happened here," Walter said.

"I won't tell them what you are," Frank whispered, and then gave himself half the shot. A moment later, his eyes fluttered closed and his body fell back with a *thump*.

He wasn't one hundred percent certain of what Frank would do once he woke up, so Walter fastened the restraints over him as a precaution. Before leaving the room, young Walter was sure to take Frank's keycard off his lanyard. Then he left, not a doubt in his mind that he would get out of the building.

Walter Reifert

My head was pounding. It hurt so bad that I couldn't even feel the pain anymore. I could still hear the thoughts of everyone in the building, so I knew I wouldn't get caught unless I wanted to. Discovering that I had the ability to control people's minds, just like my dad had predicted, was exhilarating. At first I had been really scared, not understanding how I had grabbed hold of Frank's mind. I could feel his mind as a part of my own, and simply telling him what to do—whether it be mentally or verbally—would make him do what I wanted. The fear only lasted a moment. After that, the thrill of it hit me. This power I now possessed...it was remarkable! My father had been right about a lot of things, no matter how angry his words had made me. I had to learn how to control this power. Once I could control it, I would be unstoppable. And then no one would dare mess with me or my family ever again.

I was in the elevator. It needed a code or a keycard, so I used Frank's. I was angrily ascending from an underground level to the ground floor. They had taken me, drugged me, hurt my family, and I wasn't going to stand for that anymore. I knew exactly what I was going to do. What I *had* to do.

Just before the elevator let out its high-pitched *ding* and the doors opened, I stepped to one side of the compartment, obscuring myself from the view of the soldier who was walking past at that exact moment. When I knew he had passed, I stepped out and moved briskly down the hall. I could hear my brother Tyler. His thoughts were still panicked as the doctors surrounding him continued to poke and prod him. He was at the end of the hall in room 12B. That was where I was going.

Doctors and soldiers peered at me curiously as I passed them by, but I mentally instructed each of them to ignore me and proceed with their work. I knew what I wanted to do to the doctors holding my brother, but I wasn't sure if I would actually do it. By the time I finally reached room 12B, I was fighting with myself over what I should do to them.

I came to Tyler's aid just in time. The head doctor in the room had just placed a mask over his face. By the thoughts in the doctor's head I discovered that the mask was connected to a tank full of gas to make Tyler sleep. I marched inside like I owned the place. I looked directly into the face of the head doctor, who was staring at me in surprise. "Get that thing off his face!" I snapped.

The doctor, whose thoughts were just as confused as Frank's had been, immediately took the mask off of Tyler's face and dropped it to the floor.

Tyler started gasping; he had been holding his breath. "Walter?" He tried to turn his head to look at me. His body was at an awkward angle, the bed he was strapped to turned away from the door. "That you, little brother?"

"Untie him," I said to the doctor, still holding onto his mind.

The other three, startled by my entrance and demands, hadn't spoken a word until now. "Hey," a second doctor spoke up, taking a step towards me.

My head snapped in his direction. I was still holding the head doctor, and I found that I was able to grab this one and hold them both at the same time.

"I told you to untie him," I growled, feeling my temper rising.

The two doctors who I was holding started to untie Tyler. They were fighting me as hard as they could, trying to move a single muscle at their command. But even their hardest wasn't hard enough. I was stronger than them. I was stronger than any human.

Out of the corner of my eye I saw one of the other two reaching for something under one of the counters along the wall. Hearing his thoughts told me I should be cautious. "Hit that alarm and I'll kill one of them," I warned him, and I saw him freeze.

Tyler was freed and he climbed off the table. Hugging me tightly, he demanded, "Why did you come back for me? You should have just left!"

"You're my brother," I replied simply. "I won't leave you behind." Glaring at the four terrified men, I tried to make myself look as intimidating as possible. I knew they were going to sound the alarm no matter what I did. It was my job to buy us time. "You give us sixty seconds or I'll come back for you," I snarled, and then we fled.

Tyler and I ran. I started counting in my head as soon as we left the room: one Mississippi, two Mississippi, three Mississippi. I made it to twenty-three Mississippi when the alarm sounded.

"You're not going back for them, are you?" Tyler asked me nervously. He had been counting in his head too.

"They called my bluff," I replied grimly.

I had no clue where to go, but others in the building did. I followed the map in their heads, making sure to evade soldiers and doctors as they scrambled about searching for us. We finally made it out of the maze of white hallways and found the big open room where Ethan and Anton were being held. There was a soldier inside with them; I could hear his mind. But I wasn't leaving unless my whole family was with me.

"Don't move!" the soldier yelled at us, aiming and cocking his weapon.

All I had to do was look at him and he dropped the rifle before crumpling to the floor himself.

"Did you kill him?" Tyler asked, staring at me in shock.

I peered down at the soldier, not really certain of what I had just done. "I don't think so," I said, but we didn't have time to worry about that.

"Walter! Tyler!" Ethan and Anton were yelling our names from across the room, bouncing up and down in their chairs.

Tyler and I rushed to them. I undid the straps holding Anton in place and Tyler did the same with Ethan. When my other brothers were on their feet, they grabbed me and Tyler and pulled us in for a tight embrace. They were laughing; it was their way of expressing relief.

"How did you do that?" Anton asked in amazement.

"I knew you'd come get us, little brother!" Ethan said, clapping me on the back.

"We have to go get Dad," I said, urgently trying to lead them out.

"But what about all of them?" Ethan asked me, catching my arm and gesturing to those who were still trapped in their seats. All of them were young men around the ages of Ethan and Anton. I had heard their voices from down the hall. They were all scared and had been yelling to be set free. Now, after seeing me take down a soldier with half a glance, they were all silent, watching our brief reunion with wide-eyed fascination. They were watching me. "We can't just leave them here."

I was growing more and more frantic by the second. "We don't have time!" I cried, pointing to the ceiling as we listened to the alarm that continued to sound. Somehow, the soldiers had figured out where I was, and they were all converging on this room like a giant pack of wolves. I could hear them coming. "We have to leave now!"

I quickly led my brothers from the room and rushed down another hallway. Dad was close by, and Tyler was suddenly in front leading the way. We were at my father's room in less than twenty seconds, and I shoved Tyler aside, knowing that there were two more soldiers just inside the door. They both repeated the same routine as the last soldier, so I repeated mine as well. After both were unconscious on the floor, Tyler stepped to my side and gazed at me. I made eye contact with him, and what I saw on his face was fear. My brother, my friend, was afraid of me.

"How did you do that?" he asked me uncertainly. His expression suddenly looked angry. "What are you?"

"I don't know," I whispered, answering both his questions. "But I wish that I did."

"Boys!" Our dad was calling for us from his chair.

The four of us rushed to him, Anton and Tyler untying him.

Dad was really mad. He was glaring at me. "What the hell do you think you're doing?" he snapped.

I felt a flash of anger myself. "Rescuing you," I replied, and added curtly, "You're welcome."

He jumped to his feet, and Tyler and Anton hopped out of his way when they realized just how upset Dad was. Grabbing me by the front of my shirt, he pulled me forward so our noses were pretty much touching. "Who the hell do you think you are? How dare you risk your life for me! Or any of us! You should have gotten out and gotten yourself to safety! You can't risk your life for us, Walter!"

"Well, since you're so ungrateful, I'd be glad to strap you back in," I told him, glaring back into his eyes so filled with rage.

"*Listen to me!*" Dad hissed, dropping his voice. "You need to keep yourself safe from now on, okay? No matter what happens, you have to keep pushing through and protect yourself, understand?"

"What are you talking about?" I snapped. His words were scaring me.

"I'm not going to be here for you forever, bud," Dad whispered, his eyes suddenly sad. "So you need to listen to what I'm saying."

I stared at my dad, my heart thumping in my chest and my throat beginning to close up. I recognized Dad's words from earlier that evening, and then I remembered what else my dad told me. Someone had told him what was about to go down in Hatfield. I could hear the answer in the grief-filled thoughts running through his mind, but I still asked the question anyway.

"And what are you saying?"

Dad pulled away so he could look into my eyes better. *You're important to our future, Walter. You have to keep yourself safe and help anyone that you can. But you can't risk your life like this anymore, because if you die, our people will never have a chance. Promise me, no matter how much it hurts, that you'll still push through.*

"Why would I be in any pain?" I breathed, not wanting to believe the thoughts in his head.

Walter, promise me.

My eyes filled up with tears, but I refused to let them flood over. "I promise," I whispered. "Why are you telling me all this now? You'll be there to protect me when we get out of this. Why are you telling me to be strong now?"

Dad sighed. "Because I'm not going to be there."

I stared at him in horror. "Yes, you will!"

"I'm not going to see you save our people," Dad whispered. "I just know that you will."

"You'll be there," I said firmly. "We're going to get out of here and we'll go to Canada, just like you said…"

Dad shook his head gently. He put his hand on my shoulder. "You're a good kid, Walter," he told me. "You're going to be an even better man. I'm glad I got the chance to know you for as long as I have."

I began to protest again, not willing to believe that I was going to lose my dad as soon as he was suggesting, but my brothers were arguing behind me and my dad proceeded to intervene.

"Leave them!" he ordered. "We have to go!"

"No, please!" a man about the same age as Dad pleaded. Ethan had been trying to untie him while Tyler and Anton had been insisting on leaving him be. "I have a little girl who was taken! Please, I have to find her!"

"Me too!" another father begged desperately. "I have three little ones I need to find. Please, help me!"

Every other man in the room started pleading with us all at once, and Ethan turned on my dad. "We have to help them!" he said insistently. "We can't run out without helping these people too!"

"If we let everyone out, it's going to be one huge game of target practice!" Dad replied sharply. "It'll be a bloodbath! We're leaving, just the five of us. Right now." He grabbed Ethan with one hand and me with the other. He turned towards the door to lead us out, but then stopped dead in his tracks.

"Oh, crap," Anton muttered.

"Well, it looks like the whole family has come to the rescue once again," Uncle Don said, standing with his arms crossed in the doorway. He wasn't smiling anymore.

For a few seconds, we were all silent as we stared back at Don. He was alone, but he was still blocking our escape. Finally, Dad spoke up to try to reason with him. I wasn't too hopeful.

"Don," Dad said, his voice different, unlike his usual tone with Don—angry and dismissive. He was now pleading, desperate. He was about to get on his knees and beg. "Please, just let us leave."

"You've all got the genes to carry the virus," Don said. "And you've all been exposed. Your youngest is very sick, John. You know I can't let you leave."

"I just want my boys to have a chance for a normal life," Dad told him.

"If you try to flee this building, your boys won't even have a future," Don warned, his gaze shifting and landing on me. "Walter, you shouldn't have tried to run like this. You're only making this situation worse for yourself."

"Just let me go," I said quietly, my compelling tone having no effect on Don.

"I can't," Don replied, stepping towards us.

"I'm not going to let you experiment on my kids," Dad told him, his old tone back. I was beginning to miss it.

"You need to come with me, Walter," Don said urgently. "I can get the soldiers to hold their fire on your family because the virus hasn't manifested itself in any of them yet, but they know you're sick. If you try to leave, they'll kill you without the slightest hesitation and there's nothing I could do to stop them."

I laughed mockingly. "They can't touch me," I said, my eyes narrowing.

"Walter, for your own protection, you need to trust me!" Don told me breathlessly.

"I'm never going to trust you again," I growled at him.

"You don't know what you're capable of!" Don insisted. "You don't understand the power you possess! You could hurt yourself, or someone else if you're not careful. You need to come with me right now. All of you need to come with me now."

"We're not going anywhere with you," I snarled with a harsh glare.

"Then I'm going to have no choice but to sedate you again," Don said solemnly. "That's something that's going to make us both very uncomfortable."

"You touch my boy, and I'll rip your head off," Dad warned, stepping in front of me and my brothers. "On second thought, why don't I just do that anyway?"

"You really don't want to do that, John," Don cautioned as Dad went forward. "You don't want to make a mess of things in front of your sons, do you?"

"I've been waiting for this for too long," Dad said through his teeth, looking all too eager to kill his brother-in-law.

"John," Don warned, taking a stance that said he was prepared to fight.

"Whenever you're ready," Dad replied, grinning evilly at him.

My heart skipped a beat in that instant. The hate I felt for my uncle was no secret, but at the same time I was afraid to watch him fight my father. I had grown up around Don. He was part of my family, no matter what Dad said. Even if Don had plans to experiment on me, I didn't want to see him get hurt. Dad was bigger than him, and it was very likely that things would end badly. Although my father was the bigger man in this fight, Don looked prepared to defend himself. I didn't want to see my dad get hurt either. What was I supposed to do? The only way out was past Don, and if Dad didn't fight him then the soldiers would get us. I caught a thought that crossed Don's mind for a moment, and had a sudden hope that we could escape without a conflict. He was relieved that none of us knew about the second exit. There was another door on the same wall further down, leading back into the hall and around a corner before taking us to a side exit that wasn't being guarded. It was our last chance for a quick, uninterrupted escape. I was going to take it. The soldiers were almost here.

"Out this door!" I cried, starting to run for it. I heard my brothers begin to follow, surprised by my abrupt movement. Anton caught me by the arm and told me to stop, and at first I didn't understand why. Uncle Don must have predicted my attempt, maybe even set me up for it, because he was running for me, ready to catch me before we made it to the door. Seeing this, I skidded to a stop to avoid being tackled by my uncle. To my misfortune, Tyler didn't halt as fast as me. He crashed into my back and I stumbled forward into Don's waiting grasp.

"Let me go!" I snapped. If I could make eye contact with him for just a second, I could take control of him and make him stop. He was trying to wrestle me to the floor, his arms wrapped around my shoulders. No matter how hard I twisted, I couldn't get my head around to look at him.

"Walter, come on!" Ethan yelled, grabbing my arm and trying to pull me free. We could hear the shouts of the soldiers as they drew closer.

"Get off him!" Tyler shouted, giving Uncle Don a shove.

I was suddenly slammed into the ground as Uncle Don dropped all his body weight and fell on top of me. He released me, but when I rolled over, I realized that he hadn't released me willingly. Dad had body-slammed him and now had Don's arms pinned behind him.

"Go!" Dad cried, his expression full of rage as he wrestled with Don. "Get out! Get away from this place and hide!"

"I'm not leaving you here!" I said, trying to resist Ethan and Anton as they pulled me to my feet and started to drag me to the door. I was afraid of what my father had said. I was afraid that I was going to lose him. I was afraid that this was the last time I was ever going to see him; fighting with my uncle. "We leave together!"

My father made eye contact with me for half a second. In that half a second, he said four words, but in the agony of his eyes I saw thousands more. *I love you, Walter.*

44

I let my brothers take me then. Turning to the door, the four of us rushed out, moments before the soldiers rushed in. If it weren't for the side exit, we never would have made it.

I never really believed in God, but if there was even the slightest chance that he existed then I was going to pray to him. I prayed that my dad would be okay, that we all would be okay. I prayed that we could do what Dad said; flee to Canada and stay in the Rockies. As long as I could be with Dad and my three big brothers, I didn't care where I was. I didn't really have much that was holding me here.

Several soldiers yelled for us to halt as we rounded the corner, and they even fired a few rounds at us which bounced off the walls. We ran through the door that led to the outside and kept on running. I breathed in the fresh night air, taking in the sweet scent of freedom. It was dark out now, so we would have cover until we could find a place to hide.

As we ran along the side of the building, we heard several gunshots coming from inside. I stopped abruptly, clutching my head from the explosion of pain.

"Walter, you can't stop!" Ethan said breathlessly, tugging on my arm.

"We just need to find a place to hide and then we can rest, okay?" Anton told me, taking my other arm.

"Dad," I whispered, feeling Dad's pain as my own. I could feel him slipping, slipping away from the world. He was dying. "Oh God. Dad…"

"Dad's going to be fine, Walter," Tyler insisted, but when I looked at him I saw the tears streaming down his face. He couldn't feel what I felt, but he knew it just as well. "We have to keep going."

Slipping, slipping, slipping…gone.

Dad was dead.

The soldiers burst out of the side door and came for us.

I started screaming.

My brothers pulled me forward. I kept screaming. Anton told me to shut up. Ethan let go of me. He ran at the soldiers. I heard a few more shots. I felt Ethan die just like Dad. Tyler said, "Ethan's gone!" We didn't stop. I kept screaming. Another shot. Anton went down by my side. He died. Tyler yelled. We kept running. I kept screaming.

Everything was happening in a blur. I was sobbing now, feeling out of control. I had just felt my father and two of my brothers die.

Tyler and I rounded a corner and he stopped us quickly. He turned towards me and slapped me hard across the face. I stopped abruptly and stared at him in shock. "Listen to me," Tyler said urgently. He was crying, and I realized that I was too. "You've been a good little brother, Walter. No matter what you hear me say after this, run for the parking lot. Okay? Run for the parking lot, and hide until they're gone."

I didn't say anything as Tyler hugged me quickly and then turned away from me. I didn't know what I was supposed to say. As my oldest brother rounded the corner and ran towards the soldiers as Ethan had, I heard him shout, "Run for the trees, Walter! Go for the trees!"

There were woods alongside the facility and they looked tempting. All that darkness and places to hide...it would have been perfect. But I listened to Tyler. I ran for the lot. The lot was around another corner, but I could see the start of it from where I was. I ran around the corner quickly, just as I heard a final shot. Almost instantly, I felt Tyler go as well. I whimpered, but I kept going. I kept going for Tyler, and for the rest of my family.

I ran through the rows of vehicles, vehicles that must have belonged to the doctors and other medical personnel inside. Ducking behind a black SUV, I sat down in the shadow of it and tried to catch my breath.

"He's going into the woods!" a soldier shouted from somewhere behind me, falling for Tyler's trick—his last trick that would ultimately save my life. "Go into the woods!"

Listening carefully as they tromped up the hill into the trees, I let myself cry silently. My entire family was dead, and they had all died while trying to protect me. I wanted to die too. I deserved to die.

"I love you," I found myself sobbing. "I love you all. I'm so sorry. I'm so sorry..."

The footsteps of the soldiers died off, and I allowed myself to breathe normally again. I knew I was supposed to run, to get out and hide and protect myself like Dad and Tyler had said, but I was too grief-stricken to keep going. I couldn't go any further.

"I'm sorry," I whispered again. "I'm sorry..."

Suddenly, a door on the other side of the SUV opened, and I heard someone shuffling around inside. I was on the passenger side, and when I peeked beneath the vehicle I saw that one of the doctors was at the driver's door. I could see his white pant legs, and I immediately became wary. When the doctor closed the door again, I hopped to my feet but ducked down, preparing to run in case he saw me. For several silent seconds, I waited for him to start walking back to the facility, to one of the many entrances on that side of the building. I didn't hear or see him after that, so I dropped down and peeked beneath the SUV again. I didn't see his legs, and I wondered if I had imagined him. My mind was too upset and frantic to hear any thoughts. Confused, I rose to my feet again and gazed back at the facility.

The doctor grabbed me from behind. One arm wrapped around my chest, and his other hand cupped over my mouth and nose. He had a cloth in his hand that smelled so strong it made my eyes water even more.

I grabbed at the hand holding the cloth over my mouth, unable to breathe through the horrid smell. Although I was scared and fighting this doctor, I couldn't help but think that this man was actually there to help me, not hurt me.

"Quiet, quiet, *quiet!*" the doctor hissed in my ear. "I'm going to get you out of this place. You're going to have to trust me. I'm really sorry about this."

Breathing in whatever was in the cloth—chloroform, maybe?—caused me to lose consciousness. I slumped back against the doctor's body, and he opened the door to his backseat and carefully lifted me inside. I wasn't aware of anything he did to me in that vehicle, but when I asked him about it later on, Dr. Perry was kind enough to tell me exactly what he did to help me get away from that place. He kept duct tape in his car for a scenario such as this and he taped my mouth shut while binding my wrists and ankles together. He then gave me a very strong sedative; injecting it into my upper arm; powerful enough to keep me out for the rest of the night. He left me then, closing the door and locking his SUV, going inside the facility to do his job, but also fully prepared to care for me and get me to our current haven.

Just as soon as his shift was over.

Shauna Skyler

I was strapped to a chair. I had been for a long time. An hour, maybe? There was no clock, and I had no perception of time. It could have been three days or three minutes.

After I was carried out of the tent, Sawyer and I were both taken inside the facility and down a hallway; then a soldier holding a clipboard asked for our names and ages. I refused to speak at first, but he loosened my tongue quite a bit when he held his pistol to my forehead. They were taking this virus very seriously. Once he had our names, Sawyer was separated from me and taken down another hallway, where they were running tests on younger children. I tried to claw my way free to get to him, but I was being carried by three strong men. My struggles were pointless. I was taken into a room adjacent to several other hallways. There were two rows of chairs facing back to back, at least a dozen chairs in each row. Teenagers who I recognized from my high school were strapped into every one of the chairs except for one on the end. The soldiers held me down while strapping me in. They bound my ankles and my wrists and then just left me there, but not before something strange happened. As they bound my left wrist and I screamed in protest, both rows of chairs suddenly shifted backwards at least two feet. We all looked around in surprise to see who had moved them. When we saw no one, the soldiers' eyes landed on me. They stared at me, horrified, and then they rushed away. I wasn't sure why they looked at me like that, and frankly, I didn't care. Beside me was a girl from my Algebra class, a blonde named Carly. She looked really sick. Her skin was gray and she looked like she hadn't slept in days. I tried talking to her, but she didn't even notice I was there.

I pulled against the restraints for some time as doctors and soldiers bustled about, attending to teens here and there, but eventually I gave up. None of the doctors had come to me yet, and I was getting very anxious. I had been sitting very still in my chair for a long time, staring at the floor, when I suddenly realized that the strap holding my wrists was loose. The strap was tied to the bottom of the chair, and if I could wiggle it enough it would slide up the leg of the chair and I would be able to untie the strap with my teeth. I started wiggling my arm back and forth, and the strap became looser and looser. In a few seconds my arm would be free. Before I was able to free myself, I heard a groan from my right side. Glancing over, I saw that Carly was having some sort of seizure. Her eyes were rolling back in her head, her nose was bleeding heavily, and her entire body was shaking.

"Oh my God!" I whispered as panic started coursing through me. Looking around frantically, I spotted a man in a white lab coat writing on a clipboard a few yards away with his back turned to me. "Doctor!" I cried to him. "Doctor, help! Help!"

The doctor turned towards the sound of my voice, and when his eyes landed on my desperate face his brow furrowed in concern. He had very dark, wavy hair and mahogany-colored eyes, a peculiar yet interesting eye color. As he approached me, I read the name on the gold metal tag on his chest: Dr. Shawn Perry.

"What's the matter, sweetheart?" he asked me, kneeling on the floor in front of me.

"Help her!" I pleaded, looking to Carly. "Please, help her!"

Dr. Perry looked over at Carly, and his eyes widened in surprise. "My God," he breathed, immediately on his feet. "I need a stretcher over here now! Wheel this girl to the emergency care room immediately!"

Several soldiers and another doctor came to help Dr. Perry unstrap Carly and lift her up onto the stretcher. Dr. Perry was yelling orders to anyone who cared to listen, but I wasn't paying attention to him anymore. My strap was almost ready to slide up the arm of the chair, and I wasn't going to waste any of my limited time. They were starting to wheel Carly away when the strap finally gave. Unfortunately, as it came loose, a hand snapped out and caught it.

"Whoa!" Dr. Perry said, kneeling down again and smiling up at me. "Whoever tied these didn't tie them tight enough."

As he started to retie the strap, a burst of fear filled me. I wasn't going to sit in this chair any longer! Grabbing the strap in my hand, I gave it a sharp yank. The strap was pulled clean out of Dr. Perry's hand and he snatched at it, shock written on his face. I pulled my wrist to my mouth and tried to pry it open, but the doctor was fighting me back.

"Easy, easy!" Dr. Perry said, pulling my arm back down. "Just calm down, okay? Everything's going to be fine…"

I don't know what I was thinking, but my teeth automatically came down on his arm. He cried out in surprise, and then there were several automatic rifles aimed at my head.

"Release him!"

"Stop fighting!"

"We *will* open fire!"

These threats and more were shouted at me, and I flinched away from the guns and Dr. Perry. At the same time, the chairs shifted backwards another three feet.

Dr. Perry turned to the soldiers with his hands raised. "I've got it," he told them as calmly as he could. "She's just a little nervous. Let me handle it." The yelling stopped as Perry turned back to me and gently took hold of my arm. "It's okay," he said soothingly. He placed my wrist on the arm of the chair and began to retie the strap. "Nobody wants to hurt you. Just take it easy and everything will be fine."

"Why are you doing this?" I whimpered, and found myself crying.

Dr. Perry gazed up at me, and deep sadness filled his eyes. He rose to his feet. "This is for your own good," he promised me, and smoothed back my hair.

I wasn't bothered then for maybe another twenty minutes. Suddenly, the noise in the room seemed a hell of a lot louder. I could hear everyone's voice as if they were standing right in front of me. My heart started to pound as my ears started to ring. I had no idea what was going on, but I didn't like it.

Off to my left, I saw a new doctor walk up to a soldier. "Who's next?" I heard him ask as clear as day, even though he was on the other side of the room.

"The girl on the end," the soldier replied. He was talking about me.

The doctor was writing something on his clipboard. He didn't bother to look up. "Bring her to room 6E, please. And be gentle with her, will you? We don't need any more unnecessary fatalities."

My heartbeat quickened again when I heard his words.

"I think you should give her something," the soldier said, catching the doctor by the arm. "She's a jittery one." When all the doctor did was stare back at him reproachfully, he shrugged. "But that's just if you don't want any more fatalities."

Looking rather irritated, the doctor turned and made eye contact with me. He was a few years older than Dr. Perry, with black hair and brown eyes. I don't know how, but I could read his nametag from where I was. Dr. Donald Rudolph. "This one?" he asked, nodding to me.

"That's her," the soldier said, starting to raise his weapon.

"Put that away," the doctor ordered in disgust. "The guns are the reason the last family tried to run." He started to walk over to me, and as he did so his entire mood changed. His irritated expression became warm and friendly. He knelt beside me and smiled as Perry had. "Hi," he greeted, peering into my face curiously. "How are you feeling?" When I didn't answer him, he reached into one of his coat pockets. "This is going to make you feel a little disoriented, but that's normal." He pulled out a loaded syringe.

I immediately began to struggle, but it was pointless once again. Dr. Perry had tightened the straps. I was trapped.

"Please don't," I begged as he stuck me with the needle.

He only continued to smile at me as he gave me the shot. After the syringe was emptied, he replaced it in his pocket and stood up. "Just try to relax," he told me, and then gazed down at me expectantly.

A moment later, I started to feel the effects of what he had given me. My vision started swimming, and my head began to feel foggy. I suddenly felt very tired, and my eyes fluttered closed as my head lolled forward.

"Good girl," Dr. Rudolph murmured. "I'll see you in a few minutes." I heard him repeat to the soldier, "Room 6E. I want her there unharmed and as soon as possible."

I felt the straps being undone, and then I was lifted up and placed on a hard, flat surface, and restrained again. There were voices above me, but I couldn't distinguish them. My head was too fogged up. The stretcher began to move. I felt it being pushed out of the large room and then down another hallway. Another minute went by, and I felt strong enough to open my eyes. The hallway was wide and brightly lit compared to the dim lighting of the big room. Two soldiers were pushing my stretcher, the one by my head watching me warily. I peered up at him and he stared down at me, neither of us saying a word. He looked so afraid of me, yet what threat could I possibly be to him? Even if I wasn't drugged and strapped to a gurney, I was a short, non-athletic, fifteen-year-old girl. He was a trained soldier. There was nothing I could do to hurt him.

Was there?

Doctors and soldiers were passing us as we moved, and we suddenly passed by Dr. Perry. He was speaking to another doctor about something urgent, but when I was wheeled by his gaze shifted and landed on me. When we made eye contact, that same sad look from before came to his face. "Help me!" I wanted to say to him. He was a good doctor, a good person. He didn't want to be a part of any of this. He was scared too. I had never met the man before tonight, but I knew these things. I think Dr. Perry was sick too, and he was aware of it. Whatever was happening to me was happening to him too. We were the same. When the time came, he would help me.

I lost sight of Dr. Perry when the soldiers turned to the right into a dark room. There were a couple dull bulbs overhead and some black lighting, but that was it. Inside the room, right in the center, was a surgical table with restraints attached as well. Along the walls were shelves of syringes, vials of liquid, test tubes, and numerous other things that I didn't have names for. Four doctors were in the room wearing white gloves and masks, among them Dr. Rudolph.

"Where do you want her, Dr. Rudolph?" the soldier by my head asked.

"Strap her in here," Dr. Rudolph instructed, patting the table in the center of the room before returning to his clipboard.

They pushed the stretcher so it was parallel to the table, but the soldier behind me stopped one of the doctors as they went to unstrap me. "Careful," he warned. "She's jumpy. She already attacked Dr. Perry."

"She's a child and she's scared," Dr. Rudolph snapped at him.

"She's already starting to show," the other soldier said, watching me nervously.

"Just get her on the table," Dr. Rudolph ordered impatiently.

I hadn't a clue what the soldier meant by me "showing." What was I showing? What did it matter, anyway? The drug Dr. Rudolph had given me was starting to wear off; whatever it was, it wasn't meant for anything long term. I knew because my head was starting to clear and it was easier for me to focus. The soldiers and doctors undid my restraints one by one, but I didn't move until the last strap was undone.

My first kick caught one soldier in the jaw. My second kick knocked a doctor back into the wall. I didn't get a chance to throw any punches.

"Don't hurt her!" Dr. Rudolph yelled as I was wrestled off the stretcher and onto the table. "Just get her strapped in!"

Just then, every glass object in the room rattled noisily. The room went abruptly silent, the men looking around uncertainly. Then their eyes moved to me. They all wore the same expressions that the soldiers wore when the chairs moved around in the big room. What was happening here?

I gave up after the rattling ceased. There were too many people fighting me and I was too tired to win. One thing I began to notice when I was being strapped in was that my headache had gotten much worse. My temples were throbbing and my eyes were beginning to tear up from the pain.

"Alright, now get out!" Dr. Rudolph waved his hands dismissively at the soldiers.

"Gladly," one replied, and then they were gone.

"Let's get started," Dr. Rudolph said to the other doctors. "The same procedure as last time."

Dr. Rudolph was still scribbling away on his clipboard, so the other three got down to business. One of them stuck an IV in my left arm despite my protests, and then another shined a bright light in my eyes.

I pulled against my restraints, praying that this would all end quickly.

Finally done with whatever it was he was doing, Dr. Rudolph set his clipboard down and came to my right side, where two of the doctors were. "We need three vials for the lab and a finger prick to test blood type," he said.

Another needle was stuck in my right arm and the doctors started drawing blood. At the same time, Dr. Rudolph pricked my finger with something and I cried out at the sudden pain.

"Sorry," he apologized, patting my leg. "You're doing great, sweetheart."

I wanted to hurt that man.

"We've got the three," one doctor said.

"Good," Dr. Rudolph said, walking up to my shoulder and peering down at me. "What's your name, sweetie?"

I was too upset to answer. All I wanted was to go home, see my family, and sleep in my own bed with my dog. I was so tired. And who was going to feed Kerch tonight and let him outside? My shoulders tensed and I turned my head away. I was so humiliated when I started crying again.

Dr. Rudolph seemed to understand that my behavior was out of fear and not stubbornness. "Hey," he said softly, placing a gentle hand on my shoulder. "It's okay. You're doing fine. None of us are going to hurt you." When all I did to reply was flinch away from his touch, I heard him start to walk around to the other side of me. "I have a daughter about the same age as you. I could never bring myself to hurt you." He tried to get me to look him in the eyes, but I turned my head away again. This time he simply took hold of my chin and gently turned my head back towards him. I didn't want to, but I forced myself to look at him. He pulled his facial mask down to his chin so I could see his face. "My name's Don," he told me, and smiled warmly, as he had when he approached me the first time. "And I don't want you to be afraid of me. Can you tell me your name?"

I stared into his brown eyes. Something was telling me not to trust this man, but at the moment he seemed to be trying to help. "Shauna," I told him shakily.

"Shauna," he repeated, and nodded. "Shauna what?"

"Skyler."

Dr. Rudolph nodded to someone over my head, and then one of the doctors left the room. He pulled his mask back up over his mouth and nose. "Well, Shauna Skyler, I want to give you the run-down on what's going to happen here so you aren't surprised by anything. But first I just want you to relax, okay? Can you do that for me?"

"Where's my little brother?" I demanded, not really caring about anything he had to say. "What are you doing to him?"

"You don't need to worry about your brother right now," Dr. Rudolph told me in his annoyingly calm voice.

"No!" I shouted, causing another burst of pain in my skull. "You people took him and I want to know where he is!" All the glass objects in the room rattled again, this time louder. That strange phenomenon was really freaking me out. "Why does that keep happening?" I cried.

"Shhhh," Dr. Rudolph said, leaning down closer to me. "You don't need to get so upset."

"I want to talk to my parents," I told him firmly, tugging at my restraints. "I want to talk to them now."

"I'm sorry, but that's not going to happen," Dr. Rudolph apologized.

"Please, just let me out of here!" I stared pleadingly into his eyes. "I don't want to be here!"

"I just need to confirm that you're not sick," Dr. Rudolph said, holding my gaze.

"I'm not sick," I said, even though I was pretty sure that I was. "I'm not sick!"

Dr. Rudolph smiled at me again. I couldn't see his mouth, but his eyes showed it just the same. "That's for me to decide, I'm afraid."

Tears were pouring out of my eyes, and I looked away from him.

He gave me a moment to compose myself. "I'm going to ask you a few questions, and I need you to answer them as honestly as possible. That way, things will run much more smoothly. Can you do that?"

I nodded once.

"Good," he said, taking a step back from me. "First off, how's your head?"

I hesitated. Should I tell him? "It's fine," I lied, an obvious fib.

All Dr. Rudolph did at first was stare me down. Then, he started in a low voice, "Now Shauna, I don't want to scare you, but this virus is very serious. It's nothing to play around with. If you don't answer me truthfully, then I won't be able to help you, and then all you'll be doing is suffering. You don't have to suffer anymore, Shauna." He leaned closer to me again. "Now, why don't you tell me how it really feels?"

I stared at his intense gaze, still not wanting to admit the truth. But this headache really was awful, and if he could give me painkillers that were stronger than Advil, that would just about make my day. "It feels like it's going to explode."

"Yeah?" Dr. Rudolph said.

"Yeah," I repeated quietly.

Dr. Rudolph nodded to one of the doctors. "That's were the virus starts to take over; inside your head."

"I'm not sick!" I said, but it would have helped if I actually believed it to be so. I looked up as another doctor approached me, a loaded syringe in his hands. "What are you doing?" I demanded, attempting to pull away from him.

"This is just a little something for the pain," Dr. Rudolph told me. He had gone behind me and placed one hand on my shoulder and one on my forehead to keep me still.

Painkillers in the form of a shot hadn't exactly been what I was hoping for, but I was still for it anyway. After it was over, I muttered, "How many more of those are you going to stick me with?"

"Hopefully none tonight," Dr. Rudolph replied, releasing me.

Tonight? Was that supposed to mean that I had more coming to me in the near future?

"How were her pupils?" Dr. Rudolph asked the other two.

"Dilated," one said, handing him the light they had shined in my eyes before. "See for yourself."

Dr. Rudolph leaned over me and started to shine the light in my right eye, but my eyes automatically closed and I turned away from the harsh light. "Look at my left ear," he instructed me, turning my head back towards him and prying my eye open. He shined the light in my eye a few times before opening the other one and repeating the same thing. "Almost blocking out the entire iris," he murmured, putting the light away and then pulling my shirt up to reveal my stomach.

"What are you doing?" I asked him uncertainly, finding myself asking that question a lot.

"Just tell me if you feel anything that feels different than usual," Dr. Rudolph said, and began pressing his thumbs down off to the sides of my bellybutton.

I wasn't sure what he was looking for, or what I was supposed to be feeling—whether it be pain or discomfort or something else—but Dr. Rudolph shifted the pressure down an inch or so on my torso and then I felt it. The pain I felt in my lower abdomen was excruciating. As soon as the slightest pressure from Dr. Rudolph's fingers was applied, my whole lower body felt like it was being stabbed by dozens of knives. I attempted to keep quiet, but I couldn't contain the agonized groan that passed over my lips.

Dr. Rudolph looked down at me. "It hurts?"

Was that a question or was he just telling me what I already knew? "No," I mumbled through gritted teeth, taking a deep breath to keep the tears back.

Clearly having enough of my lies, Dr. Rudolph dug his thumbs into the same place, listening to my reaction carefully.

I cried out, the volume of my yell making my ears rattle. "Yes!" I shouted, my body heaving upward from the pain. "Yes, yes, yes! It hurts! Just please stop!"

He did stop. "Was it so hard to tell me the truth?" he asked quietly as I stared back pleadingly. Pulling my shirt back down, he turned to check the results of the finger prick. "You're O negative," he told me, as if I cared to know.

"Yeah," I said. "Is that a problem? Do I need a transfusion or something?"

"No," Dr. Rudolph said with a chuckle. "No, there's no transfusion necessary."

"What's the verdict, Doctor?" the third doctor asked as he reentered the room.

Dr. Rudolph glanced up at him and nodded. "She's got it," he stated. "There's no doubt."

"No!" I said in terror, and I thrashed around on the table. "No! No, no, no, no! I don't have it! I'm not sick!"

"Shhhh," Dr. Rudolph hushed, stroking my hair in a semi-comforting manner. "Don't you worry about a thing. I'm going to take care of you until we get this whole mess figured out. The pains you feel will all be alleviated, and when we've figured out a way to treat this virus, everything will begin to go back to the way it was. I'm going to help you, Shauna. Things won't be so bad for long."

His words weren't as comforting as I'd hoped. "Please," I begged, that being the first word to come to mind as I struggled to decide what I wanted to say. "Can I please see my parents? And my brothers? I just want to talk to them for a minute. Please…"

"You're very contagious," Dr. Rudolph murmured. "I can't allow it. I'm afraid you're not going to be seeing your family for a very long time."

I let the tears come then. I saw no point in fighting them any longer. I was going to be a prisoner in this facility for who knew how long because of something that wasn't my fault. Dr. Rudolph and these other doctors were destroying my life. It was already beginning to come crashing down around me.

"I'm going to give you something to help you go to sleep now," Dr. Rudolph told me, picking something up off the ground from beside the table.

"No!" I shouted as I saw the gas mask. A long tube ran out of it and connected to a small tank on the floor. "I don't want to sleep! Please, just let me talk to my parents!"

Ignoring my plea, Dr. Rudolph stepped behind me again. "This virus is going to make you very weak and tired and will put added stress on your brain for the next several days. The best thing to do is to put you in a coma until the symptoms begin to fade and the virus has taken over completely." He put a hand on my forehead and pressed down before placing the mask over my face.

I kicked and thrashed and screamed, but it was all useless. The gas took over, and before long I felt my body relax. Moments later, I was drifting to sleep. I had no idea what would happen to me, but now that I look back on it I'm glad that I didn't. Knowing what would happen over the next several weeks would have driven anyone mad.

The last thing I was aware of before all the lights in the world winked out was that the entire room was shaking, as if an earthquake had suddenly opened up the earth beneath us.

Don Rudolph

As Shauna Skyler drifted to sleep, Dr. Don Rudolph turned to his colleagues. "It's targeting blood type," he told them, certain that they too had already put the pieces together. "Just like we were predicting. The virus is singling out a specific blood type."

"Everyone with the symptoms has O negative blood," Dr. Reeds stated, simply repeating the known facts. "There hasn't been a single host with another type, and there hasn't been a single person with O negative that hasn't had the symptoms."

"And we know what this means," Dr. Taylor muttered, looking at his shoes.

"This could become more catastrophic than we originally anticipated," Dr. Meyers said. "We *cannot* allow this to become a pandemic. This virus *cannot* leave Hatfield."

"If this gets out," Dr. Rudolph began gravely, "then everyone in the world with O negative blood will become a host to the Colician Virus."

3

Four Weeks Later

Walter Reifert

I was banging a chair against a wall. I had been for at least ten minutes before Patrick Lemoore finally came to see what the commotion was all about. But even when he asked me what was wrong, or even when I started sobbing, I couldn't tell him. I didn't know. I couldn't remember what I had watched on television that had set me off.

I was a mess. I had been ever since Dr. Perry brought me here. My family was dead. Lemoore refused to let me leave the camp. I was a prisoner, trapped in my own sufferings.

"Walter, please," Dr. Perry begged me from several feet away, the closest I would permit either of them to come. Lemoore had finally called him when I refused to stop banging the chair against the wall or speak to him. He didn't know what else to do. "Talk to us. Tell us what's wrong."

Why should I? They were the ones holding me prisoner here and forcing me to dwell on the past. It had been almost a month since my father and brothers were murdered, but it still hurt just as much as it did that night. I still wanted to die. I still felt that I deserved to die. When was this nightmare ever going to end? For more than a month I had been a freak capable of hearing the thoughts of others. For almost a month my family had been dead. For almost a month the virus had been spreading around the world. For almost three weeks, everyone in the country who had O negative blood like me was hunted down and either killed or sent to one of the many labs being established in every state. I was watching it on the news. Everyone in the country with O negative blood had fallen ill with the Colician Virus, as the doctors were calling it. Everyone who caught the virus already had or was currently developing a superhuman ability. The virus was spread by a single touch, and pretty soon, everyone in the world with O negative blood would be host to the strange new virus.

Scientists had not yet publicly disclosed how such a virus could be created, but they were passing treatment tips to doctors throughout the country as they attempted to treat those in the labs with the virus. I, thankfully, had gotten out of the Hatfield lab before the "treatments" began. Dr. Perry brought back stories every evening from inside the Hatfield lab for Lemoore. I wasn't meant to hear them, but even if I didn't want to know, I would hear their thoughts. Doctors inside the lab were doing disturbing things to their patients. Dr. Perry insisted that he took no part in any of it, and I had taken a peek into his mind to confirm that. There were some things he was forced to do that he didn't want to, but he took no part in the vile experiments that other doctors, including my uncle, were participating in. I cut Dr. Perry some slack for his actions. See, Dr. Perry was just like Lemoore and I. He had O negative blood, which gave us inside information about what was happening in the labs, but also put him at great risk.

The first day I was here, in Lemoore's hidden, abandoned military installation twenty miles outside of Philadelphia, Dr. Perry told me who and what he really was. He, his wife, and two daughters were all hosts of the virus. The Blood Registration Act quickly passed Congress; it required every U.S. citizen to get their blood type tested to confirm that they weren't an O Negative. Dr. Perry had no choice but to have himself and his family tested. He barely managed to fake the tests in time without getting caught. I wasn't really sure what he was talking about when he explained it, but he claimed he added a protein to the blood samples so when tested, their blood appeared to be O positive. Dr. Perry was worried sick at first that he would be caught, but four weeks passed and he and his family were still untouched.

Despite his concern for them, his family had to continue living their lives out in the open. If they came and hid themselves with myself and Lemoore, people would notice their absence and Dr. Perry would be incriminated. We would lose all our inside access. Dr. Perry had been unable to do so yet, but he was struggling to find a way to breach security at the lab, which would allow a small number of affected individuals a chance to escape. Dr. Perry was a very brave person for what he was doing. If he or anyone else in his family slipped up with their abilities or got their blood tested again by somebody else, the whole family would be detained, maybe even killed. I saw people with O negative blood being shot on the news every day just for trying to live a normal life. People were scared. The police or the military wouldn't hesitate to shoot any one of us who refused to hand ourselves over willingly.

Lemoore's story was a little simpler than Dr. Perry's. He was old. I think he said his age was about seventy-three. But for his age he was in great shape. He was from Scotland, having moved to Philadelphia after inheriting a good amount of money from his father twenty or so years earlier. He bought this abandoned military installation a few years ago, cleaned it up, and planned to make it into a summer camp for kids who suffered from bullying. After the outbreak, when he realized that he was infected, he decided to make it into a haven for those infected.

He was a child psychologist and spoke often to high school students about bullying, acceptance, and his new "summer camp for outcasts." He was visiting schools on the pretense of drumming up support for his summer camp (which was actually non-existent), but he was looking for anyone who seemed different. He was looking for O Negatives, to try to bring them to safety.

It was easy to spot those who were hiding. They looked scared and paranoid, and Lemoore had telepathic abilities like me, so he could hear if they were hiding the truth from the world. Those who didn't yet know were also easy to spot. Not everyone had been tested yet, but those with an ability would slip up occasionally, and if they did, Lemoore was there to look for it. He had found three at schools that had been hiding or didn't know, but he had been too late for all of them. The same day he found them, soldiers marched into the school and hauled them off to the lab. So far, it was just Lemoore and I taking asylum in the installation with Dr. Perry dropping by to check up on us almost every day.

"Walter, you have to stop that," Dr. Perry said, a little more forcefully. "Breaking things isn't going to fix whatever it is you're angry about."

I gritted my teeth, wanting to tell him off so badly. I was in no mood to have another therapy session with Dr. Shawn Perry.

When all I did was continue to bang the chair into the wall, Lemoore became frustrated. "Walter, stop it!" He came towards me.

"Just leave me alone!" I screamed, swinging the chair at him. He jumped back and stared at me in shock, and through my tears I snapped, "I don't want to talk to either of you!" I turned and slammed the chair into the wall one final time. The impact was so hard that the metal and fabric chair broke into several pieces and a chunk of brick parted from the wall. I no longer had anything else within my reach to hit, so I threw the piece in my hand at Lemoore and screamed loudly and furiously.

Dr. Perry came at me then. He wrapped his arms around my chest, pinning my arms against my body. "Just calm down, alright?" he said, holding me tightly.

He was a strong man, almost as big as Dad had been, but I was very upset and I didn't want anybody touching me. I would do whatever was necessary to get him to let go. "Let go of me!" I shrieked, pulling against his powerful grip. I broke partially free, being sure to claw Dr. Perry's arms in the process.

Letting out a cry of pain, Dr. Perry pulled his arm away from me. He clutched it to him, and I saw that I had clawed him up good. Three long scratches were set nice and deep in his forearm, and two of them had already begun to bleed. For a few seconds I stopped and stared back at him apologetically. I didn't really want to hurt him. He was only trying to help. I was just so upset. As I watched, all three scratches began to close up. The blood drew back inside his arm, and then the torn skin pulled back together. Within the course of ten seconds, Dr. Perry's arm healed itself. There wasn't even a mark to indicate anything had happened.

He looked back at me, his expression half angry. I wanted to apologize but I couldn't spit those two words out. My throat felt like it was going to close completely. I couldn't believe what I had just done. It was the middle of the night. Lemoore had called his house and summoned him. All Dr. Perry wanted to do was help me, and I had hurt him in return.

Turning away as my tears blinded me, I ran from them. I didn't know where I was going, but at the same time I did. I was taking myself to the place where I had wanted to go for a long time. Dr. Perry and Lemoore yelled my name repeatedly and I could hear them rushing after me, but I didn't stop.

When I reached that place, I hesitated—but only for a second. It was my third or fourth day here that I had found the hand gun, and its location had been locked in my mind ever since. It was in a drawer in a room I was not allowed in, but that wasn't about to stop me. I opened the drawer and took out the gun.

"Walter, what are you doing?" Lemoore demanded, fear in his voice.

I put it to my right temple. I had never held a gun before, nor did I know how to use one, but I figured it was just pull the trigger once for it to all be over.

"Okay, you need to talk to me right now," Dr. Perry said as he and Lemoore hung back. "Tell me what's wrong so I can help you."

"You can't help me," I blurted, finally finding the voice to express some of my feelings. "Just let me go…"

"Walter, listen to me," Lemoore said, his voice sounding like a hiss. When I looked at him, I could hear him inside my head. He was rattling around inside. *Don't do this, Walter. Put the gun down. It's okay...*

"Get out of my head!" I screamed, firing a warning shot into the ceiling before replacing the nose of the gun to my temple. "Stay out of there! Don't try to help me! Neither of you can help me!"

I felt Lemoore back out, afraid of what I would do should he press harder.

"I *can* help you," Dr. Perry promised, looking desperate. "But I need you to tell me what's bothering you."

"You want to know what's bothering me?" I asked shakily. "The two of you keep me locked in here all day every day and I have nothing to do but think about what happened!"

"We only keep you here for you own protection," Dr. Perry said softly. "We only want you to be safe. That's all. We don't want you to feel like you're trapped."

"I *am* trapped!" I cried. "I'm trapped in this world full of terrible people—people who turn their own families over to the lab and kill their own out of fear of what they don't understand! I don't want to be a part of this stinking race anymore! I don't want to be a human anymore!"

"You're not a part of that," Dr. Perry assured me. "You're much better than that."

"Those people killed my family!" I shouted, pressing the gun harder into my skull. "Those humans killed my family! I have nothing left in this fucking world! I don't want to be here anymore!" I put my finger on the trigger.

"Your family died to ensure your safety," Dr. Perry reminded me, for the first time daring to take a couple steps forward. "They died to protect you, to make sure you had a chance to live a good life. Do you really think that killing yourself will honor what they wanted for you?" When he saw my hesitation, he gave me a weak smile. "If you kill yourself, then your dad and your brothers will have died for nothing."

He was right. As much as I wanted to, I couldn't pull the trigger. My family's sacrifice would have been for nothing. Slowly, with a defeated whimper, I lowered the gun.

I saw Lemoore exhale a sigh of relief while Perry cautiously approached me. Reaching down, Dr. Perry took the gun from me and placed it in his belt. He then peered down at me, trying to make eye contact.

I purposely avoided his gaze. "I want to leave," I muttered. "I don't want to stay in this place another night."

"You have to, Walter," Dr. Perry apologized. "It's the only way we can make sure you stay safe." Taking my arm firmly, he started to pull me back the way we had come. "Come on. Let's go talk."

"No," I said stubbornly, halting myself. "I don't want to talk to you."

"I know you don't," Dr. Perry replied. "But you need to talk to someone."

"Well, it doesn't have to be you..." I started to snap, but Lemoore cut me off.

"Walter," he said sharply. "Come. We need to talk. It's the only way we can help you get better."

I started to tell him to just read my mind, but his stern expression caused me to give in. Defeated, I let Dr. Perry lead me to Lemoore's private study.

Shauna Skyler

Something was wrong with Shauna Skyler. It wasn't the fact that she had contracted the Colician Virus, or the fact that she had been held prisoner for nearly a month inside the Hatfield lab. No, something else was very wrong with her. At this current point in time, she couldn't explain what it was. But weeks later, when she finally found herself again, she would remember the horrific things that had been done to her.

Shauna was not in her normal state of mind. She really wasn't in any state of mind. She couldn't speak, or communicate in any way for that matter. She hadn't been able to for about a week. She was still capable of thinking, but it wasn't in the same way as before. Much of what she thought was not relevant to anything that was happening. Nothing that was done to her really registered in her mind, and her memory was not functioning properly. She knew things about herself, but there weren't any real memories to explain how she knew these things. She knew that she was a teenage girl, and she knew that she was being held against her will in a place that was all white. She knew that there was a young boy in the same place as her that she wanted to find, but she didn't know why. Most importantly, she knew she had to tell someone something. She didn't know who that someone was or what that something was; she just knew she had to do it.

There was a man with dark hair who was always dressed in white with the name of Dr. Rudolph who came into her room three times a day. He would give her shots and would speak soothing words to her, but nothing he said ever made sense to her. What was this place she was in? Why did she have to stay in the white room? Why did Dr. Rudolph give her shots every day? Why couldn't her mind function like everyone else's? Nothing made sense to Shauna, and she really wasn't certain of anything anymore. She didn't even know her own name, or what a name *was*.

There she sat, in her little white room, facing the end of her cot, her knees up to her chin and her arms wrapped around herself. For some time, hours, most likely, she had been staring at the wall across the small room. Her mind really wasn't in that room, which was why she sat so perfectly still for as long as she did. That particular day, she had been thinking about outside (most people wouldn't call her thought process "thinking," but there is no other word to describe it). What was beyond that silver steel door? What was beyond her white room? She was eager to leave that room, to stretch her legs and explore what was beyond the claustrophobic walls that had held her captive for so long. How was she supposed to do that? Dr. Rudolph never invited her to leave, and it didn't appear as if she was supposed to. How was she supposed to make Dr. Rudolph aware of her desire to leave? She didn't understand how to form sounds with her mouth like him. She had no way to communicate with him.

The big steel door creaked open and Dr. Rudolph stepped inside. He waited until it creaked closed before going to her side. She didn't look at him because she felt no reason to, but out of the corner of her eye she saw that he was carrying something in his hand. It was a big, wide cylinder shape and was attached to a tube that connected to a cupped object.

"Hey, Shauna," he said, kneeling beside her.

What was Shauna? He said that word to her a lot. She thought it might be what people called her—just like he was called Dr. Rudolph—but she didn't know.

"How do you feel?" he asked her.

How did she feel? What did that mean?

"Are you feeling any pain?"

Shauna continued to stare at the wall. She had no idea what he was saying to her, nor did she know how to respond.

Dr. Rudolph made a sound with his mouth that he made a lot. He let a lot of air out of his mouth really fast to make a soft *whoosh* sound. Reaching out to her, he put his hand on her shoulder and pushed her backwards.

Shauna understood what that meant. He wanted her to lie flat on the cot. He made her do that the third time he came to visit every day. Every time he did that, he always gave her the shot that made her close her eyes and not open them again for a long time. But that time was only the second time he had come to visit her that day. Wasn't he just going to give her another shot and then leave, like he always did on the second visit?

She did what he wanted, even though it wasn't the right time to. She stared up at the ceiling while Dr. Rudolph moved around parts of the object he had brought with him. When he stopped moving parts, he placed the cup part over her mouth and nose, making the corners of his mouth turn up as he did so.

Shauna didn't like what he was doing. He had put an object like that over her mouth before. It made the air smell bad and made her close her eyes like the third shot of the day did. When she opened her eyes again, it made the inside of her feel bad. Water with a terrible taste had come back out of her mouth and onto the floor after her eyes opened again. She didn't want that to happen again. She stopped breathing, not wanting to smell that bad smell. Dr. Rudolph would not like it if her eyes didn't close, so she closed her eyes but didn't dream.

Dr. Rudolph took the cupped object off of her face and he made the sound with his mouth again. Shauna listened to what he did. She didn't want to make Dr. Rudolph unhappy by opening her eyes. She heard the door open again and heard other people come in. She wanted to see who else had come to visit her in her room, but she still didn't want to make Dr. Rudolph unhappy. As she listened to the soft voices above her, she felt many hands picking her off her cot and setting her down on something else that felt like her cot. The hands then put things over her body, holding her against the new cot so she couldn't sit up. Why had they done that? She wasn't afraid, for she could feel no fear, but she was curious as to what was happening around her. She longed for a moment where she could no longer hear any voices so she could open her eyes and see the new things.

The new cot she was on started to move. She felt it move out the door. The door was closed again but the cot kept moving away from it. Shauna had a burning desire to open her eyes, because she knew where she was. She was outside.

4

The Effects of Time

Shauna Skyler

For an amount of time that was unknown to her, Shauna had laid perfectly still on her cot. There were several doctors, including Dr. Rudolph, who had been circling around her. All were forming sounds with their mouths, sounds that Shauna could not make. While they moved around her motionless body, she felt the occasional pinch in her arm from a shot. But even when she felt them, she didn't move. She knew that she couldn't open her eyes until there were no more people, or else she would make Dr. Rudolph unhappy. She didn't want to make Dr. Rudolph unhappy. So she waited. She waited for a long time. Her cot moved around at one point, and for a bit she could hear a low hum all around her head. The humming could still be heard when there was a sudden crash from a good distance away. Through her eyelids, she then saw the lights go out. The humming stopped as well.

The sounds that the doctors were making became increasingly louder, but then died away as all but one left the room. The one who remained wasn't Dr. Rudolph.

Loud sounds of a brawl could be heard from outside the room, and Shauna listened curiously. She wanted to see what all the commotion was about, but at the same time she didn't want the doctor to know that she was awake. Time kept ticking slowly by, but the doctor never left. She was beginning to grow impatient. Finally, when the doctor came to her side and touched her arm, she decided that she didn't care anymore.

Her eyes opened, and she looked up into the awaiting gaze of the doctor. His eyes got really big, and his mouth started to open. At the same time, Shauna did something that was based purely on instinct. Using only her mind, she made the ties over her left arm peel off of her and wrap around the doctor's neck. He grabbed at it, unable to make a sound, but he couldn't untie it. While he fumbled, Shauna made the rest of the restraints holding her down peel off as well. She sat up and hopped off her cot, taking a look around at her new environment.

She was in another white room, but it was much bigger than hers. Lined up with her cot were many more cots. On each of the other cots there lay another person. Each person wore the same clothing as her—all light blue. They all laid on their backs, their eyes closed, most of them with needles in their arms. This confused Shauna. What she saw didn't look right. Her body couldn't feel pain, so she did not remember what pain was, but it looked like whatever the doctors had done to them would cause them physical harm.

Hesitantly, Shauna approached the cot closest to hers. Laying on it was another girl like her. There were three tubes going into each of her arms, and there was a very large tube coming out of the center of her chest. Peering down at the girl as she tried to put meaning to her condition, Shauna felt an emotion that she hadn't remembered until then. The inside of her felt tight, like her body was slowly imploding. Anybody else would have called this emotion sadness or grief. That fifteen-year-old girl, who had lived through so much yet at the same time had hardly lived at all, reached up to her face to touch the tear that had trickled from her eye. She held her moist finger in front of her, staring at the tear with newfound curiosity. Looking down at the girl once again, she slowly reached out to touch the tube protruding from her chest.

As she gently ran her fingers over its smooth surface, the eyes of the girl on the table opened. Her body rose upwards, the restraints creaking in protest, and as her mouth opened a strange, frightening sound came out.

Startled, Shauna drew her hand away. She stared wide-eyed at the girl, whose breathing was hoarse and wheezy. For more than a minute, the two stared into each other, neither one moving or making an effort to communicate with the other. A steady stream of air passed over the girl's lips as she breathed, the pain from the tube in her chest visible in her eyes. Finally, the girl's lips moved slightly to form two words, words that Shauna did not understand but had a deep impact on her.

"Kill me."

Once again, Shauna experienced a new emotion. It made her heartbeat quicken and her body shake. It was an emotion she would come to experience often. This emotion was called fear. Her plan had been to take a look around and explore the world outside her room. When she'd had enough, she would lie back down on her cot and close her eyes and Dr. Rudolph would never know. But after seeing this girl, after seeing what Dr. Rudolph and the others had done, she didn't want to stay in that place a moment longer. All this time, she thought Dr. Rudolph had been a good person. She thought he had been helping her. As it turned out, he was doing terrible things to the others. How long would it be before he did something terrible to her? How long would it be before there was a tube in *her* chest? Taking several steps back from the girl's cot, Shauna let the desperation in her eyes sink in. She had to get out of there. She needed to run, before Dr. Rudolph could put a tube in her chest too.

Turning quickly, her fear propelled her towards the closest door. It was already open, beckoning her to cross its threshold. Outside that door were more white walls. This next room was very large. It was narrow, but the ends of it stretched very far. Inside this room, there were many people running in both directions. There were tall people, but there were also very small people. Some were dressed in white, like Dr. Rudolph always was, and some were dressed in blue, like Shauna. There were also new people that Shauna hadn't seen before. They were dressed in black. In their hands, they carried long black sticks that they would point at people and would make a loud *bang*. It appeared as if the people in white and black were chasing the people in blue. The people in blue were making very loud, high-pitched sounds with their mouths as they ran. Every few seconds a person in blue would be pushed inside a room and then the door would be closed.

"Hey!"

The sound made Shauna look around, her eyes landing on a man dressed in black who was looking back at her. She watched him curiously as he slowly took a few steps towards her, the black stick in his hands pointed at her. Were the men in black actually bad like the men in white, or were they good?

"You're not supposed to be out of your room, you little bitch," the man said in the strange language he could form with his mouth.

Shauna watched his face, and she saw that the man was very unhappy. He looked like he wanted to chase her. She didn't think the men in black were good people.

Without wasting any more time, Shauna ran away from the man in black. He was making very loud sounds with his mouth and his stick as he chased her, so Shauna only ran faster. She came to a place in the room where it kept going, but to the right it went another way at the same time. Shauna went to the right. There were no people going that way, and she soon realized why. The room ended suddenly, several closed doors on both sides of her but none with handles. She stopped quickly and turned around to go back, but the man in black was standing in her way.

"Where do you think you're going, huh?" he asked her as she stared at him. The corners of his mouth were turned up, his expression making Shauna even more apprehensive. "Dead end, sweetheart. Oh, that's right. You don't have half your brain to help you figure that out."

Shauna tried to run past him, but he caught her and pushed her back again.

"Whoa! Do you really think I'm going to just let you leave?" He took a few steps closer to her. "No, you and I are going to have a little fun. You owe me that much, remember?"

Backing away from him, Shauna wrapped her arms around herself. She was afraid of this man, and all she wanted was to be able to tell him that she just wanted to get out of there. She didn't want Dr. Rudolph to hurt her.

"Yeah, you're afraid of me now, aren't you? Now that you're missing half your brain, you don't even know how to defend yourself, do you?"

Just then, a large creature on four legs and covered in black fur rounded the corner. Letting out a terrifying sound that made Shauna shrink back even more, it pounced on the man in black. The creature had big white teeth that sank into the neck of the man. The man didn't make a sound before his eyes closed and his body lay limp on the floor.

It was strange. Seeing this creature with its huge teeth and body attacking the man in black put a great amount of fear into Shauna. Its body was bigger than Shauna, and it had a long nose and big floppy ears. There was also something long protruding from the back end of it, and Shauna thought it was called a tail. As it looked up at her with its big brown eyes and a thick red liquid running over its teeth and chin, Shauna felt a strange familiarity, as if she had once known a creature such as this in her past. And even though its scruffy, ferocious appearance was rather frightening, Shauna sensed a peculiar friendliness about it. She didn't think it was going to hurt her. It had just come to protect her.

Looking down at the man in black who lay unmoving on the floor, the big black creature made a low sound from its throat. It was a scary sound, but Shauna no longer felt any fear. The creature raised its eyes again to hers, and the scary expression left its face. It stopped showing its teeth and its eyes were soft as it gazed at her. Shauna peered back curiously, its brown eyes appearing oddly similar to a person's.

The two poor souls stared at each other, neither of them taking notice to the screams and yells coming from the next hallway. As they watched each other, the big black animal made another sound with its throat. It was soft and high-pitched, and Shauna felt the emotion of sadness as a response. The animal, whom Shauna felt wasn't an animal at all, was feeling sadness as well. Its sadness was putting sadness into Shauna. Slowly, Shauna walked forward and extended her hand. The animal held still as she placed her hand on its forehead. She held it there, its fur tangled but soft to the touch. There was another person behind those sad brown eyes. He was hiding in that animal's body. He was like her. Whatever was wrong with her—whatever it was that had landed her in this place, this awful place—the same thing had affected him as well.

The animal's eyes closed for a moment, and it breathed out loudly. When they opened again, they weren't sad anymore. Its eyes had hardened again, as they had while looking at the man in black, and it turned and walked back to the long room. It paused for a second and looked back at her. It moved its head back and forth several times before rounding the corner.

There were many things that Shauna didn't understand, that she couldn't understand, but she understood what the animal wanted. It wanted her to follow *him*. *He* wanted her to follow *him*.

So she did. She ran to the corner and followed him around it, but stopped when she saw that he had stopped. He was facing her, people behind him running and screaming. Extending his neck, he looked over her shoulder and made the same sad noise he had earlier.

At first, Shauna didn't understand what he was doing. She turned and looked behind her to where he was looking. There was a door at the end of the long room, with buttons beside it and red lights above it. Was that the way out? Was the animal trying to show her where to go? She looked back at him, but he was gone.

He had run back to the others in the long room, to help the people in blue.

Trusting the judgment of the black beast, Shauna went to the door. She looked it up and down and searched on all sides of it, but there was nothing she could open it with. Maybe she had to push some buttons for it to work, but instead of trying it she did something else. Raising her hands, she placed them both on the cold metal door and pictured it opening in her head. And then, after waiting for only a moment, it did.

On the other side of the door, there was a small room that appeared like it might take her to other places. She stepped inside, and a sudden voice above her startled her.

"Select your destination," a feminine voice said to her.

Shauna jumped and looked up, but she didn't see anyone. She looked all around her, but there was no one. Who had made those sounds? Her eyes landed on more buttons to the right of the door, all of them wearing a strange black symbol. Running her fingers over them, she understood what they meant. She had to push one to get the door to close and the room to take her elsewhere. But which one?

Her fingers touched every button, and they passed over the one with the symbol in the shape of a 5. That was where she wanted to go. She didn't know why or where it was. All she knew was that she needed to go there. She pushed the button.

"Shauna?"

Shauna looked up when she heard the familiar word. Her eyes landed on Dr. Rudolph, who was on the outside edge of the clump of screaming people. He was staring back at her with wide eyes, and Shauna felt that sudden surge of fear again. She pressed her back against the back wall of the room as the door started to close.

"Shauna, no!" Dr. Rudolph cried, running towards her. The door closed long before he reached it.

There was a loud bang from the door when Dr. Rudolph reached it, and Shauna heard several more follow the first. The sounds died away shortly after she felt the room begin to move downwards. A black rectangle above the door had changing symbols glowing in red light; the symbols were identical to those on the buttons.

3...4...5

When the symbol **5** popped up, the room slowed to a stop and then the door slid open.

"Sublevel Five," the feminine voice from before droned. "Holding cells for youth. Four patrons maximum per cell. Level Three clearance or above only."

Shauna stepped out of the little room and the door closed behind her. The room she now stood in looked exactly like the long one she had been in before. The only difference was that it was empty. And it was silent. There must have been several long rooms with doors on both sides stacked one on top of the other. Were there people living behind each of those doors, like she had been? Did they want to leave this place as much as she did? What was she even doing there? The big black beast had helped her so she could leave. But she was still inside that place, even more lost than before. She had felt something special about this floor, like there was something she needed to be here for. Something she needed to find. Why couldn't she remember? How did she know she needed to be here if she didn't even know for what?

She walked forward, taking a look at every door she passed. Each door had a gold rectangle in the middle of them with three symbols on it just like the buttons in the little moving room. Shauna wandered down the never-ending long room, looking at each of the symbols on the doors to see if any of them held any meaning to her. Just like the other long room she had been in before, the room led to the right but also continued straight at the same time. She took that right turn, knowing that she was lost already anyway. There were so many doors, so many symbols ...what was she looking for? A great length down that second branch of the long room, something about one of the doors made Shauna pause. It was on the left, the three symbols reading 576. It wasn't necessarily the door that caught her interest, but maybe the presence she sensed behind it. She could remember that there was a boy in this place she longed to find. Was that boy behind this door? Was he what she had been searching for?

She reached up and placed the palms of her hands on the door as she had on the door leading to the little moving room. Once again, she pictured the door opening, and then it did. There was a tone of mid-pitch, and then a whoosh of air as it swung open to reveal another white room just like hers. Unsure of what she would find, she hesitantly stepped inside.

Shauna was startled as a very short person ran at her and grabbed her legs. The little person, who was male, let out a high-pitched sound similar to what she had been hearing in the other long room with all the other people. "Shauna!" he said loudly. "I knew you'd come get me! I just knew you would!"

Confused as to who this little person was, Shauna pulled her arms up away from him as he held onto her. She peered down at him curiously. It was clear that he knew her in some way. He had called her the same thing that Dr. Rudolph always called her, and the way he clung to her suggested that they had once been friends in that time when she could not remember.

The little person raised his face and looked up at her, the corners of his mouth turned up. He was happy that she was there. "I missed you!" he said, squeezing her tighter. "But I knew you'd come get me! I knew my big sister would break out and come get me!"

Once again, Shauna wished she could understand that strange language all the other people seemed capable of speaking. He was telling her something that was probably important, but she hadn't a clue what any of it meant.

The little one continued to gaze up at Shauna. He seemed to be waiting for a response, as if he expected her to reply in the same bizarre language. When all she did was continue to stare at him, the corners of his mouth slowly went back down so his lips formed a line. What Shauna saw in his eyes put sadness into her heart again, the emotion she had felt while looking at the tortured girl and while looking into the eyes of the big black beast. She had made the little one sad, and now she was sad because of that.

"Shauna?" the little one said, letting go of her and taking a step back. "Shauna, don't you remember me?"

Again, Shauna remained silent. What was she supposed to do? She didn't know how to communicate. She didn't even know what the boy wanted from her.

"It's me," the little one said quietly. He raised his arms up to her in a peculiar gesture.

This time, Shauna took a step back. She was standing in the doorway, and she wondered if she should turn and run from this little person. But she couldn't. After all, he was what she had come here for.

The little one dropped his arms and the sadness on his face became worse. "They took your memories," he said, water running out of his eyes and down his face. "You don't even know who I am!"

Unable to bear it any longer, Shauna reached down and picked him up. She held him in her arms, and he clung to her with his. She stared into his eyes, which were blue, a blue that she had seen before. There had once been a piece of glass placed in front of her that showed her what she looked like. Her eyes were blue. They were the same blue as the little one's.

The little one stared back at her, his face filled with the dreaded sadness. "Please remember me," he said very softly. *"Please.* Remember me." He reached out to her and put his hands on the sides of her face. He then leaned his head forward and rested it against hers. His eyes closed. "Remember me."

Something extraordinary happened. Shauna gasped from the shock that hit her, and then she closed her eyes as well. The little one did something to her, something that helped her greatly. He showed her things, things about her forgotten past. She learned new words and could finally put names to things that had for so long gone unnamed.

The first thing the little one showed her was their home. Their *true* home. It was in a small village, a place called Hatfield. They were still in Hatfield, but they were inside the place that had changed them. They had lived in a small place called a house, with two older people called Mom and Dad, and two others called brothers. One was younger than Shauna, called Michael, and one was older, called Russell. They had all lived together in that house, as part of a group called a family. A creature had also lived with them—a creature that resembled the big black beast that had helped her—called a dog. His name was Kerch. They had all been happy. They had all possessed an emotion, a very special emotion, which had been directed at each other. Love. Love was beautiful. Love was something she missed. Love was something she could now feel.

The next thing the little one showed her was that night, that horrible night that tore them apart from their family. There had been bright flashing lights and men in black. The little one had been pulled out of Russell's arms, and when Shauna had tried to get to Russell, the soldiers had pushed her away from him as well. They had pulled her and the little one inside the building, the research facility that everyone in the village of Hatfield had been so afraid of. There, they were separated, and the little one could no longer show anything about Shauna. But he had more to show about himself. He had been taken into a dark room and had been tested for the virus, the virus called the Colician Strain, which had taken over them both and had turned them into something far more powerful than any regular person. The little one had learned much about the virus from a doctor, one of the men in white—just like Dr. Rudolph—because he had the ability to see the thoughts of others with a single touch. But he also had the ability to put his own thoughts into the minds of others, which was how he was showing her their past. He, the little one, one of whom she shared this emotion called love. He, the thing she had been searching for. He, her little brother.

Shauna opened her eyes and looked at her brother. He opened his and then pulled away from her to gaze back. It was very difficult for Shauna to do, because she didn't really know how, but she did her best to use the knowledge he had give her to speak a single word. After making a hissing sound with air moving over her tongue and through her teeth, she managed to say in a very shaky voice, "Sawyer."

Sawyer's face lit up in what was called a smile, and he bobbed his head up and down in what was called a nod. "Yeah, it's me."

It amazed Shauna when she realized she could understand the words her brother was speaking. She smiled back. She wasn't aware of the tears falling from her eyes until Sawyer reached up and brushed them away. Happiness was another new emotion she was experiencing, and it was overwhelming her. She pulled her little brother back to her and they held each other in a tight embrace. As they hugged, Shauna pondered everything Sawyer had showed her.

When their tests had come back positive, they had both been taken and placed in separate rooms. Unlike Shauna, Sawyer wasn't alone. There were three others that had been there with him, and they didn't get three shots a day like Shauna either. They only got one, at the end of each day when it was time to sleep. Sawyer had pulled much information from one of his doctors' head, which was information that Shauna was currently fishing through to find answers to her questions. The injections that she had been receiving three times daily were suppressants used to prevent her from using her ability; telekinesis. Doctors in the facility were running experiments on people like them. Some were harmless, but some were deadly. The doctors wanted to figure out how they worked. Shauna had already seen the results of one of the experiments. The girl with the tube in her chest was a model of an experiment that would ultimately end in death. And Shauna herself was an experiment. Her lack of memories and common knowledge was an experimental therapy for certain people who were misbehaving and needed to be controlled. She had obviously done something in her forgotten past to bring this disability upon herself. The doctors had blocked the part of her that allowed her to function like a normal human being. They had taken from her everything that she was. Was it because of the thing she knew she had to tell somebody? Had she uncovered something she wasn't supposed to uncover and she had been punished for it? On the bright side, there was still a way for her to get that part of her back. The problem was that Sawyer didn't know how.

"We have to go," Sawyer told her, pulling away and gazing at her again. Shauna didn't quite understand what that meant, and when Sawyer saw her confusion he placed his hands on the side of her face as he had before. He then showed her what he wanted her to do. He showed an image of the two of them getting out of the building and going far away from there.

Nodding to her little brother, Shauna turned to leave the room. "Wait!"

The sudden voice startled Shauna. She looked back into Sawyer's room, and realized she hadn't noticed Sawyer's three roommates. The one who had spoken was the oldest, a blonde boy named Allan. He was holding the baby girl, Megan, in his arms and the boy that was even younger than Sawyer, Daniel, was standing behind Allan. Allan had come forward and was staring pleadingly at Shauna.

"Take us with you!" Allan begged, his voice cracking. He tried to come out of the room too, but Shauna purposely blocked the doorway. "Please! Don't leave us here!"

"Let them come with," Sawyer said, touching Shauna's face and showing the three following them outside. She understood. They wanted to get out of this place too. She couldn't blame them for that, and she knew that she couldn't leave them. But would they slow her down?

Shauna decided to help them get out of the building. After that, they would be on their own. She gestured with her head in the same way that the big black dog from up above had. Allan smiled gratefully and took little Daniel's hand. They followed Shauna back in the direction she had come, moving quickly to keep up with her brisk pace. The long room, called a hallway, didn't seem so long anymore. It almost seemed like it had gotten shorter. They hurried to the point in the hallway where it split in two and took a left to get back to the little room, called an elevator. Shauna's brisk walk had changed to a run as she rounded the corner, but she jolted to a halt when she saw the huge brown dog blocking their path.

This dog was even bigger than the black one, and unlike the black one, this one didn't look like it had very friendly intentions. Its upper lip quivered as it bared its teeth at her and began to growl. Its shoulders were hunched in an attack position, and its dark blue eyes glared harshly at her.

The three young ones ran into her as they came around the corner. They stumbled back a step, and when they saw the huge dog, Allan and Daniel both screamed. Shauna felt Allan grab at the back of her shirt, and Daniel clung to her leg.

"Shauna," Sawyer whispered, fear in his voice. He turned his head into her chest so he wouldn't have to gaze upon the terrifying creature for another second. His arms wrapped around her shoulders and he squeezed her tightly.

With a ferocious snarl that made Shauna shiver and the children all whimper, the giant dog took a menacing step forward. In response to that threatening gesture, Shauna took a step back. She retreated several more steps, rounding the corner yet again and keeping a constant distance between herself and the dog. The little ones clinging to her moved with her, making sure to stay out of sight of the animal.

The dog followed her movements, looking ready to attack at any moment. At one point, it actually crouched down and tensed its body in preparation. But something changed in its eyes. It saw something in hers that made it pause, and then its eyes appeared utterly horrified. Standing up straight, it took a few more hesitant steps closer and extended its nose towards her.

Shauna stopped moving away and let it come to her. As it had realized something about her, she had noticed something about it. About him. Just like the black dog, this dog was actually a person hiding in the body of a dog. But this person wasn't any ordinary person. No, he had once been a friend to her in the past she had forgotten. She couldn't recall any specific memories of him, but his eyes had a stinging familiarity about them. He was still her friend. Was he there to protect her as the other dog had been, or had he come to thwart her escape to the world outside the facility?

Shauna still had a bit of uncertainty as she reached out to place her hand on his nose. There was something about his threatening posture in the previous moment that left her cautious. He had been in that hallway for a reason. His glare had been harsh for a reason. He had been sent down there to find her. He had most likely been instructed to hurt her, to stop her before she could leave.

His sad eyes were apologetic. Even though he had been told to stop her, he didn't want to hurt her. He cared about her, just like she cared about him. He lifted his nose to meet her touch, and he almost appeared to smile with his dog snout. A strange sound left his mouth, and although he was in the body of a dog, Shauna managed to catch the two words he spoke.

"Shauna Skyler."

Before Shauna had time to ask Sawyer to help her respond, a black blur whipped around the corner. The big black dog from the second floor must have followed her down here. He jumped on top of Shauna's friend, jaws snapping and eyes blazing.

No! Shauna wanted to say it, but she didn't know how to form the word. She grabbed at the black dog's fur to try to pull him away, but Allan was tugging at her arm. He started directing her around the mess of tangled, snarling dogs.

"Come on!" Allan screamed as Daniel ran around the dogs and around the corner again. Baby Megan had started to cry in his arms. "We have to go!"

"Run, Shauna!" Sawyer cried, and touched her face again.

The two of them were getting good at communicating with each other. The message was getting through to Shauna quicker every time. Setting down her brother, she took his hand and they followed Allan and Daniel back to the elevator.

Allan was quick. He was far ahead of all of them without much of an effort. Daniel, however, was having trouble running on his tiny little legs. He stumbled several times and finally took a header halfway down the hallway.

Sawyer had no problem running. Shauna gave him a push to go on ahead of her and then scooped up Daniel as he struggled to get back on his feet. He kicked at her at first, but when he saw it was her he wrapped his arms around her neck to hold on as she ran.

Allan reached the elevator long before Shauna did, and when he realized he couldn't open it, he punched the door angrily. "We need a card or a password!" he shouted, turning to her with a desperate look in his eyes. "We can't get in!"

While Shauna ran, she did what her gut told her to do: she raised her free hand and waved it at the door, telling it to open. And it did. Allan and Sawyer squealed in excitement and rushed inside, holding the door for Shauna until she got inside. She looked back at the fighting dogs wrestling and biting each other on the floor. With a helpless feeling inside of her, Shauna prayed that her friend would be alright.

"What button should I push?" Sawyer asked frantically as his hands hovered over the assortment of numbered buttons. "Should I push 1?"

"No, press G," Allan instructed, shifting Megan into his other arm. The baby had thankfully stopped crying. She would get them all caught if she couldn't keep quiet.

"Why would I press G?" Sawyer asked in confusion. "Isn't 1 the first floor?"

"It's the first floor below ground level," Allan said impatiently, reaching around him and pushing the button labeled G. "You push G. It stands for ground."

"Oh," Sawyer said.

Allan turned to Shauna and looked up, as if suddenly remembering she was there. He stared at her in awe. "You can control things without touching them? That's so cool!"

"Well, you can teleport," Sawyer said grumpily, frowning and crossing his arms. "That's way cooler."

"Yeah, but it hurts my head real bad," Allan replied. "I can only do it once or twice at a time before I start throwing up or passing out."

Shauna was so lost in their conversation. She could only understand a few basic words that were said to her, and it would still take a while before she was able to fully engage in a conversation. Understanding words was one thing. Learning how to speak the words all over again was completely different.

When the elevator stopped going up and the door opened again, Allan peered out cautiously. "There aren't any soldiers," he said. "Or doctors. Nobody's here. The place is empty!"

Sawyer peeked out as well, his expression nervous. "Where is everybody?"

"Do you think they're hiding?" Allan whispered.

Shauna had an idea about what was causing their hesitance. Reaching down, she touched Sawyer's face and showed him what was in her mind.

Nodding, Sawyer said, "Shauna says that all the soldiers and doctors are on her floor, where there's a big breakout."

"She told you that?" Allan said, bewildered. "She didn't say anything."

"The doctors took her memories," Sawyer explained to him. "She doesn't know how to talk and she can't understand what we say. But we can tell each other what we're thinking with our minds."

"Weird," Allan muttered.

"But she told me that they're all down below," Sawyer explained. "So that means we're safe to leave."

"Then let's go!" Allan led them out, looking around for the exit. "We can't waste anymore time. We're lucky enough as it is."

"How are we going to get away from this place?" Sawyer asked. "Where are we going to go?"

"There are woods just outside the building," Allan explained as they approached a big set of doors leading to the outside. "If we can get far enough away from here, we can hide until things settle down. I may even be able to teleport us somewhere safe if I feel okay enough."

Something was wrong. Shauna began to feel her mistake as they pushed the doors and stepped outside. It made sense that there weren't any doctors or soldiers on the ground floor. There were people running around loose down below. But there was no way that *every single one* of them was down there. That would have left the facility unguarded, allowing anyone to enter or exit. There had to be *some*one guarding the building.

The first gunshot sounded from above their heads, and the first bullet struck at their feet. Shauna jumped and stepped away from the sudden burst of heat. Allan, Daniel and Sawyer all screamed and Megan started crying again. The second shot whizzed past Shauna's left ear. She whipped around and looked up. Up on the roof, there were dozens of soldiers with large guns aimed at them. They all began shouting orders down to them.

"Don't move!"

"Hold still until one of us gets down there!"

"If you try to run, we *will* open fire!"

Shauna understood. Not what was said, but what was meant. The first shots were warning shots. The shots that would follow would not miss them.

"Run!" Allan cried, but Shauna was already running. She caught Sawyer by the arm and pulled him along with her. Allan followed after them, holding the baby to him tightly. Daniel gripped her shirt tightly, fearing she would drop him with her erratic movements.

The soldiers opened fire the moment the kids started running.

The first several shots missed them by several feet. There was so much noise. Shauna's ears were ringing with the racket. She pushed forward as fast as she was able, but when she felt the bullets nipping at her heels she knew that they wouldn't make it. If they kept moving in a straight line, there was no way they would make it to the tree line up ahead. So Shauna did the only thing that seemed logical.

Pulling Sawyer to the left, she started running in a zigzag pattern. The shower of bullets passed them as the shooters re-aimed. It seemed to be working. Allan passed her and did the same thing. Shauna continued to move in that same zigzag pattern as they neared the tree line.

Shauna heard numerous angry shouts from behind, and she knew why. In a few seconds she and the kids would reach the tree line. Once they did, they might actually get away.

"We're almost there!" Allan cried, running even faster.

Being outside was a big shock for Shauna. In the short part of her life that she could remember without assistance from Sawyer, she had never seen the outdoors. She hadn't seen anything beyond the walls of her little white room until today. The bright sunshine, the hot air, the soft grass beneath her feet, all the new sights and sounds…it was overwhelming. It was amazing. It was beautiful. She absolutely loved it. She loved it so much she could scream. But there was no time to stop and enjoy it, to stop and take in the beauty of it all. She had to keep running.

They had made it to the tree line. Allan ran ahead with the baby, and Shauna pushed Sawyer to follow him. She then paused for a moment, young Daniel still holding onto her. She turned and looked back at the facility. She looked back at the place she had thought was her home, but had ended up being her prison. The soldiers on the roof were scrambling down the ladders connected to the side of the building. When they reached the ground one after another, they began to run towards the tree line. They were coming for them.

"Shauna!" Sawyer called from up ahead. "Come on!"

Shauna turned and ran to Sawyer. Setting down little Daniel, Shauna picked up Sawyer and started to run deeper into the trees.

"Hey!" Allan cried, skidding to a halt as she ran past him while Daniel screamed in protest. "You can't just leave him here!" When Shauna kept running without looking back, Allan yelled, "Run Daniel! You have to run!"

Sawyer swiveled his body in her arms and looked at her with sad eyes. "We can't just leave them," he said. "We have to help them."

Shauna didn't stop. She didn't want to. She ran for minutes, with Sawyer telling her she needed to go back and Allan screaming at her to stop. She didn't slow down until an obstacle was put in her path. There was a steep hill in front of her, with giant rocks scattered along the side of it. The only way past it was to climb up the rocks.

Shifting Sawyer's weight to one arm, Shauna started to climb. It took her a lot less time than she thought it would, but when she reached the top she was completely out of breath. She set Sawyer down for a moment and went down on one knee, taking deep breaths as her head began to spin.

"Shauna," Sawyer said, staring up at her. "You have to help them. We have to let them come with us." He knew that she wouldn't be able to understand him, so he reached up to show her what he wanted. He didn't get a chance to.

"Hey!" Allan shouted again as he tried to climb up the rocks with the baby in his arms. "Stop! What are you doing?"

In one swift movement, Shauna scooped up her brother and started running again. Why wouldn't he leave them alone? He was supposed to stop following her! She had gotten them out of that place, and now they were supposed to go off on their own just like she decided!

"Wait!" Allan yelled as he stumbled over the last rock. "Where are you going? You have to help Daniel! *Please!*"

Shauna kept running, and she could hear Allan's continued pleas as he followed after her. She tried to speed up and leave him lost behind her, but he was faster than her and was carrying less weight. He closed the distance between them quickly, catching her arm and attempting to pull her to a stop.

In a burst of anger, she turned and pushed Allan away from her. As he fell to the ground, she stared hard at him, trying to get him to understand that he needed to leave her now. He was supposed to go off on his own. She had gotten him out, and that was as far as she had decided to take him.

His face streaked with tears, Allan held the baby close to him. "What's wrong with you?" he asked, his voice cracking.

"She doesn't understand," Sawyer explained.

"Then *make* her understand!" Allan cried, and his eyes locked on Shauna's again. "Help him, please!" He won't make it alone! You have to help him!" He looked at Sawyer again, that familiar look of desperation written all over his face. "Help her understand! They're going to kill him!"

"Shauna, let me help you," Sawyer said, turning his upper body and reaching up to her again. When he touched her, he showed her something so horrifying that her original decision changed immediately.

With a gasp, she very nearly dropped Sawyer to the ground and started to sprint back in the direction she had come. While she ran, she heard Allan yelling after her. "Help him! Don't let them kill him!"

She couldn't believe that those soldiers would ever do anything as horrible as taking the life of a child. Why? What was their motive? What was the point? Was it because they left? Was that the consequence for leaving? Would the soldiers try to take the lives of all of them? Would they try to take the life of Sawyer?

Shauna felt more anger at that thought, an anger that gave her power. She felt it moving through her, heard it echoing in her head and the trees around her. *No one. Was going. To touch. Her brother.*

A scream that belonged to Daniel could be heard from up ahead, and Shauna slowed to a stop behind a tree that sat at the top of the large rock formation. Down below, she saw little Daniel struggling to climb up the rocks. He wasn't strong enough. He was sobbing, and when he saw her he held up his arms to her so she would come down and get him. She couldn't. Not quite yet. Behind Daniel, with their guns trained on him, were three soldiers. The closest one was several feet away while the other two hung back.

"Just shoot him!" one of them hissed.

"Just shoot him and get it over with!" the other snapped.

"Do *you* want to shoot a baby?" the closest one demanded, taking a step back. Shauna saw that his stance was hesitant. He didn't want to hurt Daniel.

Daniel, although being very young, knew what the soldiers were there to do. Still crying, he ran at the closest one with his arms outstretched. The soldier froze for a moment as the toddler ran to him, but when Daniel was too close for comfort, he was knocked backwards as the butt of the soldier's gun was thrust into his face.

"Just do it!"

"I *can't!*"

"Oh, for Christ's sake!" The first soldier to speak came forward and shoved the closer one aside. "Quit being such a pussy." He aimed his gun at Daniel and fired.

At the same time, Shauna raised her hand at that soldier and told the bullet what she wanted it to do. The bullet exited the chamber, and then it froze in midair for a second before going back and striking the soldier squarely in the chest. As he went down with a thud, the soldier still hanging back traced the source of the misfire back to her and fired several times in her direction. But once again, the soldier firing ended up being the one to die.

While the hesitant soldier watched her warily, Shauna scurried down the rocks and picked up Daniel. The little boy was sobbing harder than ever, and he hugged her tightly. Shauna glared furiously at the final soldier. He wasn't aiming his gun at them, but he was still a threat to all of them. She should take his life too.

She decided against it. He backed away and nodded to her several times, telling her he wasn't going to hurt her or Daniel. When he was a good distance away from her, he turned his back on her and started walking back towards the facility.

"You saved him!" Allan said in amazement when she climbed up the rocks again with Daniel safely in her arms. "Thank you!" He hugged her leg with his free arm and then hugged Daniel when she set him down. "Thank you, thank you, thank you!"

Marching over to Sawyer, Shauna scooped him up and started on her way again. She had helped little Daniel, and the three of them would now be safe. They were fine to go off on their own.

"Wait!" Allan said in surprise, rushing after her. "You're not going to just leave us here again, are you?"

When he caught her by the arm, Shauna spun around and stared fiercely at him. She knew she was unable to make them understand, so she showed Sawyer what she wanted them to do.

"She says she doesn't want you to come with us," Sawyer explained to them. "She just wants it to be the two of us. She thinks you'll slow us down."

"Take us with you," Allan pleaded. "Please don't leave us here. We won't make it on our own."

Sawyer showed Shauna what Allan was saying, but Shauna didn't want anything else coming in between them and their safety. She shook her head at Allan.

"I can help us," Allan insisted. "If you take us with you, I can teleport us away from here. Far away. We can move farther in seconds than we could in days."

Again, Sawyer showed Shauna what Allan was proposing. But this time, what Allan was offering her in return for her companionship held deep interest to her. She thought it over carefully, and decided that accepting the three of them would benefit her and Sawyer in the long run. Allan could move them all long distances in just a few moments. If taking care of all of them meant she could have that advantage on her side, she would agree to it. She nodded to Allan.

Allan heaved a heavy sigh of relief. "Thank you," he whispered, and then took Daniel's hand. "I have to be touching all of us or else someone could be left behind," he explained.

Stretching his body towards the young ones, Sawyer placed his hand on Allan's. He glanced back to Shauna. "Come on, Shauna," he said. "This is how we get to our safe place."

Understanding what Sawyer wanted of her, she put her own hand on Allan's. She then waited, watching Allan to see what he would do next.

The boy looked slightly terrified. "Well," he said slowly and nervously after a few uncomfortable seconds. "Is there...uh...is there somewhere any of you want to go? Somewhere safe?"

"Hawaii," Sawyer replied with a giggle.

"Antarctica," Allan joked, grinning.

"Detroit," Daniel said, speaking for the first time.

"Detroit isn't a safe place!" Allan cried in protest, giving the toddler a look of disgust. "The military has control over Detroit, too!"

"My Daddy said to go to Detroit if I ever got out," Daniel explained in his surprisingly adorable baby voice. "'Cuz that's where my grandma is. He said if I found Grandma then he would find me too."

Allan paused to consider the scenario. "Your Dad is one of us too? He's still inside the lab?"

Daniel shook his head.

"Where did you say you lived again?" Allan asked curiously, a hopeful glint in his eye.

"In the country," Daniel answered. "Outside of Red Hill."

"Bloody Hill," Allan muttered to himself, and then grimaced. "Lots of our people were killed there." He sighed. "It's risky, but I think maybe we should try going to Daniel's dad first, to see if we can get some help. After that, we can go far away from here."

"But Red Hill isn't very far from here," Sawyer cautioned.

"I think for now we should just focus on getting away from Hatfield," Allan replied, taking another deep breath. "Okay, this might hurt a little bit, but it will probably just feel like you're suffocating."

"Um…" Shauna felt Sawyer tense in her arms, and she immediately became wary. What was Allan about to do?

"One," Allan said quietly, fear on his face. "Two."

"Wait!" Sawyer cried suddenly.

Shauna gasped as a tremendous pressure began pressing down on her entire body, the worst of it being on her head. Her vision went black and for a moment she thought she had died. But then the world lit up again, and they were in a different place than before. They were in a big open space filled with tall, thick grass that scratched at her legs. The area was surrounded on all sides by more trees.

Clutching at her spinning head, Shauna accidentally dropped her brother to the ground; he was also clutching his head and moaning. Shauna almost collapsed, but she somehow managed to stay on her feet. Her stomach was churning violently, and she swallowed repeatedly to keep from vomiting.

Sawyer was already lying helplessly on the ground, and Shauna saw that Daniel hadn't managed to keep his balance either. She heard a retching sound, and looked over to see that Baby Megan was throwing up on Allan.

Allan was the one in the worst condition. He swayed dangerously, still managing to hold onto the baby. His face was white, and his breathing was ragged. With a faint groan, his eyes rolled back in his head and he fell over backwards.

Walter Reifert

"Hey, will you please talk to us now?"

"No."

"Why not?"

"I'm fine. I don't need to talk to you."

"You're not fine, Walter. You need to talk about what you're feeling right now. Don't hold it in. It will only make it worse."

"What am I supposed to talk about?"

"I don't care. Whatever's on your mind right now."

I didn't want to talk to Dr. Perry. He had brought me into Lemoore's study a good ten minutes ago, but we hadn't spoken a word to each other until now. In the past, I had talked with him about my emotions. It had never made me feel any better. If anything, it made me feel worse.

Lemoore leaned forward in his chair beside Dr. Perry. "Maybe you want to talk about what caused you to break down back there?"

I didn't want to talk about that. *He* wanted to talk about that. "I don't know how to express my feelings," I muttered.

"Just talk," Lemoore encouraged. "You don't have to talk to us. Just speak aloud what's in your head. It doesn't need to make sense. You can even pretend that we're somebody else if you want, or even pretend that we're not here."

Pretend that they're not here? That sounded like a good idea. What if they *really* weren't here? That would make my day. But I still didn't know how to say what my heart was screaming at me. I didn't know how to put my emotions into words.

"You could pretend that you're talking to your dad," Dr. Perry said softly. "You could always talk to him, couldn't you?"

Yes, that was true. I had always been able to open up to my dad when I was upset. He had always been a good father. When I was six, my mom died in a terrible car accident, and after her death I'd had a hard time talking to anyone. For two years I rarely spoke, even to Dad. But halfway through my eighth year of life, something had happened. My memories of the event were foggy, but I know it was something traumatizing. After that experience, I always went to my father when I was upset, or even if I just had something on my mind. It was a great relationship my father and I had. Especially after my brothers left, when it was just me and him. My father had been one of my best friends. That was one reason why it had been especially hard to lose him. I had lost my father *and* my friend.

I tried to make myself believe he was in the room with me. I tried to see him sitting in that chair in front of me. More tears came to my eyes and spilled out over me and the old leather couch I was seated on. *Feel his presence,* I told myself. *He's here with you. You just have to believe in it.*

Dad would always remain silent, letting me speak from my heart until I was too breathless to go on. The room around me was silent. I had the floor. Even if he wasn't physically here, my father would still be listening. Taking a deep breath, I began to tell my story.

"I was watching the news again. It was late, but I couldn't sleep. I can't sleep without dreaming about that terrible night. So I went down to the den to watch the news. I know you told me not to, but I made my dad a promise before he died and I don't intend to fail him. I promised him that I would keep myself safe and keep pushing through no matter how much it hurts. But I also promised him that I would help as many people as I could. I've been watching the news, searching for signs of any of us who need help. We use that triangle mind connection to call out to others, but it hasn't been working.

"I've been stuck in this damn place for a month, waiting for someone to come here and join our little threesome. I've been waiting for someone my age, maybe even a friend, to make it to this place alive, just so I could have a friend or somebody to talk to. But since that night, that terrible, God-awful night, the military's been swarming this area. It's a miracle they haven't stumbled upon us yet. The soldiers are like parasites, hiding in the shadows of every corner within a thirty mile radius, waiting to pounce and snatch anyone who was unfortunate to get this recessive gene. People try to get here, but there's just no way they can without getting caught or killed. So I've been watching the news anyway, looking for a story that could lead me to an infected person who is struggling to stay hidden and needs my help. I thought to myself, hey, maybe if I find someone I could go to them and help bring them here, where it's safe. I thought that maybe I could save a life after so many had been lost, just like my father wanted. So I watched the news, but I didn't see what I had hoped to.

"In the Hatfield lab, there was a family who was imprisoned there. Four of the six members had O negative and were taken there after the virus spread to Philadelphia. There was the father, David, the oldest boy, Joe, the second boy, Max, and the third boy, Ben. Earlier today, around one-thirty p.m., there was a breakout at the lab. Five other kids managed to escape unscathed as a result and are out being hunted in the woods somewhere right now, but that family, the Murphys, weren't so lucky. Ben and David were both killed at the lab shortly after the breakout began. No one knows what happened to Joe and Max, but it's not too difficult to put the pieces together. Ben, the first to die, was just eight years old. He was just a kid. His life had barely started. Those soldiers killed an eight-year-old kid because he didn't want to be locked away against his will anymore.

"They killed a kid because he was a little bit different from them. They killed a kid because they don't understand that we're still people. They think we're aliens or some other uncivilized creatures, when all we really are is a group of regular people who have a bit more brain capacity than before. If they understood that, they would understand that they don't have to kill us. They would understand that they don't need to be afraid of us. And these labs...they torture innocent people in those places! We're like lab rats to them now. They use any method of experimentation and it's not considered inhumane. It all makes me sick.

"The scientists claim that their experiments are helping us, that they're 'treating' us, but they're only hurting us more. They suppress our abilities to 'keep us safe,' but all they're doing is making us sick. These labs need to come down. Either we bring them down, or their 'treatments' are going to kill us all." I paused to take a breath, knowing I was ranting on and on about many things that they already knew.

Dr. Perry was right; I *did* need to spit it all out. I was feeling a little better, but not much. I had yet to tell them what had made me snap. "You wanted to know what caused me to snap? Well, here it is. Joe Murphy, one of the kids in the family that broke out? He was one of my closest friends from school. He was also my cousin Maia's best friend. Those soldiers killed one of my best friends. That was why I cracked. We're living in a terrible world, a world that I can't understand. People kill children out of fear, and the government tortures the innocent. Humans are terrible creatures, and I'm ashamed to have been one of them. And no matter what we do or where we hide, those soldiers will never stop looking for us. Unless we do something, unless we make a stand against them, then we will die having spent our lives hiding and running from them. I'm done hiding. I'm done hiding in the dark. I'm ready to fight. I'm ready to fight for our people. I'm ready to fight for *our race*."

Both Dr. Perry and Lemoore were silent for a bit after I was finished. I know a lot of what I'd said was stuff they'd been thinking as well. I knew I wasn't the only one thinking those things.

Dr. Perry cleared his throat but didn't say anything. His thoughts were guilty, and I tried not to listen to them. I heard them anyway. My mouth opened and I spit out my question before I could stop myself. "You were the one who caused the breakout, weren't you?" I raised my eyes to meet his, but he was gazing down at the floor. I couldn't believe it. He had finally done it. After weeks of trying to find a way to break people out of that horrible place without anything leading back to him, he finally did it. And it ended in calamity. "What happened?"

"The Murphys were a few of my patients," Dr. Perry murmured, that terrible guilt hanging in his eyes. "I thought if I was careful, it would all work out fine. This afternoon, at the second scheduled dose of Suppressant, I gave Joe and Max an ordinary sedative rather than the usual injections. Since it was a lower dosage, they only slept for about an hour and a half before awaking with complete access to their abilities. Maxwell had the ability to manipulate electricity, so I knew he would be the one to break out first. He caused the electrical panels that kept the doors locked on that floor to short out. The doors all opened, but only a few tried to leave. Joe was one of them. He was a shape-shifter, so a lot of the soldiers avoided him. A few others who left their rooms retreated back in fairly quickly.

"Some of the other doctors, including Don Rudolph, had manipulated the brain of a patient to get him to be fully obedient to them. They wanted someone who would be able to sniff out hidden O Negatives and to keep those who were imprisoned in line. He's another shape-shifter by the name of Shane Gold, but I and a few others call him Beast. He's a very strong, very dangerous individual. That was why many of the patients retreated back to their rooms when they saw him coming. Those who tried to escape were either killed by Beast or taken back to their room by Beast.

"At this same time, Joe and Max broke out the rest of their family and tried to help others get out as well. David and Ben left the facility while Joe and Max stayed behind to help. Snipers shot them dead before they got halfway to the woods. Soldiers and doctors started rounding people up who were still racing about the halls. Right after the power went out, a young girl faked being gassed and broke herself out of the experimental quarters. I looked up her records, which stated that she lived in Hatfield a few blocks away from you. Her name was Shauna Skyler.

"She went down to the fifth floor, where we keep our younger patients, and used her telekinetic ability to break open the door to the room holding her younger brother, Sawyer Skyler. Inside the rooms on that floor, we keep four children to a room so they don't get too lonely and scared. With Sawyer was an older boy named Allan Brown, a younger boy named Daniel Marcus, and a ten-month-old named Megan Hopper. The three followed Shauna and Sawyer out, and they almost didn't make it. Beast found them on that floor, and if it weren't for Joe they would all be dead. The two of them had shifted and were fighting when Shauna's group made it out. Shauna used her ability to protect the five of them as they escaped, and as far as I know they made it out safely. Shauna even killed a few soldiers while protecting little Daniel. Renee and I are going out at first light to try to find the kids and bring them here safely.

"As for Joe, he was badly wounded in his fight with Beast. He and Max made it out of the facility and into the woods, but as far as their conditions are concerned, I still don't know. Soldiers claimed they put a bullet through Max before he got to the tree line, but he didn't go down immediately. There was a pursuit that went on for several hours, but I haven't been told if any bodies were brought back yet. I'm sure others have grown suspicious of me, considering Maxwell and Joe were my patients, but there have been rumors going around that people are developing an immunity to the treatment so I might still be okay." Dr. Perry paused, watching my blank expression uncertainly. "I can't promise you that he's still alive, Walter. But I guess what I'm trying to tell you is that there's still a good chance that he is."

"And if he and Max survived, that leaves...what, *seven* people who escaped?" I glared at him. "How many people does that leave dead?"

Dr. Perry sighed. "Nine deaths in all. I never thought it would end this badly. I thought with two people who had a working ability, more people would have made it out alive. I didn't think that they would actually use Beast for a situation like this..." He shook his head.

"How many people does that leave still in captivity?" I asked, trying to swallow back my fury.

Shrugging, Dr. Perry replied, "Around six hundred."

"That's way too many," I said, shaking my head in disgust. "We have to get those poor people out of there."

"We will," Lemoore piped in. "But not tonight. We need some time to organize a group big enough to take on that lab. Dr. Perry can't do this from the inside anymore, or they'll know it's him. Let's just wait until we get four to six more O Negatives, hopefully with abilities more powerful than ours. Then, we'll be able to take on that lab. How does that sound? Can you wait a few more weeks?"

I shrugged. "Sometimes I feel like we're the only ones left, like we're the last free O Negatives. What if we are?"

"We're not," Lemoore promised. "Remember what Dr. Perry said; seven probable escapees. When we find them and a few others, we'll be all set."

A buzz sounded suddenly, and Dr. Perry looked down at his belt. "I'm being paged," he explained, rising to his feet and suddenly looking exhausted. "I have to go. Will you be okay, Walter?"

"I'll be fine," I muttered, looking down.

Dr. Perry said good night to Lemoore and then left. After we heard his SUV leave and head into the woods on the hidden gravel path, Lemoore turned to me. "Are you ready to go back to bed? Because I know I am."

I nodded and yawned, realizing just how tired I was.

"Good," he said, rising to his feet and beckoning for me to follow. "I think I figured out a trick to help you sleep. Without any dreams."

5

New Hosts

Shawn Perry

The bloodcurdling screams woke Dr. Perry at around three that morning. She'd never screamed like that. He was out of his bed and sprinting to Jillian's room before he was even awake. Her room was at the opposite end of the hall, but Perry was there in a matter of seconds. He flipped the light switch and hurried to Jillian's bedside, sat beside her, and took hold of her shoulders.

She was screaming and holding her hands to her ears, her face full of pain and fear. Perry knew what was happening; Jillian had had the headache for the past week. "It's okay," he said quietly, rubbing her shoulders and shushing her as she continued to shriek. "It's okay. It's only bad for a little while. *Shhhh.*"

He managed to get her to stop screaming, but she didn't completely quiet herself. Shudders rippled through her, causing moans and sobs here and there. When she finally opened her eyes, they were filled with a terror Perry was all too familiar with.

He smiled reassuringly at her. "What's going on? Can you tell me?"

Jillian didn't answer for a while, her body heaving up and down with each labored breath. "He forgot to take out the trash today."

Perry blinked at his daughter. "What?"

"Mace," Jillian said. "The boy down the street. He didn't take out the trash and now he's grounded and he's mad."

Perry thought he had an idea of what was happening to his daughter. "Can you hear their thoughts? Hmm? Is that what's going on?"

Jillian nodded, her eyes still wide.

"Can you hear mine?"

She nodded again. "Everyone. Renee's mad because I woke Hallie up. Hallie wants to know if I'm okay."

Sure enough, Perry could hear Renee soothing Hallie, their six-year-old daughter, back to sleep in her room.

"You're okay," Perry promised her, smiling and smoothing back her hair. He got her to lay back down, and Jillian's pained and terrified noises ceased. "You're going to be fine. It's a little weird to get used to just yet, but it's not so bad once you do. In time, you'll be able to control when you hear another's thoughts. It won't be so loud."

"It's better now," she said, sighing heavily.

"You see?" Perry looked back towards the hall, where a sleepy Hallie and a frustrated Renee had come to see if Jillian was alright. "Are you going to be okay to go back to sleep?"

Jillian hesitated. "Is it okay if Hallie sleeps with me for a while?"

Perry looked to Renee, who frowned, but Hallie nodded in agreement. "Okay," he said. "Hop in, Hallie." He tucked them both in, Jillian cuddling close to her little sister.

When they were both back in bed, Perry and Renee found it difficult to get back to sleep. After a while, Perry whispered to his wife, "She's got telepathy, just like you."

"Mm," Renee replied.

"You alright?"

"Fine."

Perry could see right through her. He'd always been able to. But he didn't push it. "How's your ability? Has it been bothering you?"

"Shawn, I don't need you to doctor me."

"I'm sorry. I wasn't trying to. I was just asking if you're okay."

"And I told you. I'm fine." She rolled over so she was facing away from him. Perry had noticed she had been quite tense for a while, and he knew why. Their daughter hadn't shown the signs yet, but she would soon, and when she did, it would be harder to hide it because of her age. "When are we going to tell Hallie? She has to know sooner or later, or else she might—"

"Shawn, can we just talk about this in the morning, please?"

Perry stopped trying to talk to her, knowing it would just cause another argument. He laid awake for a long time, long after Renee's soft snores filled the silence.

The next morning, Jillian came down for breakfast early. She looked better. Peppy, even. She wolfed down three bowls of Lucky Charms before Perry finally told her to stop. "I'm just hungry," she protested.

"You're going to throw up," Perry warned. "Let your stomach settle." He knew from his work at the labs that excessive hunger right after the ability shows itself was a side effect, and he knew that violent vomiting could also be a side effect. "Maybe you should stay home today."

"I feel fine, though," Jillian said, looking a little disappointed. Since when did she ever say no to a day off of school? "Great, in fact."

"Your ability's going to pop up randomly for a little while," he explained. "Do you want a repeat of last night in the middle of one of your classes?" The look on her face gave him the answer. "If you're used to the pop-ups by tomorrow, you can go back. I can't keep you out for too long or else people will get suspicious." Renee walked into the room, her face grey and her feet sluggish. "Hey, babe," he said. "You feeling alright?"

"A little tired," she muttered in reply, going to the fridge and staring inside.

Jillian looked at her dad questioningly, but Perry shook his head, signaling her to stay out of it. "I made eggs and toast, hon."

"Oh." Renee went to the stove, her eyes not really focusing on anything. "That's nice of you."

Perry made a mental note to talk to Renee alone the next chance they got, which might be a while, but there was clearly something bothering her other than their current predicament. Renee hated when Perry tried to get her to talk about her feelings and worries, but Perry knew that if he didn't things would only escalate. He'd seen what happened to Renee when she held everything in for too long.

Hallie walked into the room ten minutes later, also sluggish. She held a hand to her head, and it wasn't until she was to the table that Perry saw the tears on her face. "What's wrong, sweetie?" he asked in concern.

Hallie went to him, sniffling and pouting, wiping the tears away. She crawled slowly onto his lap, clinging to his shirt. "My head hurts, Daddy," she whimpered. "It hurts real bad."

Renee and Perry both looked at each other, realization hitting them at exactly the same time. *I guess we will have to discuss it today,* Perry thought to himself. "Maybe you should stay home today too," he told his youngest.

Maia Rudolph

Dear Diary,

Life sucks. Life sucks a huge pair of hairy balls. My dad made me see a therapist, and my therapist is making me write down my feelings because apparently I'm a poor communicator. So here I am, writing down my feelings for you, Dr. Murtaugh. And right now I'm feeling that life sucks a fuzzy pair of mega-balls.

This entry is for you, Dr. Murtaugh. You really want to know how I feel? You really want to know what happened? Well, I'll tell you. (Actually, I'll write it down for you because I'm clearly no joy to talk to.) As you can probably guess, all this shit started after the outbreak. My dad works as a geneticist in the Hellfield Lab, where this disaster began. My father was one of those sick jerks who decided to play Match It Up! with a virus and a blood type, and now the whole world has gone to hell. But I suppose that doesn't explain my whole need for therapy, does it? You're right. It doesn't. But this should.

Why is something that doesn't directly affect me affecting me so much? I'll tell you. See, I have a friend. He's a very close friend. His name is Joe. Joe Murphy. He's everybody's dream guy. Thick black hair, dark brown eyes, flawless bronze skin, a warm, inviting smile, washboard abs, and he's six feet tall. He's HOT. The only reason all the girls at school aren't drooling over him is because of his personality. He's just like me; he's what you therapists call a "poor communicator." Joe likes to tell the truth, no matter how hurtful or angering the truth is. He doesn't have a lot of friends. Neither do I. So we poor communicators do the logical thing; we stick together.

We've stuck together since he was in third grade and I was in second. Occasionally, another loner would join our group. We were up to five before the leak at the facility. My cousin, Walter, who is quiet like me, joined us when I was in fifth grade, even though he's two years older than me. In seventh grade we gained a new member; Jazmine; and a year later Ally also joined our little group of outcasts. We were picked on and pushed around—and we still are—but it was easy to get through when we stuck together. Our chain of friendship was torn to pieces when the Colician Strain was set loose. Walter was taken by the virus, along with my other three cousins and my Uncle John. My bastard of a father took the whole family to his research facility and that's when everything went to hell. Walter somehow managed to get away, but my cousins Tyler, Ethan, and Anton, and my Uncle John were all shot dead. No one knows what became of Walter, but one can only assume the worst. Ally's family moved back to Iowa the day before Philadelphia was quarantined. They probably took the virus with them. They aren't O Negative, but at the time nobody realized that EVERYONE is a carrier, whether you're O Negative or not. Two down, three to go.

A few days after Ally left, Joe found me crying and asked me to be his girlfriend. I, of course, said yes. A week later, my stupid dad took him and his family to the Hatfield lab because they're O Negatives.

So basically, almost all my friends are gone. My boyfriend's gone. I hate my father with a fiery passion. I hope this little entry explains why good ole Daddy sent me to you, because if I have to write anymore of this sh

"Maia!"

I jerked my head up at the sudden shout and lost my grip on my pen. It fell to the floor and skittered away from my desk. Giggles were exchanged around the room between classmates, and I felt the all-too-familiar jolt of hatred begin to run its course through me. So I dropped my pen. What was so fucking funny?

My hate only intensified when I saw my classmates all grinning mockingly back at me in my back row seat. My hate changed to irritation when I saw my loser of a history teacher, Mr. Gilbert (or Bert as Joe and I used to refer to him), scowling at me.

Yes, Mr. Gilbert? Do you need some assistance pulling that oversized stick out of your ass? "What?"

"Would you care to answer the question?" Bert asked with a smirk, his way of telling me he was about to humiliate me.

I glanced around at all the jeering faces, my anger growing from a bubble to a boil. "What question?"

Bert's smirk became a mocking grin. *"Exactly."*

The giggles turned to laughs, and I ground my teeth to keep from spitting out the dangerous words that were dancing on my tongue.

Bert was laughing too. "Maybe if you had been paying attention instead of writing in your diary, you would know that I never asked a question."

More laughs. I tapped my fingers on my desk. The tears were coming; I could feel them. But I would die before I cried in front of these losers; that would only please their cruel hearts. I would gladly spend an eternity in hell before I'd please them. Why did I always cry when I was angry? And how did Bert get away with taunting me? Shouldn't he have been fired a long time ago for this? He treated Joe and I like crap all year, and still he was getting away with it. He purposely put the two of us in the back together so he could make comments about our "dorky relationship." It was fine when Joe was here; we could tolerate it and Joe always had a smart comeback for him; but now he was just pushing it. Picking on two was one thing. Singling someone out was completely different.

My eyes landed on the guest speaker sitting on a stool at the front of the room. I expected to see him laughing with the others like everyone else always did. I was surprised to see that his face was solemn. His eyes were sad. He felt sorry for me. That, in my opinion, was worse.

I couldn't recall the name of the speaker. He had a lovely Scottish accent, and I think Bert said he was a psychologist. His subject today was cyber bullying. How ironic that Bert would pick such a time to belittle me.

Even though our speaker was insulting me with his pity, I liked him anyway. I liked him because I knew his secret. He was definitely one of them. He was an O Negative. I could see it in his eyes. Beside the nervousness clouding them, I could see something in them that few people knew to look for. Being the daughter of one of the head scientists studying the Colician Strain had its perks. The guy had unnaturally bright eyes. Everybody else would just think he had neat eyes, but I knew. Would I tell anyone? Hell no. My dad took away my best friends. This was my way of getting even with him. One of them, anyway.

Bert took his good sweet time hauling his fat ass to the back of the classroom to my desk. "What are you writing, anyway? What's so important that you couldn't wait until your free period to do it? Mr. Lemoore here made some very good points that you have so rudely ignored."

I pulled my notebook away when Bert reached for it. If he read it, the embarrassment was bound to get worse.

"What is it?" he repeated, snatching it from my hand and continuing to taunt. "A love letter to Joe?" There was silence in the room for a few moments while Bert read my journal entry. I was helpless, dreading the moment the grin would appear and the laughs would begin again. I could feel the color rising in my cheeks. When the grin finally arrived and the cackle left his mouth, I stopped breathing altogether. "Oh, it's a letter to your *therapist*," he jeered. "I'm so sorry. I never realized you were having problems."

The laughter came again. It came as spurts of lava out of the mouths of two dozen volcanoes. It came as two dozen bee stings. It came as two dozen shots through the heart.

I looked around at them, the monsters who had tortured me and my friends since kindergarten. Who did they think they were? They weren't better than me! I didn't deserve to be treated this way! After what our world was suffering through, I thought this torture would end. As it turned out, I found myself wishing *I* had been changed. Being an O Negative seemed like a better way to go. They would stick together, just like my group of friends always has, and no one would be treated like this. Everyone would be treated equally, because we would all know what it was like to be shunned. To be *unnatural*. To be viewed as less than everyone else. And I could find Joe. I wasn't supposed to know, but I heard my dad talking to someone about Joe and his captive family. They had tried to escape the lab yesterday, but only Joe and his little brother Max made it out alive. They were both hurt from what I'd heard, and if I could find them I could help them and we could see this through together. I still wanted a chance at being Joe's girlfriend. His ability didn't make me want to pull away from him. If anything, I had become even more attached to him. I didn't want to be here anymore. I wanted to be with Joe.

The hot tears that stung my eyes became harder to control. Stiffly, and with pursed lips, I rose to my feet and gathered up my few belongings I brought to this lousy class: my binder complete with enough handouts from Bert to demolish a rainforest; the notebook used to jot down useless notes that didn't teach me jack shit; and the enormous text book that was a waste of energy and eight trees. I wasn't going to sit and take this shit any longer. I was done. I was done with Bert and the rest of these losers.

"Where the hell are *you* going?" Bert demanded, putting an arm out to stop me.

"FUCK YOU!" The words erupted from me before I even had a chance to consider stopping them. At the same time, I snatched my journal back from him.

Bert, in his surprise, fell over backwards onto the floor, taking several chairs and desks with him. He fell hard, harder than I would have expected him to. Almost like he'd been pushed. But Bert was a fat ass; the bigger they are, the harder they fall.

The tortoise is on its back.

I glared down at him, panting, far beyond enraged. The classroom grew silent. The losers were all watching with open mouths and wide eyes. I had just dropped the F-bomb on a teacher. Damn right they should all shut up!

Bert was staring back at me, a slight fear in his eyes. It made sense; I had never once made an effort to defend myself this entire miserable year. Joe had always done that. But Joe wasn't here anymore. I had to speak up for myself now. The first thing I ever said in response to Bert's teasing was "Fuck you."

It took me a while to catch my breath from the shout. My throat was sore; I must have used far more energy to produce those two words than I planned. Then again, I hadn't planned. I just spoke. When I was finally capable of forming words again, I once again spoke without thinking. "You can't treat me like that! Not anymore!"

I received no reply from Bert. He continued to stare up in shock at me, my high, angry voice a foreign sound to him. I then blurted out the only thing that came to mind: "I'm a person too!"

With my belongings clutched to my chest, I hurried out of the room, my cheeks hot with color. I stole a quick glance at the Scot at the front of the room as I fled, the man called Lemoore. The pity was still there, branded into his eyes.

The tears came then.

* * *

As I sat up on the roof of the school, and as mascara-filled tears splattered over the lined pages of my journal, I crossed out the last line I had written and rewrote it, expressing my true feelings.

I'm writing this, Dr. Murtaugh, because I lost the only good people I had in my life. Now I'm lost, too.

I stared at the last line for what felt like forever, and then began to sob. In a fit of frustration, I threw my journal across the rooftop. It landed about ten feet away, its open pages fluttering in the wind. Bringing my knees up to my chin, I buried my face in the legs of my jeans and cried.

Last year, halfway through my freshman year, Joe stole a master key from the head janitor so he could steal away to restricted places when he got bored. Most of the time he would just go sit up on the catwalk above the stage in the Performing Arts Center and read, but this year the two of us had made a habit of ditching Bert's pointless, required class and climbing to the roof to read, play cards, or just talk. Those had been good times.

The day before Joe was taken, taken from the cafeteria during lunch so half the school could witness, Joe had given me the key. It was if he had known what path his life was to take, but he wanted me to still be able to make our silent, much-needed escapes. Even though I would be alone.

So that was where I went in my moment of anger and grief; the one place I had always felt happy and free.

The roof had a carpet of gravel, but the nice thing about it was that it always gave away an intruder. I heard the crunching from behind me, and my heart lurched as I whipped around. If a janitor caught me up here, I was done for, but it wasn't a janitor. It wasn't even a faculty member. For a fleeting moment I thought it was Joe. But it wasn't Joe. It was that man, the guest speaker, the man who pitied me. Mr. Lemoore.

"Hi," he said as I quickly tried to brush the streaks of mascara from my cheeks. He was an older man—somewhere in his late fifties or sixties—with a full head of wavy gray hair and blue eyes.

Even at that age, he didn't seem to have a problem moving about (which was necessary if he could climb the two story ladder up to the roof). He was of average height but he hunched over slightly, making him appear shorter. Was he doing that in his uneasiness too, or was he just like me—sad? What *was* he doing here, anyway? Seeing my confusion, he held up a blue ballpoint pen. "You forgot your pen," he said. "I'm Patrick Lemoore."

"Hey," I muttered as he came to sit beside me.

His body stiffened as he sat and I caught a glimpse of mild pain in his eyes. Back problems?

"How did you get up here?" I asked him suspiciously, just now remembering that he had no key.

"You left the hatch open," he replied, a little mischievously.

"Ah." I didn't recall doing so, but it wasn't unbelievable. I had committed more reckless acts in my fits of anger that had recently become quite common. "But how did you know I was up here?"

Mr. Lemoore shrugged. "I used to go up to the roof of my school when I was upset." His cheeks took on a bit of color and he looked out over the football field that lay ahead of us.

Yeah. Right. "I think what you meant to say is that you knew I was coming up here. That was no guess." When Lemoore glanced at me, I tapped the side of my head. "You read my mind, right?"

Lemoore didn't reply, but that twinge of fear in his blue eyes became immediately stronger. For a moment, I thought of Bert, staring up at me from the floor with that same look of fear.

"I know what you are," I told him. "But don't worry." I turned my eyes to the football field, where his had previously been. "I won't tell anyone."

There was a powerful silence between us for what felt like minutes, and it very well could have been, and then Lemoore dared ask me, "How did you know?"

I snickered, and turned on him defiantly. "Read my mind."

He already was. My mouth hadn't even closed before he said with an increasing amount of fear, "You're Maia Rudolph, Dr. Rudolph's daughter."

"Don't worry," I repeated. "I'm not going to tell him anything."

"Why wouldn't you?" Lemoore demanded, but he already knew.

"Because I hate him."

"Because he took your friends?"

"Exactly."

"You're Walter's cousin." Lemoore was staring at me in disbelief.

It was the way he said Walter's name that told me he knew him. It also told me that Walter was alive. "What did you just say?"

"Walter's okay," Lemoore promised. "He's safe. He's okay."

I was still in shock. "You're…you…" I stuttered stupidly. Then I blurted, "You know Walter?"

He nodded and smiled. "I've been keeping him safe since the day he escaped from the lab."

"How is he?" I asked breathlessly.

Lemoore shrugged. "Lonely. Grieving. Depressed. Physically, he's fine."

"Can I see him?" Once again, I spoke without thinking. The look on Lemoore's face gave me my answer. I turned away, my face flushing. "Right. No; of course not."

"Don't take it personally," Lemoore said softly.

"No." I shook my head and silently cursed my father once again. "I understand."

"If your father were to somehow discover where we are…" He didn't need to finish.

"Yeah," I muttered, lowering my head.

He paused. "But maybe sometime he could come see you."

I looked up at him, my hopes high.

"I know it would mean a lot to him. Seeing you and getting out of that place would definitely brighten his spirits."

"It would definitely brighten mine too."

"Well, we'll have to keep in touch."

There was another brief silence between us. "Was there something you came up here to tell me?" I asked curiously.

"Oh, yes," Lemoore replied, remembering his true reason for invading my privacy. "I wanted to let you know that I thought your teacher's behavior was absolutely appalling. I thought you'd like to know that I will be filing a report and request for his dismissal."

For some reason, that didn't make me feel any better. I sighed. "One more month," I muttered. "One more month and then I never have to deal with him again."

"I think it will be less time than that," Lemoore said, and then asked me, "Has he treated you like this all year?"

You already know the answer to that, I thought, and I saw Lemoore smile out of the corner of my eye. "It was easier when Joe was here."

There was another pause. "I think Joe's okay, too." When I looked at him, he told me, "There are a few of us out looking for him and his brother. We're hoping to have him with us by nightfall."

Once again, his words left me no comfort. Joe would be safe, yes, but he couldn't be with me. Never again.

Lemoore took my silence to mean I was waiting for something more. "Maybe he could come visit you too."

I shrugged and looked away. In a way, I didn't want to see Joe.

"You love him," Lemoore said, sounding confused. "I don't understand your hesitance."

"I love him," I repeated. "That doesn't mean I can be with him."

Blinking, Lemoore replied, "I'm not so sure about that."

Huh? Did he really think that humans would ever allow O Negatives back into their society *willingly*? And besides, gay marriage still hadn't been legalized everywhere; there was no way they would allow this form of interracial relationship.

It turned out that that wasn't what Lemoore was referring to. "What exactly did you do before you left the classroom?" he asked, scrutinizing me carefully.

My brow furrowed. "What are you talking about? You were there. I swore at my teacher."

"That's not what I'm talking about."

"I don't understand what you *are* talking about."

"Your teacher fell over."

I snorted. "That fat fuck is about as graceful as a beached whale."

Lemoore paid no mind to my harsh comment. "Did he really fall? Was that of his own doing?"

Raising my eyebrows in amusement, I asked, "Do I need to repeat my last statement?"

"Did you push him?"

The question startled me. Was this guy trying to accuse me of something? "I didn't touch that jerk," I said defensively.

"I didn't ask if you pushed him with your *hands*."

It finally became clear to me. I gawked at him and couldn't contain a laugh. "You think I pushed that fatty over with my *mind*?" I laughed again. "You think *I'm* an O Negative?"

Lemoore gazed evenly back at me. "Are you?"

I stared in disgust. "No! If I was I would have left with Joe!"

"What's your blood type?"

"Stop interrogating me! You have no right!" Just to keep things from escalating into more serious complications, I added sharply, "I'm O positive!"

"And who was it who took your blood for testing?"

I started to snap something in reply, but I stopped. "My...my father," I answered, and I started to panic. Even if my dad *had* faked my blood type, there was no possible way that I was an O Negative. I would have felt the symptoms. My ability would have started showing. My eyes would have changed.

Lemoore was smiling a little, and it irritated me. "Do you know how easy it is for a doctor with the right knowledge to fake O negative blood as O positive?"

"My dad wouldn't do that," I protested. "He took my cousins and uncle to the lab and got four of them killed!"

"But you're his daughter," Lemoore pointed out matter-of-factly. "Forgive me for making a judgment about a man I've never met, but I think most fathers would do just about anything to protect their children."

A sudden horror sank into the pit of my stomach and slowly rose up through me. If Dad had switched my blood, he could have just as easily switched that of my little sister, Marlena. Marlena could have it too. I then reminded myself of the impossibility of it all. "I never had any of the symptoms," I blurted.

Lemoore looked doubtful. "Not at all? Not even a slight headache?"

I shook my head, almost desperately. "No migraine, no stomach pains, no insomnia, no nothing." I remembered how Joe had looked just before he was taken. He had looked like he had been hit by a train. I never came close to feeling how Joe had looked.

"Hmm," Lemoore said, looking over the football field thoughtfully. "I wonder..." He turned and looked over my shoulder. My eyes followed him as he rose stiffly to his feet and walked past me. He went over to my journal, bent down, and picked it up. He then looked back at me, his expression and body posture very different. He had changed somehow. "Well, I'll be going now. I'll just take this with me, seeing as you don't want it anymore."

"Hey," I said in protest, jumping to my feet. There were very intimate things inside that journal, things that were of no business to Lemoore or anyone else. "Not cool. Give it back."

"Oh, but you threw it away!" Lemoore's expression was mocking, taunting, and he was making me angry. "It will make a good read, I'm sure."

"Give it back!" I snapped, stepping forward and holding out my hand. Suddenly, the journal was in my hand. I hadn't made a move to snatch it back, and Lemoore hadn't stepped forward to give it back. We were both in the same position we were a moment ago. Confused, I stared down at my journal with my mouth half open. Wanting an answer, I looked up at Lemoore in hopes of getting one.

"Anger tends to be a trigger," he muttered, and I couldn't tell if he was talking to me or to himself. He was smiling at me, calmly but solemnly. "Now," he said conversationally, as if giving a lecture, "how did you do that?"

"I...didn't...what?" I stumbled over several random words, struggling to come up with a coherent statement. In the end, all I could manage was a shake of the head.

Pointing a finger at my chest, Lemoore peered across the rooftop at me and gave me a friendly and comforting smile. "I know what you are."

We both descended from the roof moments later; Lemoore was scheduled to give another speech for Bert's 9th period class, and I needed to sign in at my study hall. Neither of us spoke another word to each other.

After I signed in, I started to leave. I didn't know exactly where I was going, but when Ms. Lars called out to me in protest, I found myself automatically muttering, "Bathroom." And to the bathroom I went.

The bathroom in the Ag hallway was disgusting but rarely ever used, so that was the one I chose. It was far out of the way, but at this point I didn't care how far it was. My walk began at a brisk pace, increased to a run, and finally ended in a sprint. The final bell rang as I burst inside, panting, but I didn't hear it. I was too panicked to think of anything around me. I could only focus on me.

Gripping the sink in front of me as I tried to catch my breath, I stared at the mirror with fierce intensity. Nothing had changed. My hair was still black and shoulder blade length. My skin was still a darker tone. My face was still mildly pretty despite my lack of mascara. And most importantly, my eyes were still brown and dull. They weren't bright and full of new life.

"I'm still me," I breathed, trying to slow my racing heart. "But how did I do it?" I shook my head at the memory of the journal suddenly landing in my hand. It had to be a trick. Lemoore had tricked me. "I had no symptoms," I reminded myself. "I had no symptoms. I'm still me. If I wasn't, Dad would have taken me in. He took Walter and Uncle John and the others, and he took Joe. He would have taken me too." Wouldn't he? Of course he would have. If he cared so little about his nephews and a boy who had been in his house at least three days a week, it seemed fit that he wouldn't care any more about me. Walter and Joe were just as much a part of his family as I.

Startling me out of my reverie was a small voice, a voice that I recognized and was very glad to hear. "Maia?"

I turned and sighed with relief. "Jazmine."

Jazmine had, quite literally, rainbow hair. Her natural hair color was blonde, but Jazmine had always been of the rebellious sort. One day, she was a blonde. The next, she was a rainbow. A crimson red dye coated her straight, rigid bangs. The colors descended down her head in rainbow order, ending with a wild violet at the tips of her shoulders.

Her eyes were the palest of blue, and when she had still been a blonde people called her Snowflake. They were beautiful and gave her an air of innocence, even with the rainbow hair and the lip piercing. And just because she went against her parents' wishes by dyeing her hair with such insane colors and got piercings in places that I cringe when I think about them, Jazmine has never been a bad person. She's never gotten in trouble. Not once. Most people look at the hair and piercings and think she's a troublemaker, or that she smokes pot. Neither were true. Jazmine simply has a very colorful, artistic personality, and chooses to express that through her own body. I love it, personally. I think it's very creative, unique. She really isn't afraid of what people think of her. Even better, she doesn't care. And because of that, she had been made an outcast. One of us. Well, one of *me*. Everybody else is gone. Jazmine is one of the strongest, bravest people I've ever known. I doubt if I'll ever meet anyone braver.

I was truly glad to see her, but I saw the fear in her eyes almost immediately. "What's wrong?" I asked.

Stepping towards me, the tears began to flow from Jazmine's eyes. "I...I'm sorry," she stammered. "But I didn't know where else to go."

I saw it then. Alongside the fear, the glimmer of new life, of new power, was visible. Her snowflake eyes were more beautiful than ever. "Oh no," I whispered, my heart preparing to shatter all over again. "Not you, too."

The tears quickly transformed into sobs. "Please don't tell your dad!" she pleaded.

"Oh God, no!" I cried, and opened my arms as she came to me. Poor Jazmine sobbed into my shoulder and I stroked her hair to comfort her. For a few minutes, I shushed her until she got her emotions under control. Her sobs had died down to occasional sniffles when I pulled away and peered into her terrified, tear-streaked face. "Jazmine. Why did you come to me? Why didn't you just run?"

"I was going to!" Jazmine insisted, the tears spurting from her eyes again. "Dad and me! We were going to run tonight!"

"It's just you and your dad?" I asked.

Jazmine nodded. "Mom and Arthur are both fine. Dad and I are the only ones who caught it."

"Then what are you still doing here?" I demanded, immediately regretful that my voice sounded as harsh as it did. How could I help myself? I knew what people like my father did to people like her. Jazmine had to get the hell out of here, and fast.

"Please!" Jazmine cried out, and the tears came again. "Please help me! I know you would help Joe if you had the chance! Walter, too!"

"Of course I would!"

"Then please help *me*!" Jazmine begged, practically falling to her knees. "I know I can trust you, even if I can't trust anyone else! Even though your father—"

"I would never betray a friend to him," I almost snarled. "After what he did to Walter and Joe and my other cousins and uncle, it's all I can do to keep from killing him myself. I'm sure enough people want to do that already."

"So you'll help me?" Jazmine asked hopefully.

"Of course," I repeated. "Did something happen? Why did you come to me in the first place?"

More tears. "Arthur just called me. They got Dad at his office not twenty minutes ago. Arthur said that they're without a doubt sending someone for me."

"Then you need to get out of here," I said, my heart rate beginning to quicken. But it wasn't out of fear; it was the excitement of my own defiance. "You need to get out of here now." I told her about Mr. Lemoore and his hidden refuge for infected individuals. He was still inside the school; he said so up on the roof. If I could somehow hide Jazmine from the soldiers and inform Mr. Lemoore of the situation, Jazmine could very well be eating dinner in the company of Walter tonight. Wouldn't that just brighten their days?

"You trust this man?" Jazmine asked uncertainly. Trust was, and always would be, an issue for her.

"Yes." I decided against telling her why. I still wasn't one hundred percent certain of my own situation. "Yes, I trust him. I'd trust him with my own life."

"Then I trust him with mine," Jazmine replied, looking much more sure of herself.

"Let's get out of here," I told her, "before those soldiers come for you."

I started towards the door, but then stopped. I turned back. "Can I ask you something first? What can you do?"

Jazmine lowered her eyes, as if ashamed. "If it's alright with you, I'd rather not say."

I was dying to know, but I replied with a simple okay. How many people get to say their best friend is a superhuman? I wanted to know what it was Jazmine could do. I wanted to know badly. I kept my mouth shut.

We walked in silence down the empty hallway towards the closest side exit. If I knew my father's pack of dogs as well as I thought, they would be coming in through the main entrance in order to find Jazmine. We couldn't risk going for the front.

"Do you think we'll see each other again?" Jazmine asked suddenly. She looked to me for an answer.

I knew the answer could very well be no, but I didn't want to make her feel worse. "Yes," I replied, praying it was true. "I think we probably will."

All hope of that fled when we heard shouts from far behind us. We turned, and my stomach sank to my toes. Soldiers. Dozens of them. They were pointing and running towards us.

Knowing we didn't have a second to waste, I took Jazmine's hand and started running down an adjacent hallway. I could feel Jazmine's terror become my own, and for a few moments I thought we might actually make it out. We approached an intersection with another hall. I could see the exit in front of us, but as we entered the intersection, another group of soldiers came in from the side to cut us off. Instantly, my connection with my last remaining friend was broken. Two soldiers caught me by the arms, another prying my hand loose as three caught hold of her. Jazmine was screaming and kicking against her captors. More soldiers came to restrain her. In moments, I was screaming too.

"Get off me!" I commanded, slamming my head backwards into one soldier's nose. I heard a crack and a gasp of pain, but that was all the longer I waited. That soldier's grip loosened and I pried my arm from his grasp. I used my fist and drove it into the other soldier's throat. He let go immediately, and then I was running forward. I was quickly stopped, but not by who I would have expected.

"Maia, stop." The voice was gentle but firm. Soothing but insistent. Sympathetic but unwilling. A hand was placed on my chest and it eased me backwards, away from the struggle. The brown eyes were apologetic, but they showed intent. It was my father.

"What?" I stuttered. I couldn't believe he was actually here, coming to take away my last friend. And then he tells me to stop? Who the hell did he think he was?

"Stay out of this," Dad said, stepping away from me but pausing to make sure I wouldn't make another advance. "Please. Go back to class, sweetie. Stay out of this."

I wanted more than anything to hit him, to punch him so hard that his nose would gush for days. But my shock kept me rooted to my spot, and I knew this was a fight I could not win. I watched helplessly as my dad sedated my screaming friend before walking alongside the soldiers as they headed back to the main entrance.

Jazmine's gone.

Deep in my heart, I knew it would happen.

Students and teachers came to their doors to watch the scene unfold and to watch me stand there, completely overcome with shock, but I hardly registered their presence. I stared after my friend and my father until they were long out of sight. Hours may have passed, but I wasn't aware of time. I finally spoke, if not for myself, then for Jazmine. For Walter.

For Joe.

"Why?"

Cole Ashton

It began as an itch, an itch so irritating that my mother had to put mittens over my hands while I slept. (Even at twenty-four, my mother still felt the need to baby me.) The next morning, the first visible signs of the mutation emerged. They were only a few inches long, but I knew by the texture of them that there were feathers growing on the strange stumps emerging from between my shoulder blades. At first, I had no idea what they could be. The stumps were a strange shape I couldn't identify.

But I *did* know what was happening to me.

I knew it was happening as soon as the migraine came on eight days ago. That was the day my dad sent Mom and me up to the cabin in northern New York. He knew what was happening as well as I did, maybe even more. At least he had a warning. He knew I was O negative, so he bribed officials to keep it quiet and get me a fake ID. I didn't even know until eight days ago, when the migraine started and he told me the truth.

After the nubs began to appear, my first impression was that I was developing tumors instead of an ability. I wanted to tell my mom; maybe if we removed them right away, I would be okay. But part of me, perhaps the instinctual part of me, told me to keep my mouth shut. The migraine stopped after the third day, and whatever these things were, they were the result.

Nobody could know.

Later on the second day, the itching got much worse. I wore a baggy shirt and sweatshirt to hide what was growing out of my back, but every time I reached back to scratch at them, I'd swear they'd gotten bigger. At the end of the second day, by which time my stress was duly noted, the things on my back were each three feet long. As I gazed upon them, the strange stubs with snow white feathers popping out of them, I finally understood what was happening to me:

I was growing wings.

But the itching didn't lessen. If anything, it got worse. I slept on my stomach all night long. Well, I attempted to sleep. I would finally be dosing off when a stab of pain would erupt from my back and I'd wake up to find myself scratching at the wings. I scratched so hard, I drew blood. With my teeth gritted and muscles tensed, I resisted the terrible urge to scratch.

I was keenly aware that I could feel the wings drawing further out of my back. Sometime around 2:15 that morning, I finally drifted off. My dreams were filled with flying.

Now, here I was, standing with my back to the bathroom mirror, my head cranked over my shoulder to see the damage done. The good news: the itching had stopped at last. The bad news: I now had a twelve foot wingspan.

"Holy hell," I whispered as I took in the magnificently horrifying sight. The wings were both covered in thick, snow-white feathers. When I stretched them out, the last foot or so of each would crumple against the walls. They were beautiful, absolutely beautiful, but I could not stop the pounding of my heart. I was scared. Terrified. How the hell was I supposed to hide these from the world when I couldn't even hide them from myself? They were so clumsy that I had already broken several things in the bathroom and my bedroom. They were all but impossible to control. My body was not at all accustomed to these strange new muscles, and the slightest twitch would send a ripple through one of them and then it would thump into the wall or crash through a window.

It was 6:30 in the morning and I had already drawn plenty of unwanted attention to myself. Mom and several agents had knocked on my door to ask if everything was alright. I told everyone who came to go away. I was in one of those moods where I wanted absolutely zero human contact. I had to figure out a way to hide these wings from public eyes, and I had to do it fast. My dad was coming up from D.C. and would be here any minute. My dad, Richard Ashton.

The President of the United States of America.

Cutting them off was not an option. I knew immediately that I had nerve endings connecting them to the rest of my body. When one of the wings crashed through my bedroom window, I cut it on the broken glass and it hurt like hell. From what I'd observed, the nerves in my wings were far more sensitive than in any other part of my body. I tried drawing them in, to pin them against my back, but I was still getting used to having these new appendages. All they did was flop uselessly at my sides.

As I struggled to find a way to make them appear natural under my shirt and sweatshirt, someone gave a sharp rap at the door. "Cole, are you okay?"

Shit.

It was my dad.

"I'm fine," I lied, the shaking in my voice an easy giveaway to my fib. "I'll be out as soon as I can."

"Nick says you've been in there since you got up over an hour ago," Dad said, his voice filled with worry. (Nick is the agent who accompanies me almost everywhere I go.) "There's broken glass and feathers all over your room. What's going on?"

"Leave me alone, Dad!" I yelled at him, my voice cracking as tears started to puddle on my shoulder. He called out to me again, but I screamed mid-sentence, "Go away!" I stared at the newly grown avian parts attached to my back. Between them were barely three inches of space. Under the deep red scratches that I inflicted on myself between the base of the wings, I could see the new muscle rippling there. My back had developed more muscle for support, and the muscle at the base of the wings was far more powerful than if I had been lifting weights. It seemed fit. These wings were not lightweight.

I heard Dad say something outside the door, and it sounded like he said, "Break the door down." Scared, I looked away from my shocking image and eyed the door warily.

"Dad," I called, "what are you doing?"

"Stand back, Cole." It was Nick.

"Don't come in here!" I warned, but I instinctively climbed into the shower and pulled the curtain around my naked torso. I prayed that no one could see the bizarre silhouette behind it.

It only took Nick one kick to get the door open, and he advanced inside with his gun drawn. Nick was young; one of the youngest in the Service in fact. But even at thirty-one, Agent Nick Matheson was one of the most trusted in the Service. His gun was drawn, but I knew he did not intend to use it. It wasn't even aimed in my direction. His eyes met mine, and he lowered the gun but kept it gripped firmly in his hand. "You alright, Cole?" he asked, peering at me cowering behind the curtain.

Before I could reply, Dad was barging past him and pointing towards the door. "Give my son and I some space, will you, Matheson?"

Knowing that when Dad used his last name he meant business, Nick immediately withdrew from the room without another word.

Dad closed the door as best he could on its broken hinges and took a good long look at me. "Are you naked?" he asked rather bluntly.

"I'm wearing pants," I said, a little defensively.

"Then come out of there," Dad invited, gesturing for me to step out of the shower.

I hesitated. Dad knew what I had become, but I didn't think he was ready for this. "I don't think that's such a good idea."

"Cole," Dad said in a stern voice he hadn't used on me since I was a child. "Come out of there. Let me see you."

"No," I persisted.

"I want to see you!"

"Trust me; you don't."

"You can either come out of there on your own, or I can pull you out!"

I couldn't believe this. "I'm not a kid anymore, Dad!"

"You're *my* kid," Dad exclaimed. His face and voice both softened. "I'm sorry. Please, Cole. Come out where I can see you. No matter what it is, I'll die before I let them take you."

I sighed, knowing that fighting anymore was pointless. "Alright," I said. "You asked for it." I stepped out of the shower on rubber legs, stumbling over my own feet as I did so. My wings bumped into the wall and one of them jerked out and struck the counter, knocking my glass of water to the floor. It shattered, but my dad didn't seem to notice. He was too busy staring in amazement at my newly developed body parts.

He whistled. "Wow," he whispered after taking it in for a while. "That's...wow."

"Yeah," I replied, feeling myself becoming angry. "I guess this is going to be a bit of a problem for your campaign, isn't it?"

Dad ignored my comment, still staring at my wings. "I...wow."

"Is that all you can say?" I snapped, my face growing hot.

"No," Dad said, but he didn't look like he was talking to me. "It's just...I was hoping for something a little less...noticeable."

"I'm so terribly sorry," I muttered sarcastically, and then laughed bitterly. "I think people are going to know something's wrong with me when I walk outside with a pair of angel wings on my back."

His face lost deep in thought, Dad reached up and scratched the thick white stubble that was forming at his chin. "What are we going to do about this?" he muttered.

"We?" I squeaked. "What are you talking about? What am *I* going to do about this?"

"We're in this together, Cole," Dad said sternly, scowling a little.

"You're not the one with the wings!" I shouted.

"No," Dad said, "I'm not. I'm the President of the United States, and I lied to everyone. I kept my infected son safe while I let the sons and daughters of everyone else be taken." He gazed back evenly at me. "People have died, Cole. They've been murdered. Even worse; some have been experimented upon. Tortured. What do you think the country will do once they realize that the man who took their families from them is actually harboring his own?"

My eyes lowered in shame. I had never considered what would become of Dad if I was discovered. I had only ever thought of what might become of myself. If anyone saw my wings, both our lives were over. Mom's would most likely be as well. As I thought through the unfavorable circumstances, I repeated Dad's question: "What are we going to do?"

"Hmm." Dad's eyes never left my wings. He stood staring for a long time, completely lost in thought. After a while he started nodding, but I had no idea why. Finally, he spoke up. "I have an idea. It's a little unorthodox, and you may not like it, but I think it's the only option we have that can keep our family safe." He gestured for me to follow him and started for the door, but I stopped him.

"Why did you do this for me?" I asked. "You could have lost your career and maybe even your life. Why would you risk everything in order to kept my condition hidden when you could have just turned me in?"

Dad stared at me in disbelief. "How could you even think I would do something like that?"

Defensively, I replied, "I'm just saying that it would have been easier."

"You're my son, Cole," Dad said. "My only son, in fact. My only child. I'm not going to send you to one of those awful places." It was a very thoughtful thing to say, more thoughtful than anything he had said to me in a long time, but he ruined it by adding, "And besides, we're in too big a crisis for the American people to start losing faith in their leader."

He turned away just in time to miss the angry twitch in my lip and the hate flash across my eyes. No matter what he said or how many times he denied it, what he did would always be in his best interest. I must have acquired my selfishness and self-preservation from him. But I didn't want that. I didn't want to be a selfish liar like my father. I knew that it wasn't wise to think in such ways, but I had a thought in the back of my mind that maybe the wings were actually a gift. Maybe, just maybe, I didn't have to be this way anymore. Maybe I could start over. I could be anyone I wanted, anything I wanted. But that was crazy thinking. I would never change.

Now that I was put back in my bad mood, all I wanted to do was slam the door shut and hide in my bathroom for the rest of the day. But refusing help from my father, who just so happened to be the most powerful man in the country, would be a deadly mistake. Denying help from anyone at this point would be fatal. I saw on television what happened to those affected who had lied about their blood type, and what happened to those who had helped them lie. It wasn't just my life on the line anymore.

I guess it never had been.

I sulked out of the bathroom and froze when I saw Nick standing beside my father. He was staring at my wings, but he appeared far less surprised than my father was.

"Dad," I said nervously.

"It's okay," Dad assured. "He knows."

I relaxed a little. I trusted Nick; I always had. Even if he hadn't known—and it was impossible for him not to—I doubted he would have told anyone. Nick was calm and cooperative. Whatever Dad was planning to do, Nick would go along with it quietly. Obediently. No questions asked.

"Do any of the others know of my son's condition?" Dad murmured to Nick, referring to the other agents.

"I think some have their suspicions, but no one's made any accusations yet," Nick replied.

Oh. That's just great.

"And what's your opinion on this?" Dad asked. "Now that you've seen what my son's become."

"It's my job to protect your son," Nick said. "I've been protecting him for two years already. I'm not about to fail him now."

I exhaled a sigh of relief. It was great to know I had on my side at least *one* man with a gun.

"Are there any others you think can be trusted with this information?" Dad was listening keenly.

Nick shrugged. "I'm sure there are. Many of them are very fond of your son."

Well, that's jolly good news! Maybe if I get sent to a lab, I'll get my own little suite complete with room service and everything! Just because a few White House Secret Service agents are fond *of me!*

"But," Nick continued, "I feel that the fewer people who know about Cole's predicament, the safer he'll be."

Dad nodded. "I agree. But what to do about the wings? I can't hide him in this cabin forever. People are going to notice that my son is being hidden from the public eye, sooner rather than later."

"I've never heard of a mutation this severe," Nick replied, as if he didn't even hear Dad. His eyes drifted to the wings dragging limply behind me. "This is…different."

"Can you stop talking like I can't hear you?" I snapped.

"We're just trying to figure out how to help you," Dad said, putting up his hands in a defensive gesture.

"Well, would you mind including me in the conversation?" I'm huffing and flustered. "It's *my* body we're dealing with, after all."

"I'm sorry, Cole," Nick said, turning to me. He didn't look sorry at all. "What do *you* think we should do about this?"

I wasn't thinking anything. I had no idea what I was supposed to do about this, what *anyone* was supposed to do about this. Gritting my teeth, I lowered my eyes to the floor, feeling useless. That's what I was and always would be: useless.

There was an uncomfortable pause, and as I felt my face becoming hot again I heard my dad whisper to Nick, "Do you think there's a doctor who would be willing to surgically remove them and keep his mouth shut?"

"Whoa," I said, my body automatically on the defensive. I took a step back. "What?"

"I'm just trying to take all the possibilities under consideration," Dad told me. "And right now, this one seems like the most practical."

I was suddenly feeling very protective of my wings. My beautiful angel wings. I must have still been holding onto my crazy thoughts. Why couldn't I be a new person? Why couldn't I make a change for the better? What was holding me back? My father? Sure, he was the President. That didn't necessarily mean that he had control over my life. He wanted to cut them off. I wanted to try them out. Why couldn't I? He couldn't stop me. It was *my* body, just like I said. I got to make the decisions regarding it. I let Dad know that. "This is *my* body, Dad. I get the final say in whether or not you're cutting them off."

Dad's eyebrows went up, and I knew my last sentence was a mistake. "Do you *want* them?"

"That's not what I meant..." I looked to Nick for help, but he was peering at me in a way that made me feel uneasy. The look in his eyes...it was relief. There was no mistaking it.

"Then tell me what it is you meant, Cole," Dad ordered, his voice rising. "Do you want to be one of them? Is that what you want? You want to be a freak?"

My eyes narrowed and I growled at him through my teeth. "You've been telling me who I should be my whole life, and because of that I've turned into you. Selfish, arrogant, acting superior to everyone else. You've turned me into you. But I don't want to be you. I've never wanted to be you. Yes, I'm what you'd call a freak. I like poetry, music, art, math. I don't give a rat's ass about business and politics. Especially your business and politics. As for the wings...who says I can't have a normal life while keeping them?" I could hide them. When my muscles built up enough, I could pin them to my back under my shirt. There were ways I could get through this while keeping them. Besides...

I wanted to fly.

Dad was angry. I could see that right away. But he wasn't just angry; he was furious. "Well," he began in a shaky, dangerous tone, "if that's what you want, to be a freak with the rest of them, then you're no son of mine. You're dead to me now."

As if on cue, three of Dad's closest agents entered the room. Their hands were on their guns in their belts, and they were staring at me with suppressed expressions of shock.

I looked to Nick for help again. His eyes had changed. They were full of regret. I had only seen that look in someone's eyes once; from a man who had been harboring three O Negatives in his cellar. He had that look in his eyes right before he was shot. Right in front of me.

Was Nick aiding O Negatives?

No. He simply felt sorry for me because he knew I was about to die.

I looked back at Dad's merciless eyes. "So what now?" I demanded, proud that I kept my voice steady and even, despite knowing what was about to happen.

My dad's lips parted and he spoke two words. It was because of those two words that I would never bring myself to forgive him, even after he apologized to me live in front of the entire world.

"Shoot him."

There was a moment's hesitation from the three newcomers, and a moment was all that was necessary. Nick was already yanking out his gun while Dad was speaking. My eyes found Nick's, and I found a single word buried in them: Run. Whoever Nick really was, it wasn't who we'd all made him out to be; that was clear. I wasn't going to take any chances with the split second of opportunity I was given. I turned towards the glass door that led out onto my balcony and started to run. If I could just get it open somehow…

No. That was impossible. But Nick was taking care of the impossibility for me. His gun was the first to fire, but the bullets weren't directed at me; they were directed at the glass directly in front of me.

I prayed that there would come a day in both our futures where I could thank Nick in person for what he did for me that day. At the moment, I was focusing on escaping unscathed.

The glass shattered with the first shot, but Nick gave me two more for luck. I wanted to yell thank you right there, but then things might have gotten progressively worse for him. As I took a running leap over the carpet of shattered glass, I heard Dad shouting, "He's right in front of you! Just shoot him!"

My feet landed on the wood of the balcony, and I wasn't sure that I knew what to do next. I had never tested out my wings; I wasn't even sure that they were finished developing. They were still trailing behind me, pinned down by their massive weight, but as soon as the cool May breeze struck my bare chest they were up and flapping majestically, almost as if another entity was controlling them. Or as if they were an entirely separate entity themselves.

Giving my knees a slight bend, I pushed off the balcony and dove into the woods, my wings carrying me safely away.

If only that was how it happened.

6

Soul Mates

Maia Rudolph

For the first time in weeks, Dad was home for dinner. I knew that he had requested this night in particular, given what he had done to me today. It was too much of a coincidence that this would be his night off.

He hadn't spoken a word to me since he arrived home, and I was determined to avoid him for as long as possible. Unfortunately, staying in my room forever was not an option. Dad eventually came and knocked on my door, calling me down for dinner. It was clear he wanted to talk to me. I made a point to delay as long as possible until joining him and my sister at the dinner table.

The meal was simple—spaghetti, something I could have made myself—but my stomach was too unsettled to keep anything down. Besides, there was no way in hell I was eating anything that bastard cooked up.

For ten minutes or so I sat there, my back pushed up against the back of my chair, my arms crossed, glaring at my untouched plate of pasta. Marlena sat to my left, silent and munching each noodle one at a time. She knew I was angry and didn't want to get in the middle of the fight that was guaranteed to happen, so she avoided eye contact and refused to speak. Considering she was only six years old, my little sister was curiously smart.

Dad purposely sat across from me, glancing up occasionally to see if he could catch my gaze. I wasn't going to fall for it. If he wanted to try to communicate with me, which was something neither of us were good at—says my therapist—he would have to make the first attempt.

Finally, Dad's soft voice broke the silence, and I bit my lip to keep what I wanted to say to him to myself. "Please eat, Maia."

Through my teeth, I replied, "I'm not hungry." Immediately after the words left my mouth, my stomach growled loudly. I continued to refuse eye contact, but I saw Dad's eyebrows go up. It only made me angrier.

"Maia." Dad's voice was hesitant yet persistent. "If you're angry with me, why don't you just say so?"

I couldn't help but smile sourly. "Okay. I'm angry with you. I'm *really* angry with you."

"Let's talk about it then." Dad set his fork down and leaned forward.

I forced myself to raise my eyes. My glare intensified. "Will talking about it make a difference?"

Dad shrugged. "Why not? It can't hurt."

I snorted. I wasn't going to make this easy for him. "I think it's a little too late to start talking about something that should have been talked about weeks ago."

"Better late than never."

My mouth fell open. "*Seriously? That's* what you have to say? 'Better late than never'?"

Dad threw up his arms and gave me a helpless look. "I don't know what you want me to say!"

"How about you say you're sorry?" I retorted in a snarl. "How about you say you're sorry for getting my uncle and cousins killed, that my other cousin is still missing somewhere? How about you say you're sorry for Joe, for kidnapping him and experimenting on him? How about you say you're sorry for taking my last friend today? How about you say you're sorry for abandoning us here?" I pointed to Marlena. "You want to talk about this *now*? After you've spent weeks ignoring us and making my life hell? *Screw you!*" I shoved my chair back and stood up.

"Sit down," Dad said, his voice firmer.

"No!" I screamed, taking my plate of spaghetti and flinging it in the air. It flipped a few times, dumping noodles and sauce over the table, and shattered as it struck the floor next to Dad's chair. I pointed an accusing finger at him. "You don't tell me what to do! You're a murderer!"

Marlena cowered in her chair as I stalked to the stairs. I kicked the table angrily as I passed, which left me with a throbbing pinky toe.

"Maia!" Dad said sharply.

I rounded on him. I expected to find him glaring right back at me, but he didn't even look angry. He looked sad. He knew our relationship was falling apart, if it had ever been stable to begin with.

"I was just doing my job," he said softly. "What did you expect me to do?"

I surprised us both when I laughed. "You want to know something, Dad? The Nazis were just doing their jobs too." I turned and started up the stairs, but I didn't feel like I had left him feeling guilty enough. Once more, I turned back to him. "Joe asked me to be his girlfriend right before you took him. I…I loved him. I guess I still do. Maybe you and I should talk about *that*."

I flopped down on my bed and sobbed as soon as I slammed my door closed. Time meant nothing to me after that. I could have been in my room for days and it wouldn't have made any difference to me. Once I had my sobs under control and all that remained of my breakdown were a few stray tears, I glanced at my clock. 8:36. It had only been about two hours.

My eyes were dry and my nose was stuffed, so I grabbed a Kleenex and cleared my sinuses loudly. A dull throb was beginning at my left temple, and with a shaky sigh I lowered myself onto the side of my bed.

For a few minutes I sat staring at my feet. A gentle knock at my door brought me back. I knew who it was; only Marlena would be so quiet.

When I opened my door and gazed down on my little sister, I couldn't help but smile. She was a mini version of myself. Straight black hair that went past her shoulder blades, a thin, angular face, and dark brown eyes. She was just as quiet as I had been at that age.

At first, she looked nervous that I might yell at her, but when she saw my smile she immediately swooped in and gave me a big hug. Something in her hand crinkled against my back, and I realized she was holding a few pieces of paper. She pulled away and skipped over to my bed. I went over and sat down beside her, accepting one of the papers from her. "What's this?" I asked, but I didn't need an answer and Marlena didn't give me one. She had drawn me a picture of myself and Joe, smiling and happy. Between us was a small figure that I couldn't quite place, but could guess at. "Is this you?"

Marlena shook her head. "That's Nicole."

"Nicole? You mean Mom?"

"No. You name her after Mom." When I could give no more of a response than a blank look, Marlena shook her head again and sighed, as if I should know this already. "She's your baby."

I couldn't hide my surprise. "What?"

"You and Joe are going to have a baby," Marlena said, and giggled like it was a joke.

"What?" I said, also finding this amusing. I forced a laugh for her. "Why would you say that?"

"Because I dreamed it." Marlena was still smiling. "All my dreams come true now."

This information caught my attention. It brought my memories back to my bizarre encounter with Mr. Lemoore. Was it really possible that I had an ability? And Marlena too?

I decided to play along and not act as suspicious as I really was. "When are we going to have a baby?"

"Soon," Marlena said, going to my calendar and flipping through the pages until she found August. She pointed to the twelfth.

I laughed again, relieved that the problem wasn't even a problem at all. Marlena just had a dream. There was no possible way I was going to have a baby in three months. I loved Joe, I really did, but as of this moment I was still a virgin. "Really? So soon? I haven't seen Joe in weeks."

"You'll see him tonight," Marlena promised me, beaming.

Once again, my doubts were surfacing. "Tonight? Did you dream that too?"

Marlena nodded. "But don't tell Daddy, or else he'll take Joe away again."

I noticed that Marlena was clutching another picture to her chest. "What's that? Is that another dream?" I reached for it, but Marlena pulled away from me. She suddenly looked scared, defensive. "What's the matter? Can't I see it?" I gently pulled the picture from her tense grip. This time, I was certain that the smaller person in the picture was Marlena. There was also a man in the picture, and he couldn't be anyone other that Dad. It was a nice family picture, something I didn't see every day, but something was wrong with it. We all had sad frowns on our faces, and there were big black X's where our eyes should have been. I looked to my little sister in shock. "Marlena, what is this? What did you dream?"

Her hands fidgeting nervously in her lap, Marlena looked at the floor and whispered, "We die."

I gaped after her as she took the picture from my slack fingers and trotted out of the room. Over her shoulder she called, "Say hi to Joe for me, 'kay?"

"Okay," I replied unconsciously, unable to shake the image I had just seen. Once again, I sat staring at my feet until the next knock startled me out of my troubled thoughts. Only this knock didn't come from my door; it came from outside my window.

Puzzled, I went to the window and peered out. It was already dark, so I had difficulty seeing out, but I thought I saw some black hair blowing in the wind. If someone was really hanging there, what in God's name were they thinking?

Praying that there really wasn't some drunk dumb ass/rapist practicing acrobatics outside my room, I pulled the window up and shivered as a cool breeze raised goose bumps on my skin. Leaning over the pane, I gaped as I saw Joe barely hanging onto the thin ledge outside.

"Joe!" I cried in amazement, gaping down at him as he gazed up at me with a thick pain clouding his eyes.

"Hey," he replied, his voice shaking with his effort to hold on.

"How did you get up here?" I asked, lowering my voice. There wasn't a tree or anything else he could have climbed to get up here.

Joe attempted a shrug. "You probably don't want to know. Can I come in?"

"Yeah…yes. Yeah." I reached down and took Joe's hand to help him up. I wasn't very strong, but Joe seemed to have gained quite a bit of muscle mass. Once his hands were inside, he hoisted himself up and hopped inside, the muscles in his arms rippling as he did so. His biceps were huge! I wanted to look him up and down to see how he had changed over the past few weeks, but my eyes were drawn to my hand, the hand that had helped Joe up. It was covered in blood. "Joe?" I said weakly, looking at him in horror.

His brown eyes were bright and full of the power that all O Negatives had, but at the same time they were dull. Injured. And as I looked down to his lower body, I saw why. All he was wearing was a dirty pair of white shorts. No shirt, no socks, no shoes. His shorts were stained with dirt, grass and blood. His blood. There were three large gashes starting from the right side of his chest and ending at the top of his left hip. His blood covered his whole torso and had gone through his shorts to his knees. The blood was dried, but there were still trickles slowly seeping out of the slits. Something very big, and with very large claws, had attacked him. By the unnatural paleness his dark skin was taking on, I knew he needed help.

"Joe," I whispered, putting a gentle hand over his wound. "What happened to you?"

"Is your dad here?" Joe asked warily, looking towards my door, which was hanging ajar.

"Y-yes," I replied breathlessly. "He's downstairs."

"I need stitches," Joe mumbled, sinking to the floor.

"Joe!" I cried, dropping to my knees beside him. "Joe, I'm going to go get Dad—"

"No!" Joe clamped one hand over my arm and the other over my mouth. "Not here! I can't risk him calling the lab so they can take me back. I can't go back there, Maia!"

I saw the desperation in his eyes, and I couldn't bring myself to go against him.

"Okay," I whispered when he removed his hand from my mouth. "But we need to get you help. Maybe if we can lure him out somewhere..."

"You're so beautiful," Joe murmured abruptly, reaching up a shaky hand and brushing my dark hair behind my ear.

"What?" I said in surprise, but I didn't pull away. It had been such a long time since we last sat alone together, since he touched my face in such a way.

"I've really missed you," Joe said, his eyes terribly sad. He traced the curve of my cheek bone, leaving a smear of warm blood on my skin.

"You don't even know how hard it's been trying to continue my life without you," I replied, feeling a few tears fall from my eyes.

Joe brushed them away. "I hoped things could go back to the way they were...you know, before. I still stand by what I said before I was taken. I don't care how different we both are. I still want to be with you."

"I don't care what you are," I told him. "If anything, this ability of yours, whatever it is, is drawing me closer to you."

"I love you."

I opened my mouth to reply, but before I got a word out Joe was on his feet and running to my door. By the time my head got all the way around, Joe already had my father pinned up against the wall. Dad must have come to investigate the commotion.

He didn't look scared. He didn't even look surprised. The only visible emotion on his face was uneasiness. "Hey, Joe."

"Why?" Joe demanded, shaking him. "Why did you do it? Why did you turn me in?"

Dad blinked. "What was I supposed to do?"

"You could have lied!" Joe's face was full of blind fury, but I could see him breaking down. Whatever had happened to him in that place, it was taking its toll on him. It was going to cause him pain for the rest of his life. "You could have lied for me! I thought I meant more to you than just...just...something to play with! Something to enjoy watching scream and cry in pain!"

Dad's expression was bewildered. "You think we *enjoy* this?"

Joe's glare was hostile, but he released him. "Tell me you don't!"

The bewilderment changed to sorrow. If what Joe said was true, Dad enjoyed the experiments but he wasn't free of guilt. Guilt had still found him. "Why did you come here, Joe?"

"Because Maia's the only person I trust anymore," Joe said bitterly.

"What about Maxwell?" Dad asked, not advancing nor retreating. Whatever Joe's ability was, Dad was afraid he would use it, despite his bloodied state.

"Max is dead," Joe said, glancing at me.

"What happened?" Dad asked softly, sympathetically.

"Beast," was all Joe gave as an explanation.

Beast? What did that mean? Had the virus created a monster?

Dad nodded, evidently understanding. "I presume he's the one that got to you?" His eyes moved to the brutal slices across Joe's body.

Joe nodded in reply, exhaling wearily.

"You need help," Dad said, as if it wasn't already obvious. "Or else you're going to bleed out."

"And I suppose *you're* going to be the one to offer that help?" Joe challenged.

Shrugging, Dad said, "If you let me."

Joe laughed, a dry, agonized sound that made me wince. "Why would you help me? After you threw me in a cage and cut me apart, why should I trust you? Why should I—" His voice cut off sharply, and his head snapped back in the direction of the window. His eyes were wide and fearful.

"What is it?" I asked in alarm, following his gaze. I couldn't see anything in the dark, but Joe clearly sensed something.

"He's coming," Joe said.

"Who?" I started to ask, but Dad was already moving in on me.

"Maia," he said, taking my arm and pulling me out of the room. "Get your sister. Get out of the house."

"What's going on?" I demanded as a heavy fear began to smother my senses.

"Just get out!" Dad ordered, his tone harsh but pleading.

"I'm not leaving until you—"

"Go!" Joe ran towards me and gave me a hard shove backwards.

There was a tremendous crash from the window, and I managed to catch a glimpse of something with golden fur and huge teeth coming through before I was doing backwards somersaults down the stairs. My head struck the wood floor at the bottom and my vision turned white. As I clutched my head, the last thing I heard before I lost consciousness was a combination of my sister's screams and two big animals snarling. There was a gruesome ripping sound and a squeal of agony.

Cole Ashton

The agony was all my mind could comprehend by the time my wings gave out. Things hadn't happened as simply as I'd hoped they would in my father's cabin. I had not escaped unscathed. The bullet hole in my side was proof enough of that.

One moment I was gasping for air, my wings pumping madly to keep my one hundred seventy pound body afloat. A moment later, my wings refused to commit to another beat. As panic filled my weakened body, I struggled with all my willpower to move my strange new muscles. They hung uselessly below my horizontally positioned torso, each individual feather fluttering in the light chill of the breeze.

"Christ," I croaked, my injured side throbbing with the effort of speech. "After all this shit, this is how it's going to end?"

Because of my wings, I didn't go down as fast or as hard as I thought I would. I glided down to the ground awkwardly. Don't get me wrong; I still hit the ground hard enough to knock the wind out of me and send a wave of searing agony from my wound through the remainder of my body, but it could have been worse. Much worse. At least I didn't break anything.

I laid on the wet ground for a long time, gasping for air and from the pain. When I tried to push myself up, I found that I didn't have enough strength. I was exhausted. I was going nowhere.

The world was dark, despite the light of the full moon and a few stars that shown tonight. I had crossed the New York/Pennsylvania border over an hour ago, and the only thing I saw for miles was an endless forest. The likelihood that anybody—anybody desirable, that is—was anywhere nearby was about as likely...well, about as likely as it was for me to sprout wings and fly off my bedroom balcony.

So I just laid there on the thin carpet of pine needles, listening to the crickets and toads whose voices lit up the night. My breathing gradually slowed, and I soon felt myself slipping into the clutches of sleep.

Seconds dragged into minutes, and minutes became an hour. I was startled out of a light doze by a noise next to my head. With a jerk, my head rose and I looked around in alarm. The sound of crackling pine needles had been close—much too close for comfort. It was way too dark to see anything clearly, but off to my left a few feet, I could make out a dark shadow, blacker than all the shadows of the forest.

The silhouette of another person.

"Hey," I choked out weakly, attempting to raise myself up on an elbow.

The shadow held still for a few moments, almost making me believe it was just my imagination. Then the person came forward, slowly at first, and then at running speed.

"What are you doing?" I cried when the person knelt down beside me.

"Shh," a gentle voice whispered. Her soft hands wrapped a warm blanket around my shivering, bare body.

Whoever she was, she didn't seem to have any intention of hurting me. "Who are you?" I asked as she curled up on the ground at my side, warming herself under the blanket with my body heat.

"Someone like you." Her arms wrapped around me and her head rested on my arm.

As we began to drift off in the comfort of each other's arms, I felt an energy surge between us. It started as a tickle, and then felt as if an electrical current was coursing between us. It warmed us, made us happy, and brought us closer together. I wanted her to stay with me. I wanted to be with her forever. I knew then that this young woman was my soul mate.

7

Seeking Asylum

Don Rudolph

Dr. Don Rudolph woke up in his house alone that morning. Both his daughters were gone; they had been for almost two days, alone with a dangerous fugitive, but he wasn't worried. Joe wouldn't hurt them, and they would be found soon enough.

It was noticeably warm when he climbed out of the shower and went down for breakfast. There was an enormous hole in the side of his house where Shane Gold's inner beast had come crashing through Maia's window. Plastic sheets covered the hole, but the warm air from outside was still filtering in. He would have to call a contractor tonight. There was no more delaying that.

He ate his breakfast in a peaceful silence that he knew would not last forever. He did his best to enjoy it. He knew what he was going to do, what he would have to do to keep his daughters alive. That was precisely the deal; cooperate and the girls could live. And he would cooperate. He would do whatever he had to in order to protect his family. Did he want to do it? No.

But it wasn't a question of wanting, of free will, anymore.

A horn honked outside, and he rose. The director of the lab insisted that he be driven to work for the next week because of what happened. She was worried, as if the world would end if one of her best doctors should be killed, or become compromised. That was her greatest concern, and Rudolph knew it. She was worried that he would side with the O Negatives in order to protect his girls. Run away to join those in hiding. But he wouldn't do that. The only security was the security being offered to him right now, at the lab, so that was the only option he was willing to take. He had to protect his girls. Siding with the O Negatives would be a very poor decision on his part.

He went out to the black SUV and climbed in the back. "Would you mind parking in lot C this morning?" he asked the driver, assuming it was the same male guard as yesterday. "I need to make a quick stop at the—" He stopped, noticing that the person behind the wheel was not the driver he had yesterday. It was a girl, and he was pretty sure he knew who it was.

Maia turned around and grinned at him. "We're not going to the lab today, Dad."

Someone popped up from the cargo area behind him and held a gun to his head. "Don't try anything," the girl warned.

Rudolph looked back at her. It was Jazmine, Maia's rainbow-haired friend who went missing from a retrieval unit two days ago. Joe must have intercepted the caravan before they reached the lab and helped her escape. It made sense. No one could give a precise description, but they said something big, black, and hairy that resembled a large dog or wolf attacked and took her.

Sighing, Rudolph turned back towards his daughter. "Okay, Maia. Where are we going?"

Cole Ashton

I woke up the next morning under the bright sunshine on my makeshift bed of pine needles and fallen leaves, feeling happy, truly happy, something I hadn't felt for a very long time. I smiled to myself, knowing that my soul mate was sleeping soundly beside me, and I snuggled closer to her, pulling my wings tighter around us, only to realize that she wasn't actually there.

"Erica!" I cried, sitting bolt upright and looking around frantically. "Erica!"

I heard a soft giggle behind me, and I turned. There she was, carrying a bag of corn chips and an apple. She was grinning, making her way carefully over to me. "I'm right here, Cole," she said. "I was getting us breakfast."

"Yeah, chips," I said sarcastically. "Yum."

"Hey, it's all I could find. We should consider ourselves lucky."

"Well, I certainly do." I smiled broadly up at her.

Erica Harvard was tall, about as tall as me, with very dark brown hair, pale skin, and dark eyes. She was beautiful; long legs, soft skin. She wasn't thin but she wasn't large either. She had curves. I liked that, personally.

"Why do you wear those?" I asked her, referring to the sunglasses and earplugs she always wore. She took off the glasses at night, but they were on again as soon as the first light of dawn showed on the horizon.

"My ability," she said as she sat down, handing me the bag of chips and biting into the apple. "I have a hypersensitivity to light and sound. If I don't wear them, I could go blind and deaf."

"Yikes," I muttered. "So…you see and hear really well? Is that how it works?"

"Well, I see and hear things very well that are up close, but I can also see things or hear things from very far away. Like now." She nodded over my shoulder. "There's a search party with dogs and guns, looking for the winged man who fell from the sky last night."

"Aw, shit," I muttered. "Should we get going?"

"We're fine for now," Erica said. "They're six miles north."

"Oh," I said thoughtfully. "You're right. That's quite handy."

She smiled, and we ate in silence for a while.

"How's your ouch?" Erica asked, nodding to my wound.

I looked down. It hurt pretty damn bad, and it wasn't looking too pretty either. "I don't know. I'm no doctor."

"We should probably get you looked at."

I laughed. "By whom? Who would help me?"

She shrugged, and then didn't say anything for a few minutes. Then, "I think I'm pregnant."

I choked on the chip I was swallowing. Erica patted me on the back until I managed to cough it up. Eyes watering, I cried, "*What?*"

Erica was snickering. "I said I think I'm pregnant."

"Oh," I said, feeling very disappointed. "So...was it your boyfriend?"

Smiling, Erica assured me, "I don't have a boyfriend, Cole. I think it's yours."

I stared at her, thinking that maybe she was playing a joke on me. "Did we...? Last night...?"

She laughed. "No. We didn't. I'm not sure how it happened, or how I know, but I just do. Here." She took my hand and placed it over her belly. "Do you feel him?"

I couldn't feel anything physically, such as a kick, but I could feel something there. Yes, our son was there. *Our* son. "Whoa," I whispered. I looked up and found myself smiling at her. "That's amazing!"

"I know."

It was in that moment that I realized I loved that girl—and that unborn baby—more than I had ever loved anything else. I would do anything and everything for them, no matter what the cost.

I would die for them.

Maia Rudolph

I held Joe's hand as Dad stitched up the wound in his side. It was almost finished. The good news was that it wasn't infected. Joe looked up and smiled at me. I smiled back, and then looked up at the rest of the group. Marlena, sitting quietly by a tree and playing with some twigs and fallen leaves. Jazmine, still holding the gun in her hand but no longer pointing it at Dad's head. (I didn't think it was necessary anymore; Dad was more than willing to help once he saw the gun.) And Max, Joe's little brother, standing a few feet away, watching Dad's hands intently. Yep. Max was alive. Joe lied, saying Max was dead in case he was captured again and his brother would still have a chance to escape, when in truth, Max looked perfectly fine—just an occasional bruise and scratch.

Dad finished stitching Joe's wound. He smeared anti-biotic ointment over it and then placed a bandage over that. "Okay," he said from his tree stump seat. "It's done."

"And how is it?" I demanded.

Dad shrugged. "It looked clean to me, considering where he's been since he got it. No signs of infection. He looks healthy." He glanced down at Joe. "Just be sure to change the bandages twice a day. I don't know where you'll find them, but..." Dad looked like he couldn't care less if Joe found any or not.

"We'll find some," I said, helping Joe as he gingerly sat up.

"*We?*" Dad peered at me, as if he still thought he could tell me what to do.

"Yeah," I said. "*We*. All of us."

"You and Marlena are going to come home with me, Maia," Dad told me.

"No," I said defiantly. "*You* are going to come with *us*."

Raising an eyebrow in amusement, Dad asked, "Really?"

"Yeah. You're not in charge anymore. You're not taking us anywhere."

"And why not? It's safer at home."

"We're all O Negatives, Dad!" I snapped. "Even Marlena and I, even though I don't know how. Nowhere *you* take us is safe."

"I can keep you safe."

"Did you hear what I just said?"

"Yes," Dad said, "I did. And I'm saying that I have the power to protect you, but you have to come with me. *Now*."

"Have you considered that maybe I don't want your protection?" I demanded. "I haven't wanted your protection for a long time. I never asked for it. You shouldn't have protected me and Marlena. Why would you protect us and let them take Joe and Jazmine?"

Dad peered at me with a don't-be-stupid look. "Because you're my daughters. I would do anything to protect you."

"Well, I'm telling you, *don't*." I helped Joe to his feet and started to lead him away, but he held back. He was glaring at Dad.

"What are we going to do about him?" he asked me.

Dad's eyes narrowed at Joe's harsh stare. "Yes, Maia, what are you going to do about me?"

"Just leave him here," I muttered, barely throwing him a glance. "I changed my mind. I don't want him with us."

"We can't let him go." Joe held his ground.

I turned on him. "What are you proposing we do, Joe? Hmm? What the hell are you suggesting?"

Joe looked away, not wanting to start a fight. "Nothing."

"We *should* take him with us," Max said thoughtfully.

Everyone glanced at him.

"He's a doctor," Max explained, "and Joe's hurt. What if he gets an infection before we get where we're going?"

"And where exactly *are* you going?" Dad asked curiously.

Joe, Max, Jazmine, and I all looked at each other. We knew where we were going, but we weren't going to tell him. "You're right," I said to Max. "We'll take him with us." When Dad rolled his eyes in frustration, I told him, "And there's some stuff I'd like to talk to you about." I don't know what it was about me and Marlena, but we didn't work the same way as the other O Negatives. We didn't feel how they felt, or see how they saw. We didn't have the same connection that the others did. Why that was, I didn't know, but I had a feeling that Dad did, and I wanted to know one way or another.

Cole Ashton

We were running now. Well, Erica was trying to run while helping me limp along. My wound had gotten worse. Much worse. I had tunnel vision and the slightest movement made me cry out.

"Come on, Cole!" Erica pleaded, trying to get me to move faster. "They're almost here! We have to get out of here!"

"I...can't..." I crumpled to the ground.

"Cole!" Erica cried. "Get up!"

"Go!" I ordered, trying to push her off me. "I can't go any farther. Just get out of here!"

"I'm not leaving you!"

I could hear the dogs now, barking ferociously somewhere not too far behind us. They were going to kill us both if I couldn't get Erica to leave. "I said go!" I shouted.

Erica screamed suddenly, and then a strong pair of hands was around my chest, hauling me to my feet.

"Let go!" I sputtered, pulling at the hands.

"Come with me!" a man said urgently. "I'll help you!"

"Let go of him!" Erica shouted.

"My wife and family are infected! Come on! I can help!"

I really couldn't fight him, and Erica stopped screaming and went with us. The dogs were getting closer, and we could hear the distant shouts of those searching for us.

I'm not sure how far we went, but we eventually arrived at a van parked on the side of a country road that weaved in and out of the woods. The man helped me into the back seat while Erica went around to get in the other side. Three women were in the car, watching us intently. One woman, the oldest, and presumably the man's wife, sat in front. Two younger girls, one a teenager and one in her twenties, sat in the middle two seats. All three of them had blue eyes and light brown hair, except for the wife who was graying. Luggage was tossed here and there around the van.

I groaned as the man pushed me into my seat, and Erica held me in her arms, stroking my hot forehead. I forced my eyes to stay open, taking a look at the man for the first time as he got into the driver's seat. He glanced back at us quickly, his gray eyes nervous behind his glasses. He had light hair, a sandy color, and thick facial hair that almost hid his entire mouth.

"How did you find us?" Erica asked as the man got the van going and sped away.

"We heard you," the teenager said, tapping her left temple. She was a telepath. Maybe they all were.

"Who are you?" I choked out, my tunnel vision worse.

"My name's Graham," the man at the wheel said. "Graham Odau. This is my family."

"I got shot," I panted, my eyes closing automatically. "I think it's infected."

The car was silent for a moment. "I think I know someone who can help you," Graham said.

Then I passed out.

Maia Rudolph

We'd been walking for hours. We were heading toward the old military compound owned by Patrick Lemoore, the man I'd met at my school the day Joe came back to me, and also the man who was hiding fugitive O Negatives. The compound was in the outskirts of Hatfield, a suburb of Philadelphia and the town where Dad's lab was, but we drove Dad's vehicle far from Philadelphia to get some distance between us and the authorities who were surely looking for him. We drove in a big U, hoping to throw off any tails we might have before arriving safely at Lemoore's place. Unfortunately, the vehicle blew a tire before we reached the compound, so we were now forced to walk the distance between us and our haven.

I'd been walking up front with Joe and Marlena, while Jazmine and Max walked behind Dad to make sure he didn't run off and report us, but now I was beginning to lag back a bit. I wanted to talk to Dad about why Marlena and I were so different, so odd compared to the others—which was a funny way to put it considering the O Negatives were supposedly all odd—but I just didn't know how to phrase my question. I didn't even realize Dad had caught up with my pace until I felt his dark brown gaze upon me.

Looking up, I snapped, "What?" at his curious expression.

"What do you want to ask me, Maia?" he asked patiently.

"What makes you think I want to ask you anything?"

"Because you said you wanted to talk to me, and you have that look on your face."

"What look?"

Dad smiled. "That look you always wear when something's bothering you."

I glared at him. "I don't have *a look*."

Dad snickered. "Yes, you do, sweetie."

"You don't know anything about me!"

Sighing, Dad replied, "As much as you hate to believe it, I really do know quite a lot about you, dear."

I glared at the ground, angry at him, angry at myself…angry at the world. Why was the world so completely full of bullshit?

Dad gave me a moment before pestering me some more. "So what do you want to ask me?"

"Why are Marlena and I so goddamn different from the others?"

Dad frowned. "Watch your mouth, please. Your sister's right there."

"Shut up," I grumbled. "Are you going to answer me or not?"

"So you understand that you two are different?" Dad said quietly, lowering his gaze to the ground.

I scoffed. "It'd be kind of hard *not* to notice!"

"That's a very long story that you probably don't want to hear right now," Dad said.

"Why wouldn't I want to hear it?"

"Because it would make you angry."

I stared at him in horror. "Oh God. What did you do to us?"

Dad refused to speak anymore after that. I was too flustered to threaten him properly. I wasn't even sure that I wanted to know the truth anymore, with the possibilities running through my head. I walked far ahead of the group, trying to clear my head with the crunching of the leaves beneath my feet as the only sounds. Eventually, I became tired and my pace slowed. Joe caught up to me, and he was staring at me in a really weird way. He was staring at my *stomach* in a really weird way.

"What?" I asked him, confused.

"Maia," he said, reaching out and putting a hand on my stomach. We stopped walking, and he held his hand there for several long minutes.

"What is it, Joe?" I asked again, growing exasperated.

"Maia," Joe whispered, looking up at me with wonder. "You're pregnant."

8

Closer Together

Walter Reifert

My eyes blinked open. Bright rays of sunshine filtered in from the window to my right. I felt extremely well rested and refreshed. There hadn't been a day since the outbreak where I'd felt this good.

Confused, I turned my head to the right and shaded my eyes from the harsh glare that welcomed me back to Earth. The clock on the desk beside the window read 12:13. But that wasn't all. I had no proof, but I knew that I'd slept for several days without waking. There were no dreams to be remembered.

Flooded with relief, I laid my head back down and let out a joyful laugh. Laughing was something foreign to me nowadays. Nobody laughed anymore. After five weeks of misery, I finally felt capable of laughter again. Maybe, if my sleep cycles became more regular and I avoided painful reminders (mainly the television) of my life before O Negatives, I could slowly but surely begin to heal.

"Thank you," I whispered to Lemoore, my broad smile causing my facial muscles to cramp. "Wow. Thank you so much. *Wow.*"

Memories of what Lemoore had done to me were foggy, but it had clearly worked. I vaguely recalled him putting his hands on my face and telling my mind to rest, to go to sleep, to stop working for the time being. And then it had. My mind shut down, and now here I was, awake, feeling better than I had since before my family died.

My family…

I felt a horrid pang in my chest, but I did my best to push it aside. My grief would be with me for a long time; I knew that much. But maybe, after I started a life for myself, maybe by getting married and having a family of my own, my pain would begin to dull to a throb, and then that throb would simply become remembrance. The memories I had of my family were good ones. The ones of them alive and happy should be the ones I held onto.

I climbed out of bed and worked my way out into the hallway. My stomach growled ravenously. When was the last time I'd eaten? I didn't know, but I was starving now. And with Lemoore's overflowing fridge and pantry…anything was possible.

I reached the long staircase connected to the balcony that overlooked the front entrance of the compound. As I began to descend, I heard three separate voices talking excitedly down below. Lemoore's voice was distinguishable, but the other two male voices were not. Both were English accented, and as I hurried the rest of the way down I picked up a few fragments of their conversation:

"I am just *so* enthused that the two of you made it here safely!"

"We couldn't have made it so far without your help."

"I don't mean to be so forward, but do you have anything to eat? We're starving!"

When I reached the bottom, all three turned to look at me in surprise. Both newcomers looked between the ages of twenty and twenty-five, and they seemed to resemble one another. Were they brothers? Cousins? They were both tall, and although I could tell they were related, their features were very different. One was bigger. Not fat, just *big*. His hair was closely cropped and a dark red in color. His face was rounder and he looked a lot tougher than the other. I wouldn't want to get in a tussle with him. The other had curly blonde hair and a much thinner face. They did, however, have the same eye color. A deep, calming brown. Both wore tattered shorts and t-shirts, and although they looked worn out and underfed, they still appeared overjoyed to be here.

"Walter," Lemoore said with poorly hidden excitement, "this is Damien and Berry Burnett. They traveled here all the way from the London area."

He didn't say it, but I understood. They were O Negatives. They had survived the brutality of both countries and made it here safely. They heard our call. They were alive and well, and that could only mean one thing:

We weren't the only ones left.

Berry and Damien turned out to be twins. They were twenty-three years old and amazing cooks. To celebrate, we had a huge brunch of omelets, bacon, toast, strawberries, and orange juice. For the remainder of the day, Lemoore and I laughed with the Burnett twins as we told each other stories of what our lives were like before the outbreak. Before bed, we watched comedy sitcoms and hooted and howled in our over-the-top excitement. Dr. Perry showed up around eleven—off early—and was just as surprised as I. Soon he was making friends with the twins as well. Lemoore showed them to a room that they could share, and I went to bed with a smile on my face.

The twins had no parents, just like me. After the virus attacked the U.K., they hid in a safe house outside of Manchester until it was discovered and everyone associated with it killed. Everyone, that is, except for them. Their abilities were not easy to hide; Damien was pyrokinetic and Berry could control water. The twins, fire and water. They did their best to hide until they could find a safe haven. They heard our call and then stowed away on an ocean liner that was destined for Cape Cod. They then followed our call until they arrived here, exhausted and starving but alive.

The arrival of the twins foreshadowed the arrival of three more groups. The first group came two days later. It was a group of three, consisting of two women in their thirties and a boy who said he was thirteen. Three days later, a group of seven arrived. Two guys and five girls, all of varying ages. We celebrated with chocolate cake and wine, even those who were underage (by that time it was just myself and Scotty, the boy from the first group). Even though there were things we should have been attending to, our party lasted for exactly two days, until the third group showed up. We were ecstatic when the group of six arrived. That was, of course, until we saw that one of them wasn't one of us.

His name was Graham Odo, or Odau, or however it was pronounced, and he was a retired lieutenant in the Philadelphia PD. He had fled Manhattan with his wife Jane and two daughters Sarah and Caroline, who were all O Negatives. While evading the authorities, they stumbled upon a young couple, Cole Ashton and Erica Harvard. It was easy to see that the two of them were O Negatives; Cole had a large set of wings and Erica always wore sunglasses and ear plugs due to her heightened senses. The family decided to take the couple along to Philadelphia, their destination.

Although his intentions seemed pure, Graham was still unwelcome among a growing group of O Negatives. He was on the verge of being attacked by the Burnett twins when Dr. Perry suddenly entered and yelled, "Stop!"

It turned out that while Dr. Perry was still in the FBI, he had worked with Graham Odau on his last case. He didn't give specifics, but Dr. Perry said that the ex-cop could be trusted with our secret.

To me, it appeared that something personal had gone down between them, but that was just me. They simply regarded each other with a single nod before Dr. Perry rushed Cole down to the small infirmary in the basement.

Cole was suffering from a terrible infection as the result of a gunshot wound in his right side. "If they'd gotten here a day later, Cole wouldn't have made it," Dr. Perry told me when I joined him with Cole and Erica in the basement.

Currently, Cole was lying face down on the table, his wings spread wide and sagging to the floor. He was still unconscious but he would be alright; Dr. Perry was healing his wound and infection with a vial of his blood. "How did he grow wings?" I asked curiously. "I've never heard of anyone growing a new body part, especially one from another species."

"I've never seen anything like this either," Dr. Perry admitted. "I didn't know this was possible. Maybe he spent a lot of time around birds...or maybe he was touching a bird when he was infected? I'm only speculating. I can't give you an actual answer. Do you have any idea how this happened, Erica?"

We looked at her, but she only shrugged. "He hasn't told me much about himself yet. We just met a few days ago and he's been fighting this infection for most of that time. Maybe he's just a special case."

"He can't be the only one," I said to Dr. Perry, but how could I know that? "If one of us has a bizarre mutation like this, then others must have had the same thing happen to them."

"We all have bizarre mutations, Walter," Dr. Perry told me. "This case is just more bizarre than usual."

"Is he going to be okay?" Erica asked nervously, inching closer.

"He'll be fine," Dr. Perry assured her. "He was near death when you brought him in, but my blood can heal anything. As long as you're still alive, that is. He'll be alright. He just needs to rest a bit."

Erica exhaled loudly, and I had a feeling she'd been holding her breath for a while. "Thank God," she whispered, and then looked to Dr. Perry. "Thank *you*. Thank you so much."

"You two are a couple, I take it?" Dr. Perry asked her.

"We're soul mates," Erica murmured.

I glanced at Dr. Perry, confused. "Soul mates?"

"Yeah," Erica replied. "We met each other, and I can't explain it, but there was this connection we felt. We're supposed to be together. We're soul mates."

Dr. Perry nodded, as if he understood. "Why don't you come lay down on the table over here so I can take a look at you?" He saw the hesitance in her eyes and smiled reassuringly. "Don't worry, Erica. I'm one of you. I just want to check you out to make sure you're alright."

"I'm fine," Erica said tersely.

"It's just a routine checkup that I do for all newcomers," Dr. Perry said. He was minding her nervousness, but I also saw his hesitance.

Erica paused for a few moments longer, and then she gave in and went to the table. She sat on the end and wrapped her arms around herself, watching Dr. Perry carefully. "Forgive me," she said, "but I'm not the biggest fan of doctors."

Dr. Perry chuckled. "That's quite alright, dear. I just want you to know that I have no intention of hurting you."

"I know."

"I know you have heightened senses, but would I be able to take a look at your eyes?"

"Um..." Erica winced. "I suppose if you turn the other lights off."

It took a few minutes, but Dr. Perry managed to get a decent look at Erica's eyes before she just couldn't keep them open anymore. He checked her vitals and looked her over for any injuries. She seemed fine, although she was very protective of her stomach area and refused to let Dr. Perry touch her there.

"If you're hurt, I have to help you," Dr. Perry kept telling her, but eventually Erica just showed him what she was protecting. "You're pregnant," he said in awe.

The bulge was small, but it was definitely there. Erica was pregnant.

Dr. Perry didn't understand how, because when Cole awoke, Cole and Erica both claimed that Cole was the father, yet they had only met a week earlier and Erica already appeared to be six weeks along. Also, they had not yet slept together. For one reason or another, Dr. Perry believed them. I heard jumbled thoughts again about how we were reproducing through touch instead of sexual intercourse and the incubation period for the fetus would be one-third the time of a human fetus. If Dr. Perry's theory was correct, and I believed it to be, then Erica would be giving birth to her baby by mid-August. He—Erica insisted that the baby was a boy—would be one of the first O Negative-born children.

Lemoore and Dr. Perry had a small conference in Lemoore's study after Cole was taken care of. The rest of us avoided the Odau family like they were deathly ill. When the two men returned to the group, we were dismayed to learn that Graham Odau would be staying with us for two nights, until his family got settled in. I knew the man wanted to stay longer from the look in his eyes rather than the thoughts in his head, but he had a son back in New York he promised he would go back to (who apparently didn't like our kind very much—Odau's reason for not bringing him along).

Due to the sudden increase of residents in the compound, it was logical to believe that many more would soon be arriving. To make room for the people that would soon be here, we all began to share rooms. I shared with Scotty and the Burnett twins. The entire Odau family stayed together, while Cole and Erica shared with another couple. The others assembled their own groups.

Late that night, the small group of us that possessed telepathic abilities assembled in the break room on the first level. The group consisted of myself, Lemoore, Scotty, Jane and Sarah Odau, and two from the second group; Eric Dawson and Sophie Hansen. We all sat in a circle on the floor, hand in hand. What we were about to do, Lemoore and I had done numerous times before the new arrivals. After Lemoore explained it to everyone who was new to such a connection, we all held hands and closed our eyes, allowing Lemoore to lead us in the call.

For those of you who are still free, who haven't yet been taken or who have managed to escape, this message is meant for you.

Lemoore spoke the words clearly, aloud and in his head, and the rest of us projected his voice, pushing it beyond the compound, as far as we dared send it.

You may fear that you are alone, that you are the last O Negatives left in the outside world. You are not alone. There is a safe haven, here just for you. Come. Join us. It is the only place we can truly be safe. Here. Together.

Lastly, Lemoore projected an image of the compound and instructions for how to get here. The call had taken less than thirty seconds, and we all opened our eyes and released each other's hands.

"Now," Lemoore said, giving his head a shake to bring him back to the real world. "If we send this message every night, and we continue to pull in refugees, we should be able to bring in people from all over the world within a few weeks."

"What are we going to do once we fill up the compound?" Jane asked.

"Well, things might get a bit cramped, but we can set up tents around the perimeter. There's enough space here for a few thousand, but beyond that..." Lemoore shrugged.

Everybody nodded in agreement. After bidding each other good night, we all dragged our feet upstairs to bed. I caught Lemoore's arm at the bottom of the stairs.

"How are you, Walter?" Lemoore asked me, having not spoken with me about my emotions since before the twins arrived.

"I'm doing pretty well, actually," I replied, realizing that I had been smiling and laughing a lot since Damien's and Berry's arrival.

"Still having problems with sleep?"

I shrugged. "On and off. It's been a lot easier ever since Scotty and the twins moved in with me."

Nodding, Lemoore said, "I guess we were right about you needing other company. I'm glad you're feeling better, Walter. Now, did you have something you'd like to speak to me about?"

Lemoore knew that I did, obviously, and knew what I was going to say, but it was best if I said it aloud. "Do you remember what Dr. Perry told us the day of the breakout? About Beast?"

Glancing away uneasily, Lemoore nodded.

"I'm not sure if sending the message is safe anymore," I concluded. "Maybe it never was. If he hears us...if he finds us here..."

"Then nothing would stop him from leading the soldiers here." Dr. Perry had arrived silently, as usual, and had come to join our conversation.

"I've already taken the issue of Beast under consideration," Lemoore replied solemnly. "I've decided that we cannot delay the union of the O Negatives because of one single threat."

"If Beast finds us, it won't just be one threat!" I said. "It will be thousands! Is risking the lives of everyone here the right thing to do because we have a small hope that more of us are out there?"

"There *are* more of us out there," Lemoore insisted.

"We know," Dr. Perry interjected. "And if you want to continue the call, then you need to start setting up a defensive strategy in case we *are* attacked."

"Fine," Lemoore snapped wearily. "We'll work that out tomorrow." He left Dr. Perry and me at the bottom of the stairs.

I turned to Dr. Perry, but he was speaking before I could blurt out my question: "So, you're doing better, I see."

"Yeah," I muttered, shifting my weight from foot to foot. "I am, thanks."

Dr. Perry nodded, but he continued to stare me down. "You want to ask me something?"

"Yes." I paused, trying to come up with the proper words. "You and the ex-cop. Something big happened between you two during your final case, didn't it? Something bad."

Biting his lip, Dr. Perry replied, "You could say that."

"What happened? If you don't mind me asking."

Dr. Perry lowered his eyes from mine. I didn't look directly into his mind because whatever happened was clearly a life altering experience, but I couldn't help overhearing the terror that was leaping out of him. After a long time, he finally answered. "We saw a lot of people die," he whispered. "We saw a lot of people die in a lot of terrible ways. I saw awful things in my ten years as an agent, but that last case...it was the first time I truly saw the evil that the human race was capable of."

"What happened?" I repeated, eager to know.

Dr. Perry stared at me. I caught a thought on the edge of his mind: *He doesn't remember.*

What didn't I remember? And why should I remember? Was I *there*?

"There was a girl," Dr. Perry began, and I knew he was intent on only letting me know so much, "very much like you, actually. Strong. Hard-headed. Her family was murdered, and cruel people hurt her in unspeakable ways. She went to Philadelphia and started killing the people she believed were responsible for what was done to her."

"So you saw the first evil in her?" I asked.

"No," Dr. Perry said, "I didn't. Not in her. I saw it in the people who committed the crimes against her."

"What happened to her?"

Pausing, and giving me a look that suggested he had more to say, Dr. Perry replied, "She died."

I didn't like the ending to this story. I could sense that Dr. Perry was both lying and telling the truth. Something more had happened. "What about the people who killed her family? What happened to them?"

Dr. Perry shrugged. "They paid the price for their actions. Don't ask me how; I took no part in that."

"What did *you* see that was so awful?"

"I saw what grief and hate can do to a person. I saw what that person will do to others to deal with grief and hate. I saw..." His voice cracked and he cleared his throat. "I saw good people deteriorate in front of me. It was terrible—painful—to see."

"Did anyone you knew die?"

"Yes. I saw several murdered, right in front of me."

"And the girl? What...I mean...I don't understand."

"What don't you understand?"

"Why did she have to die? It's not fair."

Dr. Perry shook his head and smiled. "No. It wasn't fair. But you know what? It's okay, because I think that at the end, she was finally at peace with herself."

I supposed that was an okay ending. "And that was why you left the FBI?"

"Yes."

"Because of what you saw?"

"Yes, but not for the reason you think." He glanced out one of the windows. "I was disturbed for a long time after it was over. I still have nightmares sometimes, even after ten years. But the fact that I was traumatized wasn't the reason I left. I left because the girl warned me about what was coming for us. I left because I knew I needed to be a doctor, so I could help our people when the time came. And look at what I've done so far. I'd say it was all worth it in the end."

"Wait." Something about his story wasn't making sense, didn't sound right. "Are you saying that the girl *knew* this was going to happen?"

Dr. Perry nodded, suddenly wary.

This story suddenly sounded familiar: A girl who knew the future. Before the outbreak. Where had I heard that before? "How is that possible? How could she know?"

After giving me one last look of reproach, Dr. Perry said, "She just did." He turned and started up the stairs, going to check on Erica and her unborn son.

My mind was buzzing. *The girl warned me about what was coming for us.* How could she know? How *did* she know? Why in God's name did I feel like someone had told me this story before?

And then it hit me. I gasped, and turned to Dr. Perry in surprise. But he was already gone. That didn't matter. I knew what I knew, and nothing he said would change that.

Dr. Perry once knew my father.

Shauna Skyler

It was terrible, this thing called pain. Every waking moment was pure agony for Shauna. The slightest of movements would cause her to cry out as the hole in her side protested angrily.

A week had passed since Shauna's small group of children stumbled onto the property of Alec Marcus, and it had also been a week since Alec Marcus put a bullet in Shauna's side. A week had passed, and Shauna still hadn't been able to get out of bed.

You may fear that you are alone, that you are the last O Negatives left in the outside world. You are not alone. There is a safe haven, here just for you. Come. Join us. It is the only place we can truly be safe. Here. Together.

Shauna understood what the message meant. She had to get herself and the kids to the place in her dream. It was the only place they would be safe, the only place where people wouldn't shoot at them. They had to go there. Now.

She awoke from her uneasy slumber to the feeling of a cold, wet cloth being pressed to her forehead. With a pained groan, she forced her eyes open. Alec loomed over her, his concerned face swimming before her eyes. How long had she been asleep? Why did her side hurt so much? It hadn't hurt this much when she'd gone to sleep...

"You're burning up," Alec murmured, cooling Shauna's face, neck, and arms with the cloth.

With Sawyer's constant help, Shauna was now able to understand speech. She was not yet capable of forming words, but she was easily understood with simple hand gestures or Sawyer's interpretation. Alec said it was only a matter of time before she would be able to speak again too (assuming she didn't die first). Had she really been able to speak before all this happened? It was hard to believe. Her current life of silence was all she knew. But Sawyer insisted that she could, and she believed Sawyer.

Reaching up a shaky hand, Shauna pointed to her wound and winced.

"I know it hurts," Alec said apologetically, leaning over her and taking a look at it. "It's infected. I had to get all the gunk out before it made you even sicker."

"Is she going to die?"

Alec turned to Sawyer, Allan, and Daniel, who were all worried and had come to look on. "I don't know, kiddo," Alec told Sawyer, sitting on the bed beside Shauna. "I hope not. She's holding through it, but if this infection gets any worse..." His voice trailed off.

"She needs a doctor," Allan said, his eyes tearing up. "She can't die! She said she would take care of us!"

While Alec comforted Allan and Daniel, Sawyer went to Shauna's side. He took her hand, and Shauna did her best to give him a smile. It morphed into a grimace, but Sawyer responded with a smile of his own. "What should we do, Shauna? How can we help you?"

Shauna showed him the picture of the compound, the compound that would be their haven.

Sawyer's eyes lit up. "You dreamed of it too?" he asked in a hushed whisper.

"What did you dream of?" Alec asked.

"The compound," Daniel piped in.

"We all dreamed of it," Allan added.

"Why are you all dreaming of the same place?" Alec asked, a little reluctantly.

"That's where our people are," Sawyer said. "That's where we'll be safe."

"Mr. Lemoore and Walter told us to come and be safe with them," Daniel said.

"They told you this in your dreams?" Alec was skeptical, but he heard the truth in the boys' words.

"Yeah," Allan replied, and then his face lit up. "They...they have a doctor there! Dr. Perry! He has healing blood!"

"We have to take her there!" Sawyer chirped.

"Whoa!" Alec put his hands in the air. "Let's not get ahead of ourselves. Even if we knew how to get there, we can't move her."

"We *do* know how to get there!" Daniel insisted.

"But we can't move her!" Looking down at Shauna, Alec's face softened again. "She'll start bleeding again, and then she *will* die."

"Then bring Dr. Perry *here*." Allan stood defiantly, demanding that Alec save Shauna's life. "You shot her, so now you have to help her."

Alec's jaw tensed. "Get out," he said, his voice shaking.

Angrily, Allan stomped off. The two younger boys lingered in the bedroom.

"All of you."

Daniel quickly left, but Sawyer stayed behind. "Dr. Perry is one of the doctors working in the lab. Shauna's seen him. He pretends to be on their side, but really, he's on ours. He lives in Philadelphia. Do you think you'll be able to find him?"

Alec sighed. "I'll do my best, kid. I suppose I owe her that much."

Nodding, Sawyer left the room. Alec looked down at Shauna's weak form again, and his expression became pained. "I'm so sorry," he whispered. "I'm so sorry I shot you. I thought...I thought you were...I don't even know what I thought. And then Daniel and the boys ran out of the bushes, screaming for me to stop, and I realized that you were only checking to make sure it was safe. You were trying to protect them. You were trying to protect my boy." He was crying now. "Thank you so much for saving Daniel. His mother was murdered a few months after he was born by some guy stalking her, and after they came and took my son...I thought I was going to lose my mind. Thank you for rescuing him. For what you did for my boy, I am going to do whatever I can to save your life. You're going to make it, okay?"

Shauna nodded and gave him a thumbs up.

"You get some more sleep now," Alec told her. "I'm going to see if I can track down this Dr. Perry."

* * *

Dr. Shawn Perry lived in the suburbs of Philadelphia with his wife and two daughters. It wasn't too far from Red Hill, but Shauna's condition was getting worse with each passing minute. Any movement on her part caused her pure agony, and moving her from the bed to the truck would be torture. But if they didn't move her, she would surely die. The infection, not the wound, was killing her. Pus kept filling up in Shauna's side, and each time Alec tried to drain the wound, Shauna's screams became louder and more pained. The window in which they could move her without killing her was closing. Alec had to make up his mind, and fast.

His mind was made up for him when a knock sounded at his door. It was the Sheriff.

"We have to get her out of here," Alec said urgently when he managed to get rid of him. "People heard Shauna's screams and saw one of you outside. They know I'm harboring O Negatives. The Sheriff is going to contact the Hatfield lab, and they're going to send a retrieval team. We have to get out of here before they arrive, or God only knows what will happen to all of you."

"Is it safe to move her?" Shauna heard Allan ask from the other room as Alec ran around, frantically collecting supplies the children would need.

"We don't have a choice," Alec replied grimly. "Sawyer, take the baby. The two of you and Daniel get in the truck. Allan, stay here and help me move Shauna."

Alec and Allan came into Shauna's bedroom, their faces stiff with worry. "We have to go now, Shauna," Allan said.

"I'm sorry," Alec apologized. "But we're going to have to move you." He nodded when Shauna shook her head quickly. "If we don't, they're going to come and take you back to the lab. We have to get you to Dr. Perry."

Alec did his best to raise her without irritating her injury, but Shauna still screamed, and it was the loudest one yet. She dug her nails into Alec's arm and shook her head furiously, pleading with him to stop. He wanted to, but he couldn't.

"I'm sorry, baby," he murmured as Shauna screamed and cried. "I'm sorry. It will all be over in a minute." He looked down at Allan. "I'm going to carry her. There's no way she'll be able to walk."

Shauna's sobs lessened but didn't cease as Alec carefully carried her outside. He halted on the porch. He cocked an ear out away from the farmhouse, listening. "Shit," he muttered. "They're already here." He started running, sending Shauna into a new fit of screams.

When Allan heard her loud cries, he turned. "What's wrong?" he asked in alarm.

"They're here!" Alec cried.

Allan sprinted for the pickup and started to cram into the back with the three young ones. Alec stopped him.

"No! You have to drive."

"What?"

"I have to hold them off or you'll never make it! Sorry Shauna…"

Shauna groaned as Alec set her in the passenger seat. Glancing down, she saw that her bandages were soaked in blood.

"I don't know how to drive!" Allan protested. "I'm only ten!"

Alec hesitated before going to Sawyer and taking his hand. "Show him," Alec whispered, and tossed Allan the keys.

Sawyer reached forward and took Allan's hand.

Allan nodded and took a shaky breath. "Okay," he said, climbing into the driver's seat. "Here we go."

"Follow the GPS," Alec instructed, turning on the dashboard GPS and plugging in Dr. Perry's address. "Get out of here. Stay safe." He looked to Shauna. "Thank you for saving my child. Get better and look after him, okay?"

Shauna made an effort to nod but couldn't.

Alec then turned to Daniel, his expression pained. "I love you Daniel. Don't ever forget that."

"I love you too, Daddy," Daniel replied, tears dripping from his eyes as Alec slammed the doors shut.

Trucks were already roaring down the gravel driveway. Alec ran back towards the house, and Allan did his best to start the truck and then work the pedals and steer at the same time. They made it through the cornfield and into the woods when the gunshots began.

With a groan, Shauna raised her head enough to see Alec out of the rearview mirror. He had a shotgun in his hand and was firing at a long line of trucks coming up the road. She only saw him for an instant, but she saw him stumble backwards and fall to the ground. A moment later, Daniel started crying, saying, "Daddy's dead! Daddy's dead! They killed him! Daddy's dead!"

Shauna couldn't stay awake any longer. The pain and exhaustion were too overwhelming. Slumping down in her seat, she passed out.

About thirty minutes later, Dr. Shawn Perry received a text from his wife, Renee. It was on his urgent line. It read:

The strays got in.

Dr. Perry knew what the message really meant, and his heart leaped in excitement. He texted back:

Stray cats?
No. Kittens. And one of them was bit by a dog.

By the time Shauna regained consciousness, the shadows of sunset were dancing on the peach-colored walls around her. She couldn't remember ever lying down on the bed she was in. To her surprise and relief, her wound felt remarkably better. It still hurt, but nowhere near as much as before.

She turned her head to one side, and saw Sawyer lying beside her, watching out for her. He smiled when she looked at him, and then hopped off the bed and ran out of the room. A few moments later, he came back with a middle-aged blonde woman and a dark-haired girl that looked to be about Shauna's age. The woman was smiling and carrying a tray with a bowl of soup on it.

"Hey," the woman said. "It's good to see you awake. You weren't looking too great when we brought you in."

Shauna watched cautiously as the woman set the tray down on a table beside the bed and sat down beside her. She pulled away when the woman reached towards her.

"You don't have to be afraid," the woman told her, gently placing a hand on Shauna's forehead. "I don't want to hurt you. My name's Renee Perry. This is my step-daughter, Jillian. We're like you and your brother."

Nodding, Shauna allowed her to put a cold cloth on her forehead.

"You're still pretty warm," the woman said, "but your fever's gone down, which is very good. I gave you a shot of penicillin to help contain the infection. It looks like it's already beginning to do its job. How do you feel?"

Shauna didn't answer.

"She doesn't talk," Sawyer explained.

"Oh," Renee said. "That's okay."

"The bad doctors hurt her," Sawyer added.

Renee paused, and then addressed Shauna again. "You came looking for my husband, right? Dr. Perry? You heard the call?"

Shauna nodded.

"Well, I'm sure he can find a way to help you get your voice back." Renee took the bowl of soup in her hands. "Do you think you can eat?"

While Renee fed Shauna her first meal in days, Shauna met Renee's daughter, a sweet little blonde girl who was between the ages of Allan and Sawyer. Her name was Hallie. Such a pretty name for such a pretty girl.

Dr. Perry was working a very long shift and would not arrive home until after 11:00 p.m. After finishing her soup, Shauna decided she needed to sleep some more; the food made her feel much better, but she was still exhausted. She awoke sometime after eleven to many voices in her room.

A cold hand pressed against her forehead and a man's voice said, "She's still burning up. I need to get her back to Lemoore's and give her a vial of my blood. The penicillin isn't working anymore. This infection is out of control."

"Is she going to die?" A boy's voice, maybe a few years older than herself.

"If I don't treat her quickly, she will," the first man's voice replied. "Without a doubt."

Forcing her eyes open, Shauna squinted up at her visitors. There were four men in the room along with Renee. Two were standing at the door, so Shauna couldn't see their faces. One was standing at her feet. He was the young man she heard. He had brown hair and a kind face, but Shauna couldn't see much because the lights were dim and her vision was swimming in and out of focus. He made eye contact with her and smiled.

The oldest man, a man with dark hair and dark eyes, looked down and also smiled. "Hi, there," he said softly. "We're going to take you somewhere where I can get you help."

There was something wrong with this man. Shauna had seen him before. She had seen him inside the lab, where doctors hurt her people. How could she trust a man like that?

"It's okay," Dr. Perry soothed as Shauna's eyes grew wide. "You're safe now." He looked at the two men by the door. "Berry, Damien, will the two of you get the younger ones and start the car? Walter, I may need your help with her." He looked down at Shauna again. "She looks a little jumpy."

Shauna pulled away from them when they tried to pick her up. "No!" She heard the word come out of her mouth, and still couldn't believe it was her own voice, even when she started shouting. "No, no, no!"

Dr. Perry scooped her up quickly before she could climb off the bed. He held onto her, even when she thrashed and screamed.

"It's alright, Shauna," Renee assured her, rubbing her shoulder as Dr. Perry passed.

"No!" Shauna cried.

"Shauna, you have to be quiet or people will hear you," Dr. Perry told her. "And then I can't help you."

Shauna shut up, but she kept squirming. She didn't want to go anywhere with him. "No," she whimpered.

"You're fine," Dr. Perry said as they left the house. He carried her to a big black vehicle and set her inside.

One of the other men, the blonde, sat in the back with the four little kids, Meg and Daniel on his lap. The red-haired man sat in the passenger seat while Dr. Perry got behind the wheel.

Shauna tried to get out the other door, but Walter had gone around to that side and climbed in beside her. She then attempted to get out the way she came, but Walter caught her and pulled her back, holding her to him. Shauna screamed loudly.

Dr. Perry looked back at them. "You need to calm her down, Walter. You need to calm her down now."

"I've got it," Walter said, and then leaned his head against Shauna's.

Instantly, Shauna felt calmer. Her body relaxed against Walter's, and she lost all ability to scream and move. She laid against Walter, his warm breath on her hair comforting her more.

Something was happening between the two of them as the car drove down the dark road. Something...magical. Shauna suddenly felt as if she had known this boy, Walter Reifert, her whole life. She loved him. And he loved her.

Walter drew in a deep breath and then tilted his head down, so he could speak into her ear. "Shauna," he whispered.

"Walter," Shauna breathed, and then their arms were around each other.

Walter Reifert

Shauna Skyler...

She was all I could think about. Her red hair, her innocence, her fear. And most of all, the ability to only speak a few words. The doctors in the lab had hurt her, and I was going to do whatever it took to bring her back.

Because I loved her.

And she loved me.

Poor Shauna was so terrorized that she ran screaming through the compound for twenty minutes after our arrival. She woke everyone up, and the only thing we could do was try to catch her. In the end, Lemoore was the one to intervene. He caught her head in his hands and knocked her out with his thoughts. She was on the floor, unconscious, in an instant.

By that time, all four of the younger kids had started crying. Dr. Perry took them to an observation room where he and I were checking them over.

The baby girl, Megan Hopper, whom the boys had nicknamed Meg, seemed the healthiest of the bunch. Her eyes were clear and she had no visible injuries. Dr. Perry checked her over briefly before moving on to Daniel.

Daniel was a sweet toddler with dark hair and blue eyes. The boy was nice enough, but I knew something was wrong with him. Dr. Perry did too.

"Daniel, can you tell me what's the matter?" Dr. Perry asked him. "Do you hurt somewhere?"

The boy, who had a constant stream of tears running down his face, didn't answer. He didn't even acknowledge them.

"His daddy died," Sawyer said quietly from his chair. "They killed him."

Dr. Perry sighed. "Listen, Daniel, I know you're sad, but everything's going to be okay now. We'll find someone to take care of you, and no one's going to hurt you again. But if you're in pain, you need to tell me so I can help you. I'm a good doctor. I won't hurt you." He waited for Daniel to meet his gaze.

Eventually, the boy did. And when he did, he laid back on the table and pulled his shirt up to his neck.

"Oh," Dr. Perry said. "That's...ow."

There was a massive bruise covering Daniel's chest. It must have been there for a while, because it had turned a sickly yellow-brown color. I grimaced at the sight of it. "How many broken ribs do you think there are?"

"I don't even want to guess," Dr. Perry muttered, taking a syringe full of his blood from his jacket. "I'm going to give you a shot, Daniel, but it will make you feel better."

Daniel pulled his arm away and whined, but in the end he held still. Moments after the injection, his face calmed and the bruise vanished altogether.

"Good boy," Dr. Perry said, picking him up and setting him in a chair. "Your turn, Sawyer."

Sawyer climbed up on the table, shaking his head to get his mop of sandy hair out of his eyes. "Where's my sister?" he asked as Dr. Perry listened to his heart.

"She's fine," Dr. Perry promised. "She's resting. She was really sick."

"She doesn't really talk," Sawyer told him.

"I know. Renee told me. I'm going to try to get her voice back as best as I can."

"Why is that?" I demanded. "What did you do to her in that place?"

"I don't know," Dr. Perry answered, but then he said, *Don't expect me to answer that in front of her four-year-old brother! I'll explain it to you and Lemoore later.*

So it was that bad?

"And how are you feeling, Sawyer?" Dr. Perry asked.

Sawyer shrugged. "Fine, I guess. I want to see my sister."

"I need to take a look at her first. You can see her tomorrow."

Sawyer frowned, but he didn't say anything more.

Dr. Perry concluded that Sawyer was in perfect physical health. It then took Dr. Perry a full five minutes to convince Allan to get up on the table. He was less than cooperative after that.

"I don't want a shot!" Allan screamed as Dr. Perry wrestled with him.

"Walter, help me," Dr. Perry ordered, and I went to hold the boy down. The poor kid shrieked until we both released him, upon which time he leapt off the table and pushed himself into a corner. He refused to move or speak after that.

"Jane and Sarah will take good care of them for now," Dr. Perry told me as we left the two women with the children.

I wasn't worried about them. All I cared about was understanding what was wrong with Shauna. "What did you people do to Shauna?" I demanded, a bit more harshly than I intended.

Dr. Perry stopped and glared at me. "I had *nothing* to do with *this*!" he snapped. "I never hurt anyone like that!"

"Like *that*," I shot back. "Sure, tell them all you're a good doctor, but you still hurt people in that place!"

"If it weren't for me, she wouldn't even be here! *None* of them would be here!"

I couldn't admit that he was right. I was too angry. "Answer me! What happened to her?"

"They put a chip in her head. It blocks certain parts of the brain, depending on what it's programmed for. The one in her head has blocked her forms of communication. It probably also blocked a good chunk of her memories before her escape as well. This way, she can't speak to anyone and can't remember much of anything."

"But why would they do that?"

"Because she learned something she wasn't supposed to."

I stared at him quizzically. "What?"

He shrugged. "I don't know."

"Then how do you know that she *did* discover anything?"

"Because I've seen this before." Dr. Perry ran a hand through his hair. "I've only seen it in one other case, and the reasoning was because he got out of his room and found something he wasn't supposed to see. I don't know what it was; I doubt many people do. But whatever it was was very bad. He killed three doctors and tried to kill every member of the staff in the facility."

"And who was this person?"

"Shane Gold."

I raised my eyebrows. "Beast?"

Dr. Perry nodded. "Now they're using him as a weapon to protect their secret. It's very dangerous, but evidently it's also very important."

We walked in silence to Shauna's room. I asked Dr. Perry as we reached the door, "Do you think you can fix her? Make her the way she was before?"

Dr. Perry sighed. "I don't know. But I stand by what I said before; I'll do what I can."

As soon as we entered the room, Shauna started thrashing against the restraints binding her wrists and ankles to the table. Dr. Perry had made the ties out of belts to keep Shauna from overexerting herself. Her eyes were wide and she whimpered as we approached.

"Help her," Dr. Perry murmured to me.

I went to Shauna's side and took her hand in mine. She immediately calmed down. She looked up into my eyes and said my name. I smiled at her and told her everything was okay.

"I gave her a small dose of my blood to clear up the infection, but I didn't heal all her injuries because I wanted to look for the place where they inserted the chip." Dr. Perry took Shauna's head in his hands and gently turned it from side to side. Shauna flinched, but with my hand in hers she allowed him to examine her. After brushing the hair off of her left temple, Dr. Perry paused in his search.

"Is that it?" I asked, peering down at the small, circular scar.

"No," Dr. Perry said, and took a deep breath. "This is where they drilled through her skull to take a sample of her brain tissue."

I felt nauseated. "They did *what*?"

"Some patients had samples of their brain tissue taken for research. The sample was most likely taken while she was conscious. Anesthesia was used, of course. It's good to see that this hasn't gotten infected. A lot of patients who had a sample taken died due to an infection in the brain." He turned Shauna's head back and gently lowered it back to the table. Shauna was hyperventilating, staring up at him in terror. He whispered soothingly, "*Shhh.*"

"It's really bad for us in that place, isn't it?" I asked quietly.

"Yes."

"Are you sure she's unable to talk because of the chip? What if she's like this because of what happened to her in that place?"

"Trust me; it's the chip. Remember that I've seen this before." Taking another look, Dr. Perry lifted Shauna's head again and sifted through her hair on the back of her head. Finally, he said, "There it is."

"Can you take it out?"

"I won't be able to without killing her or giving her permanent brain damage." Dr. Perry paused, thinking. "I think Lemoore might be able to shut it off. There's no guarantee, but it's worth a try."

So I went and brought back Lemoore. Shauna didn't like being touched by him either, but she allowed him to if I held her hand. Lemoore held her head in his hands while looking down into her eyes. He stood like that for a while, searching through her mind for the signal that was suppressing the real Shauna. My Shauna. Then, suddenly, both Lemoore and Shauna gave a little gasp. "I've found it," Lemoore murmured, and Shauna's lips formed the same words.

"Can you turn it off?" I asked eagerly.

"I'll give it a try," Lemoore said. About a minute passed, and nothing happened. I was not prepared for what happened next.

Shauna started screaming, a shrill, animal sound. Lemoore was thrown several feet backwards until he struck the wall and then crumpled to the floor. Dr. Perry ran to him as he clutched his head. I held Shauna in my arms as she convulsed violently.

"It's okay," I whispered to her and the seizure grew worse. "It's going to be okay." *Be okay. Please be okay. Don't die. You can't die.*

I held her through the worst of the convulsions. I held her as she grew still. I held her as she vomited.

I held her as she stopped breathing.

9

Don's Confession

Maia Rudolph

I awoke in Joe's arms, as I had every morning for several days. At first I smiled at the warmth, the love my soul mate was giving me. But then I opened my eyes and the smile left me. The piercing eyes on me from across the burning coals were only a threat, nothing more. Why we still kept him with us, or alive at all, was beyond me.

In the shadows of the sunrise, a mouth opened and asked me softly, "When are you going to let me go, Maia?"

I glared at him. "Do you deserve to be let go, Dad?"

Don Rudolph stared at me helplessly. "It's been three weeks. Joe and Max are fine. Your baby's fine. Just let me and your sister go."

"You really think I'm going to let Marlena leave with you?"

"You can't take care of her."

"I'm pregnant, Dad. I have to learn sooner or later."

Dad's eyes left mine and landed on something over me. Joe was awake and glaring at him with me. "You get paid to hurt children," he snarled. "You don't deserve to keep yours."

His expression unchanging, Dad said, "Who are you to decide that, Joe?"

Max was awake now, and Jazmine was stirring beside him. Marlena still dozed beside me. I could feel Joe's hate radiating in waves from him. I took his hand to calm him down. He relaxed, but the fury was still with him.

Why is he still with us, Maia? What further use is he to us?

It's not that we need him. It's that I'm afraid he'll be able to lead his people to us.

You really think he'd do that? You're his daughter. So is Marlena.

I'm an O Negative, Joe. So is Marlena. We're both different, but we're still a threat to them. I can't risk the life of my sister. Or our baby.

Our baby. Our baby girl. How I had become pregnant with Joe's daughter, and how I knew our baby was a girl, was a mystery. It just happened. Joe said we were soul mates, but that didn't explain the pregnancy. Our anatomy had changed. We no longer reproduced through sex.

Either way, it didn't matter. We were having a baby, and nothing could prevent that from happening. Our baby was going to grow up free of the labs. She was going to live a normal life. As normal of a life as was possible.

Marlena sat with Dad for a while by the tree he was tied to while I talked with the other three. Dad had removed the stitches from both Max and Joe more than a week ago, and their wounds were healing nicely. Joe intercepted the truck carrying Jazmine to the Hatfield lab immediately after her capture and she was hiding with the rest of us in the woods.

"I say we kill him," Max said, and then glanced at me. "No offense, Maia."

"No one's killing anyone," I snapped. "We're not going to become like him."

"You were the one who thought we should keep him with us in the first place!" Jazmine said to Max.

"You're right, though," Joe told me. "If we let him go, he'll lead the soldiers to us."

"Then what do you want to do about him, Joe?" I demanded. "He's my father. I don't care what he's done; *we're not killing him.*"

"He wouldn't hesitate to kill any one of us," Jazmine said softly.

She was right. Dad would kill any three of them without blinking. But I couldn't kill my own father. Especially not with Marlena present.

I turned and looked at my father. Marlena was busy chatting with him, but he was watching me. Carefully. As if he were planning something. As if he knew something.

He did know something. He knew why Marlena and I were so different, and he was going to tell me. I wasn't going to back down this time.

I rose and went to my father. Marlena looked up and then dove out of the way as I lifted my hand and made the ropes fall away from my father. He only continued to sit, staring at me with those knowing eyes. "You're going to kill me?" he asked, his voice holding no fear. "Joe finally talked you into it?"

"Shut up," I snapped, seating myself in front of him.

"Maia, what are you doing?" Joe demanded.

"Talking to him," I replied. "Marlena, go with Joe."

"I'm not going anywhere," Joe said stubbornly.

"You will all leave while I speak to my father," I ordered.

Joe obeyed, taking Marlena's hand and leading her back over to Max and Jazmine. They were all out of earshot, so I turned back to my father. "I want to know," I said.

Dad knew exactly what I was talking about. "If I tell you, will you let me leave?"

"That depends."

"On what?"

"Your answers."

Dad sighed, but seemed to take the hint. "I never planned for the experiment to go as it did."

"How did it go wrong?" I asked, already impatient. "What did you even do?"

Dad paused. "You mother didn't agree to it at first, but eventually I convinced her. I told her it was to help the human race, to strengthen it, and that was true. I didn't lie to her. I never lied to her." Dad sighed again. "Things went smoothly with you. Your birth was quick, quicker than expected, and the delivery was easy. But the experiment failed. You were exposed to the chemical compound, but nothing happened. It didn't harm you, but it didn't enhance you either. You were just the same as before. You were six when we realized our failure. A few more years of study and manipulation brought about a new strain, a new virus. We were certain it would work. I convinced your mother to have another child so we could try again. Marlena was a healthy fetus, but your mother had difficulty carrying her. She was constantly sick, and by the eighth month she began to bleed internally. We had to perform an emergency C-section, and Marlena was just fine. You mother, on the other hand..." He shook his head. "She didn't make it."

I didn't reply. I was too full of shock and anger to speak. Dad thought my speechlessness was his cue to continue.

"Marlena's first test was when she was four. It was successful. The premonitions began a few days later, and have been noticeable ever since. You wouldn't have noticed. You would have disregarded them as child's talk."

I thought about the pictures Marlena had drawn the night Joe found me.

"And then, when there was the leak at the lab, and everybody with O negative was affected, we saw progress in you. You didn't notice it until it was pointed out to you, but I saw it. Maybe it was the extra dose of Colician Strain that finally set you off. I don't know. All I know is that it worked. After all these years, it finally worked.

"The thing with you and Marlena is that you have little or no control over your abilities. You seem to be able to control yours when you're angry, but Marlena's premonitions come and go as they please. The drug we nurtured you with as fetuses was meant to give you more control, but instead it gave you less. You don't have the same bond with the others as the rest do. You never had symptoms. You still managed to become pregnant due to something we refer to as the Bonding Effect, but you never felt the connection to Joe that he did to you."

"I feel it," I said curtly.

"Not the way that Joe does," Dad told me.

I took a moment to try to process everything Dad said. It was a lot to take in, and I was so angry. "What did you do to us?" I demanded. "When we were in the womb?"

"We gave you drugs that would allow your body to accept the Colician Strain once you were born. You see, we never thought that anyone would live without the treatment administered before—"

"You killed my mother so you could experiment on me and my sister?" I shouted, each word louder than the last.

Dad closed his eyes briefly. "I didn't kill her," he whispered.

"Yes," I snarled, "you did! You *killed* her!"

"That wasn't how it was supposed to happen…"

"Well, that *is* how it happened! How do you *live* with yourself? You killed your wife and fucked up both your kids!" I stood and kicked him in the face, knocking him on his back. I then stomped off, yelling to the others, "Leave him here! We're leaving."

"Maia!" Marlena shouted fearfully, running to me and hugging my legs. "Maia, I'm scared!"

"Scared of what?" I asked, but that was when Jazmine started screaming.

"They're coming! I can hear them! We have to leave now!"

I was shoved forward suddenly, and I stumbled before rounding on my father. He was gazing defiantly at me, holding Marlena in his arms. "Let her go!" I said.

"Are you really going to risk everyone's freedom for hers?" Dad asked me, backing away. "They're here, Maia. You'd better run."

"I don't want to hurt you," I told him.

"You already have," Dad replied harshly.

I stared at him in surprise, and then I looked at Marlena. "I'll come back for you," I promised her. She nodded at me, and then I turned and ran.

10

Old Friends and Past Lives

Shawn Perry

Dr. Perry rarely saw his family anymore. Few of the doctors working at the labs did. When he wasn't at the lab, he was at Lemoore's. And when he wasn't at Lemoore's, he was sleeping. So when he finally had a break, he was more than ecstatic.

"Hey," he called when he opened his front door. "I'm home early."

No answer. He couldn't hear anything.

"Hello?" he said, a little uncertainly. Where was everyone? The other car was still in the garage...

The closet doors to his left suddenly burst open, and Dr. Perry instinctively reached for the gun on his belt. He relaxed when little Hallie sprang forth, yelling "Boo!" and grabbing his legs as she squealed in delight. "Hi, Daddy!" she said, jumping up and down.

"Hey," he said, scooping her up and smiling. "How's my girl doing?"

"Fine," she said, beaming.

"How long were you waiting in there?" Dr. Perry asked curiously.

"Not long," Hallie said breathlessly. "I heard you coming." She tapped her forehead, their code gesture when referring to one of their abilities.

"Ah."

"I miss you, Daddy." Hallie wrapped her arms around his neck and hugged him tightly.

"I know," he replied sadly. "I'm going to try to get home more. Where's your mom and sister?"

"Mommy's sleeping and Jillian's in the living room," Hallie said, more concerned with other matters. "How's Shauna, Daddy?"

"She's doing fine," Perry told her. "At least she was the last time I checked. We had a little accident with her a few days ago when we tried to get her memory back, but she's okay now. Walter's taking good care of her."

"Did she get her memory back?" Hallie asked hopefully.

Perry paused. "No. I don't think she ever will."

"Oh." Hallie's face fell.

Hallie went to play while Perry went into the living room to see Jillian. Jillian was sitting on the couch, doing her homework while she listened to music. "Hey, Jillian," he called from the doorway. His eldest didn't respond, so he walked to the couch and waved his hand in front of her face. Jillian still didn't respond. Perry was confused, knowing she wouldn't purposely ignore him like that. He went around to the other side of the couch and leaned down to see her eyes. Her pupils were dilated, blocking out both irises. Knowing what was happening, Perry reached out and pulled the buds out of his daughter's ears.

She blinked and looked around. "Huh? What?" she stuttered, and met her father's concerned gaze. "Oh, hi Dad."

"You okay?" he asked her.

"Yep," she said, still blinking to clear her head. "There's a boy down the street who's hiding just like us. I was talking to him."

"You should tell him your father can get him to a safe house."

"I have. He's going to talk to his parents about it and get back to me."

"Is he the only O Negative in his family?"

"Yes."

"What's his name?"

"Mace. Mace Campbell. Do you know him?"

Perry shook his head. He recalled the name from Jillian's first episode, but he had never met the kid. "How old is he?"

"Thirteen. Will you help him?"

"Of course." Perry sat next to his daughter. "How are you doing?"

Jillian shrugged. "Okay, I guess." She shrugged again. "I don't like hiding this."

"I know. I won't be able to keep up my act for much longer. Soon, we can join Lemoore and the others."

"Good," Jillian said, and then leaned forward and hugged him.

"What was that for?" Perry asked when she pulled away. He was grateful, but surprised. Fifteen-year-old girls didn't exactly make hugging their dads a daily ritual.

Again, Jillian shrugged. "I love you, Dad."

Perry smiled. "I love you, too. I'm going to see how Renee's doing."

"She threw up again when she got home."

"Yeah, I know," Perry said grimly, and left the room to go upstairs.

Renee had been sick a lot lately. Perry assumed it was stress, having to deal with the horrors she had seen while in the FBI, but she insisted she was fine. Perry saw through her, though. Something was bothering her, and she had yet to tell him what.

Perry went into his room, finding Renee exactly where he expected her to be; curled up on the very edge of the bed, a bucket and towel resting on the floor beneath her. Her hair was matted and dull, not its usual golden shine. Her face was pale and stressed, purple splotches under her eyes from exhaustion.

Her eyes were closed, but Perry was certain she knew he was there.

"I'd like to be alone, please," Renee muttered at him, unmoving.

"Are you okay, babe?" Perry asked, coming over and sitting by her feet.

"Did you hear what I just said?"

Sighing, Perry said, "Yes, I did, but I know something's wrong, and you're going to tell me what."

"Oh so persistent," Renee said sarcastically, glaring up at him.

"Come on," Perry said, frustrated. "I don't need the attitude. I'm trying to help. You've been sick for weeks, and I know something's bothering you. If you don't tell me then it's going to get worse and then you're going to get worse. Hallie needs you, hon. She misses you."

"You're really going to use Hallie to make me feel guilty?"

"That's not what I was doing!" Perry took a deep breath. He didn't want to fight. "Look, Renee, I just hate seeing you like this. I like seeing you as your peppy, happy self, and so do the girls. They're worried about you too. We all just want you to get better."

Renee's face suddenly became sad, dreadfully sad, and she sat up. "I don't know how to say it," she said, her voice cracking.

"Just say it," Perry whispered.

Tears fell from her eyes. "I feel like something horrible is about to happen," she said. "No; I *know* something terrible is about to happen. To all of us. I want to get out of this house, Shawn. *Please.* Let's just pack our bags and go to Lemoore's tonight!"

"Hey," Perry said, taking her hand in his. "Everything's going to be okay. I just have a little bit more work to get done at the lab, and then we're out of here."

"Please, Shawn!" Renee sobbed. "I want to leave *now!*"

"Nobody knows about us," Perry whispered, kissing her gently. "We're safe. We'll be alright." He smiled reassuringly. "We'll be out of here in no time, alright? Nothing's going to happen to us. I promise. Trust me."

Renee wanted to argue more; Perry could tell, but she simply nodded and laid back down. "I'm scared, Shawn," she whispered. "I'm scared for our children."

"They'll be fine. They're going to grow old and happy, just like we will." He kissed her again. "You're going to be fine, too. Just try to relax a little. Are there any leftovers in the fridge?"

"Jillian ordered pizza for her and Hallie," Renee said. "I wasn't hungry. They'll probably let you have some if you ask nicely."

Perry chuckled. "Okay. Try to eat something later, okay? It'll make you feel better."

"Whatever you say, Doc."

Perry flinched and inhaled sharply. Renee didn't mean it in the context Perry took it, but she recognized her mistake immediately.

"I'm sorry," she said quickly. "I didn't mean—"

"I know you didn't mean that," he assured her. "It's okay."

He left her in peace then. He got her to talk to him, so now he was going to let her be alone like she wanted.

He made it halfway down the stairs when the doorbell rang.

"I got it!" Jillian called.

"No, that's okay!" Perry replied, descending the last of the steps. "I'm right here." He went to the door and opened it. His heart skipped a beat when he saw his visitor.

"Hey," a very drunk Graham Odau mumbled. "I was in the neighborhood. Thought I'd stop by and say hello."

Perry knew that was a lie. The two men had purposely avoided each other for ten years. "You've had a bit too much to drink," Perry replied, stepping back as Odau stumbled inside. He took his arm and led him into the living room.

"Well, what else am I supposed to do?" Odau muttered. "My whole family is gone."

"Dad?" Jillian said uncertainly upon seeing Odau.

"Would you mind giving us the room, honey?" Perry asked her, helping Odau into the armchair.

Jillian nodded, gathered up her things, and quickly left.

"Who's that?" Odau asked lazily as he fell onto the couch.

"My daughter," Perry said. "Jillian."

Odau's brow furrowed, thinking hard. "Yeah...you mentioned her when we were working on...that case. So you won custody?"

"No. I never won it. Her mother and step-father died in a car accident a few years back. She's been living with me and Renee ever since."

"Poor kid."

"She's coped well. She never had a close relationship with either of them." Perry didn't like referring to Kyra as Jillian's mother, because in truth, she had never been much of a mother.

"And you and Renee are married now?"

Was Odau going to ask about his entire life over the past ten years? "Yes. We married not long after…that case."

"Good for you. Good for you…"

"I thought you were staying in New York with your…with Jackson," Perry said, taking the opportunity to shift the subject off of himself and his family. He wasn't sure either of them really wanted to move on to the subject of Jackson Odau, though.

"Jackson joined the Marines right out of high school," Odau said, slumping down on the sofa. "And he knows what I did. He knows that I took his mother and sisters to a safe house. He's angry, Shawn. He…I think he hates me."

It was the first time Odau had ever used Perry's first name. This was serious. "You don't think he'll tell, do you?"

Odau snorted. "It's hard to say. He certainly could."

"You know what they'll do to you if he does."

"That doesn't really matter. My boy's going to kill me anyway."

"You don't know that!" Perry whispered fiercely.

"Yes, I do," Odau grumbled. "I've seen it in his eyes every day for the last ten years. The Doc's already in him, Shawn. Do you want to know what he said to me before we left? He told me I was a traitor for taking Jane and the girls to Lemoore's. He told me I should report the compound to the authorities. He wants them all dead, even though his mom and sisters are among them. He told me he'd kill me if he ever saw me again. I didn't believe him at first, but now…I'm scared to go home." He sighed.

"Graham," Perry said, "why did you come here? Why did you come back to Philadelphia?"

"I came back to see my family. But mostly, I came to see you."

"Why?"

"I've been thinking a lot about this year…"

"You've only been thinking about it because of what Hara…what Hallie told us all that time ago."

"Yes, exactly. I…" Odau suddenly burst into tears. "I miss them! I miss my family! Nothing's been right since the day I found out who my son's going to become!"

"Hey," Perry said, putting a comforting hand on his shoulder.

"I need help," Odau sobbed. "I need help, but you're the only doctor I trust."

"What do you need from me?" Perry asked. "Please tell me. Anything you need. I *want* to help you."

"I want to be with my family," Odau said as he got himself under control. "But the others at that place all hate me. I don't know what to do or where to go."

"Why don't you just stay with me for a while?" Perry offered. "Renee would be more than happy to have you here. Then you can come with me when I go back and forth between here and there."

"Thank you," Odau murmured graciously. "But I can't stay with you. This is your home."

"What we saw ten years ago brought us together," Perry said. "Even though we never spoke of it. What we saw cannot be forgotten. It's a part of both of us, of all of us. You are welcome here. Please stay."

"Where would I stay?"

"I can have the my youngest move into Jillian's room and then you can have Hallie's room."

Odau's head snapped up suddenly. "You…you named your daughter after *her*?"

"Yes," Perry replied, a little defensively.

Their conversation was cut short as the phone rang.

"Sorry," Perry apologized, getting up to get the phone. "I have to take this. It's either the lab calling for me or the FBI calling for

Renee." He went to the phone and answered politely, even though he was annoyed by the interruption.

There was a pause before an elderly woman replied. "Hello, sir. Is this the residence of Dr. Shawn Perry?"

"Yes, this is him speaking," Perry said.

"My name is Margaret Benson, Dr. Perry," the woman said. "I'm a nurse here at the Hospice Center in downtown Philadelphia."

"Alright." Perry already knew what this woman wanted. There was probably an elderly patient there with an ability, and she wanted him or her extracted immediately.

But why the hell was she calling his house?

"There's a patient here who'd like very much to speak with you," Margaret explained. "He says that you and he are old friends. He says he'd like to speak with you before he passes away."

"Okay. What's his name?"

"Ivan Long."

Perry didn't recognize the name, but he *did* know the name Long. He could never forget it. Was somebody from his last case trying to contact him? He doubted it. The only people left alive were in his house or... long gone. "Okay. Put him on."

"Just one moment please, sir."

Perry waited, and then he heard the heavy breathing of the man on the other line. "Hello?" he said, but received no reply. "Mr. Long? I heard you wanted to speak to me."

"Yes, I did," an old, English man said into the phone, his voice heavy with death. "But my name's not Long."

"Oh my God," Perry breathed. It was Noah Travis.

Dr. Perry didn't understand why he was getting himself so worked up. He knew this man. They were friends. At least, they had been for a short time ten years ago. But it was one stressor after another, one more reminder of that last case. The year, the outbreak, Walter, Graham, and now Noah.

The woman at the front desk told him to go to the third floor, room 318, on the left side of the hallway. "There may be a nurse in there with him," she said, "but she'll leave you. Mr. Long said that it's very urgent he speaks with you."

Perry didn't know what could be so important, but he could make time for a dying friend.

He paused when he found the room. He wasn't sure if he would be able to go in, to face his past again. Reaching up, he knocked gently on the open door.

"Just go right in, sir," a man at the floor's help desk told him.

Taking a deep breath, Perry did as he was told.

Noah looked awful. Most of his hair was gone, as were his teeth, and he had dark brown patches all over his skin, making his skin appear stained. He was very thin—uncomfortably thin—his eyes were drooping and tired, and his hands shook violently when he gestured for Perry to come to his bedside. Perry hesitated at the condition of his old friend, but then he went to him, taking his hand gently in his own. "Noah," he greeted quietly.

"Shawn Perry." Noah's voice sounded worse than when they had spoken on the phone the day before. It had a throaty sound to it, as if he needed to cough quite hard to clear it. But he didn't cough. He just kept on smiling, even though he was hooked up to an IV with several bags of medicine and had a respirator to help his breathing. He pulled the mask away from his face so Perry could hear him more clearly. "It's good to see you again."

"You look terrible." The comment was out of his mouth before he could stop himself. "I mean, it's good to see you, it's just…" He looked away.

Noah chuckled, sounding more like a kitten being strangled than anything. "Pull up a chair, my friend."

Perry did, trying to avoid looking at Noah's face. It pained him to do so. "Why did you call me here, Noah?"

"I wanted to talk to you before I died," Noah replied, patting Perry's hand. "I figured this would be the best time to do so, before you get caught."

Instinctively, Perry looked around quickly to make sure there were no cameras or lingering nurses. "I'm not going to get caught," he said in a whisper. "My family and I will be out of Philadelphia before that happens."

Noah smiled weakly at him, a smile that had a little bit of pity in it too. "Okay. If you're so sure. How's your family?"

"Fine."

"You and your partner are married?"

"Yes, but she's not my partner anymore."

"I know. Your *former* partner."

"Yes, we're married."

"And your daughters?"

"They're fine. They're both—"

"Telepaths?"

Perry kept forgetting that Noah knew everything about him, even though Perry hadn't told him these things yet. "Yes."

"And how are your abilities going for you?"

Perry found that to be a rather odd question. "What do you mean?"

"Is your family able to hide them well?" Noah asked.

He shrugged. "They've been doing fine with it, as far as I can tell."

Noah nodded, a deeper knowledge hidden in his eyes. "Maybe your should leave sooner than you planned."

"Why's that?"

Noah shrugged. "I just think it would be safer. You can't hide forever, you know."

"I know," Perry said. "I just have a little more work I need to get done in the lab before I disappear."

"Too much work will kill you, you know."

Sighing, Perry asked, "Did you just want to chat, or are you trying to tell me something?"

"I'm trying to indirectly tell you something," Noah said. "I can't tell you your whole future, remember. I can only tell you certain pieces."

"And what are you trying to indirectly tell me?"

Noah smiled again. "If I told you directly, it wouldn't be indirect, would it?"

Perry was growing frustrated. He stood up. "I have a lot of work to do, Noah. I don't have time for guessing games."

"No, wait!" Noah cried, grabbing Perry's arm and making him sit again. "I'm telling you to quit your job. That's what I'm trying to tell you."

"I thought you couldn't be direct."

"That wasn't the part that was supposed to be indirect."

Biting his lip, Perry asked, "Are you saying something's going to happen if I don't?"

Noah hesitated. "I can't tell you that, remember?"

They sat in silence for several minutes, Perry thinking over what Noah had said. He knew he really should pack up his family and leave, but things were fine now. Another week or two, and they would be able to join Lemoore and the others.

"I'm going to die," Noah said, as if that wasn't already obvious. "Very soon. I'm glad you came, Shawn. You're the only friend I have left."

Perry hated it, but that was the truth. All Noah's other friends were... elsewhere.

"I'm glad you called," Perry said softly. "I'm glad I get to say goodbye."

"It won't be goodbye forever, you know."

"For you, it is." Perry took his hand again. "Do you want me to stay with you?" he asked. "Until... you know."

"Until I die?"

"Yeah."

"No. I'm not going to ask you to do that."

"I don't want you to die alone. That's not fair."

"Life isn't fair, Shawn. And that's okay. I won't be alone. I'll have my nurses."

"That's not the same thing."

"It's alright. I'll be alright."

Perry laughed scornfully. "No you won't. You'll be dead!"

"Everyone dies, Shawn."

"Not me," Perry whispered. That was the thing he feared most. Never aging, never being able to die. Would he live on, watching everyone he loved die, having no relief from his pain, his misery?

"Excuse me, sir," the male nurse from the desk said, stepping into the room awkwardly. "It's lunch time."

"That's fine," Perry said, even though he had been hoping to stay longer. "I have to get to work. My boss is going to fire me if I don't get back."

"That's all for the better," Noah replied.

Perry rolled his eyes, but let the comment slide. "It was good to see you," he told Noah, forcing a smile. "One last time."

Noah nodded, and smiled in return. "Only for me," he whispered. "Only for me."

Perry nodded, but as he left, Noah stopped him.

"No matter what happens," he said, "no matter what you have to go through, don't ever give up."

"I would never," Perry said. "You know that."

"I know that," Noah replied. "But you don't."

Two days later, Dr. Perry got a call at work. It was the woman who had called about Noah before, regrettably informing him that Ivan Long had passed away.

That same day, Dr. Perry ran into someone who he prayed every day he would never have to see again.

"Afternoon," Don Rudolph said brightly as they both clocked in after their lunch break.

Perry mumbled a reply, having no desire to start a conversation with him. He tried to walk away from him, but they were both going the same way. "Back from your vacation?" he asked Rudolph as they both rode the elevator to the sub levels.

Rudolph glanced at him, and smiled as though Perry was making a friendly joke. He certainly was not. "I'd hardly call it that," Rudolph replied.

"Well, while you were off on your adventure with your kids, some of us have been stuck here working overtime in your place," Perry snapped. The elevator stopped and the doors opened at the perfect moment, and he didn't linger.

Rudolph called after him from inside the elevator. He had to go to the lowest sublevel, to work on some special secret project. Probably more torture devices. "You don't like me very much, do you?"

Perry turned back to him, scowling. Rudolph was holding the elevator door open, and was still smiling at him. Perry hated that smile, more than he hated Rudolph. "I've found that I don't like many of the people here."

"Why's that?" Rudolph asked, scrutinizing Perry carefully.

"Take a wild guess," Perry muttered, and turned to leave. Rudolph caught him off guard with his final comment.

"My guess is that you have something in common with the people here," he said, "which is why you don't like the other doctors here."

Perry whipped around, a bubble of panic bursting in his chest and making it difficult to breathe. He caught one last glimpse of Rudolph as the doors closed between them. His eyes were full of knowing.

The next morning, Perry was awakened by the sound of his doorbell ringing. He went downstairs to answer it, but Hallie had gotten there first. The door was hanging wide open, revealing a smiling Don Rudolph gazing down on her. "Hallie!" Perry called sharply, taking her arm and pulling her behind him.

Rudolph's gaze rose lazily to meet Perry's. "Morning, Perry."

"Go upstairs," Perry told his daughter, who had a look of sheer terror on her face, and she ran away as fast as she could.

"Cute kid," Rudolph complimented as Hallie disappeared from sight. "What's her name?"

"What do you want, Rudolph?" Perry demanded, his tone hostile and uninviting.

"Can I come in?" Without getting an approval, Rudolph stepped inside and closed the door.

"I'll ask you one more time," Perry warned, "before I call the cops. What do you want?"

"So aggressive," Rudolph said, smiling innocently at him. "What have I ever done to deserve such treatment?"

"Gee, where to start? Get out of my house."

"I actually came about your daughter," Rudolph said, holding his ground. "What's her name?"

"Which one?" Perry snapped.

"The cute little blonde who answered the door."

"Her name's Hallie."

"Hallie? Huh. That's funny. My brother-in-law's wife's name was Hallie."

"Fascinating," Perry muttered, knowing he was talking about Walter's dead mother.

"Her first grade teacher filed a report to me last week," Rudolph continued, a little too pleasantly. "The teacher claims that the girl has extraordinary knowledge for a child her age. She also says that she knows things. Things she shouldn't."

"So?" Perry tried to keep calm, but his heart was already pounding. "She's a smart kid."

"No," Rudolph said, his too-cheerful smile reminding Perry of someone he once met. It made him shudder. "That's not what I meant. The girl knows things that are *impossible* for her to know. You understand what I'm saying, don't you? I'm certain you do."

"She's a very observant child. She's always been that way."

"It's just suspicious, don't you think? What with the timing of this report. It just makes me wonder…"

"You shouldn't wonder anything. My daughter's fine." Perry's voice was clipped, agitated. Rudolph could hear it.

Rudolph smiled kindly. "When are you going to stop lying to me? It's pointless, you know. It's all over."

Perry couldn't help but be afraid of this man. "What are you talking about?"

Rudolph was still smiling. "I know what you did."

"Shawn?" A sleepy Renee was coming down the stairs, Hallie in tow. "Who's here? Hallie said—" She stopped short upon seeing Rudolph in the doorway.

"Renee," Rudolph said pleasantly.

Renee looked to her husband. "What's going on?" she asked nervously.

"Oh, I was just leaving," Rudolph answered before Perry could open his mouth. "I was just telling your husband he should be a little more careful." He turned to leave. "Have a nice day, Dr. Perry. Renee. Hallie."

When he was gone, Perry slowly turned to his family, which had assembled at the foot of the stairs. Odau had also felt the tension and stood at the top of the stairs.

"Who was that?" Odau asked.

"What did he want?" Renee demanded. When she received no reply, she said sharply, "Shawn!"

"Get your bags," Perry said quietly. "All of you."

"Why?" Jillian asked uneasily.

"Because we're leaving. Get the bags you packed and any other things you'll need. I'm going to drop Graham off at Lemoore's and when I get back, we're leaving and never coming back."

Kill

Walter Reifert

I awoke to Shauna stirring restlessly in my arms. Blinking, I gazed into her awaiting blue eyes and smiled. She smiled back. "Hey," I whispered.

Shauna still had difficulty speaking, but her voice was steadily coming back. "Hello, Walter," she said slowly and shakily.

"You're getting better," I complimented, my smile broadening.

"Yes," she whispered, nuzzling up against me.

I held her close and stroked her hair. She suddenly gasped and pulled away, putting a hand to her belly. I reached out and placed my hand over hers. Beneath her touch, our son was stirring. "He's moving," I said in awe.

"Yes," Shauna said. "He moves. Restless."

"What do you want to call him?"

"Early?"

"It's not too early. Dr. Perry said that he thinks gestation will be less than three months. Erica's already showing. It's been almost two weeks for us."

Shauna thought for a moment. "John."

"What?" I said in surprise.

"Your dad."

"I don't want to name our son after my father," I said, even though—in a way—I did.

"Tyler? Ethan? Anton?"

"No," I said, wishing she would stop. I was feeling the familiar pang in my chest, the pang that had left me for a little while. "We could make his middle name Jonathan. I like that idea."

"Why not first?"

"Because...I want—I *need*—to move on."

Shauna nodded as if she understood, but I doubted she did. "What you want to call baby?"

I thought. There were a few names I liked, but I wanted Shauna to like one of them too. "There's a couple I like."

"What?"

"Well, there's Jake. I've always liked Jake. I also like Lawson, Flint, and Peighton, because they're not as common, but also Ryan..."

"Flint," Shauna said thoughtfully, nodding. "Flint Jonathan. I like."

"I like it too," I said, repeating the name. "Flint Jonathan. It's a good name."

"Good name for baby," Shauna repeated, smiling and rubbing her belly. "Flint Jonathan."

"I think it's a keeper," I whispered, wrapping my arms around my soul mate.

A commotion from downstairs pulled us apart.

"Going on?" Shauna asked, her eyes wide.

"It's okay," I assured her, climbing out of bed. "If it were a problem the alarm would have gone off."

Shauna followed me out of our room, gripping my hand tightly as we descended the stairs. Why was she so nervous? There were so many of us here now that this compound was easily protected.

"Bad," Shauna said, tugging my hand. "Bad person!"

"There's no bad people here," I insisted as I struggled to listen to the conversation below. When we reached the bottom of the stairs, I told her, "I'm sure it's just some more refugees..." My voice trailed off as I caught a flash of rainbow hair at the doorway.

"Oh my God," I whispered, and then I was running through the crowd of people who had assembled to greet them. "Jazmine!" I shouted. "Jazmine!"

Jazmine met me at the edge of the crowd. We hugged and laughed. "You're okay!" she cried.

"You're an O Negative!" I replied.

"I guess so," she said, beaming. "Guess who else made it here?" She stepped aside, and then both Joe and Max Murphy were jumping on me.

The four of us exchanged more hugs and laughs, and then I caught sight of Maia behind them. I went to her, no words capable of describing my ecstasy. "Good to see you, cuz," I said, and we hugged too. When I pulled away, I saw that her expression was troubled. "What's wrong? You're an O Negative, aren't you?"

"Yes," Maia said, "but Dad's got Marlena."

"We'll get her back," I promised her quickly. "We've got a big group here. We're going to coordinate an attack on the Hatfield lab." I caught a glimpse of Shauna out of the corner of my eye. "Oh! Maia, this is my soul mate, Shauna." I turned towards Shauna and gestured to her. Shauna's face was grim, sick. And there was something in her hand...

Maia smiled weakly. "Hi, Shauna. I'm Walter's cousin, M—" Her voice cut off and her eyes widened in shock as blood began to trickle from her mouth.

People gasped. Some screamed. I think I screamed. Maia's hand fumbled over the knife jutting from her chest, the knife that had been in Shauna's hand a moment earlier. Maia collapsed into Joe's arms, and Joe screamed her name. I turned to Shauna, my eyes wide and disbelieving. Shauna saw my face and shook her head quickly. She pointed at Maia and cried, "Maia Rudolph! Kill! Maia Rudolph!"

"Why?" I whispered.

"You killed her!" Joe screamed at Shauna, clutching Maia to him. "You killed her, you crazy bitch! She's pregnant!"

"Somebody get a vial of Dr. Perry's blood!" I shouted. Maia was holding on, but just barely. "Somebody help her!"

"I've got it, Walter," Lemoore said, weaving his way through the crowd. He had a syringe in his hand, filled with Dr. Perry's blood. How he had reacted so quickly, I didn't know, but I was beyond grateful for it. "Everybody back up! This isn't a show."

"Kill! Kill!" Shauna screamed. "Maia Rudolph! Kill! Kill! *Kill!*"

"Get her out of here," I choked out, crouching down beside my cousin. I heard Shauna scream louder as she was dragged away, but I ignored her. "Hang in there, Maia," I whispered as Lemoore removed the knife from her chest and quickly injected her with the blood. Moments later, the wound pulled closed and Maia's eyes fluttered open.

"How do you feel?" Lemoore asked her.

Maia looked down at her belly, and her lips parted to form the words, "My baby…"

Lemoore put a hand to Maia's stomach and listened. "Your baby's fine."

Both Joe and Maia breathed sighs of relief. Maia looked up at me and forced a smile. "That's quite a babe you got there, Walter."

I wanted to say something, to apologize for Shauna, but my tongue had gone numb. All I was able to do was hug my cousin.

Shawn Perry

Dr. Perry had only meant to drop off Graham Odau and then quickly return home to get his family, but when he arrived a swarm of people dragged him inside. Within five minutes, he had heavily sedated Shauna, sedated a hysterical Joe Murphy, and performed an ultrasound on Maia Rudolph, who had been stabbed by Shauna. The shit that happened when he wasn't there…

"What happened?" Perry asked Walter when it was all over.

"I don't know," Walter replied weakly. "The four of them got here, and I introduced Maia to Shauna and then Shauna stabbed her and started screaming her name and how she needs to kill her.

I don't understand what happened. She was fine when we woke up…"

"Shauna's mind had been derailed," Perry told him. "That makes her extremely unpredictable. I was worried that this would start happening…"

"Do you think she's going to try to kill others, too?" Walter asked quickly.

"I didn't say that. What I'm saying is that we should be very careful with her from now on. Keep Maia far away from her. I'd like to have a guard with her from now on, and I want to keep her on mild sedatives until I can determine the cause of the outburst."

Walter nodded. "I agree."

Perry took a moment to look Walter up and down. "And you? What about you? How are you holding up?"

Walter shrugged. "I was really scared for a moment there. I was so sure that Shauna had killed her, and Maia's pregnant. That would have been two lives lost!"

"Well, they're both fine," Perry promised him. "It was close, but they'll be alright."

"I need to talk to Shauna when she wakes up," Walter said. "I need to figure out why she did this."

"There may not be an answer," Perry told him.

"But there has to be! It's been a long time since she's been like this, and this is the first time she's reacted to someone this way."

Perry put a hand on his shoulder. "We'll both try to talk to her later. Until then, spend some time with Maia. Joe, too. They're both pretty shaken up from this episode."

Walter nodded. "I'll do that. What are you doing here so early, anyway? Don't you have to be at the lab soon?"

"I came to drop off Graham so he could see his family. He's having a hard time coping with this. I have to run home to get my—" Perry stopped suddenly and stumbled backwards. Something was wrong. Very wrong. Renee was calling out to him from home. No…she was screaming. Jillian's and Hallie's screams soon joined hers. "Oh, God," he breathed. The horror, the terror, was taking him over.

"Dr. Perry?" Walter said in alarm, taking Perry's arm. "Dr. Perry, are you okay? What's happening?"

Perry turned and started running. He felt blinded, deafened by his family's screams. He ran into several pieces of furniture as he went, and didn't stop even when people caught him by the arms to ask what was the matter. Nothing could stop him now. He had to save his family.

He was in his SUV and speeding down the gravel drive. Walter ended up in the passenger seat somehow and was screaming questions at him. At one point, Perry remembered telling the boy, "Your uncle knows I'm an O Negative. He went after my family."

It wasn't until he felt the tug, the terrible agony of death, that he finally came back to the world. His foot found the brake pedal and he brought the vehicle to a stop in the middle of the road. Drivers behind him honked angrily, but he took no notice of them. He was more than halfway home, but he was too late. Renee and Jillian were already dead, and Hallie was badly hurt.

"No," Perry choked out. "No…please, no!"

"What happened?" Walter asked, but he went unheard.

Images of Renee flashed across Perry's vision, images of their time together. The two of them being assigned as partners in the bureau. Their case when they finally decided they were meant to be together; the case where they met the future daughter of Walter Reifert and Shauna Skyler. Their wedding day. Buying their house in Philadelphia. Finding out that Renee was pregnant with Hallie. Living together. Happy. It was always happy.

But not anymore.

Jillian's memories came next. Memories that Perry would forever cherish, even when he struggled to forget his past life and move on. The first time Perry saw his infant daughter, and got to hold her in his arms. Fighting for custody of her, and losing, but sneaking calls to her whenever he could. Her mother and step-father dying, when she finally came to be with him. Jillian panicking when she was first able to hear thoughts. Perry going to calm her down.

He loved his daughters. He loved his wife. Why did they have to die? What had they ever done to deserve it? And in such a brutal manner…

"No!" Perry screamed, stamping his foot on the gas pedal. He sped the remaining distance to his house and jumped out without putting the SUV in park. Walter went after him, knowing what happened.

The people who attacked his family were already gone; there were no laboratory vehicles anywhere in sight. It wouldn't have mattered. No number of bullets could have stopped him in his state of heartbreak. He ran to his front door, his front door that was smashed in and hanging off its frame. He realized he was screaming.

He found Jillian's body right away. She was lying face down on the stairs. She must have tried to make an escape, but was shot down in the process, a single gunshot to the back of her head. Perry went to her, waterfalls pouring from his eyes.

"I'm sorry," he whispered, kneeling beside her and stroking her back. "This is my fault. I should have saved you when I had the chance. This is my fault."

Walter put a hand on Perry's shoulder, but he didn't say anything. The boy knew better than to speak.

Perry followed the trail of broken glass and toppled furniture into the kitchen. That was where he found Renee. She was sprawled on her back, her gun resting beside her. She had attempted to fight back, and had taken five bullets to the chest as a result. Perry held her head in his lap and rocked her for a while. He cried, and Walter let him. Eventually, Perry had to get up. He could hear the weak telepathic cries coming from somewhere else in the house. When he raised his eyes, Walter pointed solemnly towards the living room.

Perry went to Hallie. Her eyes were closed, but she was still with him. Just barely. He gently lifted her and then sat on the couch with her resting in his arms. There were two bullet wounds in her stomach, and a good amount of blood covered her body and now Perry's arms.

"Get me a vial of blood," Perry whispered to Walter. "They're in the fridge on the top shelf."

Walter went to the fridge, but then called out, "They're all gone! There's nothing left!"

Perry closed his eyes. He should have known. He left the compound in such a hurry that he didn't bring any vials from there. He didn't even have a syringe to take blood from his body. Even if they took Hallie back to the compound, she wouldn't survive the trip. When he opened his eyes again, he saw Hallie's sky blues looking back at him.

Her young, innocent eyes were cloudy and disoriented, but she didn't take them off of Perry. Perry, her daddy. Her pale face struggled to form a smile, and she forced out, "Daddy…"

"*Shhhh*," Perry whispered, stroking her blonde hair.

I'm scared, Daddy, she told him, no longer able to speak.

"Don't be scared," Perry tried in as soothing of a voice as he could muster, also forcing a smile. He realized that Walter had left them, leaving Hallie to share her last moments of life with her daddy.

I am, Hallie whispered.

"It's just a bad dream," Perry said, rocking her on his lap. "It's all just a bad, bad dream. Close your eyes. Go to sleep. When you wake up again, you'll be with Mommy and Jillian."

And you, too? Hallie asked hopefully.

Perry's heart broke all over again. "I'll see you soon, baby. But I'll always be with you. As long as you remember me, I'll always be there."

And you'll remember me?

"Yes. I could never forget you. Or Mommy or Jillian."

I don't want to go without you.

"You have to, baby. Go, so you can be happy. You'll be happy. No more bad dreams." He leaned forward and planted a kiss on his daughter's forehead. He held his lips to her for a long time, all the while listening to her last, distorted thoughts about how she forgot her favorite sweater at school and wouldn't get it back, and how she left her bike outside even though she was told over and over again to put it away and felt bad about it now because Daddy was upset and she should have done what she was told, and how she had really been looking forward to meeting Daddy's friends at the compound, especially the other kids with powers. The thoughts continued, and faded away to nothing.

When Perry finally pulled away, Hallie's eyes had closed.

Holding Hallie after her birth. Watching her take her first steps. Hearing her speak her first word (it had been teese, in place of cheese). Taking her to the park and pushing her on the swing, her favorite. Driving her to her first day of school every year.

Everything.

Gone.

All that remained were the memories.

Tucking Hallie in at night. Watching Hallie's soccer games. Hugging Hallie after she scored the final point in the final game…

Holding her as she died…

Walter helped carry the bodies to the SUV. They silently loaded Perry's family into the back. Just before getting in themselves, Perry spotted a boy a few years younger than Jillian hiding in the bushes of the house next door. Perry gestured for him to come over, and when he did, he stole a glance into the back of the truck.

"Jillian?" he asked quietly.

Perry shook his head gently, and the boy lowered his head sadly. "You're Mace?"

Mace nodded. His face looked terribly sad. By then, Perry's emotions had extended beyond sadness. All he felt now was numb.

"Why don't you come with us?" Walter said.

Mace hesitated for a moment, stealing one more glance into the back. "Okay."

The three rode in silence for the entire trip. Perry was grateful for it. He didn't have anything to say. The slightest sound made his head foggy, anyway.

When they made it back, an eternity later, everyone had gathered outside. They were waiting for Perry. They knew what had happened.

Perry didn't want their sympathy. He didn't want to hear them say they were sorry, or that it would be okay. No matter how many times it was said, he knew he wasn't going to be okay.

Thankfully, they didn't give him any of that. Erica Harvard reached him first. There were tears in her eyes, but she didn't say anything. She wrapped her arms around his neck and hugged him tightly. Cole Ashton joined the tearful embrace. It was then that Perry realized that they weren't there to give him sympathy; they were there to grieve his family with him. That made it all the easier.

The Odaus came next. Even Graham jointed the embrace. Sawyer, Daniel, and Allan snuck their way in. Other small children clung to his legs. Baby Meg was crying somewhere in the group. Erica's unborn child kicked him from her belly. Hundreds of people surrounded him. Walter's hand rested on his shoulder. Perry saw Lemoore's sad face across the crowd.

They were all there for him. They were all there *with* him. He had lost his family, but this family was still here. It would be difficult, but he could survive. He could make it through this, because this family was there to help him.

The following week was the most difficult. Perry knew he had to get up and help the people that needed him, but he had no strength to even move. He laid in bed most of the week, and the others let him. No one asked him to come downstairs to work. No one even asked him a question about the medical equipment. Everyone who had taken his place for the time being figured it all out themselves or asked others for their advice.

He really appreciated the solitude. He couldn't face anyone, not while he was like this. Eventually, though, someone had to get him moving again. He assumed it would be Lemoore or Walter, but it wasn't either of them. He was grateful when his visitor came to him.

"Hey, Perry," Graham said, quietly closing the door behind him and pulling a chair up to the bed.

Perry didn't know how Graham knew to call him by his last name, but he was grateful for that, too. Anyone who called him Shawn just reminded him of Renee.

"I came to see how you're doing," Graham continued, "even though I can guess it's not too great."

He received no answer. Perry wasn't sure he was even capable of speaking anymore.

"I can't say I know how you feel, but I know that being separated from your family is the hardest obstacle for a person to overcome." Graham leaned forward, and took Perry's hand. There were tears in his eyes. This surprised Perry. The Graham Odau he'd been introduced to ten years ago was an angry man, a fighter. Now, he was an emotional mess. "I'm so sorry," he whispered. "I'm so sorry this happened to you. They didn't deserve it, and you don't deserve this." He paused. "Please say something."

"I thought Renee was Jack's mother," Perry murmured, barely even aware he was forming words.

Graham's mouth fell open. "What did you say?"

The thought had been on his mind for a long time, almost half the time he'd spent in solitude. Renee was supposed to be Jack's mother. He'd never said she wasn't, so she must have been! Why didn't he say anything? "I thought Jack was our son. Me and Renee. Jack never told me who his mother was, and I'd always assumed it was her. That's why I thought they'd be fine if I dropped you off at the compound first. I assumed Renee was Jack's mother, and that she and the girls would be okay in the short time I was gone. But now..." He shook his head. "I don't understand how he could have a different mother. I could never love anyone else the way I loved her. She was my soul mate. No one else could ever be."

Graham hesitated before speaking again. "You don't think...you don't think this event changed anything, do you? Do you still think Jack will be born?"

"I know he will," Perry said. "I feel his presence all the time, even though he's not here. He'll live. I just don't understand how." Neither of them spoke for a long time, but then Perry sat up, his eyes wide with realization. "Oh my God," he breathed.

"What?" Graham asked in alarm.

"Jack," Perry said. "He told Renee. He knew, and he told Renee!"

"Told her what?" Graham was confused, and he looked a little frightened upon seeing Perry's wild expression.

"That she was going to die!" Perry leaned closer to him. "Just before you came to my house that night, she told me that she knew something bad was going to happen. She wanted to leave the house and come here. And she'd been sick for a long time, full of anxiety and depression. Don't you see? Jack told her all those years ago that she and my children were going to die around the time of the outbreak, and she was trying to tell me." He dug his nails into his legs, hating himself. "And I didn't listen to her. I told her it would all be okay. And now they're dead!"

"You couldn't have known," Graham whispered. "It's not your fault."

"It is," Perry said. "I didn't listen to her. I followed my own faulty logic and it got my family killed." He fell back against his pillows, and for the first time since his teenage years, he wanted to kill himself. He wanted to so badly. Unfortunately, he couldn't die. That theory had been tested a long time ago. He could do whatever he wanted to his body and it would still regenerate. That only made him angrier. "Get out," he mumbled.

"What?" Graham said again.

"Get out!" Perry screamed, and Graham was quick to comply. Once again in his solitude, Perry thought about his sudden realization. So Renee had known, and she never told him. In all their years of marriage, she never told him she and the girls were going to die. How could he have tried to help them if she never told him? He suddenly felt a blinding fury aimed at his dead wife, so awful that he bit down on his tongue until blood flowed freely. But then he found that he could not be angry with her. His anger turned onto two other people, people who had tried to protect him ten years ago and then didn't tell him of this awful thing that was to come.

His future son, Jack, hadn't told him this. How could he not? Perry hated his son in this moment, and there was only one person he hated more.

That person was Hara.

12

Moving On

Walter Reifert

Renee Perry. Jillian Reynolds. Hallie Perry.

Those were the names written on the gravestones. They were buried under a willow tree on Lemoore's property. It was peaceful there, and as beautiful as any other.

More than a month had passed since Perry's family was murdered. The mood in and around the compound had taken on a sepulchral atmosphere after that. People were quiet, sad, and they had a right to be. Perry wasn't the only one suffering from the loss. It was a terrible thing that such a peaceful, innocent family had been slaughtered like stray dogs in an alley. The event caused everyone to stop and think: Would they come to the compound and strike them all down? Would anyone be spared? The solution was clear. We needed to take action before they took us down.

I dropped the daffodils to the ground, one over each grave. The flowers were growing along the walls of the compound, and they looked so nice that I decided to pick some and come here. Beautiful flowers for a beautiful family.

I had attended their funeral, but I still felt that my duty to them was not yet complete. They needed more than simply being put to rest. They needed assurance.

"I wish you all could be here with us," I whispered to the gravestones. "I'm sorry it had to end this way. I'm sorry you never had a chance." The sun peeked out from behind the clouds, and I raised my head to it, soaking in the warm rays of sunshine. I looked down again. "It wasn't fair. You never did anything wrong. It wasn't your fault the virus affected you." I sighed and brushed away my tears. "I'm going to make a promise to you, and I hope to God I can keep it. You didn't deserve to die. None of us did. Not my father, or my brothers, or anyone else. I am going to dedicate the rest of my life to our people. I am going to protect our race, to make sure that no one else dies the way you did. I'm going to find a place where we can all live in peace and without fear, somewhere where there are no humans. Not one more O Negative is going to be murdered. Not one."

A branch crackled behind me, and then Shauna stepped up beside me and slipped her hand into mine. She, too, had brought flowers. Wildflowers. Beautiful, purple wildflowers. She dropped one beside each daffodil, and then rested her head against my shoulder.

"No more," I whispered.

"No more," Shauna repeated.

I put a hand on Shauna's bulging belly. Flint's hand pressed outward and touched mine. I smiled lovingly. Shauna was six weeks pregnant. We were halfway there.

"Sad?" Shauna asked quietly.

"Yes," I said. "I'm sad."

"Reason?"

"They didn't deserve to die. I don't want anyone else to die like that."

"Die like John Tyler Ethan Anton? Renee Jillian Hallie?"

I smiled at her. "I don't want anyone else to die like them."

"You save them?"

"We're going to start making plans on a new strategy tonight. We're going to save as many as we can."

"Good person," Shauna said, hugging me.

"Thanks," I whispered into her hair, kissing her head.

Shauna abruptly pulled away from me and stumbled back, tripping over a tree root and falling to the ground.

"Shauna?" I said, alarmed. I crouched beside her and put a hand on her shoulder. "What's wrong, baby?"

Clutching her head, Shauna's entire body started shaking violently. "No...no... no..."

"Shauna, tell me what's going on!" I cried helplessly as I held her trembling body in my arms.

That was when she started screaming.

Shauna wasn't the only one Dr. Perry had to sedate. At exactly the same time, Sawyer had also started screaming. The siblings laid beside each other on separate tables in an observation room.

"What happened?" I asked Dr. Perry after they had both drifted off.

"It's hard to say," Dr. Perry replied. "But it was something that has a connection to the two of them, because they both felt it. I have an idea, but I won't know until they're calm enough to communicate."

He turned away, and so did I. "How are you?" I asked him softly. The first week after his family's death had been awful for him. He hadn't even gotten out of bed.

Dr. Perry shrugged and pretended to ignore me.

"Shawn," I said.

"Please don't call me Shawn," Dr. Perry whispered, still avoiding my gaze. "Renee was the only one who called me that."

I sighed. "Okay, but will you please answer me?"

Slowly, Dr. Perry raised his eyes to mine. His shattered heart was visible through them. "It still hurts," he said.

I nodded. "I know. It will never really stop, but it will get easier."

"That's how it's been for you?" he asked.

Again, I nodded.

"I never fully understood how it was so hard for you...why after a month you still hadn't improved. Now I get it."

"It will get better," I repeated. "And we're all here for you. We all love you. You're not alone."

"Thanks, kid," Dr. Perry whispered.

"But if you're ever feeling down, I mean, *really* down, please come talk to me. My biggest mistake was trying to deal with it alone."

Dr. Perry glanced my way. "You're a good kid, Walter."

For the next few hours, I talked to Erica and Cole. They were one of the quietest couples, but also one of the cutest. I asked about their baby. They were going to call him William Richard Ashton, after their fathers. Both Cole and Erica were very excited for their baby, who was due in a month. They then asked about my baby.

"Flint Jonathan Reifert," I said.

"Oh, that's a great name!" Erica said.

"Your dad's name was Jonathan, wasn't it?" Cole asked.

"Yeah, John. Shauna wanted to call him John, but..."

"You need closure," Erica finished for me. "It's understandable. It's a good name though."

"Is Flint Shauna's father's name?" Cole asked.

"No," I replied. "We just liked that name."

"What are Joe and Maia going to name their baby?" Erica leaned over her plump belly, resting a protective hand over William.

"They're going to name her Nicole, after Maia's mother," I said. "Her mom died during childbirth with her sister, Marlena. Maia was ten. I'm not sure what the middle name will be, though. Maybe Rebecca? That's Joe's mom."

"It seems like everyone's naming their babies after their parents," Erica said with a chuckle.

"That's because everyone's parents keep dying," I replied dryly. I glanced at Cole. "Why are you calling him William *Richard*? I thought your father tried to kill you."

"He did. But the father I had as a child was a much better man than he is now. I'm naming my son after the good Richard, not after the *new-and-improved* Richard."

I nodded. "That's understandable."

"Have you heard?" Erica piped in excitedly. "We now have six compound babies coming!"

I liked that term. Compound babies. It was catchy, and had a double meaning.

Glad to be back on the baby subject, I smiled. "Really? Who?"

"Well, there's an older couple—Jen and Nathan—who are due around the same time as Maia and I. They're naming their daughter Jaya. Such a pretty name."

Maia, Jaya. Different spellings, same sounds.

"Then there's Abe and Tracy. They're also having a girl. Ashley. A new couple bonded the other day. Your pal Scotty and a new girl named Marta. So young, yet so cute. They're what, fourteen? They're having a boy, and I think he said they're naming him Cody."

"I haven't seen Scotty in a while," I said thoughtfully. "It's good to hear he's found love too."

We talked more about what we thought our sons would look like, and then I was summoned back to the observation room.

Shauna and Sawyer were both awake when I got there. Sawyer sat playing with a toy car in Shauna's lap, while Shauna's mind wandered elsewhere. Her eyes were glazed over and nothing about her suggested to me that she had any idea what was happening around her.

"Well, I found out what's ailing them," Dr. Perry said grimly. "Their mother was just killed."

"What?" I said in horror. "When? Where? How?"

"I don't know what the circumstances were, but she was killed in the lab." He shook his head. "They felt her go. The feeling was so foreign and horrifying to them that they panicked."

I nodded, remembering that awful feeling. "How are they now?"

Dr. Perry glanced at the brother and sister. "As you can see, Sawyer is doing much better. He'll need some time to cope, but he'll be alright."

"And Shauna?" I whispered. "She's...elsewhere."

"Yes," Dr. Perry said. "But that's for an entirely different reason. About the same time that Angelina Skyler passed, Shauna and your baby made the mental bond that most pregnant women seem to make with the fetuses."

"Mental bond?" I hadn't heard about this yet.

"It's different with everyone, and in Shauna's case the bond happened very suddenly. That's why she started screaming. Her mind and the mind of your baby are now connected, and that's a very shocking thing to experience. She doesn't appear to be all there just now, but she'll come around. She just needs some time to process that she and the baby are now one mind."

"Why haven't I heard about this before?" I asked, confused. "From what I've heard, there are five other pregnant women here besides Shauna."

"It happens around the last half of the pregnancy, from what I've observed. Erica went through the same episode, but hers was very mild. Jennifer's case was bad, but she pulled through it before I arrived. Maia never felt anything, but that's not surprising. She doesn't feel a lot of things."

"Walter."

I looked over. Shauna was calling me from the table, her hand outstretched. I went to her and held her in my arms. "Everything's going to be okay, baby," I whispered, stroking her hair. "I'm here. Flint's here. We'll be alright."

"Mom," she whispered, resting her head against my chest. "Dead."

"Yes," I said sadly. "She's dead. I'm sorry."

"Mom," she repeated. "Dead. We. Dead."

"What?" I said, pulling away and staring at her. What did you just say?"

"We," Shauna said, her eyes blank. "Dead. All us. Dead."

"What is she saying?" I asked Dr. Perry as I began to grow scared.

"I'm not sure," Dr. Perry replied with concern.

"Maia Rudolph." Shauna looked at me. "Kill."

The next day's incidents left many of us wondering: Just what exactly did Shauna see in the lab to earn her a lobotomy? What did she mean when she kept saying we needed to kill Maia? What was Maia's part in my girl's broken mind?

It started when I was walking with Shauna through the den in the main residence. If I had known Joe and Maia were there, things wouldn't have gone so sourly. But I didn't know, and Shauna saw Maia.

I saw Maia to, but Shauna was already screaming and running towards her before I could react. "Shauna, stop!" I cried, even though it was pointless. The only thing she knew was that she had to get to Maia. And kill her.

Maia and Joe both started running when they heard the scream. They didn't need to look to know who it was. Joe pushed Maia through a door and slammed it shut. He turned and quickly transformed into a big black dog (He was getting better at shifting. He could complete a transformation in a matter of seconds now). The hair on his back rose and he snarled ferociously.

Shauna stopped a few feet from him, hesitating at the sight of the creature. I hung back a few feet. There wasn't any point in startling her; she would only start screaming and running again.

A look of recognition crossed the black dog's face, and the viciousness left him. He whined and stepped towards Shauna. Shauna reached out a hand and petted Joe's forehead.

I knew what was happening. The two of them had encountered each other in the lab before, and in this situation they were remembering it. As long as this reunion wasn't interrupted, Shauna would at least be calm enough to listen to me.

"Shauna!" Dr. Perry shouted from across the room.

Shauna shrieked and ran away from Joe. I groaned and rolled my eyes. Such excellent timing, Dr. Perry.

The chase for Shauna lasted roughly twenty minutes. Lemoore ordered everyone out of the den so he, Dr. Perry, and I could deal with her. All the doors were locked, so Shauna couldn't get out, but still she tried to escape. I didn't chase her. I knew it would only frighten her more. Lemoore and Dr. Perry refused to listen to me.

When Shauna finally sat down at a table to catch her breath, I waved the two men away so I could try to talk some sense into her. "Hey, Shauna," I called softly, hoping she wouldn't feel threatened by my approach. "You tired?"

Shauna's head snapped up, and she was out of her chair in a flash.

"No!" I started to shout, but she wasn't running away from me.

Her arms wrapped around me and she clung to me tightly. "Walter," she whispered.

"Hey," I said, hugging her back. Flint kicked in between us. "You've worn yourself out, haven't you?"

"Maia Rudolph," Shauna said, looking up at me desperately. "Kill. Kill Maia Rudolph."

"We're not going to kill Maia," I told her. "She's my cousin. Do you understand that? She's my family."

Shauna shook her head frantically. "Kill Maia Rudolph. Maia Rudolph kill!"

"I'm not going to let you—" Shauna put a hand over my mouth before I could finish. She then spoke very slowly.

"Kill Maia Rudolph." She paused, staring hopefully into my eyes. "Maia Rudolph *kill*."

That was the moment I started to understand. "Wait…what did you say?"

Shauna was suddenly ripped out of my arms by Lemoore, who then sat in a chair and held her on his lap. Shauna screamed and thrashed to no use.

"Hey!" I said angrily. "Let go of her!"

"We're just trying to help her," Dr. Perry assured me while pulling a syringe out of his jacket.

"Kill!" Shauna screamed as she thrashed. "Maia...*kill!*"

"She's trying to tell us something!" I protested, grabbing Dr. Perry's arm.

"She needs to be sedated!" Dr. Perry insisted.

"She needs to *speak*!" I shouted back.

Shauna took a deep breath, and then the words erupted out of her. "Kill Maia Rudolph or Maia Rudolph will kill us all!"

The silence that followed her declaration was vast. I was sure that people in adjacent rooms had heard and were pondering over the claim, listening in for more of an explanation. Actually, I think everyone in the compound had heard.

"What?" Dr. Perry breathed, the needle hovering over Shauna's arm.

Shauna saw the needle and shook her head furiously. She started whimpering. "No more drugs! Please...no more drugs!"

Dr. Perry paused at her words, and then put the syringe away. "Walter," he said, his eyes glazed over. "Take her to bed, please."

We laid in the dark together, hand in hand, nose to nose. For a while, we were silent. Eventually, I had to ask.

"What you saw in the lab, it was something about Maia, wasn't it?"

I felt Shauna nod in the dark.

"Something that told you she's going to kill us?"

Shauna nodded again.

"But you don't remember what you saw, do you? You just know that she's supposed to kill us."

"I'm supposed to tell you something," Shauna murmured. "But I can't remember what. They've kept me from remembering. I remember enough to warn you, though. To tell you what we have to do to survive."

"We're not going to kill Maia," I said. "I love her. We can keep her safe so she can't do whatever it is she's supposed to do."

Shauna shook her head. "We can't keep her safe. They're going to come for her, and when they do, it'll be too late. We have to end it now. We have to end *her*."

"We'll find another way."

"There is no other way, Walter."

"We're not going to kill her, Shauna."

There was silence, and then Shauna rolled over, turning her back on me. "It's her or all of us, Walter."

The shouts from outside woke everyone around three that morning. Shauna whimpered in the dark and clung to me. I told her to stay in bed and I, along with Lemoore, Dr. Perry, Cole, Joe, and Graham, went to investigate.

Outside the front door, screaming and pounding on the glass, was a man in his thirties. He was covered in blood. We knew he was an O Negative, so we opened the door and helped him in. His body had taken two bullets, and he collapsed moments after he came inside.

"Nick?" Cole said in confusion.

We all looked at him. "You know him?" Joe asked.

Cole nodded skeptically. "He's one of my father's secret service agents. Or at least he *was*. He helped me escape when my father ordered me killed." He knelt beside Nick. "Nick? Can you hear me? It's Cole. You remember me, right?"

Nick's eyes eased open, and he stared up at Cole. He was disoriented, but recognition flashed across his face. "Cole," he said, and smiled. "You have the beautiful wings."

"Yeah," Cole said. "The bird wings."

"No," Nick corrected. "The angel wings."

Cole paused, contemplating that. "What happened to you, Nick?"

"Your father found out what I am and what I did for you. He sent me to the Manhattan lab. I heard in their heads what they were planning to do, so I escaped and came here to warn you. They're coming for you!"

"How do they know where we are?" Lemoore asked in alarm.

"They don't yet, but it's only a matter of time before they figure it out. And they're planning a strike on your camp. That's why I'm here. You have to get ready for a fight. They're coming for a girl, and they'll kill anyone they can in the process."

"What girl?" Dr. Perry asked.

Nick thought. "I can't remember her name..."

"Maia Rudolph?" I knew it was her even without an answer.

His eyes lit up. "Yes! That's her! Maia Rudolph!" He looked around. "Do you know her?"

We all exchanged glances, but no one answered before Nick suddenly coughed up a mouthful of blood.

"I'm taking him downstairs," Dr. Perry said, getting help from Cole to lift Nick. "I have to remove the bullets or he won't have a chance."

Dr. Perry, Cole, and Joe took Nick away. Graham and Lemoore turned to me once they were gone. "I guess Shauna was telling the truth after all," Lemoore said.

"I knew she was," I replied curtly. I looked up and saw Shauna standing at the top of the stairs. I smiled, and she came down and sat with me while we waited. Nick screamed as Dr. Perry removed the bullets, and it felt as if the screaming went on for hours. Finally, it stopped, but it didn't ease the tension.

Joe came up a few minutes later and shook his head. "He didn't make it. He had lost too much blood. It was too late for Dr. Perry to save him."

Even though Nick died on Dr. Perry's examination table, we made sure that his death meant something. His warning didn't go unheeded. After a quick breakfast, everyone organized themselves into groups with people who had similar abilities to help each other train. Those with more experience would teach those with less. My group was the biggest. Of the three hundred or so people we had at the compound, over a hundred of us were present. Telepathic abilities were the most common ability among us, clearly. Lemoore and I split the group in half, each teaching about fifty. I took the liberty of talking to the younger kids, seeing

224

as I could relate to them better. Among my group were Scotty, Sawyer, Mace, Caroline Odau, and even little Daniel. It made me sad to think that even the toddlers had to train. None of us were safe. But it was comforting to know that even Daniel, who was not yet three years old, was at least as powerful as the others. At least the boy could protect himself when the time came.

There wasn't another shape shifter among us, or another person who had grown another body part, so Joe and Cole partnered up to work together. Joe worked on shifting into a winged animal, and Cole helped teach him to fly. Cole also had to work on his take-offs and landings, because so far they had been really clumsy, and hilarious to watch. Later, I saw them teaching each other how to use the sky and trees to their advantage.

Maia and Shauna were both telekinetic, so they took turns training so they wouldn't cause another squabble. Right now, Shauna was inside with Dr. Perry. Maia and two other women—I think their names were Heidi and Christiana—were working on keeping an object hovering in midair while fighting each other at the same time. I didn't know how they could multitask like that, because I sure as hell never could.

I paused in my teachings to watch Maia. She seemed to be having great difficulty controlling her ability. Unlike the other two, she couldn't fight and keep the object hovering at the same time, and was having a hard time just doing one of those things. I could see she was getting very frustrated. She kept biting her lip and scowling in a way that made me grin every time I saw it. Eventually, Heidi suggested to Maia that she take a break, and Maia plopped down on the ground with an angry sigh.

Erica and her small group of people were sitting around in the grass, talking and laughing. They were waiting to train after dark, when they would be most useful in a fight.

Practice went all day. We took breaks only at lunch and dinner times. By the end of the day, everyone except the group with super-senses trudged off to bed, completely exhausted. Shauna and I curled up in each other's arms and were asleep in no time.

Everyday more O Negatives were arriving. By the due date for Erica's and Maia's babies, we had over eleven hundred residents. The place became overwhelmingly crowded. Hundreds of people were sleeping outside and on every available floor space inside. We needed to move some place with a lot more space. People were going to keep coming and coming, and we were running out of room. We only had a tiny fraction of the O Negatives in the world living in our little, crowded community.

We prepared for a month, but there was still no sign of the supposed attack. Eventually, we were forced to address other matters.

Shauna, Erica, Cole, and I were sitting in the den with dozens of other people, watching the weather forecast. We monitored it closely because of the number of people sleeping outside. Erica had been acting strangely all day, and it got worse by the hour. Now, she was resting against Cole, squirming uncomfortably. Cole was tense too. He knew something was wrong with her. Finally, she let us know what it was when she started screaming.

"He wants out!" she shrieked, jumping to her feet and clutching her head. "He wants out! Out! Out! Out! Let him out!"

"Is she having the baby?" I asked, alarmed.

"Dr. Perry!" Cole shouted, and several others began calling for him as well. "Erica's going into labor! *Dr. Perry!*"

Dr. Perry came running. We all helped Erica downstairs and onto an exam table. Her screams had become low moans, but she was still clutching her head.

"Alright," Dr. Perry said to the rest of us. "I don't know what to expect with this birth, but I'm going to do my best. We need to get her prepped—"

"There's no time for that!" Erica cried, and moaned in pain.

"Just relax, Erica," Dr. Perry told her. "You're going to be fine. We're going to prep you now."

"No!" Erica shouted. "Willy's coming now! He's coming *now!*" The screams began again, and I looked away in embarrassment as Erica shoved her skirt and panties down to her knees.

Dr. Perry was so surprised that he barely managed to duck down and catch the baby as he slipped out. There were a few choked cries from William, but then he only cooed sweetly. I looked over at him and couldn't help but smile. He had tufts of black hair on his little round head, and had Cole's blue eyes. As Dr. Perry turned to hand William to Cole, I caught a glimpse of the pink, naked, wrinkly wings on William's back. They were featherless, tiny, and useless, but I knew that one day they would be just as beautiful and powerful as his daddy's.

Shauna and I left them then. They were both so happy to see their son, and neither of us wanted to interrupt that bond.

As we left, I looked at Shauna. I realized that we were both smiling, too.

We held hands as we returned upstairs.

Maia's baby came in the middle of the night. The screams from downstairs woke me up. I made sure that Shauna stayed in bed and I went to go see the new arrival. What would Maia's daughter be to me? My second-cousin? Whatever the relation, I was considering her my niece.

I missed the birth, and Dr. Perry reported that baby Nicole came just as quickly as William.

Nicole looked exactly like Don. The same thin face and slim body, the same hair and eyes. I didn't say anything about it, but when I looked at Maia I knew she was thinking the same thing.

Joe came up to me and slapped me on the back while I was holding the baby. He was grinning broadly from ear to ear.

"Congratulations," I told him, smiling in response.

"You're her godfather, right Walter?" Joe said enthusiastically.

"Uh..." That question caught me off guard.

"You have to be!" Maia declared from where she laid on the table. "Walter, *please*! I want Nicci to get to know you the way we know you!"

"Nicci would get to know me whether I accepted or not," I protested. "But okay. I'd be honored to be Nicci's godfather."

I went back to bed shortly thereafter. Erica accompanied me. Cole was upstairs asleep with William, so I walked her back to her room. As we climbed the stairs, she slipped her arm into mine. "You do realize that you're also William's godfather, don't you?" she whispered to me.

I laughed. Not only was I going to be a father at eighteen, but I was also going to be a godfather. To two children.

Two days later, Jen and Nathan were proud to present Jaya Alexa Thayer to the community. Everyone was thrilled to see the babies, symbols of hope for our people. The three families were constantly swarmed by admirers.

Regardless of Dr. Perry's fears, the O Negative babies seemed to be completely fine. They didn't show any signs of abilities yet, and Dr. Perry predicted those would start showing between ages one and four. The only problem was with poor baby William's wings. By day three he was crying around the clock as the feathers began to grow in. It was an incredibly itchy and painful process, according to Cole, but he claimed that as soon as the feathers grew in, William wouldn't be so fussy.

Our next surprise came the day after Jaya's birth. Maia, who had never had the telepathic bond to those she loved, suddenly started screaming.

"Marlena's dead!" she cried, and started sobbing. "She's dead! My baby sister! They killed her! *He* killed her!"

I knew who she was talking about. Uncle Don killed his own daughter. I was in shock, unable to believe my little cousin was dead. I watched silently as Joe and Erica tried to calm Maia down, and as I did so, Shauna came from behind me and slipped her hand into mine. I looked down at her. Her expression was scared. "Marlena's dead," she whispered. "Now they come for Maia."

13

Divided Families

Walter Reifert

They came two mornings later.

We received the warning from Cole, who had been flying with Joe. They were still several miles away, but they were coming all the same. They had guns. What did we have?

"We have our abilities," Lemoore assured the frantic crowd that had assembled in front of the compound. "We've been training for more than a month. We're ready."

"Not all of us can fight!" a woman in the crowd protested.

"No," Lemoore agreed, "we can't. But the majority of us can. We have powers that none of those soldiers have seen. We've learned to control the fire within. They've only seen what we can do when we're out of control. Let's show them what we can do when we're *in* control."

Murmurs of approval surged through the crowd.

"They're the ones who changed us!" Lemoore exclaimed, looking around at all of us. "They changed us, and then they took us! They took us away from our families, our friends. They locked us away. They tested us. Experimented on us. Tortured us. *Murdered* us." He looked around again. "Now, after all they've done, they're hunting down those of us who are still free and trying to live peacefully. They're coming for one of our own, and they're planning to kill as many as they can!"

"Why don't we just hand over Maia Rudolph?" a man demanded.

Maia tensed on one side of me, and Shauna gripped my hand on the other.

"Yeah!" another man agreed. "Maia's the only one they want! We hand her over and they'll leave us alone!"

There were shouts of agreement, but Lemoore just shook his head in disappointment. "Really?" he said. "You want to hand over one of your own? After what you've seen them do, you want to sink to their level?"

Silence.

"We will not give away our own," Lemoore said firmly. "Ever. This is how we are strong; when we're together. Our bond is one that cannot be defeated. We will stand together. We will stand together and fight them. We will show them that we will not stand by and let them take us down. We will show them that we are not weak. We will show them that we are strong! We are stronger than they think! We are stronger than *we* think! We are stronger than they are!"

Cheers and applause.

"We are not a threat, or a weakness, or a disease!" Lemoore pumped his fist in the air, and his voice boomed on. "We are O Negatives, and we are people, too! Our time to stand against them is now! Let's go show them—and the rest of our kind—just how willing we are to fight for our own freedom!"

Fight we did.

Win, we did not.

I made Shauna promise me she would stay inside. She was almost due, and I didn't want to risk her or our unborn child. So she hid in the basement level with the children, elderly, and anyone else unable to fight. There was a guard positioned at the top of the stairs to protect them, should anyone get inside the compound. But we weren't going to allow that to happen.

Erica and Maia were instructed to stay inside with their babies, but both insisted on fighting.

"You need me," Erica told Cole when we attempted to dissuade her. "I'll be a stronger pair of eyes and ears for all of us."

"This is my fault," Maia told us. "They're fighting for me. I'm not hiding inside."

When the shooting began ten minutes later, I lost sight of everyone I loved. I had never believed in God, especially since April 4, 2018, but I prayed to him anyway.

Dear God, if you exist, please take care of the people I love. Take care of my family. I don't care if I die. Let me die if it means they'll live. You already took my first family from me. Take me and let my wife and child live.

I was ready to die. I went into that fight knowing there was a good chance I wouldn't come out of it. I meant what I said in my prayer. I would gladly die if it meant the people I loved would live.

As I fought, I repeated their names in my head, so I'd always remember who I was fighting for.

Shauna, Flint, Maia, Cole, Max, Erica, Lemoore, Dr. Perry, Scotty, Damien, Berry, Jane, Sarah, Caroline, Graham, William, Nicole, Jaya, Allan, Daniel, Sawyer, Meg, Jazmine.

And in the back of my mind, another list of names was echoing from my subconscious.

Dad. Tyler. Ethan. Anton. Marlena. Renee. Jillian. Hallie. Nick.

Maia Rudolph

I don't know how it happened. I couldn't understand it. I froze. He caught me by surprise. It wasn't my fault!

Joe and I stuck together throughout the fight. At least, until Beast showed his butt-ugly face. Shane Gold and Joe had met twice before, and they apparently had a score to settle. Both had transformed into enormous dogs, and for a moment after making eye contact, the two of them were a tangle of fur and teeth.

I left Joe to settle his score with Beast. That was one quarrel I wasn't going to interfere with. I joined Erica, who was taking on three soldiers on her own. We dealt with them and continued onward. We were separated some time later as the fight backtracked into the woods, and I never saw another O Negative again. It was when a twig snapped behind me, and I whipped around, ready to fight, that I hesitated.

"Dad?" I said in surprise.

Why it surprised me so much to see him, I don't know and I never found out. But the surprise led to my hesitation. The hesitation led to my end.

Dad raised his arm and pulled the trigger of the strange-looking weapon in his hand. I expected to hear a bang and then feel horrible pain somewhere inside my body, but that wasn't what happened. There was an audible click, and then the dart struck my neck. I was on the ground a moment later, and unconscious a moment after that.

Graham Odau

Graham wasn't sure what he was doing in this fight. He had no ability. He couldn't fight like the others could. Sure, he had a gun, but what use was a hand gun against the automatic weapons the soldiers had? But his wife and girls were fighting, and while they were, so would he.

So far, the fight seemed to be going in their favor. Graham even managed to take down three soldiers without getting fired at. But he had lost the crew he'd been fighting with. He was entirely alone, and he hadn't seen a soldier in a while. Had he taken a wrong turn in the woods?

Fallen leaves crunched behind him. He jumped and whipped around, preparing to fire at will. He immediately lowered his gun. "*Jackson?*"

"Hi, Dad," Graham's son replied curtly, keeping his gun trained on his father.

"Jackson," Graham whispered. "What are you doing? Your mom and sisters are here! You're willing to risk them?"

"You're the one who brought them here," Jackson snapped.

"Have you killed anyone?"

"What's it to you?"

Graham shook his head helplessly. "Jackson...this isn't the way. Killing these people is not the solution."

"Then what is?"

"There are good people here, Jackson."

"There are good people out there, too, Dad."

"Please put the gun down and go home, son."

"No. You don't tell me what to do anymore. You have no right."

"I'm your Dad, Jackson! I'm just trying to help you!"

"You don't need to help me anymore, Dad. I'll help myself."

Graham sighed. "I'm trying to help our family too, Jackson."

Jackson's eyes narrowed and his lips turned up in a smirk, and suddenly Graham was afraid. "So am I."

Walter Reifert

I heard the gunshot, and although I didn't feel anyone go the way I had felt my family go, I knew someone I cared for had just died. I ran in the direction of the shot. There were no soldiers or O Negatives there. I saw a body lying face up on the ground. It was Graham, with his eyes still open and a bullet in his forehead. I gagged, but there was nothing in my stomach to throw up.

I noticed the young man standing a few yards away. He was a soldier, and his gun was trained on me. I didn't bother putting my hands in the air. These men were told to kill, and my surrender would mean nothing but an easy kill for them.

But the boy didn't shoot me. He stared at me for a long time, hard, pondering. And then I took a good look at him. Long, sandy-brown hair, and cold gray eyes. Those eyes... I had seen them before. I had seen this boy somewhere before.

The recognition was in the other boy's eyes too. Eventually, the boy lowered the gun and turned away. As he did, he called back to me, "Just this once, O Negative. Never again."

I stared after him. Had this boy, this boy who I recognized yet couldn't place, this boy who had just murdered another man, let me live?

Yes. The soldier let me live. But that didn't really matter.

More were coming.

Cole Ashton

Erica was screaming. I could hear her, but I couldn't see her. After the soldier shot me while I tried to protect her, I had lost all sight of her.

My heart was pounding. Blood was pouring out of my stomach. I blinked as fog obscured my vision, and then I realized it was my eyes failing me. I was dying. I was dying, and Erica was taken. At least William was safe...for now.

"Erica!" I tried to shout, but a clump of blood flew out of my mouth instead. I pushed myself up, only to be pushed back down by another soldier.

"You're dead already," the soldier said with a sneer, pointing his gun at my head. "I'm doing you a favor." His head snapped up to look at something behind me, and then he crumpled to the ground. A moment later, Walter was at my side.

"Cole!" He looked down at my bloodied body. "Oh, God! Cole!" He pressed down on my wound to stop the bleeding, making me cry out again and spit out another mouthful of blood.

"Took Erica!" I choked out through the blood clogging my throat. "Get Erica!"

"What?" Walter said in a panic. "What did you say? They took Erica?"

I nodded and spit out more blood. "Save...my family. Protect...William. Save Erica." I was unable to take another breath. I fell back against the ground, listening to Walter scream my name from above. I was sinking, falling away from the world. Walter was pounding his fist on my chest, but I couldn't feel it.

Because all the lights had gone out.

Walter Reifert

"Cole!" I screamed, and hit his chest again. "You are *not* dying on me! Wake up, God damn it!" I started chest compressions, but for several minutes I received no response from him. His glazed eyes stared up at me helplessly, and my anguished tears fell into them. Not Cole. Please, God, not Cole. I can't lose anyone else.

While I pumped, I looked around me. Most of the soldiers fell back several minutes ago, allowing me to finally observe the death toll. Bodies were covering the ground, almost like a carpet. The worst part was that most of the dead were from our side. We had trained for a month, but that hadn't made a difference. Our abilities meant nothing in this fight. They were nothing against guns. We had lost. We had lost our own to death, and Maia was taken anyway.

"Not you, too," I whispered to Cole, pumping harder. "I'm not going to lose you, too! Nobody else is going to die today!" Cole still wouldn't wake up. "Cole, please!" I sobbed. "If not for me, then for Erica! And William!"

A splatter of blood struck me in the face, and Cole's body heaved under me. His heart was started, but he was choking on his own blood.

"Look out, Walter." Dr. Perry was suddenly there, pushing me aside to do his job: saving lives. He injected Cole with a syringe full of regenerative blood, and when the gunshot wound was healed, Cole spit out the remaining blood clogging his airways. "Good boy," Dr. Perry breathed, patting Cole's shoulder.

"Erica," Cole said, his eyes pleading with ours.

"We'll get her back," I promised him. I turned to Dr. Perry. "You had perfect timing. What are you doing here, anyway? I thought you were staying near the compound."

Dr. Perry's eyes were haunted. "They got inside," he whispered.

"They—*what*?" My heart was pounding again. No. They couldn't have gotten inside. Because that was where—

I jumped to my feet. "I have to find Shauna," I said.

"If she's not dead by now, she will be soon," Dr. Perry replied. "Trust me. They opened fire on all the children."

"William!" Cole cried, and started sobbing.

"I'm going to find her," I repeated firmly, but froze when I heard a low growl. I slowly turned, and there was Beast, in the form of an enormous sandy-brown dog, back hunched, hair raised, teeth bared. Nervously, I retreated a step. Beast didn't seem to care who posed a threat and who didn't; he lunged for me anyway, jaws snapping.

I fell over backwards onto the ground and covered my face with my hands, but there was no need. A dark shadow fell over me, and then another dog, this one black, slammed into Beast and tackled him to the ground.

Shauna Skyler

Shauna knew what was going to happen before it did. She heard the gunfire and shouts from upstairs, and then the pounding on the stairs from above. So when the first soldier came through the door, Shauna had babies William and Nicole in her arms and had everyone else behind her.

She waved her hand at the soldier and he flew across the room, but his gun still went off. Several times. Screams erupted as bodies of children and parents fell. More soldiers came in, their guns already firing. Shauna waved them out of her way and made a run up the stairs, calling for the others to follow. Allan was right behind her, holding Meg and tugging Daniel after him. Jen followed with Jaya, and it wasn't until more kids started coming that Shauna realized she had lost track of Sawyer. At the top of the stairs, she stepped aside to allow others their escape, and she called down, "Sawyer! *Sawyer!* Up here!" And then she gasped. She gasped because she felt the exact same feeling she'd felt when her mother died. Only this time, it was her brother dying instead of her mother. She choked back her sobs, and then she started running. She was too late to save Sawyer, but she had others she needed to protect, too. She held the babies close to her, and ran.

She herded those she could outside, away from the soldiers. Outside, she took them to a place she and Walter had once found, a place in the woods where they could hide. But on the way, she was tackled. One soldier ripped William from her arms, and the other went for Nicole. Shauna waved him aside. She jumped up again, but the soldier who had grabbed William was already gone. So was Daniel.

She didn't waste any more time. She hid the dozen or so who remained in the brush and handed Nicole to Jen. She did not hide, though, no matter how much Allan pleaded with her. She had to find Walter. He was in danger; she could sense it.

To Walter she went.

Walter Reifert

Joe lost. Beast lifted him off the ground and threw his mangled body through the air. Poor Joe, who was dying, lay at our feet, unmoving. Beast, bloody but still strong, came for us next. I raised my hands and screamed, "Stop!" Only when Shauna jumped in front of us, shielding our bodies with her own, did I realize that I hadn't been the one to speak. But after she cast herself between us, I did scream. "No!"

I started towards her, but Dr. Perry caught my arm and pulled me back. Then I saw why. Beast had stopped his advance. He was staring at Shauna, his blue eyes wide in his dog face. I realized that he, too, had once met Shauna in the lab, and he, too, would not hurt her. He would not hurt her because they had both been hurt for the same reason.

Beast whimpered and lowered himself to the ground, his paws over his eyes. He didn't move again.

Shauna turned back to me, grief and fear written all over her face. "Sawyer," she whispered.

I saw the thought in her mind. "Sawyer's dead?"

Shauna nodded. She came to me, the tears flowing from her eyes. "Maia?"

"They took Maia," I told her. "Erica, too."

"They took William," Shauna said.

I looked back at Cole, who was being carefully lifted to his feet by Dr. Perry. "It's going to kill him," I whispered.

"They took Daniel, too," Shauna told me. "And lots of other people. Many more are dead."

"Walter."

We all turned at the sound of the voice, because everyone except for Cole had heard it before. And none of us liked that voice. "What the hell are you doing here?" I snarled.

Uncle Don trotted down the hill and stood before us, smiling his sick smile. "I came to see you. It's been a while. I'm glad to see you're looking well."

Shauna started to advance menacingly, but I stopped her. "Go," I said, pushing her away. "All of you, go. Please. Leave us."

Dr. Perry helped Joe, who had transformed into his regular form, to his feet, eyeing Uncle Don furiously.

"Hello, Dr. Perry," Uncle Don said cheerfully. "I'm glad you finally found your place of refuge. Sorry your family isn't here to experience it with you."

I was so impressed that Dr. Perry managed to turn his back on Don. He helped Cole and Joe back towards the compound, from where the last of the soldiers were retreating. Shauna hung back.

"Please be careful," she begged me, backing away slowly and placing her hand over her belly. "Please come back to me. I need you. *We* need you." Then she turned and ran.

"How've you been, Walter? It's been a long time."

I turned back to him and glared. "Well, I was doing great. That is until I came face to face with the man who killed my family."

Don blinked at me. "I didn't kill your family, Walter."

"You killed yours."

The smile never left Don's face, but something else flickered across his eyes. Anger. Sadness. Regret. He didn't comment, but he started walking towards me.

"Why did you take Maia?" I demanded, moving away from him. "What do you want her for?"

"That's none of your concern, Walter."

"Yes, it is. These are my people you're taking and killing. I'm trying to protect them."

"And you're doing a terrific job of that so far."

I stopped, my expression furious, allowing Don to come closer. "I know you're planning to use her to kill us. How do you plan to do that?"

Don also stopped. His smile became even more inviting, even more terrifying. "Why don't you come back with me, Walter? You'll be safer there and I can take care of you. You won't have the stress of protecting anyone else. You'll be free."

I laughed scornfully. "*Free*? I won't be free! I'll be in a prison cell! This place, here with my people, *this* is me being free."

"Come with me, Walter," Don insisted.

"I'm not going anywhere with you," I snapped, and I made the mistake of turning my back on him.

I heard him running for me, and I started running before he could catch up. It didn't work out so well. My foot slipped over a rock and I stumbled. Don tackled me, like he had tackled me all those months ago inside the lab. "All things end so much cleaner if you lie still and *stop fighting*!" he shouted at me as he struggled to pin down my squirming body.

"Get off!" I shouted back, but my arms were pinned beneath me. I could only try to wriggle myself free. "Get off—*ow*!"

Don had stuck me in the arm with a needle. "How many times do I have to tell you, Walter?" He asked as he injected me. "I'm only doing this in your best interest."

"Fuck you!" I replied through my teeth as the sleepy haze took over my mind.

"So ungrateful," Don said, and then leaned down to speak in my ear. "But do you know what? I'm saving your life. I know that you would try to come after me if I didn't take you, and you would be shot on sight if you did that. I'm saving your life, Walter."

"Saving my life so you can kill me, like you did the rest of us?" I retorted angrily, my eyes slipping closed.

Don started to reply, but a series of loud screams interrupted him. Someone tackled Don and I heard her slapping and kicking and screaming at Don. I heard Don run off, and then I was turned over onto my back. I blinked up and saw Shauna's scared face looming over mine.

Her voice was foggy, but I understood what she said. "Walter! You need to find me! You need to bring me back!"

14

Bringing Her Back

Walter Reifert

The sedative didn't keep me out for very long.

The body count was at fifty-six, many of them children. I knew it was a big number, but I could have sworn I'd seen more bodies than that while saving Cole.

Alongside the body count, there was also the count of those who were missing. Twenty-seven O Negatives were taken by the soldiers. Among them were Erica Harvard, William Ashton, Maia Rudolph, Daniel Marcus, and Max Murphy. No one knew if the missing were dead or alive, but we could only pray for the best and assume the worst.

After I woke up from a mid-morning nap, I took a walk outside. I took a walk down the rows of the dead.

I recognized every face. That was the hardest part; I knew all of them. I only saw a few faces that I had been truly close to, but I'd loved all of them. Berry Burnett was the first I came across. Damien was sitting beside him, holding his twin's hand. That was when the tears began. Unfortunately, Berry was only the beginning. A few bodies down was Sawyer. His pale face looked pained, and the rest of his body was bloodied and tattered. I shook my head at the sight of the young boy. "Why?" I whispered. Why did a child who had just started life have to have his life abruptly ripped away from him? It wasn't fair! None of it was fair!

A few rows down, I saw Jane, Sarah, and Caroline crowded around Graham's body. They were all weeping and holding each other, and I couldn't blame them. Word was that Graham's son, Jackson, was one of the soldiers who came here. Jackson had been the one to put the bullet through Graham's head. I'd be crying too if Tyler, Ethan, or Anton had been the one to kill Dad.

The last two people I laid my eyes on were the two who impacted me the most. Side by side, Scotty and Marta laid together. Their expressions were peaceful, and I knew they were in a better place together. Scotty held Marta's hand, and their hands were resting over Marta's belly. Over the bump that had just started to form. Over Cody.

Cody. The O Negative who would never be.

Covering my face, I ran inside. I bumped into people and walls as I did so, but I couldn't let anyone see me cry. I was one of the leaders; I was supposed to be strong.

When I reached my room, I was relieved to find it empty. I locked the door, sat on my bed, and sobbed. I sobbed for everyone we had lost, everyone I loved. I sobbed for everyone who was taken. I sobbed for everyone who was grieving.

I sobbed for all of us.

I cried for an hour and threw up twice. I almost threw up a third time, but all that came up was spit and stomach acid. After that, I managed to pull myself together. It was hard, but I managed.

I slowly and painfully made my way down to the basement, where I knew I would find Shauna. Somehow, when the two of them saw each other during the fight, Shauna had deactivated the chip in Shane Gold's brain. He was recovering under the watchful eye of Dr. Perry; however, when I arrived, I was relieved to find that Dr. Perry was absent.

"Shauna," I murmured, and went to her by Shane's bedside. Shane was awake, but just barely. Dr. Perry wanted to keep him sedated until we were sure Shane was no longer a threat. I smiled at him. "How're you feeling?"

Shane forced a smile in return. "Okay," he said. "But I've been better."

"I'm glad to hear it," I replied, slipping my arm around Shauna's waist.

"I'm sorry I tried to kill you," Shane said. He lifted his hand slightly.

"No problem," I said, reaching out and shaking it. "It wasn't your fault."

Shane was a tall, slim man in his twenties with shoulder-length golden-brown hair and blue eyes. His hair and eyes reminded me of the giant dog that tried to take my life, but I shrugged the feeling off. That wasn't Shane; that was Beast. And Beast was gone now.

Reaching up, Shane scratched his beard that was too long and heaved a sigh. "So you're Shauna's mate, right? And it's Walter?"

"Walter Reifert." I nodded. "Pleased to meet you."

"And you." Shane peered at me for a while. "You're probably wondering how I know your girl."

"You met in the lab," I said.

Shane nodded. "We got busted for the same thing. They put these damn chips in our heads to shut us up."

"What you saw has something to do with my cousin," I told him. "Maia Rudolph."

Wincing, Shane asked, "Maia Rudolph's your cousin? *Ooooh,* sorry 'boutcha."

"What did you see?" I asked.

"We have to kill her, man," Shane said. "Or else she'll kill us."

"What did you see?" I demanded impatiently.

Looking at Shauna, Shane nodded. "That's something she needs to tell you."

"She can't tell me," I snapped. "She doesn't remember."

"That's why you need to help her remember," Shane said.

I looked at Shauna, who was staring pleadingly into my eyes. "I could kill you," I whispered, caressing her cheek.

"If you don't do it, everyone will die," Shauna replied softly.

I glared at Shane. "If one of us dies, it's on you."

Shane smiled. "I trust you, man."

I turned back to Shauna again. "You're sure you want to do this?" I was scared. I didn't want to kill myself in the process, as Lemoore nearly had. But most of all, I didn't want to kill Shauna and our son.

Shauna nodded. "Please," she whispered. "I owe my mother and brother that much."

My hands shaking, I reached up and placed them on the sides of her head. "Close your eyes," I whispered. "And breathe."

She closed her eyes and took a deep breath, and I did the same. *Please*, I prayed, this time to my father. *Give me the strength to save her and our unborn child.*

"Walter?" Dr. Perry came into the room and saw what we were doing, and he started shouting, "Walter, no! You'll kill the both of you!" But by the time he pulled us apart, I'd already found what I was looking for.

We both crumpled to the floor.

Shauna Skyler

When I finally woke up, the shock caused me to clutch my head and scream. The shock passed quickly, but the shivers didn't. I wrapped my arms around me and curled into a ball. Why did everything hurt? Why was everything so bright? Why was everything so loud?

"Walter!" Dr. Perry and Lemoore were both screaming the name.

Oh, no. Walter was hurt. But as much as I loved him, I couldn't worry about him right now. There were bigger, worse things to worry about.

Before I rose, I put a hand to my belly. It was so huge, something that would take getting used to, assuming I didn't give birth in the next few days. Flint. That was our son's name. He was going to be beautiful.

"Shauna?" Dr. Perry was peering down at me in concern. "Can you hear me?"

I couldn't help it. I started screaming again. Dr. Perry sedated me a minute later.

"It's a machine," I told them all after I woke up again.

Walter was fine. He had a seizure after bringing me back, but he was okay now. Thank God.

"What kind of machine?" Lemoore asked dubiously.

I took a deep breath. "Dr. Rudolph did something to Maia and Marlena while they were still in utero. He mutated their genes and then gave them a dose of the Colician virus when they were about five."

"The what virus?" Walter said.

"The Colician virus," Dr. Perry said. "It's what the virus that changed us is called."

"Since their genes were mutated inside the womb, they were different from us," I continued. "They never showed any symptoms, and their abilities were very difficult to use. Maia could only use hers when she was under emotional pressure, mainly when she was angry. Marlena could only use hers when she slept. But there's something more to them, something deadly."

"They're far more powerful than any of us," Lemoore concluded, nodding. "They just never knew it. Neither did we."

"You don't even understand the extent of their abilities," I said. I looked at Dr. Perry and Walter. "None of you do. They never felt it, but their connections are there. Maia has a connection to Joe, and to Nicole. And to everyone else."

"What are you saying?" Walter asked nervously.

"They don't just have a telepathic connection to the ones they love," I said grimly. "They have a telepathic connection to every O Negative in the world."

I gave them a moment to process it all. Everyone was silent for what felt like minutes, and then Walter asked, "That's what you saw, wasn't it? You found out about Maia and Marlena and they put the chip in your head."

I nodded. "They already tried to kill us using Marlena, but it wasn't likely that it would work. She's young; she couldn't handle the strain. She died in the process."

"The process of what?"

"They built a machine that connects to Maia's and Marlena's minds. The machine amplifies their abilities, allowing the connection to all of us to be thousands of times stronger. Now, the humans fear that we've become too dangerous, too unpredictable. With the machine and Maia's mind combined, the doctors will amplify Maia's ability and send out a high frequency pulse...that will shut down the brain of every O Negative."

There was more silence, longer than the last. Finally, Lemoore muttered, "Kill Maia Rudolph or she'll kill us all."

I nodded. "I never wanted to take an innocent life, but no matter where we run... no matter where we hide...they'll keep coming for her."

"So what do we do?" Dr. Perry asked the group.

"It's obvious, isn't it?" Walter said. "We're going to the lab. We're going to get Maia back and destroy the machine."

He left the room quickly, and I knew he was angry. The others left soon too, and I sighed to myself. Sure, we could go to the lab to get Maia. But getting her back wasn't as easy as any of us thought.

Walter Reifert

"You saw what just happened to us in a fight!" Dr. Perry protested. "Fifty-six dead, twenty-seven missing!"

"We have to go, Dr. Perry," I insisted.

"More of us will die!"

"We'll all die if we don't!"

"We are not prepared for this! We couldn't defend our own home! Do you really think we'll be able to lead an assault?"

I stood defiantly. "Yes."

Dr. Perry shook his head. "You're crazy!"

"Maybe so," I said. "But I'm not going to hang around here, waiting to die."

"Walter, he's right," Lemoore said softly. "We're not capable. We'll all be killed before we even get close."

I shook my head. "Well, *I'm* going to fight. You two can do what you want. But I *know* there will be people who will stand with me."

Lemoore's eyes narrowed. "We'll see about that."

Everyone was silent after I finished explaining the situation. They were scared, scared of dying but scared of fighting. I looked around, hoping—*praying*—that somehow there would be those willing to fight.

"We have to take the fight to them this time," I insisted, my voice becoming more and more desperate. "It's our turn to strike."

Again, only silence.

"We all know someone who has died," I said, losing faith in them. "We've seen people we love die. If we don't fight, that'll be all of us." Nobody responded. "I'm going to fight. I'm going to fight for my family; John Tyler, Ethan, and Anton Reifert. They were all murdered in the Beginning. Whoever's with me, and will fight in honor of those who have died, please step forward. *Please.*"

Shauna immediately stepped forward. "I'm fighting for Angelina and Sawyer Skyler." She took my hand.

We looked out at everyone hopefully. We waited, but no one came forward. I looked at Shauna hopelessly. Would we be the only volunteers? I wouldn't let Shauna go if that was true. I wouldn't risk it. I sighed in defeat and lowered my head, but then I heard a voice in the crowd.

"I'm fighting for Berry Burnett." Damien stepped forward.

"Nick Matheson," Cole said.

"Marlena Rudolph." Joe. "Ben and David Murphy."

"Scotty DuPierre and Marta Thomson."

"Graham Odau."

"Alec Marcus."

There was a pause, and I looked around at who we had so far. Cole, Joe, Damien, Sarah, Jen, Allan, Shauna, and I. We weren't doing bad, but we needed more than that.

Suddenly, I heard a voice I was certain I would not hear.

"Renee and Hallie Perry, and Jillian Reynolds." Dr. Perry had come forward.

I smiled at him gratefully, and he nodded in return. *I'm with you until the end,* he told me.

Glad to hear it, I replied.

Following Dr. Perry's move, Lemoore also stepped forward. "Every Colician who has died as a result of this fight."

In the end, we had enough volunteers.

I held Shauna close to me that night, as I had every night, but this time was different. The connection was stronger. Shauna was back. *My* Shauna. The frightened, broken girl I'd first bonded with was gone. In place of her was the woman with whom I was meant to be. With whom I was always and forever meant to be.

"Thanks for finding me," she whispered in the dark.

"'Twas my pleasure, ma'am," I replied, my embrace tightening.

"I'm scared," she said suddenly.

"Of what? What we're going to do tomorrow?"

"No. I'm afraid that I'll go to sleep and won't wake up again. That that other girl will take my place again. I'm afraid I'll fall asleep and be trapped in the depths of my own mind again."

"That won't happen," I promised her. "And if it does, I guess I'll just have to go find you again."

Shauna turned over in my arms. We locked eyes in the darkness. "I'm scared for our child, Walter. For our people."

I leaned forward and kissed her. "We can't live our lives in fear, Shauna. I know it's easier said than done, but a life of fear is no way to live. It's just what they want."

"What happens if we can't free our people?" Shauna asked me restlessly. "What happens to us?"

I shrugged. "I don't think about it. I don't like to think about the alternative."

"Where will we go?" she whispered. "When we are free, where will we go? How will we keep our lives separate from the humans? We can't live together; that's clear enough in itself. Where could we go where we'd be at peace with ourselves and the world?"

Again, I shrugged. "Maybe we could all relocate to a part of the world where we could all stay, and the humans could move away to someplace else."

Shauna shook her head. "That won't work. Remember after World War II? The Jews moved to Israel and pushed the Palestinians aside. Do you also remember how that ended? The Arabs exterminated them all."

She had a valid point. "I don't know what we'll do," I admitted. "But we'll figure something out. We should sleep now. We've got a lot going on tomorrow."

"What are you going to do when you see Don?" Shauna asked me as she closed her eyes.

I didn't answer. I didn't know.

It was me who had difficulty sleeping that night.

15

The Counterattack

Maia Rudolph

I was so tired. My eyelids were blocks of concrete. When I managed to lift them, I could barely see anyway. Everything was white. I couldn't move. Dad moved into my small field of vision and peered into my eyes for a while. "Maia?" His voice was distant, hazy. "Can you hear me?"

The blocks of concrete came crashing down.

When I awoke a long time later, I was still exhausted but I could keep my eyes open. I was still in the white place, and something was buzzing around my head. I tried to move, but my entire body was paralyzed.

"Maia."

My eyes drifted to the left. Dad was sitting in a chair, watching me. His eyes were tired, and sad. He should be sad. He killed his daughter. My sister. "Why am I so tired?" I demanded.

"That's just the drugs we gave you," Dad replied.

"Why can't I move?"

"That's the drugs, too."

I stared at him. "Why are you doing this?"

Dad lowered his eyes. "You had the baby?"

"Yes."

"What does she look like?"

I paused. "She looks like you."

Dad raised his eyes again. "What's her name?"

"Nicole," I said. "But Joe and I call her Nicci."

Dad didn't reply. He walked over to me and started futzing with something over my head. The buzzing grew louder.

"Dad," I said as loudly as I could, "why are you doing this? Why are you going to kill everyone?"

Sighing, Dad said, "Because you're dangerous to yourselves and to everyone else."

"So you're going to kill us? Is that really the only solution?"

"Yes."

Angrily, I shouted, "You already killed your wife and your daughter! Are you really going to murder you granddaughter, too?"

Dad hesitated. "You'll kill every O Negative with this machine; every O Negative except for you. And I'll do whatever I have to to protect you."

That was when the world went black forever.

Walter Reifert

We were in the woods, hidden from the snipers on the roof of the lab. This was it. If we failed, our kind was doomed. We knew what to do; we were waiting for the signal. Joe and Cole would tell us when to advance.

Shauna stood beside me, her hand gripping mine. When I looked around, I realized that everyone was holding hands. It made me smile. We finally accomplished what I believed would have won us the last fight: we connected. Not just our bodies, but our minds. This connection was what made us strong. It was what made us *us*. It was what made us capable of winning this fight.

The snipers on the roof all looked up suddenly, and then they were shouting and pointing their weapons towards the sky. A moment later, Joe and Cole landed, and easily took out the eight men. Cole then looked out at us and motioned for us to move in. Our presence was still unknown. That wouldn't last for long, though. Better get moving…

Silently, we all ran into the lab. All six hundred of us.

Getting in unnoticed was the easy part. It was continuing to go unnoticed that was the hard part.

The alarm sounded less than two minutes after our entrance. A doctor saw us and set it off before we could stop him. Once the buzzer went off and the red lights started flashing, screams of excitement and eagerness sounded throughout the building. I even heard some improvised battle cries.

Shauna, Joe, and I left the group to work on disarming the doors to allow all imprisoned O Negatives to escape. Cole would have gone with us, but he was too eager to find Erica and William. In the meantime, we went to find Maia.

Shauna was the only one in our group who knew where the machine and my cousin were. She was our greatest asset. She knew every turn, every door. For miles we seemed to run, following Shauna as she took us into elevators, through doors, and down hallways. All was going well; at least we thought so.

The first doctor came out of a prisoner's door, brandishing a tranquilizer gun as he did so. Joe was unconscious on the floor in a second. The next second, Shane was running out of the elevator, yelling for us to run. I was knocked unconscious after taking an elbow to the face a moment later.

Shauna Skyler

I knew where I was going. I'd lost Joe and Walter, but that didn't stop me. Getting to Maia Rudolph and the machine was the best way to help them right now. We didn't have long. Maia had been missing for a day; the machine would be activated soon.

The doctors weren't following me anymore. Shane was holding them off so I could get down to the bottom floor. I was grateful, but I couldn't help but think that he had probably given his life to ensure that I fulfilled our mission.

I made better time on my own. My pregnant belly slowed me down, but I didn't have Walter and Joe to worry about losing. I'd already lost them.

The room I was looking for had a door like any other in this place, but the inside was much bigger and much different. Walter and Joe would have wandered past it, searching for a door that stood out, maybe made of a different material or color, or maybe with a sign that read **AUTHORIZED PERSONNEL ONLY**. I knew better. This whole facility was for authorized personnel only; there needn't be signs saying so.

I found it quickly, and I waved my hand to make it open. When I stepped inside, my blood turned to ice.

Being in this room was bringing back all the memories I had of my time in captivity. My time with Dr. Rudolph. All the needles, the drugs, the restraints… I wrapped my arms around myself and shivered. But I had to get a grip quickly, because the thing that frightened me the most was right in front of me. And it was already turned on.

Maia was pumped full of so many drugs that she was in a coma. IV's protruded from her arms, her legs…her neck. All around her, the mighty machine roared with life. The machine was in the shape of a transparent dome, surrounding Maia in order to amplify her deadly brain waves. A metal plate cupped Maia's head, waiting to suck all the juice out of her. Computers of all sorts were situated around the dome, flashing lights and messages and equations.

I knew what I had to do. I didn't want to, but I didn't have any other choice. Walter would understand. He would forgive me. It was what I had to do in order to save our people.

I went to the biggest computer and began typing. The process would take a while to get through, and would have multiple failsafes, but I could do it. That is, assuming that no one interfered with me.

The gunshot made me jump. The pain made me clutch my stomach. The cough made me spit out a mouthful of blood.

Walter Reifert

The pain caused me to wake. I gasped and clutched my stomach, but when I pulled my hands away, there was no blood. And no wound.

"Walter?" Shane was in human form again. He was gently slapping my face, trying to bring me out of my daze. "Walter, it's okay. They're gone now. Can you stand up? Joe's still unconscious..."

"No," I whispered, but I wasn't talking to Shane. Shauna had been shot in the back, with an exit wound over her belly button. Shauna was bleeding to death. And so was my baby.

Shauna Skyler

My baby was screaming. I could hear his cries of pain in my head. I tried to scream with him, but there was too much blood in my mouth. And the blood kept coming. I was dying. So was Flint.

I have no idea how I turned, or how I even managed to stay on my feet that long, but I did. And when I did, I saw Dr. Rudolph was the one holding the gun. His eyes wandered over my pregnant belly, but his calm, resolved expression never changed. Go ahead, Dr. Rudolph. Shoot a pregnant girl. It makes no difference, because she's an O Negative.

"Shauna," he said, and caught me as I went down on my knees. "You're still fighting. You were always fighting. Why?"

My pain gave me anger. My weakness gave me strength. Taking Dr. Rudolph's hand, I placed it over the wound on my belly. Over my baby. He resisted, but I held him there. Leaning forward, I managed to choke out in an airy whisper, "Because I have something worth fighting for."

Dr. Rudolph pulled his now bloody hand away from me, and he held the gun to my head. "I'm sorry," he said.

The gun went off, but after Walter tackled him. The bullet whizzed past my head and struck the wall. I tried to speak, but I was choking on my own blood. I collapsed to the floor, writhing as I gasped for breath.

Walter Reifert

I had never been so angry in my life. Even when my family was murdered, that anger couldn't be compared to this rage. I punched Uncle Don. I beat him until his face looked like it had gone through a meat grinder. And even when I knew I'd gone too far, I continued to pummel him. I couldn't stop. He put a bullet through my girl and my baby. I was going to kill him.

In the end, Joe peeled me off of him. I was still punching and kicking, but Joe calmed me down. "He's not worth it, Walter. Leave him. Go be with Shauna."

It was at that time that I realized I was crying. Silently. The tears ran down my face in rivers and formed pools on the floor. It wasn't enough that Don killed my father and brothers. No; he had to kill my girl and child, too. Why not? Just kill them all and you'll kill me, too.

I fell to my knees beside Shauna. Her eyes had closed, leaving a gaunt, bloody corpse in her place. But she wasn't dead. Not yet. I took her bloody hand and held it in mine. She opened her eyes and gazed up at me, her blue eyes distant. There was nothing I could do for her or our son. Nothing to do but hold them until they passed. Would I be able to bear letting them go in the way I'd let go of Dad and my brothers? Could I keep it together enough to find a safe place for our people? The answer was no. If Shauna died, I would die.

Shauna tried to speak, but more blood came out of her mouth instead of words. Slowly, she reached up and touched my face. Caressed it. Her blood left a streak on my cheek, but I didn't mind. It was a part of her. I closed my eyes and willed myself to stay in this moment. I couldn't. My grief was too much.

Shauna held my face, and she whispered two words in her head. *Finish it.*

My eyes opened. I beheld Shauna's pleading gaze, watched in agony as her eyes closed again. She would be dead, along with our son, in a matter of minutes. The best thing I could do to honor them would be to complete what they died for.

I went to the computer, the computer beside which Shauna had fallen. There was a series of options available to me on the screen, but I didn't know which I needed to select.

"Walter," Shane said hesitantly.

I turned on him. "You found this machine before. How do I shut it down?"

"Walter…" Shane's face was pained. "It's not as easy to shut down as you think."

"What are you talking about? Just tell me what I need to do!"

"Don't do it, Walter," Don said from his bloody pool on the floor.

"Shut up!" I snarled. "Give me a reason not to!"

"If you shut the machine down before its purpose is completed, you shut Maia down, too."

I stared at him, the horror of the decision I would have to make coming into focus. "You're saying that if I shut the machine down now, I'll kill her?" I looked to Joe. The same horror I was feeling was written all over his face.

Don nodded. "Yes. You'll kill her. *So don't do it!*"

"If I shut the machine down, my cousin dies. If I don't, then we all die." It wasn't fair. Making that choice wasn't fair. But it was one I had to make. With a terrible grief in my heart, I turned back to Shane. "Show me how to shut it down."

"No!" Joe cried.

Shane caught him as he rushed forward. "Joe, you won't get to be together either way," he whispered. "She's going to die one way or the other. Don't let it be for nothing."

Joe's face held the worst grief I had ever seen. He turned away slowly, walking stiffly towards the door.

Shane turned back, pain in his eyes too. "Let me do it," he pleaded.

"No," I said forcefully. "She's *my* cousin."

"All the more reason for me to do it."

"No," I repeated. "I have to do this."

Sadness clouded over Shane. He reached out a hand and grasped mine. He showed me what I needed to do. "I'm so sorry," he whispered. "No one should ever have to make the choice that you're making."

Without replying, I went to the computer. I ignored Don's pleas for me to stop, until he blurted, "Don't kill my family!"

I turned to him in shock. Angry tears popped into the corners of my eyes. It was a horrible thing to say, but I said it anyway: "You killed mine."

Don was speechless, and I didn't wait for him to argue more. I selected the option labeled END PROGRAM. When the next box popped up, I clicked yes and then typed in Don's password: mytwogirls. The computer screen went black, as did all the other computers in the room. As the machine began its shutdown procedure, I looked to my beautiful cousin. She was so peaceful where she sat. "I'm sorry, Maia," I whispered, and then I felt her go.

Joe started wailing and crumpled to his knees. He clutched his head and sobbed. Back at the compound, I knew baby Nicole was crying just as hard.

I held in my tears. I was not going to show Don any more emotion. This was his fault. I may have been the one to pull the plug, but he plugged her in. *He* was the murderer. Maia's death was on *his* hands, not mine.

A hand landed on my shoulder. It was Dr. Perry. He looked at Maia's lifeless form across the room. "She's gone?" he asked quietly.

I nodded.

"Shauna too?"

"Not yet."

Dr. Perry started to go to Shauna, but I caught him by the arm. I stared at his belt, where a stolen gun now hung. My anger returned. I took the gun and rounded on Don. For ten seconds, I allowed my fury to take control of me. I pointed the gun at his head, and thought about how great it would feel to pull the trigger. But I didn't. No; I didn't give Don that satisfaction either.

When he realized that I wasn't going to—that I was *unable* to—pull the trigger, Don asked me to. "Do it. Please. There's no point in letting me live."

"No," I said, unmoving, "there's not."

"Then kill me," Don whispered. The blood on his face made him look all the more pathetic.

I wanted to. I *really* wanted to. But I had never killed anyone in this war and I planned on keeping it that way. "Your life isn't mine to take," I said, and I handed the gun back to Dr. Perry.

Dr. Perry stared at the weapon, both desire and hesitation in his eyes. He looked to me in confusion, but he found the answers written on my face. Stepping forward, he dropped the gun on Don's chest. "Take Shauna and wait for me outside," he told us.

"What are you doing?" Don asked as Shane scooped up Shauna.

I heard him tell Don as we left, "You killed your family. Not only did you kill mine and Walter's, but you killed your own. *Your own family.* How can you live with that?"

Just outside the door, I lingered behind to hear the rest of the conversation.

"There's one bullet in there," Dr. Perry continued. "I'll leave the decision up to you what to do with it." A moment later, Dr. Perry came out and ran into me.

"Where do we take Shauna?" I asked. "Is there any chance we can save her and the baby?"

"There's always a chance," Dr. Perry told me, and we followed after Shane and Joe.

It wasn't long after that that we heard the gunshot. I knew who was dead.

I didn't feel him go.

16

The Revival

Walter Reifert

Shauna was awake when we detoured into an operating room. She woke up because she needed to cough up another pint of blood.

"Set her on the table," Dr. Perry ordered, and went to retrieve the necessary instruments for the operation.

"Is there absolutely no way to do a natural birth?" I asked again.

"They'd both die before the baby made it out," Dr. Perry said.

Shane set Shauna on the operating table. Shauna coughed up more blood and struggled to sit up. "She can't breathe when she's laying down," I told him when he tried to push her back down.

Dr. Perry came back with a scalpel, a scissors, a syringe, and a role of gauze. "Sit on the table so her head will rest on your leg," he instructed me.

I did what he said. Shauna had an easier time taking in air, but it was still difficult. She managed to smile up at me.

"She needs anesthetic," Dr. Perry said, nodding to me.

Nodding in reply, I placed my hands around Shauna's face and took away all her ability to feel pain. Her face smoothed out, even looked relieved.

"I'll have to do this quickly," Dr. Perry muttered to himself. "Neither of them have much time." He looked up at me as he raised the scalpel. "Don't let her look."

I looked away as he started cutting, and Shauna and I held eye contact for the entire operation. Shauna was calm, relaxed. Blood continued to flow out of her mouth, but that didn't faze her. She smiled up at me. *Flint's going to be okay,* she whispered, and she sounded...happy.

"I know," I whispered back.

After listening to some very unpleasant sounds coming from Dr. Perry's operation, I heard Dr. Perry call, "Shane."

Shane came and accepted what Dr. Perry gave him. I only caught a glimpse of it, but a glimpse was all I needed to know we were too late. Shane bundled the snow white baby in his own shirt. He rocked him in his arms. Blood stained through his shirt. Shane looked up and caught my eye. His face said it all.

The baby, Shauna said urgently, trying to sit up. *Where's my baby?*

"Shhhh," I shushed, keeping a steady hold on Shauna's mind. "The baby's...the baby's fine."

Don't you dare lie to me!

I didn't want to, but I had to. "He's fine."

"It's not too late, Walter," Dr. Perry said as he loaded a syringe full of his blood.

"Yes, it is," I whispered, shielding our words from Shauna.

Dr. Perry shook his head, and suddenly, he smiled. "It's never too late." He injected Flint's dead, shriveled body with the blood.

We waited. It felt like years passed, and still, nothing happened. I shook my head finally. "He's gone."

"No," Dr. Perry said firmly. "Don't give up on him. Give him some time."

I gave him time. I gave him plenty of time. And then, miraculously, I heard his first cry. "Oh, dear God," I breathed, letting the tears come. We all laughed and cheered and cried as Dr. Perry injected another dose of regenerative blood into Flint, and then a third into Shauna. "Thank you," I whispered as the wounds from the bullet and C-section healed. "Thank you for saving my family."

Dr. Perry was still smiling. "Don't give up on them," he told me. "Don't ever give up on them. Now go meet your son."

That night, there was a celebration at the compound. We rescued exactly seven hundred and eighty-five O Negatives. Before we led our counterattack, seven hundred and eighty-five O Negatives were being held in the lab. We went around and counted the people who led the attack. Six hundred and eighteen. Before we left, we had six hundred and eighteen volunteers. We had rescued everyone from the lab. Other than Maia, we had no fatalities.

We had won.

Everybody from the lab wanted to meet the young man who led the attack. They all wanted a glimpse of the eighteen-year-old who defied the soldiers. They all wanted to see me. I spent hours introducing myself to newcomers. People grasped my hand. People hugged me. People cried when I told them how I almost lost my child and soul mate during the attack. The best thing I saw on the faces of everyone that night were the smiles. The love. There was no emotion other than happiness that was exchanged that night. Seeing such a love, such a bond, between my people left a light feeling inside of me. I found that I was beaming, but it took me seeing Cole, Erica, and William in a tight embrace to notice it. My eyes wandered over the crowd, and I spotted Joe cradling Nicci. He met my eye and forced a smile, but I could see the sadness there. The emptiness. It was the first negative emotion I had seen since our return.

My heart ached for my cousin and her grieving family. Her child would never know her mother. Maia would never get to watch her daughter grow up. Joe would never have another love. All these thoughts and more crushed my heart, but I told myself that Joe and Nicci would be okay. We would all be okay.

I drew my eyes away from them, just in time to see Daniel running up to me on his chubby toddler legs. My smile returned, and I scooped him up into my arms.

"You came to get me!" he cried joyfully, hugging my neck.

"Of course I did," I said. "I couldn't just leave you there, pal."

Also beaming, Daniel whispered into my ear, "I've got a new mommy and daddy!"

"What?" I looked up and saw a smiling couple walking towards me.

Their names were Mariana and Kelsey. The two were soul mates who bumped into each other before being taken to the lab. Mariana'd had a baby, but the little girl was taken by the doctors and never seen again. They said they knew she was dead.

"We never got to meet our Emily," Mariana said sadly, "but there's no point in living in sorrow forever. Daniel needs us."

"Thank you," I said gratefully, holding her hands in mine. "He really does."

And it was truly beautiful to see broken families coming together to form new ones. Allan and Meg were also adopted by couples who had lost children. The new families seemed very happy together, and that was when I was certain everything would be okay. Not all the O Negatives were free, but if we could pull together like this in such a terrible time, then we would have the strength to free our remaining brothers and sisters.

It was dark when I finally managed to excuse myself and go inside. I received tremendous applause that made me blush, but I accepted it because I knew it made them happy. The celebration continued outside and inside, but where I was going there would be no people. No people except for two, the two I cared for most. "Hey," I said as I entered the observation room.

Shauna was exhausted from the birth and the loss of blood, as was Flint, so Dr. Perry let them rest down here where it was quiet. She looked up at me sleepily from her bed and smiled, Flint nuzzled warmly in her arms. "Hey," she said. "How's the party?"

"A little too much hero worship," I replied, sitting on the edge of the bed. "Everyone wants to meet 'the boy who led the rescue party.' It's a little ridiculous."

"Why? You *did* lead the rescue party. Without your bravery, those poor people would still be trapped in that awful place. Most likely, we'd all be dead, too."

"But I wasn't the only one who went," I protested. "I wasn't the only one who *fought*. You could have died while trying to save us, and I don't see anyone giving you praise."

"If you hadn't been there to motivate us, then there wouldn't have been a fight." Shauna reached up and caressed my face. "It takes hundreds to fight. It takes one to lead that fight."

I looked down as Flint made a cooing noise. He was smiling up at me, showing off his pink, toothless gums. I took him and rocked him in my arms. "He's beautiful," I whispered.

"He looks like my dad," Shauna said. "I bet you anything he's going to be a blonde."

"I'm just glad he's okay," I replied, setting our baby in the cradle beside Shauna's bed. As I slipped my hand into Shauna's, I told her, "I'm just glad that you're both okay."

Shauna sat up a little and gave my hand a squeeze. "While I was still...well, *not me*, I overheard you asking Dr. Perry about what it was like in the lab. Now that I remember what happened to me..." She shook her head and sighed heavily. "We didn't have it good in that place, Walter. No one did."

"I want to know what happened to you in there," I said.

"Some of the things were horrifying. I'm afraid to sleep for fear the memories will haunt me there, too. But I don't want there to be secrets between us, Walter. I want us to trust each other."

"Tell me."

"I can show you." She reached up and placed her hands on my head. She was hesitant, and she asked, "Are you sure you're ready? There's no turning back once we start."

"I've been ready since I saw what was done to you," I told her.

She nodded, and closed her eyes. I did the same and then we were off.

17

Shauna's Time

Shauna Skyler

The brightness of the room around me woke me up. My headache was gone, but the lights still hurt my eyes. I covered my eyes with my arm and carefully sat up. All my aches and pains were gone, but a few new things were affecting my body. My skin felt tingly and my head felt woozy. I tried to stand up, but I was uncertain on my feet so I sat back down. Glancing down, I took a look at myself. I was now in an outfit of pale blue, and had no shoes or socks. There were numerous red spots on my arms, where needles had penetrated. The cot beneath me was hard and unsupportive. My back was stiff from lying on it for so long.

How long *had* I been lying on it for? A day? Two? *Longer*?

Once I was certain I wouldn't fall over, I stood up to take a look around. I went to the door first. It was big, made of steel, and I knew it was thick by the thudding sound it made when I pounded my fist on it.

"Hello?" I called, but my throat was so dry that I started coughing. Once I started, I couldn't stop.

There was a chemical toilet and sink in the far corner of the little room. I went to the sink and drank greedily from the faucet until my stomach was sloshing. Feeling better, I looked around again. Other than the cot, toilet, and sink, there was a table and two chairs in the room. There were no windows, and there was no handle on the door. I was boxed in.

A moment later, there was a loud whoosh of air and the huge door swung inwards. Startled, I sprinted to the bed and hopped onto it, pushing myself into a ball in the corner. I watched uneasily as a man with dark skin and black hair entered. He looked familiar. What was his name? Dr. Don Rudolph. He was the one who knocked me out, who drugged me.

He saw my nervousness and hesitated at the door. In his hands he had a blanket and a tray of hot food. The food looked good and I was starving, but I wasn't going anywhere near him. Not yet.

He smiled at me, but didn't come to the cot. Instead, he went to the table and set the tray and blanket down. He took a seat in one of the chairs and simply sat there. He didn't look at me or speak to me.

Eventually, I got up the courage to approach the table. Dr. Rudolph didn't look at me until I sat down, upon which time he smiled warmly at me. "Hi, Shauna. It's good to see you up and about."

"How long have I been here?" I asked quietly.

"Four days," Dr. Rudolph replied. "You should eat." He pushed the tray to me.

I was suddenly scared. "I've been here *four days*?" I hunched down in my chair.

"Don't be scared," Dr. Rudolph said, giving me another one of his smiles. "You're safe now. The virus has been contained."

"Then why am I still here?"

"The only way the virus will stay contained is if we give you a dose of suppressant every three hours."

I was so confused. "What exactly is this virus?"

Another smile. "It's nothing you need to concern yourself with."

"Um, if you're going to keep me here, then it *is* something I need to concern myself with!"

"Please eat something." Dr. Rudolph nudged the tray again.

In exasperation, I shouted, "I'm not eating anything until you tell me what the hell is going on! What is this place?"

While I stared angrily at him, Dr. Rudolph waited patiently for me to calm down. When I did (somewhat), he said, "We're still in the facility where you were gassed. We're just underground. There are rooms down here for everyone who was infected, so you're not alone. As long as we continue to give you the suppressant, the effects of the virus will not show. You'll be healthy as long as you accept the treatment. Do you understand me?"

I didn't answer. I didn't believe him. There was something wrong about this virus. Something different. I didn't think that they were suppressing it to keep us healthy; I thought that they were suppressing it because they were scared of it. Whatever it was.

Dr. Rudolph continued. "With that being said, I'd like it very much if you'd accept your treatments willingly. You probably won't like them, but it's for your own good."

"I want to talk to my parents," I said dismissively. "I want to hear what they have to say about this."

"I'm afraid you're not allowed to have visitors," Dr. Rudolph said. "From outside or inside the facility."

"Why not?" I demanded shrilly.

"Because we have yet to fully learn how the virus functions," Dr. Rudolph explained. "Interaction with other infected patients may result in unwanted side effects."

I buried my face in my hands. "You can't do this. You can't hold me here!"

"I'm afraid that I can."

I looked up at him. "How long are you going to keep me here?"

Dr. Rudolph didn't answer me for a while. "Indefinitely."

That was when I knew I had to get out. Somehow, and soon, I would need to get out of this place. I knew that if I didn't escape, I would die here.

"You'll see me every couple of hours," Dr. Rudolph said, "but in between visits you'll be on your own, although there is a hidden camera keeping an eye on you, so I wouldn't try anything silly. I'll bring you some books the next time I come." He stood up and pulled a syringe out of his lab coat. When I shrank back, he asked me, "You're going to hold still for me, right?"

I held still. I was going to cause him trouble, but I needed time to come up with an effective strategy.

The injection left me feeling dizzy, weak, and disoriented. Before Dr. Rudolph left me, he urged me to eat what was on the tray. For a long time after his exit, I stared at the food. I was hungry, but I wasn't going to eat their food. I wasn't going to eat anything until that doctor explained to me what the hell was happening and on what grounds he was allowed to hold me.

On wobbly legs, I went back to the cot and laid down.

For the next three days, Dr. Rudolph tried to coax food and water into me. I refused. Each visit he became more and more concerned for my health. He even tried to force feed me once. When he seemed to realize that I had no intention to do anything other than lying on my cot, he took matters into his own hands.

At midday on the fourth day of my fast, Dr. Rudolph entered my room, only this time he wasn't alone. Two men wearing black padding came in with him. They must have been security guards, and they looked like they could wrestle an elephant and come out as the winners. Their stony expressions didn't make my uneasiness subside.

"Planning to eat today, Shauna?" Dr. Rudolph asked me, folding his arms.

I didn't answer, but the entrance made me wary.

"Didn't think so," he murmured, and then gestured to me. The guards (or were they orderlies?) came at me. I immediately sat up, prepared to fight back. But what was the point? One man took each arm and hauled me to my feet. I let my body go limp, but they continued to pull me, only now I was more uncomfortable. For the first time during my stay, I was taken outside my room.

I fought the men as they loaded me onto a stretcher and tied me down, but I was so weak that I gave up rather quickly. My lungs were already burning, and as I gasped for air Dr. Rudolph patted my shoulder.

"You see?" he said. "You're not even strong enough to fight. You'd feel a lot better if you'd eat. But since you're not going to do that willingly, well…" He shrugged and placed a blindfold over my eyes. I was wheeled down a long hallway and into what felt like an elevator. We ascended a floor or two, and then I was wheeled down another hallway. We came to a stop after taking a left, and then the blindfold was removed.

I gasped, and gave a weak tug at the straps.

"Just relax, alright?" Dr. Rudolph hooked two separate IV's into my arm, pumping different fluids into me.

That wasn't what bothered me. What bothered me were the rows of stretchers, each with an unconscious body lying there. I clenched my fists and squeezed my eyes shut, wanting more than anything to go back to my cot in my room.

"You're going to be fine," Dr. Rudolph told me, and when I opened my eyes again he was injecting a syringe-full of something into the saline drip.

"No!" I cried feebly. The drip was moving quickly, and I soon lost all will to move.

Dr. Rudolph fed me fluids through the IV's, but when we got back to my room he tried to feed me orally as well. Ten minutes passed and still I refused to eat. The orderlies were getting tense, waiting for Dr. Rudolph's order to hold me so he could force bread and cheese into my mouth.

"Shauna," Dr. Rudolph said, and leaned back in his chair. He was frustrated, but I could also tell he was tired. "You may think that refusing to eat is a good way to defy me, but really, all you're doing is hurting yourself. We're not planning to hurt you. We're not planning to force you into anything. All we're asking is that you take care of your body so we can take care of the virus. All we're asking is for you to eat. Now please. I really don't want to force feed you. I know you're plenty capable of feeding yourself."

I didn't reply. I stared hard at him. Why should I listen to him? He wouldn't even tell me what the virus was.

He raised his eyebrows. "This'll be a lot messier if you don't cooperate."

My eyes wandered to the door, which stood ajar behind the orderlies. My body tensed in anticipation. How I wanted to get outside that door of my own free will.

An orderly shifted his position slightly, so he was blocking my view of outside.

"You want out?" Dr. Rudolph asked me, his thumb cocked towards the door. "Well, your situation hasn't shifted in that direction at all. If you want any chance at all of leaving, you'd better start eating."

But I didn't want to. I looked down at the plate of cheese and bread, a simple meal made for an uneasy stomach. Dr. Rudolph's statement would have worked on me two days ago, when my stomach was snarling and I was ravenous. Now, I didn't really even feel hungry. I just felt sort of empty, almost like I could feel in my body where my deflated stomach sat.

Alas, I gave in. Dr. Rudolph was right, after all. If I wanted out, I would need to be stronger. More energetic. It was difficult for me to walk five paces without having to stop to catch my breath. I gave in and ate slowly, under the smug eye of Dr. Rudolph. I couldn't eat it all, but that didn't matter to him. I ate. He broke me.

Or so he thought.

For two days, I did my best to eat as much as my stomach would hold. I threw up once, but then I asked Dr. Rudolph for more food to try again. He looked a little confused, even suspicious, but he brought me a little more anyway. Each meal he watched me until I ate enough. Or what was enough in his eyes.

I felt my strength coming back. When Dr. Rudolph wasn't around, I did what I could to exercise. I walked briskly in circles around my room—trying to make it look like I was pacing if anyone was watching me—until I got too dizzy to continue. After walking I'd do push-ups and sit-ups on the cot. Dr. Rudolph's suspicions eventually got the better of him.

"I'm just trying to take care of my body," I told him when asked about my excessive exercising. "Like you said I should."

Dr. Rudolph peered across the table at me, searching my face for something. He stared at me for a long time. "What are you doing, Shauna?"

I blinked innocently at him. "I just told you."

Dr. Rudolph's suspicions didn't leave him. He continued to bring in orderlies when he came with the food and injections, and even warned me about the camera a couple more times (something which I had yet to find in my room). I did my best to be cooperative and appear innocent whenever they arrived, but I think that only made Dr. Rudolph even more suspicious. After a couple of days, though, he started coming alone again. I gave him three meals of peace by himself before I started acting up again.

"Shauna, move away from the door, please." Dr. Rudolph's voice was exasperated, and I knew that he would come in whether I moved or not.

I stood beside the door, waiting for it to open. Dr. Rudolph always told me to back away from the door when he entered so he wouldn't have to worry about an escape attempt. But now I was being stubborn. If he wouldn't tell me what this virus was, I would figure it out for myself.

My injection was already overdue because I'd been standing there for fifteen minutes already. How long did it take before the virus started functioning again? How much longer could Dr. Rudolph wait? Clearly not much longer, because the door whooshed open a moment later. I lurched toward the opening, but at the same time I was body slammed by Dr. Rudolph. I stumbled backwards and landed on my cot. The door swung shut behind Dr. Rudolph and he pulled the syringe out of his coat, gripping it tightly in his hand. His eyes were challenging, something I had never before seen.

"We're not going to have any of this, now, are we?" he asked breathlessly. "We were having such a good week. You're not going to start causing trouble again, are you?"

"As long as you keep me here," I replied, and I ran at him.

I don't know how he did it, but he somehow managed to flip me over his shoulder and knock the wind out of me as I hit the ground. He sat on top of me and pinned my arm behind my back, driving the needle into my arm with such force that I screamed.

After it was over, we both laid on the floor, panting. I was sore all over, and even after the scene I'd just made, Dr. Rudolph still helped me to my feet. His hands were gentle. He said to me as he lowered me onto the cot, "This fighting isn't going to get you anywhere good, my dear. Look. I hurt you. I don't want to hurt you. Please don't try that again." He stood and patted my knee. "I'll see you again in a few hours. I'll have a guard bring in your breakfast."

"Leave me alone," I muttered from the floor. It seemed like a pretty pathetic thing to say, but when Dr. Rudolph answered me his voice was emotional.

"I can't, sweetie," he said as he left the room. "You know I can't."

One of the guard/orderlies brought in a tray of food a few minutes later. I didn't even glance at it. I stayed on the cot until Dr. Rudolph came in three hours later for the next injection. When he asked me why I didn't eat, I could finally say, "I'm not hungry," and tell the truth.

I didn't try anything for a couple days; I was too mad. Plus, Dr. Rudolph started bringing in the guards/orderlies again to make sure I behaved myself. Then a day came later that second week of my stay when I realized I *had* to start fighting again.

"We're going for a walk," Dr. Rudolph said that morning after injection time.

"I don't want to go for a walk," I said, stubbornly wrapping my arms around my knees and glaring up at him.

He just smiled, and the two guards/orderlies came in and forced me to my feet. "It wasn't a request," he replied. "Let's go."

By walk, Dr. Rudolph meant that he would walk and I would get to take another ride on the stretcher, complete with blindfolds and restraints! "So much for a walk, Rudolph," I grumbled.

He chuckled and gave me a reassuring pat on the shoulder.

We went to the same floor where I had all those fluids pumped into me, but I think we went to a different wing. The trip was a bit longer, and the sounds I heard were not at all like those I heard before. Last time, I only heard silence. Now, the screams, cries, and drills I heard made my heart run away. I was practically hyperventilating when Dr. Rudolph took off my blindfold.

The lighting in this wing was darker, and Dr. Rudolph and I were separated from the others in the room by thick curtains. I looked around frantically, the screams and drills continuing. "What's going on?" I demanded, trying to wriggle out of my restraints. "What the hell is this place?"

Dr. Rudolph loaded a syringe. He gave it two sharp snaps.

"Stop!" I cried as he injected it into my arm. "Stop! What are you going to do to me?"

"Let the drug do its work," Dr. Rudolph murmured as my thrashing grew weaker. "Let it take you over, and you won't feel the pain."

"What are you doing?" I squeaked, my body numb and motionless.

"Just breathe deeply," Dr. Rudolph said, turning my head sideways to expose my left temple. "And please don't scream."

Just then, a horrible cry echoed throughout the room, and I whimpered. What was going to happen? Why could I hear drills?

Something was placed on the exposed part of my head. I couldn't tell what it was because my skin had gone numb. My guess was that it was gauze.

"You're going to feel a slight pressure," Dr. Rudolph told me, and then I heard the drill.

I gasped when I did feel the pressure. The buzz of the drill became muffled as the bit penetrated my skull. I wanted to scream. The urge was great, but when I opened my mouth, no sound came out. A trickle of blood escaped the gauze and rolled down my cheek. It went over the bridge of my nose and started dripping onto the stretcher in front of my face. The drill was loud, its vibrations rattling through my whole body, but I could still hear the light tap each drop made as it fell from my face.

Tap...tap...tap...

Drip, drip, drip.

Walter pulled away from me with a jerk and a gasp. He slipped off the bed and fell to the floor in a heap, clutching his head and moaning. "Oh my God!" he cried, and I saw tears on his face. "Why? That's the most horrible thing I've ever seen!"

Flint was crying in his cradle. My own heart was pounding. "Walter," I said, climbing down gingerly to the floor. "Walter." I took his head in my hands again. "It's okay. It's over."

"But it still happened!" Walter sobbed, clutching my shoulders. "My own uncle! I never knew just how bad it was..."

"Shh," I soothed, stroking his hair. "Walter, it's over now. That's not going to happen to me again. Or to anyone here. We'll get the others out of those prisons and then it'll never happen to any of us ever again."

Walter finally raised his eyes to mine. The tears had stopped, but his face was moist. "How could you bear it? Didn't it feel—"

"Awful?" I raised my eyebrows. "Yeah. But I dealt with it. I dealt with it because I knew I had to get out of there. I had to get to you." I caressed his face, something I did quite often. Walter said he liked it. It comforted him, made him feel at peace.

"I don't know if I can handle the rest of it," Walter whispered.

"You can," I promised him. "That's the worst of it. Everything else is what led up to my punishment."

Walter nodded, taking deep breaths. "Okay," he said. "Okay. Just don't show me how they carried out the punishment."

"Even if I wanted to show you, I can't remember. It's all in pieces." I paused. "Are you okay now?"

Walter nodded again.

I raised my hands. "Ready?"

I didn't move from my cot for two days after the drill went through my head. My head ached too much and the procedure left me…well, I suppose *traumatized* was the best word. I ate a little when Dr. Rudolph brought food, and I allowed him to change the bandages on my head when he wanted. But other than that, I didn't move. Not even when I had to pee.

I had absolutely no desire to move until I was paid a little visit one evening by one of the guards/orderlies.

He came in quietly. His footsteps were so soft that I wouldn't have heard him if the door hadn't given him away. He came to my bedside where I laid curled into the corner. He leaned forward and peered into my face. For a while he did this, before he waved a hand in front of me. I blinked and tried to focus my eyes on him.

"Oh," he said mildly. "You *are* awake."

I shrugged. I wished I wasn't awake. This headache was killer, and Dr. Rudolph hadn't given me any pain meds so far.

The guard/orderly was one of the men who had dragged me out of the room both times. I recognized him. Tall, big, blue eyes, closely-cropped blonde hair. What did he want now?

"Your head hurt?" he asked.

"Yeah," I muttered. And then, "What's it to you?"

He shrugged. Out of the corner of my eye, I could detect a grin creeping onto his face. "I can probably fix that. I'm David."

"Shauna." I squinted up at him. "What do you mean you can fix it? Can you get me pain killers?"

Another shrug. "Sure. I can get you anything. Whatever you want, really."

I breathed a tremendous sigh of relief. "Thank you. Thank you so much. I can't begin to tell you how much…what are you staring at?"

David was staring at me. Hungrily. The expression would have made me take a step back, had I been standing. "I can get you pain pills," he said, his grin broadening. "I can get you so many fucking drugs that you could be high for the rest of your life. But you have to do something for me first. A favor, you might call it."

I knew where this was going. "Forget it," I snapped, closing my eyes and doing my best to ignore the throbbing in my head. "Piss off."

"Oh, no," David said, and before I knew what happening he was straddling me and cupping a hand over my mouth. "Nope. Besides, you know you want those drugs."

I was too weak to fight. I watched helplessly as David fumbled with my pants, trying to figure out how to get them off. Was everything really going to come to this? Was I really about to be raped by one of the men who was supposed to be protecting me?

"I'm going to give you the ride of your life, baby," David said, panting.

When I heard the thump, I thought I was blacking out or somehow blocking out what was about to happen. But then David fell off of me and onto the floor, groaning and clutching his head.

A terrifying sound escaped my throat, a cross between a moan and a scream. Over David stood Dr. Rudolph, and on Dr. Rudolph's face was the most fearsome expression I'd ever seen in my life. The gun in his hand only made the appearance even more terrifying.

"Get out," he said to David through his teeth. As David stumbled to his feet, Dr. Rudolph added, "If I ever see you on this floor again, I'll have you shot. Do we understand each other?"

David didn't say anything, but he was out of there quickly. I didn't realize I was sobbing until Dr. Rudolph sat beside me, the fury in him gone. "Don't let him come back!" I begged him, crawling onto his lap and clinging to his jacket. "Don't let him hurt me!"

"Nobody's going to hurt you," Dr. Rudolph whispered, holding me to him. "He's never coming back." He held me for a while, shushing and rocking me. Then, he asked me, "He didn't...did he?"

I shook my head but gripped him tighter. "Don't leave me," I whispered.

He rested his chin on the top of my head. "I'm not going anywhere." He took a syringe out of his pocket, hesitated, and then put it away again.

We stayed like that for a while, until my sobs died away. I looked up when I felt something wet dripping on my face, and I realized that they were tears.

He was crying, too.

A few days later, I met Shane. I was sitting on my cot, as usual, when I suddenly heard a noise from outside. Lots of shouting, a couple of crashes. There were even a couple of gunshots. I started to get up, to go to the door and press my ear against it, but my door swung open before both feet were on the floor. I watched, puzzled and wary, as a man stumbled inside and quickly pushed the door shut. He turned to me, eyes wide and breathing rapidly. His hair was long and golden, tied behind him in a ponytail. He had a beard and mustache of the same golden color. "Hey there," he said breathlessly, striding over to me.

"Who are you?" I asked him, pushing myself into the corner. "What are you—"

"*Shh!*" the man hissed, putting a finger to his lips and sitting on the opposite side of the cot. He pointed to the door, and we listened as the voices from outside grew louder, and then grew distant again. He chuckled to himself and leaned back against the wall, relieved.

He was wearing the same light blue scrubs as me, and he was running away from the doctors. "You're a *prisoner* here?" I whispered, scooting closer to him.

"We're matching, aren't we?" He pulled at his shirt.

I laughed joyfully, and then we were hugging. "I thought that Dr. Rudolph was the only person I'd see for the rest of my life!"

The man made a face. "You've got Rudolph too? What a dick."

"How did you get out of your room?"

He shrugged. "They were taking me out for tests. I just used my ability to get away from them."

"Ability?"

"Yeah, my ability. What can you do?"

"What are you talking about?"

He stared at me, half in bewilderment and half in pity. "You really don't know, do you?" He sighed and scratched his head. "Well, I guess there isn't an easy way to say it. This virus they say we're infected with…well, it's not, like, an illness. Not exactly. The virus changed us. That's why they give us those shots three times a day and then sedate us at night; they're afraid we'll use our abilities."

I remembered back to the night I was first taken here, when chairs and things kept moving for no apparent reason. Only now, it seemed there was a reason: I had been scared. So, so scared. "What kind of abilities?"

The man sighed again and stood up. "Okay," he said. "This is going to freak you out a little, but it's necessary." He smiled reassuringly at my hesitant expression, and then he wasn't him anymore.

One second he was a man, and the next he was a huge, golden dog. The dog wobbled on its feet a little, but then balanced itself and came forward. I was terrified of it at first, pulling myself away as it advanced. But then I looked a little closer. The dog had blue eyes; the same blue eyes as the man. My mouth fell open. "*What*?"

The corners of the dog's mouth turned up. It was smiling. *He* was smiling.

I sat forward and reached out, still not believing what my eyes were telling me. I reached out towards the dog, and he stuck his nose out towards me, so that we touched. It was then, when I was actually touching the dog and looking into the man's blue eyes, that I believed it. This man had just shape-shifted into a dog, and for some reason, I found that incredibly awesome. I couldn't help but smile back at his goofy dog grin.

My door was thrown open suddenly. The dog changed back into the man as the orderlies rushed in and grabbed him. As they pinned him down, he looked up at me, and I was surprised to see him still smiling. "I didn't catch your name, dear."

"I'm Shauna," I said, watching from my cot.

"I'm Shane," the man said. "It's nice to meet you, Shauna."

I nodded in reply, watching sadly as the orderlies forced Shane to his feet and out the door. It was disappointing, but he would have been discovered sooner or later. I couldn't keep my new friend forever.

Before he was dragged out of my room, he glanced back at me. "Hey Shauna, don't forget about your ability."

Shane was taken away, and that was the first and last time I saw him in the lab as me—my normal self. Just before my door closed, I glimpsed Dr. Rudolph standing outside, watching me.

He was glaring.

I wanted to use my ability. I tried the next morning.

"Shauna, this is really unnecessary," Dr. Rudolph said sternly from the other side of the table.

"Is it?" I snapped back, mirroring his movements.

"I don't want to hurt you."

"You know, you keep saying that. I think you already *have* hurt me. I think your drugs are hurting me."

"Is this because of what Shane told you?"

"About our abilities? Yeah. And I want to use mine."

Dr. Rudolph's eyes were scolding, but I saw something more in them. I saw fear. Fear of me.

"Don't bother telling me that he's nuts," I said. "I saw him shift forms. That was no delusion."

"What do you think you'll gain from using your ability?" he asked me.

"Freedom," I replied.

"No." He shook his head. "These abilities are dangerous to everyone, those with an ability and everyone who doesn't have one. Do you want to hurt people, Shauna?"

"That depends. You, I doubt I'd mind hurting."

Dr. Rudolph ran around the table at me, snatching at my shirt. Instinctively, I waved my arm at him. The table slid across the floor and blocked his path. He stared at me as he ran into it, the fear in his eyes more obvious.

I looked down at my hands in amazement, and then looked back up at him, the smugness showing on my face. "Huh," I said. "That's pretty cool."

"Don't," Dr. Rudolph said, but he was no longer stern. He was pleading.

With another wave of my hand, the table flew backwards and shoved Dr. Rudolph into the wall. He let out a cry of pain and struggled to free himself, but he was pinned. I gave him a sly wink when he met my gaze. "See you around," I said. "Then again, hopefully not."

"Shauna, stop!" Dr. Rudolph cried. "You don't know how to control it!"

"I guess I never will if you don't let me practice," I replied, waving my hand at the door. It swung open, and I stepped out into the unknown world.

"Shauna, stop!" Dr. Rudolph repeated, but I was already outside.

I was in a long, white, brightly lit hallway. It seemed to stretch on for miles. There were a few people in the hallway, mainly doctors, and they all looked at me when I stepped out.

"Someone grab her!" Dr. Rudolph yelled from inside.

A few doctors started to advance on me uncertainly, but I quickly and confidently waved my hand at them. They toppled to the floor and into walls, and I started running. I made it five paces when the alarm went off. I ran faster, but I think that was where I went wrong. Because I rounded the corner too fast, preventing myself from ducking out of the way as an orderly thrust a hard, blunt object into my face, knocking me unconscious.

I awoke seconds later, as two orderlies were dragging me back into my room. Dr. Rudolph was glaring at me, a syringe in his hand. "I didn't want it to have to come to this, Shauna," he said. "I thought we'd be able to get along okay."

The orderlies hoisted me up onto my cot and pinned me down. "What are you doing?" I mumbled as he came towards me.

"If you're going to fight like this," Dr. Rudolph said, "then I have no choice but to keep you under sedation for the remainder of you time here."

"And how long is that?" I asked fearfully, eyeing the loaded syringe.

Dr. Rudolph locked eyes with me and told me something he told me a few weeks ago, although it felt like months had passed since then: "Indefinitely."

So that was how it went. I was kept under sedation for twenty-three and a half hours of the day, every day. The other half hour was the time I got to eat and use the bathroom. Even when I was awake, I felt like I was asleep. The drugs kept me drowsy and disoriented.

The routine became old right away. I begged Dr. Rudolph to give me another chance, to let me be awake, but I had blown it. He didn't give in to anything, no matter how much begging I dished out. So, out of concern for my own health and sanity, I tried something new.

"Please," I pleaded, the tears streaming down my face. "I haven't seen my family in weeks. Just let me talk to my brother."

"I'm sorry," Dr. Rudolph said, "but that's not going to happen."

"*Please.*" I was sobbing now. "I just want to see him for a minute."

Dr. Rudolph's face remained impassive. "No."

"Just...just..." I didn't know what else to do. "Just let me give him a hug!" I gasped for breath, feeling like I had just run a marathon.

With a small shake of his head, Dr. Rudolph said, "I'm sorry." He took the familiar syringe out of his pocket.

"No more drugs," I whispered, shaking my head desperately as the orderly took hold of my shoulders. "I don't want any more drugs."

Dr. Rudolph didn't say anything. I had a feeling that even if he did, it wouldn't be very nice. I struggled and screamed as he gave me the injection. Soon, my cries died away and my eyes fluttered closed. My body went limp against the orderly and he laid me down. Dr. Rudolph said something under his breath. A few more shots, and then they both left me.

The room was silent. Minutes ticked by.

I waited for thirty.

My head was pounding when I allowed myself to open my eyes. I looked down at where Dr. Rudolph inserted the needles, and gave a gentle push with my mind. The liquid that was injected into me slowly seeped out of my body and ran down my arm. When only blood came out, I stopped pushing. I'd finally managed to outsmart Dr. Rudolph, and he didn't even know it. I grinned to myself. My stalling had given me enough time for my ability to be turned back on, and I held the injection under my skin and faked unconsciousness until I was sure no one was coming back. As for the cameras…I just had to hope I was having a lucky day.

I went to the door and opened it with my mind. Slowly. I was surprised to find that nobody was in the hall. What time was it? I had no clue anymore. Carefully, I wandered down, keeping an eye out for anyone who could get me in trouble. At one point, I had to duck into a doorway when a doctor detoured into my hall and then turned into a room. I encountered no one else. I found the empty hallways rather curious, but I didn't question my luck.

I wandered and wandered until I found a strange looking elevator. It needed a code or a key, but it still opened when I waved my hand. Once I was inside, a female voice asked me where I wanted to go. I was so surprised, I pushed the first button I saw.

"Sublevel 7," the robotic voice droned.

"No!" I said in protest, pushing several other buttons, but that didn't have any effect. I could feel the elevator descending, and it stopped and opened again, refusing to let me go anywhere else.

Maybe I'm supposed to be here, I thought to myself, peering out. *Maybe I'm supposed to see something.*

I stepped out, allowing the doors to close behind me. It looked almost the same as the hallway I'd stepped into from my room. Almost the same. There were fewer doors, and the lighting wasn't as bright. It felt...dangerous. Threatening. Deadly. Black. Something was wrong here.

Uneasily, I crept down the hall, my ears and eyes peeled for any signs of movement. Nobody was down here; my ears were ringing in the silence.

I passed several doors, each one leaving me with a more ominous feeling. I rounded a few corners until I came to a dead end. At the end was a door, a door like any other. And I knew, somehow, in my gut, that whatever I was supposed to see was behind that door. It was beckoning to me. I waved it open and entered. There wasn't much light, but I could see well enough. Around the room were dozens of computers, all hooked up to a machine in the center. The machine I needed to destroy.

My feet took me to the only computer that was turned on. I sat down and began clicking through files, unsure of what I was looking for but certain there was something. Random files flashed across the screen and then flashed away again.

For a long time, I sat at the computer looking for something significant. When I found what I was looking for, I didn't realize it at first. Then I looked a little closer. I looked closer at the names. The names that I didn't know yet were so familiar to me.

MAIA/MARLENA RUDOLPH

Rudolph. Were these Dr. Rudolph's daughters? He'd mentioned them once or twice, but never said their names. If they were his daughters, then why was there a file about them here?

Were they affected too? I clicked on it to open it, and I started to read. At first, I was confused, but when I finished, I was horrified.

"What?" I breathed, pulling myself away. "They…they—"

"Shauna."

I turned. Dr. Rudolph was just inside the doorway, watching me calmly. Calmly. How could he be so calm, knowing what he was going to do? "You—you—"

"I do what I have to," he said.

"You're going to kill us all!"

"Only if people like you continue to fight us. None of us *want* to hurt you. But we may have to, if it means humanity's survival." He gestured for someone to enter, and two orderlies came in. "And now that you've seen the plan, I know you'll try to leave and warn others. Shane tried when he found this."

"What did you do to Shane?"

"Exactly what I'm about to do to you," Dr. Rudolph said, and the orderlies advanced on me.

That was the last thing I remembered; the screaming, the struggling, the fear. Fear was the last thing I felt before the girl I was disappeared, only to be replaced by a soulless being. An empty person.

18

The Silver Lining

Walter Reifert

I pulled away from Shauna, more tears in my eyes. "I still can't believe Uncle Don would do that," I said. "My own uncle…" I shook my head.

Shauna pulled me to her, held me in her arms. "It's okay," she whispered. "It's over. He's gone."

"His memory isn't," I replied, lying down beside her. "No matter how long I live… no matter where our lives go…I'll never forget Don Rudolph."

"No one expects you to. But we have to move on."

"How? How do we move on? If Don could do it, someone else could. It's only a matter of time before someone else decides we're still a threat and creates a new strategy to wipe us out. What then?"

Leaning her head back so we could look each other in the eyes, Shauna told me, "We fight. We did it once. We sure as hell can do it again."

"But for how long? Our entire existence? How many times will it take for them to leave us be?"

Shauna didn't answer. She couldn't, even though we both knew the answer. As long as we lived on the same planet as the humans, we could never be at peace. Our two species could never coexist.

"Walter!" Cole and Damien stumbled down the stairs, their eyes wild and excited. "Shauna, the two of you won't believe this!"

"What's going on?" I asked nervously, but it couldn't be bad. Their expressions were too happy.

"You've got to come see this!" Cole insisted breathlessly. "Both of you. Shauna, we'll carry you."

"I'm fine," Shauna said, but Damien had already scooped her up. I protested when Cole picked up Flint, but then let it go.

"Come on!" Cole said urgently.

We went upstairs, Shauna and I uncertain of what we would see. I was surprised to find the compound extremely quiet. People were packed in every available space while others peered inside through the windows. Their attention was all turned to the giant television mounted on the wall in the den. The news was on, and as I watched, my mouth dropped open in amazement. There was footage of the damage we'd done to the Hatfield lab, and it was quite extensive. Not only had we destroyed that lab, but we'd also unintentionally destroyed four others.

"After irreparable damage was done to the O Negative laboratory in Hatfield, Pennsylvania, the original O Negative lab, O Negatives and O Negative supporters from around the world have begun to follow suit," the reporter began gravely. "Four other labs from around the world have been destroyed, all patients either dead or missing. From San Francisco, California, to Madison, Wisconsin. From Berlin, Germany, to New Delhi, India. There were reports that O Negatives and their supporters teamed up to bring down the only places that keep our world safe from the threat of those infected with the Colician Virus."

"What threat?" someone in the room shouted, but he was quickly shushed as the reporter continued.

"All four masses of people appear to be converging on the same central point: the location of the rebel O Negatives who took down the Hatfield lab. The exact location of the O Negative rebels has not yet been confirmed, but the military believes it to be within a fifty mile radius of Philadelphia." A map of Pennsylvania popped up on the screen, and a big red circle was drawn around Philadelphia.

"Great," I muttered. "Now everyone in the world knows where we are."

"We'll be fine," Cole assured me, waving his hand dismissively.

The reporter replaced the map. "If any civilians come into contact with any of these groups, do not attempt to fight. Military forces are being mobilized and will be dealing with the O Negatives as they see fit. Again, do not attempt to fight any of these groups. Our society cannot begin to comprehend the amount of destructive force possessed by them.

"The Hatfield Regime is led by rebel Walter Reifert, a former Hatfield inhabitant," the reporter continued.

"That a boy, Walt!"

"Walter Reifert will kick your ass!"

"You've got your military, but we've got Walter Reifert!"

More shouts echoed around the room, but I was intent to hear the end of the report. A picture of my face was onscreen, the awful yearbook picture from my junior year, and I struggled to pick up as many fragments as possible.

"...avoid all contact...being dealt with...threat the world has ever faced...being labeled as leader of the O Negative uprising..."

Loud cheers erupted around the room, and it took a moment to realize they were applauding *me*. I'd been spotted, and now everyone was praising me for my big accomplishment of the day. I, however, did not feel like celebrating.

"Is this how they see me?" I asked Cole as people thumped me on the back. "As a threat that needs to be dealt with?"

Cole's face became solemn. "Yes," he said, "but that's not how *we* see you. We see you as a leader. Our leader. And our judgment is all that should matter to you anymore."

"How am I supposed to lead these people?" I asked, gesturing to the crowd. "I'm only eighteen."

The compound went silent. The few who had heard my comment passed it along to those who hadn't.

"*Only* eighteen?" a woman to my right said.

"That's not all you are," another woman said.

"You lost your family, and still you kept fighting," Cole told me, placing a hand on my shoulder. "You saved Shauna from that empty place she was trapped in. You led an unarmed group of civilians against the lab and got everyone out alive. You sacrificed someone you loved to save the rest of us." He smiled weakly.

"So what?" I whispered.

"It takes true bravery to do what you did," Damien said. "And for what you did, we're all grateful."

Everyone did something then that left me stunned and speechless. They all got down on their knees, gazing back at me lovingly. They were all serious about this; they wanted me as their leader. An eighteen-year-old boy with no past leadership experience.

"Not boy. *Man*." Lemoore came up from behind me and patted me on the back. "You haven't been a boy for a long time."

Shauna's hand slipped into mine and she gave it a reassuring squeeze. She smiled at me.

And that was how it began.

We started calling ourselves the Colicians. The virus that created us was called the Colician Strain, so we thought the name fit. It was a relief to not hear "O Negative" thrown around so much anymore.

As elected leader of the Colician race, I had the honor of greeting the group from Madison. It was led by a woman and two men, all several years older than me but they insisted that they wanted me as "Supreme Leader." The woman's name was Peighton, and the two men were Klaus and Garrett. The four of us spoke in private as the arriving group of nine hundred attempted to get settled in what little space there was left. I told them that I didn't want to be the only person of authority among our people. I wanted their help. "Supreme Leader" reminded me too much of the Nazi Holocaust anyway. Peighton suggested the idea of a Cabinet, a committee of nine members who aided the President— me—in decision making. Peighton, Klaus, and Garrett made the first three, and they said I should pick the remaining six from my group. I already knew exactly who I wanted.

Dr. Perry and Lemoore both agreed, but reluctantly. Cole required a little more persuasion, but I wanted him. He was the only person I knew who had a political background, so he was going to be very helpful. Damien gave it some thought, but then turned the offer down. Shauna said no before I even asked her, as did Jane and Erica. And Joe... he was too heartbroken to give me an answer. Joe hadn't been the same ever since Maia's death; silent, mourning in seclusion with his daughter.

Could anyone blame him?

By that time, I, the President of the Colician Race, had a Cabinet of six. We all agreed to wait a few days until the refugees from San Francisco arrived to pick the remaining members.

We received devastating news once the San Franciscans made it. A flustered young woman by the name of Alicia reported that two of their buses were struck by missiles. One bus was completely destroyed, killing everyone on board. The second bus suffered numerous fatalities, but seventeen people lived. Alicia was one of those seventeen. Ash and black scorch marks covered her arms and face, but otherwise she appeared very strong and durable. When asked who was in charge, she said, "No one. Our leader, Kaden, was on the first bus."

"Who's been giving instructions, then?" I asked her.

She shrugged. "Me, I guess."

So Alicia agreed to become number seven.

Our people from overseas were having difficulty getting to us. The leader of the Germans, a man called Killian, was also a telepath. We sent messages back and forth to give updates on what was happening with our groups. The Germans had suffered few fatalities throughout their journey due to a very powerful pyrokinetic, but they had hit a recent roadblock. They were on the coast of Portugal, and were currently trying to get a ship big enough to transport their group across the Atlantic.

We are working on coming to you, Killian assured me. *Do not count on us for another few months, but we will see each other soon.*

We'll be waiting for you, I promised him.

That was really all we were doing right now. Waiting. From what we last heard, the group from New Delhi was massacred, but seven other enormous groups were coming to us from around the globe, and we would wait for them. Perhaps not at the compound, which was long since overcrowded, but we would wait.

That was the next problem we faced. Our population was dramatically increasing, and considering how many infants and young children we had, we couldn't be crammed together or live outside anymore. The solution came to us when four young humans wandered into our camp, looking for the man in charge.

I'd called a Cabinet meeting about twenty minutes earlier. We were discussing more efficient ways to bring our people to us from long distances, and also what to do about our lack of shelter. Our group of seven stirred uneasily when we heard an uproar from outside.

"Let me go look," Klaus said as I stood up. But before he could leave Lemoore's study, a furious Damien burst inside, dragging a boy behind him.

"What's going on?" I demanded, taking in the scene. I didn't recognize the boy, who looked to be no older than thirteen, but there were now a lot of people whom I didn't recognize.

"This human and three others came to the edge of our camp in a big pick-up," Damien explained angrily. "The other three got away when they saw us coming, but this one wasn't in the truck and got left behind, along with this crate." A man I knew as Coltrane dragged a large crate inside after them, resting it in front of our table. "It's probably full of weapons and explosives!"

The boy shook his head quickly, his eyes filled with terror, but he didn't say anything in his defense.

"Is this really what it's come to?" Damien snarled at him. "Even the kids of your kind want to kill us?"

"N-no!" the boy stammered. "We didn't—"

"Stop talking!" Damien shouted.

"Damien!" I cried when he raised his hand to strike the boy. "Please. Leave us. I want to speak to him."

"He's dangerous!" Damien protested.

"No," I said, "he's not. Please." I nodded to the door.

Damien huffed, but he and Coltrane left, closing the door behind them.

"P-please!" the boy whimpered, hugging himself. "We didn't want to…we weren't going to…"

"Why don't you come and sit down?" I offered, pulling out a chair next to me.

The boy hesitated, but then came to me and sat down. Maybe it was my charming smile or my good looks that comforted him, but whatever it was, I sensed he felt calmer by me.

He was African-American and had very dark eyes. His t-shirt and basketball shorts were splattered with mud, as was his face. He wasn't very tall, but he looked strong.

"What's your name?" I asked him.

"Danny," he said, glancing at everyone at the table. "Danny Bennett."

Dr. Perry stiffened in his chair, and Danny's eyes shifted to him.

"Hello, Danny," I said, extending a hand. "My name's Walter. Walter Reifert."

"I-I know," Danny said, and looked away in embarrassment. "I've seen you on TV."

I nodded. "And what do you think of me from what you've seen?"

Danny kept his eyes averted. "I don't know. I don't think you're as bad as the government's made you out to be. Maybe you've done some bad things, but you did it to protect your people." He shrugged. "I don't know you, so I can't judge."

Again, I nodded, and I noticed that the others were beginning to loosen up. Their first impression of the boy was not complimentary (I heard that in their thoughts), but now they were beginning to think that he was here for a good reason. I, for one, knew he was here to help us.

"So why is it you came to us today, Danny Bennett?" I asked curiously. "Who left you behind?"

"My brother, Brandon," Danny said, "and my cousins, Rose and R.J."

"That wasn't very nice," I commented.

The boy shrugged again. "That big red-haired guy scared them."

Everyone in the room laughed. "He grows on you, trust me," I said.

Danny forced a smile, and then pointed to the crate at the foot of the table. "We came to bring you these."

Cole glanced at me, and I nodded to him. He opened the crate and then gasped.

"What is it?" Alicia asked.

"Food," Cole said, his expression full of disbelief. "And...is that—?"

"Medical supplies," Danny confirmed, nodding. "Our whole truck is full of those."

"Where did you get all this?" Peighton asked him dubiously.

"My family started a fundraiser for the O Negatives in our area," Danny explained. "We didn't know what your conditions were like, so we thought we'd try to help out. Most of the donors were people who had lost a family member. After we got a lot of money, we went shopping for stuff we thought you might need. My truck has food and meds, and we've got a few more trucks coming with clothes. I doubt it's enough, but I hope it'll at least help." He glanced at us warily again. "If-if you want our help, that is."

"Thank you very much, Danny," I said, amazed at what this boy was offering us. "We really appreciate it."

"Did you lose a family member?" Garrett asked.

Danny shook his head.

"Then why are you helping us?" Lemoore peered at him curiously.

Danny shrugged. "You didn't ask for any of this. Those doctors gave you those abilities and then took you away. An ability doesn't make you a bad person. It's not fair that they're treating *you* like the enemy."

We stared at him for a while. I caught myself, as well as the rest of the Cabinet, smiling. This was where the good of the human race remained, in people like this boy.

Danny was right. It was nowhere near enough, but it definitely helped. Especially the milk. Gallons and gallons of milk were brought, because they knew we had lots of babies and young children.

We did our best to ration the food and other supplies, but there was nowhere near enough for everyone. Danny and the others promised to bring more soon, when they got more money, and we all thanked him graciously. Before the humans left, Danny's father, Jordan, told us something that was really helpful.

"You know they evacuated Philadelphia, don't you?" he said, climbing into his truck with Danny.

"I do now," I replied, intrigued. "There wasn't anything on the news."

"No," Jordan said. "They want to keep it quiet, so they don't provoke or encourage you or whatever. But everybody's gone. There're houses and grocery stores just sitting there, waiting to be used." He raised his eyebrows at me.

I thought over that new information for a moment. "Why did they evacuate? We weren't making any threats…"

"That doesn't matter," Jordan said. "You attacked the Hatfield lab and won. They're afraid you're going to start attacking major cities next, starting with Philadelphia. They're afraid of you now, Mr. Reifert. That's a good thing, but that's also a very bad thing. You've already seen what terrified humans will do to defend themselves."

He drove away, leaving me with the brilliant possibility of expansion. Philadelphia was big enough to house our current population and the incoming population of Colicians.

A hand slipped into mine. Shauna peered up into my thoughtful face. She was holding Flint, our boy who now had a thick head of blonde hair and lively eyes. "What is it?" she asked me. "What did he say to you?"

The smile lit up my face. "Philadelphia's empty."

The next day, we used the buses from San Francisco to start relocating our camp. Everyone was excited, and the relief ran through all of us. There were only five buses that were still fit for use, and with our population of nearly three thousand, it would take multiple trips to transport us all.

By high noon, almost everybody was gone. I'd sent Shauna and Flint on ahead with Erica and William. Both girls were reluctant to leave without their boys, but Cole and I had a few things to do before we left.

I asked the Cabinet to stay behind and help take the remaining things we might need. I also wanted to say goodbye to the compound with them.

"This was our home," I told Lemoore as we sat at his desk in his study. "Long before any of the others arrived."

The scene felt so familiar. Lemoore spoke to me like this in this room so many times while I was struggling to overcome my anger and grief. This was how it had been before; just me and him.

"You're going to miss it," Lemoore said softly. It wasn't even a question.

"Yeah," I sighed. "But I knew we would have to leave it eventually. It's a damn big place, but not big enough for all of us. Not by far. I just never thought..." I let my voice trail off and I shook my head sadly.

"You never thought it would be so hard."

"No," I said, and laughed at myself. "Is that naïve of me?"

"Not at all," Lemoore replied. "It's perfectly normal to grieve a place you love. In a way, it's similar to losing someone you love."

I felt a sharp pang in my heart, but it was not as awful as when it was just the two of us, living day and night in the empty halls that were once again barren. I had lost my family, yes, and even now it was hard to think about. But now I had a second chance, a chance that made my pain hurt a little less every day. I had a new family. And it was wonderful.

"Yes," I agreed. "I suppose it is."

"You're doing a remarkable job, you know," Lemoore told me. "They all love you."

"Well, I love them, too."

"That's why they love you. You went from losing everything you loved to defending an entire race of people. You wouldn't have believed me if I told you this four months ago, but you're the strongest person I've ever known."

"Thank you," I whispered.

A low honk that reminded me of a fog horn could be heard from down the gravel road. Jane, Sarah, and Caroline were back with our bus.

"We'd better get going," I said, standing up.

"You go on ahead," Lemoore said. "I'm going to stay behind for a few minutes." He suddenly looked very tired, and he ran a hand across the wooden surface of his desk.

"Are you alright, Lemoore?" I asked.

He offered me a weak smile. "This may have been our home long before any of theirs, but it was my home long before it was yours. I'm going to miss it, too. I just need a minute."

I nodded. "I understand. We'll wait for you. Come whenever you're ready."

"Hey, Walter," Lemoore called as I went to the door. "We're family now. We've been family for a while." He gave me a stern look. "So please stop calling me Lemoore."

I smiled. "Okay, Patrick."

Something was wrong. I knew that as soon as I reached the front door. The thoughts of everyone outside were panicked, and a frantic Peighton hurried up to me as I stepped onto the front steps. "Walter!" she cried. "They're coming! Human planes. They're going to bomb us!"

"Bomb Philadelphia?" I asked in growing horror.

"No." Her expression was very grave. "They're coming to bomb *us*."

The rest of my Cabinet hurried up to me from the bus pickup point. "We need to get out of here," I told them.

"It's too late," Cole said breathlessly. "They're almost here."

We could hear the roar of the jet engines getting closer and closer with each second.

"I can put a force field around us," Peighton announced. "But we all have to be fairly close together."

"Oh God," I breathed. "Patrick." I turned and started running back inside. "Get the Odaus! I'll get Patrick!"

"Walter, stop!" Peighton shouted as Garrett ran to the bus that was pulling up behind us. She and the others started following me. "We have to stay close together!"

"I'm not losing him, too!" I yelled back, taking the stairs two at a time. I whispered to myself. "I can't lose him, too. I'm not losing another father."

"Walter!" Dr. Perry shouted, catching up to me. He caught my arm, but didn't try to stop me. We ran towards Patrick's study as fast as our bodies allowed, all the while the roar of plane engines growing louder and louder in our ears, until the sound blocked out the rest of the world.

19

The Declaration of Independence

Richard Ashton

People were cheering and whistling. Reporters were smiling boldly and shaking his hand. President Richard Ashton, the forty-fifth President of the United States, had never felt so pleased with himself. His speech addressing the American people was taking place inside the wreckage of Patrick Lemoore's abandoned military installation, the haven that the O Negative rebels had sought out. Ashton was sitting in the chair that was presumably the final resting place of Walter Reifert, where Reifert had presumably been on the night three days ago, when he burned in the fiery inferno that descended upon the compound.

The air around Ashton still had the detectable scent of smoldering ashes, so powerful that his eyes stung and watered. And what was even worse; the smell was faint, but it was definitely there; President Ashton could smell the charred remains of O Negative flesh. The clean-up crew had done its best to clear the bodies from the scene—what little remained of them, anyway—so the report would be appropriate for all audiences, but the smell still lingered. He could almost taste them, the dead O Negatives who perished in that place. How many were killed in the air strike? A hundred? Two hundred? More? The O Negative remains were so small and so scattered that it was impossible to know.

It was highly probable that his son was there at the time of the strike. Was he inside the compound? Was he one of the bodies that appeared to be running towards the bus that was still smoldering out on the lawn? President Ashton had murdered his own son. It was a terrible loss, and he felt a little sadness when thinking about it, but the fact that he had allowed his son to die would give a powerful message to the rest of the world.

The United States of America would do anything—*anything*—to protect her people. And she would not back down. Not ever.

Although questions were being asked about the death of the president's son, most people were concerned with the matter of the death of Walter Reifert. The lead rebel—an eighteen-year-old boy, surprisingly—was dead. With their leader dead, the rest of the O Negatives would begin to lose hope. They would be back under control again shortly.

A majority of the compound was reduced to piles of black rubble, but the desk and chair where Reifert had sat had remarkably survived. The debris around the furniture had been cleared away, and that was where Ashton would make his speech, behind the desk where the dead rebel leader once sat. Ashton thought the image would have a strong effect on both Americans and O Negatives alike. The government was still on top, and that was how it would stay.

The audience of reporters and other civilians hushed, and then the man behind the camera said, "Mr. President, we're live in five…four…three…" He fingered two and one.

"Good morning, my fellow Americans," Ashton said into the camera. "As most of you are aware, three days ago, the United States Air Force led a strike on this military installation where we are now. Inside were a majority of the O Negative rebels, led by Walter Reifert, who is believed to have perished here in the compound." He went on, explaining what had happened, and explained how it would benefit the world's current situation. His speech went on for an hour, utter silence befalling the audience.

Ashton pictured his citizens sitting in front of their televisions, listening as intently as his live audience was. He pictured the O Negatives watching as well, grieving their lost rebel leader. Would they try to avenge Reifert's death? Would this situation become all-out war? Those questions didn't matter right now. Reifert was dead. That was the most important thing.

His speech ended and he asked for questions. A woman asked a question regarding what to do about the escaped population of O Negatives. Another asked if he would use this event to his advantage in the next election. Ashton did his best to answer patiently, but after the fifth question, it was clear he was growing annoyed.

"Yes," he called, his impatience now audible. "You sir, in the back."

The hand in the back lowered, and several heads turned to face the speaker. Ashton didn't have a good view of the reporter, but he did when everyone around him gasped and moved away from him as fast as they could. Ashton gasped too, staring at the man at the inside of the circle. The *boy* at the inside of the circle.

"I was dismayed when I didn't receive an invitation, Mr. President," Walter Reifert said harshly, his voice and body quivering. "After all, this was *my* home."

"*O Negative!*" someone shouted, and then the Secret Service agents were pulling out their weapons. Not a single shot could be fired before the guns flew out of their hands and clattered away into the woods.

"Don't bother," Reifert snapped. "I brought my own protection." Men, women, boys, and girls came out of the crowd and stood behind Reifert, all glaring at Ashton. A girl with red hair took Reifert's hand, but he didn't return the gesture.

The cameras were all focused on Reifert and his band of O Negatives, so at least the viewers wouldn't be able to see Ashton's shock. "You—you're supposed to be dead!" he blurted. "You were supposed to be in here!"

"I was," Reifert said curtly. "But I'm sorry that I disappointed you so." He continued to glare at Ashton, but didn't say anything more.

"What do you want?" Ashton asked him nervously.

"How dare you," Reifert whispered, so softly that Ashton almost didn't hear him. "How dare you sit in *his* chair, behind *his* desk! *How dare you!*"

Ashton was so confused that he remained speechless. Wasn't that Reifert's chair?

"I knew you wouldn't tell the truth about what happened here," Reifert continued, his voice back under control. "So I decided to come and tell it myself." He turned to the camera. "For those of you who care enough to hear the rebel story, then listen up. We don't want to hurt your people. We never did. Yes, the labs were attacked, but that was the only way to free our people. Don't you see? It's always been in self-defense! *Your* people were the ones who turned us into this. *Your* people were the ones who locked us up and experimented on us. *Your* people were the ones who started murdering us. I hate to say it, but *your* people started it. The only reason we fight is to protect ourselves. We have rights, too."

"You have no rights!" Ashton cut in.

Reifert looked at him sharply. "I am an American citizen, am I not?" He looked around at his O Negatives. "Almost all of my people here are American citizens. We have the same rights as everyone else in this country!"

"You lost your rights when you became contaminated freaks!" Ashton replied.

"Contaminated by a virus that *you* created!" Reifert countered. His voice was shrill, but when he spoke again it was calmer. "Is this really what this country's come to? You infect people with experimental viruses and then take away their rights as Americans? As *people*?" He shook his head in disappointment. "If this is what the United States of America has become, I suggest you tell them." He pointed to one of the cameras, which was now aimed at Ashton.

Ashton stared at it, completely speechless.

Reifert looked into the camera aimed on him again. "That's what your president, your great protector, did to my people. He turned them into 'freaks' and then took away their rights. And when we finally fought to get those rights back, he responded by bombing our place of refuge. Lucky for us, and unknown to you, almost everybody was gone by the time the bombing took place."

There was an uproar in the audience, and Ashton found himself very angry. Everyone had left?

"Philadelphia was evacuated because your government has made you believe we are going to attack your cities. This is not true. But since the city is empty and our population is rapidly increasing, we are making Philadelphia our temporary home."

"You can't do that!" Ashton protested. "That's *our* city!"

"Then where the hell are we supposed to go?" Reifert demanded. To the camera again; "This is who your president is! This is who *you* elected! Do you want to know what happened here three days ago? We were relocating our people to Philadelphia, and a few of us, the people who form *my* Cabinet, stayed behind to clean up. As we were preparing to leave, your great leader bombed our home. He only killed six of my people, and that may seem like a small number, but it's not. We loved them. *I* loved them. They are irreplaceable. Therefore, I want to tell you their names, so you'll remember them. Jane, Sarah, and Caroline Odau. Half of a family. All dead. Garrett Mikkelson. Dead. Peighton Stone. Dead. Patrick Lemoore." Reifert lowered his eyes. "Dead." He looked up again, his eyes hard. "Because it is clear that our two races can never live in peace, we will be branching away from you. Where we will go is uncertain, but it will be away from you. This is the Declaration of Independence for the Colician race. We will find on our own what you will not give us. Freedom." He and his O Negatives turned away, and the crowd parted to let them through.

"You know I won't stop until we're rid of you," Ashton threatened, rising from his chair.

Reifert stopped. He turned around. "Well, if you're going to kill us all, why don't you start now. Show the world what you're really capable of, Mr. President." He took something from another O Negative, an object wrapped in cloth. He approached the desk and set the object down carefully, taking the cloth away. It was a baby. A baby boy with black hair.

Ashton looked up in amusement. "You're going to let me kill this baby? Just give him to me? You deserve everything that's coming to you."

Reifert smirked. "Look a little closer."

Ashton did, and his eyes widened in horror. The baby had blue eyes. *Ashton's* blue eyes. As he watched, Ashton saw two small wings unfurl behind him. Angel wings.

"Meet your grandson," Reifert said. "William *Richard* Ashton. If you're going to slaughter us, why not start with him? Show the world that you have no mercy. Show the world that no one will be spared."

The baby, Ashton's grandson, gazed up at him. He gurgled and made baby sounds. Ashton hadn't placed the boy at first because of the hair, but those eyes and wings were unmistakable. This was Cole's son. There was no doubt.

"Go ahead," Reifert said. "We won't stop you. What are you waiting for?"

Ashton stared at his grandson for what felt like forever, taking in every detail. He knew he would never see William Richard Ashton again, and he wanted to remember the boy. He may be an O Negative, a mutant freak with wings, but he was Ashton's grandson.

"Take him away," Ashton choked out at last.

"What was that?"

"Get him away from me," Ashton ordered, looking away from the baby.

Reifert smirked again. "You're pathetic," he said. "Stay away from my people." He picked up the baby.

"I have fire power," Ashton said weakly. "You can't hide forever."

Reifert looked amused. *"You* have fire power?" He laughed scornfully.

Just then, an O Negative with dark red hair stepped forward and held out his palm. A series of bright orange flames erupted from it.

Reifert leaned across the desk. "So do I."

Ashton couldn't control his anger. How dare that boy walk onto *his* soil, in *his* country, and threaten *his* people! "Hey!" he shouted, and pulled out a handgun from inside his coat.

Reifert, who was walking back to his freaks, turned at the shout. He didn't even flinch when he saw the gun. The red-haired O Negative, the girl who had taken Reifert's hand before, lunged forward and screamed, "No!"

A shadow fell over Ashton, and then a figure fell from the sky and landed between him and Reifert. Ashton jumped, his finger squeezing the trigger. He quickly let off the pressure when he realized who it was. "Cole?" he said in surprise.

Cole's angel wings folded behind his back gracefully, a change from the last time they'd been in each other's company. He looked older, more mature. And there was something in his eyes, a burning hate, that told Ashton that Cole wasn't his boy anymore.

Cole stepped forward so the nose of the gun pressed into his bare chest. "Pull the trigger, Dad," he growled. "Because you'll have to kill me yourself before you touch him."

Shakily, and still stunned by Cole's bizarre entrance, Ashton said, "I've ordered you killed once already."

"Yes," Cole agreed, "but can *you* do it?"

Ashton stared at him, the boy who was no longer his boy. Could he do it? Could he murder his own son? It was easy to order someone else to do the dirty work, but could he do it himself? Could he *really*?

No.

His hand shook so hard that the gun fell and clattered to the desktop. A sound that was half a sob and half a groan left his mouth. Full of shame, he lowered his eyes from his son's. The son he had pushed away. The son he had tried to kill. The son he had lost. The son he would never love again, and who would never love him.

With one last hateful glance, Cole turned and followed the boy who held his son. They then joined the other O Negatives, the group leaving the torched remains of their past haven.

"Cole," Ashton called weakly, and then louder; "Cole!"

His son didn't answer. He didn't say goodbye. He didn't even look back.

"I'm sorry," he whispered, allowing the tears to flow. He didn't care that all the cameras were now turned back on him.

As they left, Walter Reifert paused and turned back. A single camera focused on him, and he sent a message to his people through that camera.

All of you who belong with us: Come. We're waiting for you.

Walter Reifert raised his eyes to the president, just in time to see him pick up the handgun from the desk and raise it again. Walter didn't have time to react before the deafening bang echoed through his brain and the bullet lodged its way deep into his skull.

20

Picking Up the Pieces

Walter Reifert

I gasped and sat straight up in bed, my eyes shooting open. The echo of the gunshot was still ringing in my ears, and my body shook violently from the vividness of the dream.

"Shh," Shauna said soothingly, sitting up and rubbing my back. Her eyes were bleary, clouded over with sleep. "It's okay. You're okay. We're safe."

"I know," I said breathlessly as I got myself under control. I let out a deep breath and laid back down.

Shauna rocked and hushed Flint, who was beginning to fuss between us. "Was it that dream again?"

"Yeah."

"The same one?"

"The same."

"I can't imagine what I would do if that had actually happened..."

"Well, it didn't," I told her, rolling over to face her and the baby. It was dark, but I could see the fear in her eyes. The fear of losing me. "I'm here. I'm not going to leave you or our son."

She reached up and brushed my hair back, and then pulled her hand back sharply. "You're all sweaty," she said, wiping her hand on the sheets.

"Sorry."

"Why do you keep having that dream? He never even fired at you."

I shrugged. "Probably because he easily could have shot me." I shrugged again. "And I'm afraid that something will happen to me and you'll be left alone with the baby. I'm scared too, Shauna."

We laid in silence for a while, holding hands and helping Flint get back to sleep. I knew there was something on her mind, and I let her wait to say it aloud instead of listening to her thoughts.

"Walter…I've been thinking a lot. I know we're young and we already have a baby, but…do you want to have more kids?"

"Right now?" I asked, startled.

"No! It's too early, and it's hard enough knowing we'll have to raise Flint under these conditions. I'm saying later, when we're free of the humans, is there a possibility for a bigger family?"

"There's always a possibility," I replied. "I had three siblings, you had three siblings, my father had three siblings… I don't see why we can't give Flint a few more."

Shauna smiled.

"But not until we find a more permanent home for our people," I said. "And until we're sure the humans won't send a missile at us every chance they get. Our race…we need a few years to get on our feet."

Nodding, Shauna nuzzled up against me and said, "I love Flint, but I really want a little girl."

"Me too. In time, we'll have one."

"I don't know about you," Shauna said at the breakfast table that morning as she spooned mashed fruit into Flint's mouth, "but I really like this place. I wouldn't mind staying here for a while."

Shauna and I were sharing a three bedroom apartment with Erica, Cole, and William. We offered the extra room to Joe and

Nicci, but Joe declined the invitation. All he wanted was to be alone with his daughter. No other social contact was necessary, he said. Since we had an extra bedroom, we used it as the baby playroom. Flint and William had developed a brotherly bond, and enjoyed each other's company.

The babies were growing fast. It was early October, so the boys were about two months old, but they were already crawling around, making lots of noise, and even standing up. Dr. Perry took a biweekly look at them, and said they should be walking and talking before four months. "Our children mature more quickly than humans, mentally and physically," he said.

"I don't know about you," Cole replied, spooning mush into William's mouth, "but I'd prefer to have my own home with just me and my family. No offense."

"I agree," I said. "I love you guys, but we'll have to split eventually."

We all laughed, and the babies banged their little fists on their highchair trays.

I went for a walk after breakfast to clear my head. It had been more than a month since we lost Patrick and the others, but my pain wasn't getting any better. It wasn't until I slammed into Peighton's force field and watched Patrick burn that I realized just how much I loved him. He was my adopted father. And now he was gone.

Garrett and the Odaus hadn't made it into the radius of Peighton's force field when the bombs fell. They burned outside, running away from the bus. I was so close to reaching Patrick, but I was a few seconds too late. Another couple of feet, and I would have burned, too. And Peighton, poor Peighton, died saving the rest of us. She had never made a force field so wide or so strong before, so when the bombs hit, the strain was so great that it killed her. I couldn't help thinking it was my fault... She didn't burn, so we buried her body in a flower garden here in Philadelphia. My

Cabinet was down to four, but that wasn't the part that hurt me. A part of me died every time one of my people died.

I shivered in the crisp October air and pulled my jacket tighter around me. I looked up at the houses and apartments that were filled with my people. More free Colicians were coming in every day, and we had yet to learn how many of us there were. To preserve space for the new arrivals, we didn't waste any space.

Dr. Perry calculated the expected number of Colicians that might be coming into our city. "Approximately eight percent of the earth's population has O negative blood," he said. "There are approximately eight billion people living on this planet. Therefore, approximately six hundred and forty *million* people on the planet have O negative. That's not subtracting the casualties we've sustained."

I repeated the number in my head, bewildered by the size and implications of it. "How the hell are we supposed to fit six hundred and forty million people into Philadelphia?"

Dr. Perry shrugged. "We can't."

I lowered myself to a bench facing a small pool between some office buildings and watched a trio of mallards paddle along. It was nice and quiet here, a relaxing place. A peaceful place.

"Did you know that ten years ago, much of this area was destroyed by a huge fire?"

I looked up as Alicia sat down beside me. "Yes, I remember it."

She wrapped her arms around herself and shivered. "All the buildings and homes within a mile radius of this point were destroyed. It took years to rebuild." She pointed out at the water. "It's rumored that the fire started here."

I raised an eyebrow. "In the water?"

She shrugged. "Or *something in* the water…"

I peered at her curiously.

She smiled and explained, "It's also rumored that someone—a girl around your age, actually—had extraordinary abilities and started the fire in some bizarre way."

Thinking about that, I said, "It sounds like she was one of us."

"Yeah," she agreed, "but it was ten years ago, so it's impossible." She laughed. "Just one of the many legends the humans will tell their children about our people."

I nodded thoughtfully.

We sat in silence for a bit, until Alicia turned to me. "How're you doing? Are you okay?"

"Yeah," I muttered, tossing a rock into the water and watching the ripples go on and on. "Why wouldn't I be?"

Alicia wouldn't speak again until I met her eyes. "You've lost a lot," she said softly, her eyes sympathetic.

I nodded. "I think about it a lot. More so recently."

She put an arm around my shoulders. "You're an incredibly strong person for holding on like this. To stand up and lead these people in such an uncivilized time. I admire you. You don't hear them say it, but the others do, too."

"Thanks," I said, glancing back to the water.

Alicia leaned in and whispered, "I miss Patrick, too."

A tear slid down my cheek as Alicia got up and walked away. She may miss him, but she didn't know him like I did.

"The Canadians are arriving tomorrow," she called back to me. "The Mexicans and Brazilians the day after. Our German friends will be here next week."

"What's your point?" I asked.

"There's strength in numbers," she replied. "When we get all our people here, then we can find our way out of this shit hole."

I looked up into the sky as a shadow fell over me. Cole was flying with William, showing the boy how to use his underdeveloped wings.

Flying...

"Why didn't anyone think of this before?" Klaus asked when I ran my idea by the Cabinet.

"I don't know," Dr. Perry replied, "but it's perfect."

"We'll get everyone here faster and safer," Alicia agreed.

"And we'll get people here who wouldn't be able to get here otherwise." Cole nodded. "It's brilliant, Walter."

"You're the one who gave me the idea," I told him. I looked around at them. "No objections?"

"None," Alicia declared.

I grinned. "Then I hereby declare Colician Airlines officially open."

21

One Last Stand

Walter Reifert

There were twelve airplanes at the airport that were airworthy. We found nine Colicians capable of flying them. Seven humans volunteered to help. We decided we could only put ten planes in the air for now.

But only ten planes was not such a terrible thing. After day two we'd found four more Colicians from overseas with piloting experience. After a week we'd found sixteen. After two weeks of the airline's existence, we managed to get a total of twenty-two planes in the air from all across the world.

By the end of October, we had several million Colicians sheltered in Philadelphia, and I had nine members on my Cabinet. Killian from Berlin agreed to join me as soon as his ship arrived. He was easy to convince because he and Alicia turned out to be soul mates. Damien changed his mind and joined me, as did his French soul mate, Olivia. My last two members came from Manchester and Baghdad. Johanna, from Manchester, was twenty-nine, and Sayid, from Baghdad, was twenty-three. On November 2nd, I changed my mind and made my Cabinet ten Colicians strong instead of just nine. I met a young man from Somalia, whose name was Marcos, and I wanted him working with me. He, too, was eighteen and had lost his entire family. He then led the entire Colician population of Somalia to the United States. He belonged on my Cabinet. He was my Somalian parallel.

Day and night, I could hear plane engines roaring overhead, bringing in new arrivals. Before Peighton died, Dr. Perry harnessed her ability to create force fields without her present. She was dead, but her presence was still felt. There was an enormous force field around the city and around each plane as they traveled. Humans had attacked us numerous times, but with no resulting fatalities. Beneath Peighton's force fields, we were untouchable.

There was a celebration in the streets on November 8th. It wasn't for any particular reason; everyone was just so happy to be free. The air was chilly, but spirits were warm. Everyone was drinking and dancing. It was then that I realized that even if there wasn't peace between us and the humans, there was peace among our people. There was a group of Japanese mingling with the Germans. A pair of Americans were speaking with a trio of Afghans. Nicaraguans and Canadians, Sudanese and Pakistanis. Chinese and Russians, Filipinos and Indians. Here, there were no separate countries or races. No separate colors. Here, we were all one race.

One people.

I found Shauna and Erica with the boys a few blocks down. "Hey babies," I said, kissing Shauna and then Flint.

"Have you seen Cole?" Erica asked me, a note of worry in her voice.

"No," I said. "Why? Can't find him?"

Erica glared at me. "You're lying." When I stared back at her, confused, she rolled her eyes and groaned in disgust. "If you see him again, tell him not to come home until he's cleaned up his mouth. He's not going to talk like that around our son." She turned away and then disappeared into the crowd.

I looked at Shauna. "What was that?"

Shauna shrugged. "I think they got into a fight. She didn't give me all the details."

"What would they fight about?" I asked, having never seen them so much as disagree before.

"I don't know. I wasn't there, but apparently he said some things in front of William that she didn't like."

"That's too bad," I muttered.

"Da!" Flint said, stretching his arms towards me.

"Flint!" I replied, grinning and taking him from Shauna. "So other than Cole being a dick, how's the party been?"

"Dick!" Flint cried, causing several heads to turn and earning a few laughs.

Shauna frowned. "This is exactly what Erica's mad about; Cole swearing and William repeating him."

Embarrassed, I looked down at my son and told him sternly, "Don't say that. It's bad."

"'Kay," Flint replied, sticking his fist in his mouth.

Shauna sighed and rubbed her forehead. She seemed irritable, and she was never like this. "Are you alright, babe?" I asked her in concern.

She shrugged. "I don't know. I'm tired, I have this headache, and all I've wanted to do all day is hit someone."

"Maybe we should go see Dr. Perry," I suggested. This wasn't normal behavior for Shauna, and it bothered me.

Again, she shrugged. "Yeah, that sounds like...like...like a..." Her eyes suddenly rolled back in her head and she crumpled to the ground.

"Ma!" Flint shrieked, reaching a hand out to her.

"Shauna!" I cried, getting down on my knees and shaking her shoulder. "Oh my God! Somebody help!"

"Ma!" Flint screamed, beating his tiny fist on her back to try to wake her. "*Ma!*"

People all around us realized what was happening and started calling out to each other, trying to find someone who could help.

"Somebody get some help!"

"Go get Dr. Perry!"

"Oh my God! It's Shauna Skyler!"

A man I recognized but whose name I didn't know crouched down beside us. "Give me your baby," he said. "I'll stay with them while you find Dr. Perry."

"Thank you," I said breathlessly, passing Flint to him and taking off through the crowd that was parting for me.

I did my best to run, unsure of exactly where I was going. As I ran, I could hear the steady approach of plane engines, and it crossed my mind that we were getting seventeen planes of Colicians to Philadelphia today. The thought left me quickly, the steady murmur of thoughts growing louder as people realized what was happening to Shauna. I thought I heard my name being called, and I ignored it until a heavy hand landed on my shoulder. "Walter!"

"I can't talk now, Damien!" I said hurriedly.

"Walter, stop!" Damien grabbed my wrist and spun me around. "Dr. Perry knows about Shauna; he's on his way."

"Then what's the problem?" I asked, impatient.

"We just got word from one of our planes," Damien said, his eyes afraid. "The plane from Moscow that should be arriving any minute. Apparently, the human pilot's been compromised and he's planning to bring the plane down on top of us!"

"What?" I said in disbelief. I'd questioned all the pilots myself and their intentions were pure. How could this have happened?

The drone of the plane I'd heard before was now a roar, and in a few seconds that roar was deafening. People screamed and put their hands over their ears. I looked up, and there was the plane. It was bearing down on us quickly. After considering almost every violent possibility the humans could give us, this had never crossed anyone's mind. I never thought that one of our own planes could be hijacked and brought down over our heads. Philadelphia's entire population was in the streets; so many of us were going to die. My presumption was that the incident at the compound would be the end of attempted extermination (after my conversation with Ashton, that is). I was so wrong.

People covered their faces with their arms, but that wouldn't do any good. We were done.

Something happened. The plane slowed in its descent and then came to a stop in mid-air only yards above us, with its nose pointed (I swear) directly at me. It was so close that I could see the pilot and copilot in the cockpit, staring out at us in fear and confusion. For a moment it hovered there, suspended above our city. The streets were deathly silent, everyone watching the bizarre incident unfold. Then, with a heavy groan of shifting metal, the plane began to back up. A murmur swept through the crowd, curious thoughts and whispers being exchanged between neighbors. I, too, watched with wonder.

That is, until I heard Flint scream.

I don't know how I got there, but one moment I was watching the plane float backwards through the air above the city and the next I was back to where Shauna had fallen. She wasn't on the ground anymore.

"Ma!" Flint cried, reaching for her from the arms of the man with whom I had left him. While everybody else watched the plane's movements, the people around Shauna watched her as she held the plane above our heads.

"Shauna?" I whispered in a mixture of shock and horror.

Shauna stood in the middle of a circle others had made around her, her head tilted towards the sky and her arms outstretched with the palms facing up. For the tremendous weight of the object she was holding, she didn't have a very strained expression on her face. She looked calm, entranced. She looked like she was someplace else, and another being had taken over her body, just like before. I knew it wasn't her because of her eyes. They were red. Blood red. Her eyes were blood red flames.

"Ma!" Flint cried again, quieter this time. He hiccupped and started crying, his soft sobs the only noise around us. It was then that I realized the plane engines had stopped. Shauna had turned them off. She was in control now.

"Shauna," I said to her, a bit steadier. "What are you doing? Are you...are you okay?" I started to reach out and touch her, to calm the blazing fire within her, but I was stopped by a hand that shot out and grabbed my wrist.

"Don't," Dr. Perry warned from my side, watching Shauna hesitantly. "Don't touch her."

"What's wrong with her?" I demanded.

"I'm not sure," he replied. "But don't touch her. Who knows what might happen."

So we watched. We watched as Shauna's eyes and hands shifted and the plane began to groan loudly with her movements. The plane floated through the air, over the buildings, over all of us. We shifted ourselves to see where Shauna was taking it.

I heard a single word being repeated in Shauna's mind: *bridgebridgebridgebridge bridgebridgebridgebridge.* I looked around and saw where she was going to put it. There was an overpass a block west of us. As we looked on in amazement, Shauna brought the plane to a shaky rest on top of it. The bridge shook uneasily and a chunk or two of concrete fell to the road below, but it looked as if it would hold.

Once we were certain the bridge wouldn't collapse with the full weight of the plane of Russian Colicians resting on it, a clamor of voices erupted through the streets.

"Get those people off that plane!" I shouted, but I knew no one could hear me. It didn't matter; people were rushing for the bridge as I spoke. "Don't let that pilot get out of this city!"

"Walter." The man holding Flint handed my baby back to me and nodded to Shauna. I looked back and saw something horrible. The red of Shauna's eyes was leaving her. In the form of bloody tears.

As the blood leaked down her face, she swayed on her feet. The blue of her eyes came back, and I saw my Shauna come back to me. But something was very wrong.

"Shauna?" I said, reaching out to her. I tried to catch her as she fell, but Dr. Perry beat me to her.

"I've got her, I've got her," Dr. Perry said, setting her down gently and wiping the blood from her face. He glanced up and spoke to someone in the crowd. "I need a vehicle here immediately. She needs medical attention now."

"Yes, sir," a woman replied.

Flint was still crying as I knelt beside Shauna's fallen body, and I realized I was too. I stroked her hair, smoothed it behind her ears. "You'll be okay, baby," I whispered. "Dr. Perry's going to take care of you. Everything's alright."

But then I heard gunshots coming from the plane.

22

The Solution

Walter Reifert

There was a riot in the streets. The happy party had turned into an angry brawl. My people were very angry. They wanted me to execute the pilot who'd tried to murder us. I didn't want to think about what I needed to do about him. Right now, I just wanted to focus on my family.

"Ma," Flint said, poking my nose and smiling crookedly.

"Ma's going to be okay," I promised him, tickling his tummy. "She just has to stay here for a little while." Dr. Perry came from around the corner and I stood up quickly, clutching Flint to my chest. "So?" I asked anxiously. "How is she?"

"Well," Dr. Perry sighed, "I've got good news and I've got bad news. The bad news is she had a stroke and needs to stay in intensive care for a few days. The good news is it wasn't life threatening. She'll be alright."

"What happened?" I demanded, my head ready to burst. "I mean, she just had a headache…"

Dr. Perry put his arm around my shoulders and sat me back down. "I know this whole situation is very difficult to deal with, Walter, and understanding what happened to Shauna isn't easy. She subconsciously knew what was going to happen. Her body was preparing itself for what she would have to do to stop the plane, hence the headache. But the strain of holding an object of such weight for so long was still too much for her to handle. If her body hadn't already been preparing for it, she would probably be dead."

"But how could she know?" I whispered. "How could she possibly know?"

Dr. Perry shrugged. "It's not uncommon for one of us to predict an upcoming event. Others probably saw it coming too, but not with the intensity that Shauna did. The people who sensed it probably just had a bad feeling in their gut, and didn't come to the party. Who knows? The abilities of our people—and the extent of their powers—are incomprehensible. I don't fully understand what happened to Shauna. Somehow she saw the event coming, and somehow she stopped it. She did those things, so I think we should just accept it and move on." He gazed out the window at the sounds of the riot outside the hospital. "Move on and focus on that problem. What are you going to do, Walter?"

"I don't know," I muttered. "I honestly don't know what I *should* do. They want me to kill that human."

"Do *you* want to kill that human?"

I couldn't answer him, because I didn't know the answer.

"Shoot him!"

"Make him suffer!"

"He tried to kill us! Let's show him who's in charge!"

I stood in front of the human who had tried to drive the plane into the ground on top of us. He was tied to a chair in the street, one eye blackened. He shot two people before suffering the blow to the face. Thankfully, no one died in this incident that very well could have ended in devastation. But my people wanted justice, and their definition of justice was butchering this man in the street.

The gun I had been handed was like a lead weight in my hand. It felt heavy, weighing me down. Would I use it? Could I use the same kind of weapon that killed my family? Could I do what my people wanted me to do?

Did I want this human dead?

Do I want to kill this human?

"I don't know what I want," I breathed, letting the gun fall to the ground.

There was an uproar from the crowd surrounding us.

"Kill him!"

"You can do it, Walter!"

"*Stop!*"

The word was screamed so loud that it took a moment to realize it was me who screamed it. I looked out at my people, my angry, vengeful people. They grew quiet from the force of my scream, so quiet that I was sure they all heard me wheezing as I struggled to catch my breath.

"Stop!" I gasped, my voice cracking. "Stop it! What's *wrong* with all of you?"

There was an immediate atmosphere of guilt and humiliation that swept through the crowd. Many eyes averted to the ground.

"Why are you doing this?" I croaked. "Why are you trying to make me kill this man?" I stooped down to pick up the gun. I held it up for all to see. "One of these killed my father. My brothers. My mate's brother. Your families. And you're asking me, your leader, to use one against this man? Yes, he tried to murder us in cold blood, but killing him won't prove anything except that we're just as bad as the humans. I thought this new race, this new family, was going to be something different. I thought we were going to be peaceful. Just." I shook the gun above my head. "You see this? We start using these and we only prove that we're no better than those who hurt us. I thought you would understand that." I lowered the gun, gazed upon it with sad, remorseful eyes. "These weapons have no place among us. If you choose to use them, I have no objection, but you will then have no place in this city. We will not kill. That's not who we are. If any of you want to be killers, then I suggest you leave now, because there is no place for you here." I threw the gun to the ground and it skidded away several feet. "I want this man taken to the edge of the city and set free. And you." I marched up to the man where he sat and got in his face. "You will go to President Ashton. Tell him what you tried to do here. Then, tell him what *I* did. Tell him I let you live." I went behind him and untied him. As I walked away through the crowd that parted without protesting, the man called out to me.

"Hey!" When I turned, I could see the fear in his eyes. I also saw something else in them. Gratitude. "Thank you," he whispered.

"Walter?"

I sat up with a jolt when the hand landed on my shoulder. "What?" I said, still half-asleep. "What's wrong?"

"*Shh, shh,*" Dr. Perry said, smiling down at me. "Nothing's wrong. There are a few people here to see you."

"Now?" It was the middle of the night and I was resting beside Shauna's hospital bed. Couldn't it wait until morning?

"It's really important," Dr. Perry insisted. "You'll want to hear this. Trust me."

I rubbed the sleep from my eyes as three people came in. Two were men I didn't recognize, and the third was little Allan Brown.

"This is Nickolay," Dr. Perry said, gesturing to the older man. "He came in on the Moscow flight today."

"Sorry about the rough flight," I muttered.

"This is Nathan." Dr. Perry gestured to the other man. "He used to be a mechanic before the outbreak. And you know Allan."

"How've you been?" I asked the boy.

Allan shrugged. He was sleepy too, and didn't look too happy about being awake so early.

"So what do you need to talk to me about?" I asked them, leading them out of the room so Shauna and Flint could sleep in peace.

"When put together, I think the four of us can be very useful," Nickolay said, including Dr. Perry in the group of four. He spoke in a thick Russian accent but in very good English.

"And how's that?"

"My ability," Nickolay said eagerly, "is to create a parallel earth and take items from it. I've created my own food, water, anything you can think of, really."

"That's nice," I replied. "You plan to take items from there and distribute them here?"

"Not exactly," Dr. Perry said, grinning at Nickolay.

"This land I created is expansive," Nickolay continued. "It's the same size as this earth. The only difference is that it's empty."

The puzzle pieces suddenly snapped into place. "You want to move everyone there?"

Nickolay nodded. "But I can't physically travel to this world. I can only take things from it."

Groaning, I dropped my head in my hands and shook it hopelessly.

"That's where Allan comes in."

When the Russian said that, I knew there was still hope. We could have our own world. We could start over. We could live in peace.

"We can build a machine to harness Allan's teleportation ability, like I did before with Peighton," Dr. Perry said, gesturing to himself and Nathan. "Then, we can combine his and Nickolay's abilities, so we can transport all our people to this parallel earth."

"And you think this will work?" I asked.

"I know it will work," Dr. Perry replied. He shrugged. "Even if I wasn't sure, it's worth a shot."

I nodded, a huge weight lifting off my chest. "Get on it as soon as you can. I want to start moving our people as soon as possible."

I told our people the plan two days later. I heard no objections. Dr. Perry had what he called "The Rift" open three days after that. He told me he wanted to send someone through first to test the place out, to make sure The Rift worked and that the new earth was habitable. Basically, he wanted to make sure The Rift didn't transport you to nowhere and that the new earth actually had a breathable atmosphere.

To everyone's surprise, Joe was the first to volunteer. No one saw much of Joe these days. He kept himself and Nicci isolated at the edge of the city and didn't speak to anyone. But he spoke up at the city meeting held in the street in front of the hospital. Normally, I wouldn't have let a single parent try something this risky, but I let Joe go through first. If he was coming out of isolation to help us, I wasn't going to turn him down.

"If anything happens to me," he said as we stood in front of The Rift, "take care of Nicci, okay?"

"I promise," I said.

"And don't ever tell her about Don. I don't want my daughter to grow up knowing her grandfather was a murderer."

"I won't, if that's what you want."

Joe passed Nicci to me and gazed through The Rift, a circle of metal surrounding what looked like blue fire. He took a deep breath and stepped into it. The blue fire swallowed him and he vanished. The few people who were allowed to observe the test held their breath, as did I. The basement of the hospital felt very cold as we waited to find out whether Joe survived.

I could hear each second ticking by on the clock above my head. I counted eighty-seven of them before the blue fire parted in the middle and Joe stepped out, a dazed expression on his face. He stumbled forward and fell to his knees.

"Joe!" I cried, rushing to him and kneeling beside him.

"Joe, can you breathe?" Dr. Perry asked him, looking into his glazed eyes. "Are you alright? Answer me!"

"Joe." I reached out and touched his shoulder, my brow creased in worry for my friend.

Joe's eyes met mine and we held each other's gaze. Then, his face lit up in a huge grin. "It's amazing," he whispered.

23

Crossing Over

Shauna Skyler

Walter was speaking to a human reporter. He chose a young college student who contacted him requesting an interview. Her intentions were pure; she wanted to hear Walter's view of the world's situation, or the War as she put it. Walter agreed to speak to her in our apartment, to tell her our plan to relocate. He wanted her to tell the world that we could all finally move on. The humans could keep their planet, and we could move to our own.

While Walter spoke with the reporter, I was helping our people cross The Rift. Thousands already had and were setting up camp a few miles from The Rift's opening.

Dr. Perry suggested to Walter a few days ago that we move The Rift to a more open location, where our people could access it easier. He recommended a church outside the city, a church that had recently been rebuilt after a fire destroyed it a little over a decade earlier. The church had a lot of open space around it for our people to wait their turn to cross over, but a lot of us thought of the place as something else. Something more. The Rift rested in the middle of the sanctuary. People thought it symbolic because The Rift was leading us to *our* sanctuary.

Although Walter was currently informing the world of what our plan was, he let the authorities around Philadelphia know earlier so they wouldn't be alarmed at the large gathering of Colicians outside the city. In response, the National Guard put up a six-foot-tall barbed wire fence to separate humans and Colicians as we relocated. They guarded the fence with guns, but we seemed to come to at least a somewhat mutual understanding of each other. They had no intent to use them.

Hundreds of humans had gathered on the other side of the fence to watch our progress. The noise was deafening, so I almost didn't hear the voice screaming my name from the other side of it.

"Shauna! *Shauna!*"

I looked around, unable to pinpoint the origin of the shout.

"Shauna, to your left!"

My eyes wandered over every face outside the fence until they landed on someone I recognized. My mouth fell open. *"Russell?"* I ran to him, startling two of the guards as I did so.

"Hey!" one said, raising his rifle slightly.

"Get back!" another one ordered.

"It's okay," Russell told them as I reached the fence. "She's my sister."

The guards relaxed, but they kept a wary eye on me.

"Russell," I said as we entwined our fingers through the fence. "What are you doing here?"

Russell looked sad, broken. He rested his head against the fence. "I heard you're all leaving. I was hoping I could see you one last time."

I smiled weakly.

"Mom's dead," Russell said, his eyes dull and lifeless.

"I know," I replied.

"They sent us her body. Said she overreacted to a drug. That's not what happened, is it?"

I shook my head.

Russell glanced up hopefully. "Sawyer…?"

Again, I shook my head. This time, *I* looked down. Russell sighed, and I asked him, "What about Michael and Dad?"

"They're fine." He stopped himself. "Well, they're alive. Our family's broken. We'll never be okay again."

"Sure you will," I whispered as I began to cry. "You've got each other. We'll be in different places, but we'll make it. We'll be alright."

Russell glanced up again. "What about you? Who've you got?"

I smiled. "I have Walter."

Russell perked up, interested. "Walter Reifert?"

"Yes. We're what we call soul mates."

I saw Big Brother Russell enter the playing field. "Is he good to you?"

"Oh, yes," I promised him. "He's wonderful. Don't ever believe any of the awful stuff you hear about him. He's the kindest, bravest man I've ever met."

Russell forced a smile. "Well, if he's your soul mate, then he couldn't be a bad person. He wouldn't deserve you."

I smiled.

"So how are you?" Russell asked.

"Fine." I shrugged. "I miss you guys, but I've already accepted that we can't stay together anymore."

Nodding, Russell said, "If this world wasn't so damn racist, we could still be a family."

"You can't blame them for being scared."

"I blame Ashton for making you into monsters!"

I gripped his hand through the fence. "Come with us," I whispered. "All three of you. Come stay with us and our son."

"You have a son?"

"Yes. His name's Flint. He's beautiful. Please, come with us."

Russell shook his head. "I can't. *We* can't. We don't belong with you."

I gaped at him. "You were just bitching about racism, and now you're—"

"Shauna." Russell hissed my name, pulled me close. "I've seen what you are. Your people...your people are good. My people... Our pain and destruction can't follow you. Don't ever let us taint your society. Don't ever let us take that goodness from you." He lowered his voice even more. "Don't ever give up."

"Russell!" I said, clinging to him as he pulled away. "*You're* not bad!"

He turned to me, the emptiness still there. "I'm not good, either. I'm human, and there's bad in all of us."

We stared at each other for a long time, neither of us quite sure what to say next. Then, Russell said, "I was going to bring you your dog, but we had a hard time letting him go."

"That's okay," I replied. "Keep her. Where are you guys staying?"

"We're staying in New York with Grandpa Monroe."

"I love you, Big Brother," I whispered. "Tell Dad and Michael and Grandpa for me."

Russell nodded. "Of course I will."

It pained me to turn my back on him, but I managed to do it without breaking down. Russell called my name one last time, but I refused to look back. I knew that if I did I'd never be able to let him go.

Russell was never one to say, "I love you," but when he spoke his next words, the last words I ever heard him speak, I knew that was what he meant.

"Have a great life, Little Sister."

I cried as I stood there with my back to him. It was unclear how long I waited, but when I finally turned back around, I was certain I would see Russell still there, also crying. But he was gone.

I waited.

I waited for a long time.

I waited until both humans and Colicians alike had vanished altogether.

But he never came back.

I stood staring at the place where I last saw Russell until the sky turned black.

Joe Murphy

Joe Murphy had crossed over with his daughter Nicci the first chance he got. He had to get away from that world, the world where everything he saw, everyone he met, and everywhere he went, reminded him of Maia.

He was currently staying in the camps set up for new arrivals. That's where everyone went to start, but people were leaving left and right at all hours of the day and night. Joe was planning to do the same, but he wanted to make sure he had enough supplies to support himself and his daughter.

Three days after his arrival, which was also the last day of his stay in the camps, Joe was pushing his way through the crowd, hoping to buy one of the cows that had been brought over from Earth. It took over an hour of negotiating, but eventually he managed to cut a deal.

On his way back, trying to convince the stubborn cow to go with him, he paused at a water tent. It was hot, and he had neglected to bring a bottle or a canteen. As he sat with his drink, gazing out at the busy crowd, a flash of black hair caught his eye. Plenty of people had black hair here, but it still left a throbbing pang in his heart. He squeezed his eyes shut, willing the tears away, and then looked back up, expecting to see a random girl with black hair walking by.

He gasped.

Maia was walking by, swept away with the crowd. Joe blinked several times, but it was her.

"Maia!" he shouted, standing up abruptly and spilling his water all over him.

Maia stopped and looked at him. She looked the same as she had the last time Joe had seen her alive; beautiful, powerful. Happy.

They stared at each other for a long time, Joe refusing to blink for fear that she would disappear if he did. Neither one said a thing. But after a long time, Maia smiled at him.

And then she was gone.

Joe dropped the rope holding the cow and ran to where Maia had just been, screaming her name. He looked everywhere for hours, but Maia was nowhere to be found. She was gone.

Joe knew that Maia had been there to tell him something, but he couldn't for the life of him understand what. For years, he sat in the chair on his porch, gazing out on the open fields and pondering over what he had seen. He even asked Nicci, when she was old enough, what her thoughts were. She didn't have an answer either.

It took Joe sixteen years, took watching his daughter fall in love with her soul mate, took seeing his granddaughter for the first time, for him to finally understand what she meant.

Life goes on.

And Maia was very wise, indeed.

Epilogue

There wasn't peace between the O Negatives and humans. Not in the way Walter Reifert wanted. The people of Earth didn't help the O Negatives as they relocated. They didn't give them food, water, or shelter. Anything they needed, the O Negatives were expected to pay for, and expected to pay a ridiculous amount. But the stubbornness went both ways. The O Negatives refused to give the humans anything from their new world, from the Parallel Earth.

The killing stopped. Philadelphia was repopulated. Each race heavily guarded their side of The Rift, but with negotiations, people from each side could cross over. Humans were allowed to relocate to the Parallel Earth when governments began falsely accusing their own people of aiding the other side. O Negatives were allowed onto Earth to bring stragglers of their race to their new home.

The Colician virus never went away. It never stopped affecting the lives of those on either side. Any O Negative who was born to a non-O Negative family developed an ability. For years, the humans allowed the new O Negatives to relocate peacefully to their designated home.

No, there was not peace, but there was mercy.

* * *

August 19th, 2034

It was the sixteenth anniversary of the Colicians' Independence Day.

It was also the day the Colicians remembered those they'd lost.

Walter Reifert crouched down and ran his hand across the brick street that went around the capitol. He had declared all those years ago when their world had just begun, that the names of the dead, those who died in the Beginning, would be etched into bricks. Those bricks would form the street surrounding the capitol and the main street leading through the capital city.

The capital city was named Reifert City in honor of their leader and all he had sacrificed to save his people.

It took almost ten years before the street was finally finished. Over five million people died following the outbreak. That meant that over five million names were etched into over five million bricks, and then over five million bricks were laid to rest in the street. Walter said he didn't care how long it took; they would forever honor the ones who never made it home. This road, these bricks, were the way.

Walter gently brushed the dirt off of the bricks he knelt before. It was Independence Day, and he, too, had dead to honor.

MAIA RUDOLPH

He smiled. "You'd have loved it here, cuz. It's wonderful." He laughed, and looked up at the sky, the sky that was always blue and beautiful on this day. "You wouldn't believe how big Nicci is now. She just turned sixteen. She found her soul mate, at the same age you found yours." He sighed. "Joe misses you. He doesn't say it, but...we can see it. He doesn't talk much anymore. I hope you're in a great place, surrounded by your family and friends. I hope that when Joe passes, he'll find you there. You deserve to be together. It wasn't fair that you were taken away from each other so soon." He lowered his eyes again, and he gazed upon the names of those who had disappeared from existence, but whose memories would be with Walter forever.

MARLENA RUDOLPH. PATRICK LEMOORE.
JANE ODAU. SARAH ODAU. CAROLINE ODAU. GRAHAM
ODAU. SAWYER SKYLER. ANGELINA SKYLER.
JOHN REIFERT. TYLER REIFERT. ETHAN REIFERT.
ANTON REIFERT. SCOTTY DUPIERRE.
MARTA THOMSON. BERRY BURNETT.
GARRETT MIKKELSON. PEIGHTON STONE

He looked up, and saw Dr. Shawn Perry not too far from him, kneeling and resting his hand on the bricks beneath him. Walter knew whose names were there.

RENEE PERRY. JILLIAN REYNOLDS. HALLIE PERRY

The names went on forever, as did the memories. The pain of losing so many had long since dulled in Walter's heart, but he would never forget, and neither would any of his people. With these names etched into the street, Walter felt that a part of them was still with him. He knew others felt it too. Walking on their names brought them back to life, personified them again. Walter glanced up further. In a huge, golden circle centered in front of the steps to the capitol building, there was a phrase carved in deep letters:

WE DEDICATE THIS MEMORIAL TO THOSE
OF US WHO NEVER MADE THIS FAR, SO THAT
THEIR HEARTS MAY LIVE ON IN US.
WE WILL NEVER FORGET.

Walter smiled.

A hand reached past him and touched two of the names in the street; Angelina and Sawyer Skyler. Walter looked up at his soul mate, who had aged with him but still remained as beautiful as the time of their bond. His pain had scarred, but Shauna's was still bleeding inside her. He reached up and brushed the tears from her reddened cheeks.

"Sixteen years," Shauna whispered. "It's been sixteen years, and it still hurts."

Walter pulled her close to him, comforted her with his arms, his lips. "It will never go away," he told her. "But it gets easier with time."

Shauna raised her eyes to his. "I'm scared," she breathed.

Walter's brow furrowed. "Of what?"

"I don't want our children to know of the world we were born into," she said. "The world that *they* were born into."

Walter smiled reassuringly. "We can't hide the world from them, Shauna. They have to know, so their descendants won't make the same mistakes those before them made."

"But it's just so hard…" Shauna's voice cracked. "To explain it to them is like reliving it all!"

"Sometimes," Walter whispered, "reliving it helps you come to terms with it."

Shauna forced a smile, and she looked up. "Hey!" she called to someone over his shoulder. "Come see our old friends."

Walter looked and saw their children approaching, laughing and eating treats from the celebration. Walter wished that's how this day could remain to them; a celebration. Something fun and happy. But his children would have to learn the truth. His children. Flint, who was tall and strong like Walter. Katherine, who was beautiful and deadly like her mother. Malcolm, who had John Reifert's pride. And—

"Where's the munchkin?" he asked, looking around for her.

"Oh!" Shauna glanced at him. "She's with the boys."

"What boys?"

"Jack, Rhett, and Davey."

Walter searched every face of every child in the street, until his eyes landed on a familiar boy. The boy looked just like Dr. Perry. There was Jack. Beside him, with her back turned, was Walter's youngest child.

"Hallie!" he called. "Come here for a minute and take a look at this."

The little girl with long, curly dark hair turned at the sound of her name. When her eyes landed on her daddy, her face lit up. On her skinny, four-year-old legs, she ran to him, giggling.

"There's my girl," Walter said, beaming at his beautiful child. He scooped her up and she hugged his neck, so hard that she choked him. Laughing, Walter held his little girl. The girl with his mother's name.

And his eyes.

Dear Walter,

Things on Earth have gotten far worse than we anticipated. The economy is still in a slump, people are starving, and the states of Florida and Georgia are at war. The same is happening in other countries around the world. We're suffering over here, my friend.

Unfortunately, this isn't what we need to be worried about right now.

I've received information through a reliable source who wishes to remain unnamed. I'm sure you understand. She's given me some very troubling news.

The government thinks that the world might have a better chance at coming out of its turmoil if they can bring all the O Negatives back. However, they still don't want your abilities to be a part of our world. Scientists are trying to find a cure for the Colician Strain by mutating it. We both know what could happen if scientists begin experimenting with the Colician Virus again. You have to help us put an end to this, and fast.

I don't think either of our worlds could survive another catastrophe like the last.

Good luck,

Danny Bennett

ABOUT THE AUTHOR

Author photo by Amber Blanchard Photography

Ms. King resides in Southern Wisconsin with her family. She enjoys writing, reading, long walks, and spending time with friends and family. To contact the author visit CSJ King Publishing at www.repeatproductions.samsbiz.com.

www.ingramcontent.com/pod-product-compliance
Lightning Source LLC
Chambersburg PA
CBHW071201020726
47502CB00002B/495